The story of Josephine Cox is as extraordinary as anything in her novels. Born in a cotton-mill house in Blackburn, she was one of ten children. Her parents, she says, brought out the worst in each other, and life was hard – but not without love and laughter. At the age of sixteen, Josephine met and married 'a caring and wonderful man', and had two sons. When the boys started school, she decided to go to college and eventually gained a place at Cambridge University, though was unable to take this up as it would have meant living away from home. However, she did go into teaching, while at the same time helping to renovate the derelict council house that was their home, coping with the problems caused by her mother's unhappy home life – and writing her first full-length novel. Not surprisingly, she then won the 'Superwoman of Great Britain' Award, for which her family had secretly entered her, and this coincided with the acceptance of her novel for publication.

Josephine gave up teaching in order to write full time. She says: 'I love writing, both recreating scenes and characters from my past, together with new storylines which mingle naturally with the old. I could never imagine a single day without writing, and it's been that way since as far back as I can remember.' Her previous novels of North Country life are all available from Headline and are immensely popular.

'Hailed quite rightly as a gifted writer in the tradition of Catherine Cookson' *Manchester Evening News*

'A classic tale . . . a born storyteller' *Bedfordshire Times*

'[Jo Cox] out-writes and out-sells most of the opposition . . . unmatched since Catherine Cookson burst on the scene some 40 years ago' *Peterborough Evening Telegraph*

Also by Josephine Cox

Queenie's Story

Her Father's Sins
Let Loose the Tigers

The Emma Grady Trilogy

Outcast
Alley Urchin
Vagabonds

Whistledown Woman
Angels Cry Sometimes
Take This Woman
Don't Cry Alone
Jessica's Girl
Nobody's Darling
Born to Serve
More than Riches
A Little Badness
Living a Lie
A Time For Us
Cradle of Thorns
Miss You Forever
Love Me or Leave Me
Tomorrow The World
The Gilded Cage
Somewhere, Someday

The Devil You Know

Josephine Cox

headline

First published in 1996
by HEADLINE BOOK PUBLISHING

First published in paperback in 1996
by HEADLINE BOOK PUBLISHING

18

ISBN 0 7472 4940 7

Printed and bound in Great Britain by
Mackays of Chatham plc, Chatham, Kent

HEADLINE BOOK PUBLISHING
A division of Hodder Headline
338 Euston Road
London NW1 3BH

DEDICATION

I wrote this story while my house was filled with big handsome men. Most of the time covered in dust and dirt and wearing boots the size of barges, they cheerfully went about their labours, drinking gallons of tea and chatting while they worked. They always had a smile, even when I constantly caused 'little' changes in their schedules: such as asking for extra windows, or the moving of an airing cupboard with all its paraphernalia from one side of the house to the other; re-positioning of doors, and moving ceiling lights from their designated areas in the kitchen. They didn't even complain when I 'lost' an item of their equipment while trying to secure a flyaway tarpaulin in a high wind.

There were times when I almost reached screaming pitch; when the rain came down and mud was walked in all over my floors; when the hammering reverberated in my brain until I couldn't think straight; when next door's cat swung from the scaffolding, squaring her black hairy shoulders at my own poor confused moggy, who was prepared to defend her territory to the death.

Every day I marvel at the skill with which my humble cottage is being transformed. I give a heartfelt thank you to you all with your tousled hair, grimy, smiling faces and hob-nailed boots – every man a hero. How could I dedicate this book to anyone else?

CONTENTS

PART ONE

1956

Fear

Chapter One

With trembling fingers Sonny picked up the receiver for the third time. Again she hesitated. How in God's name could she expect anyone to believe her? What she had overheard was so bizarre, so unreal, she could hardly believe it herself.

She laughed, but it was a dry harsh sound. 'You always had a talent for picking the wrong man,' she told her reflection in the hallway mirror, 'but this time you've found the devil himself!'

A tide of emotions rippled through her as she recalled the conversation she had just heard. She was angry. Angry with him. Angry with herself. But more than that, she was desperately afraid.

Tony Bridgeman had deceived her, in a way so cruel and evil she could never have envisaged it.

Tears sprang to her eyes. Impatiently she brushed them away. 'You should go to the police,' she said aloud. But then she dismissed the idea. 'They won't believe you either. You're not talking about being battered or raped. You haven't been robbed or threatened, and as far as you know Mr Tony Bridgeman has never broken the law in his life.' She spoke his name bitterly. Her expression hardened. 'In fact, the bastard's done nothing that would interest the police; except to plan a murder, and no one would ever believe that.'

She didn't know which way to turn. 'You can't deal with this on your own, Sonny,' she decided aloud. 'This isn't the age-old tale of a man choosing his wife over his lover. This is far more sinister.'

Shuddering, she glanced round, as though fearing he might be in the room, watching her. Listening.

She couldn't understand why she hadn't suspected anything. Dear God, she must have been blind. But then love *was* blind! But, oh, if she hadn't gone there today . . . ! Her heart turned over. Laughing nervously, gazing at her own image in the hall mirror, she quipped, 'You know what they say, don't you? Eavesdroppers never hear good of themselves.'

It was ironic. She'd gone to his house, full of excitement at the thought of their snatching a few minutes alone. She'd wanted to share her wonderful news. The news they had both been waiting for. Well, now she knew, didn't she? Knew him for the monster he was; his wife too. She remembered how they had laughed; what they had planned. Her blood turned to ice. Even now, with the shock subsiding and her reason returning, the truth was too awful to contemplate.

She had gone to his house, her heart brimming with hope for the future. She had left in a daze, filled with dread as she drove down the road like a maniac. Funny, she thought, how love could turn to hate. But then, they did say love and hate were two sides of the same coin.

She glanced at the door. 'Hurry, Martha,' she muttered. Her gaze shifted back to the mirror. Her own image stared back, white-faced and stark. In the eerie silence, the insistent ticking of the grandfather clock was the only note of reassurance. The soft rhythm mingled with the beat of her own heart. And that of the child inside her.

Instinctively she laid a hand across the gentle mound of her stomach. 'Ssh!' In calming the unborn, she also calmed herself. 'Think, Sonny,' she whispered. 'What to do? What to do?'

Frustrated, she dropped the receiver into its cradle and began pacing the floor. 'I should go to the police,' she muttered bitterly. Deep down she prayed she was wrong; that tomorrow would come and everything would be normal, that he would smile at her and all her fears would melt away. She thought about his smile, that wonderful handsome smile that had won her to him. 'Evil bastard!' In that moment she could have killed him with her bare hands. Hands that couldn't stop trembling. Hands that had caressed every inch of his body.

Reaching into the dresser drawer, she took out a packet of cigarettes and a lighter – a slim gold lighter engraved with the words 'To my lovely Sonny'. Impulsively she threw it to the far end of the room, where it bounced off the carpet and slid beneath the jardinière.

A shadow crossed the glazed front door. Nervously she swung round, peering through the glass. 'Martha?' She stepped forward, waiting. Praying it was not him.

A moment passed. There was no one there. She reached into the drawer once more, groped around and swore. 'Bugger it!' Having thrown down the lighter, she couldn't find any matches.

Snatching up the pack of cigarettes, she strode into the sitting room and went to the fireplace. On tiptoe she searched the high mantelpiece, her fingers creeping from one side to the other. With a sigh of relief, she took down a box of matches. While she lit the cigarette her hands shook uncontrollably. Hurry, Martha! Where was she?

Pausing a moment, she considered her options. But there was no real choice left to her. Frustrated, she seated herself in the wicker chair beside the door. This morning she had woken and thrown open the curtains to another beautiful late-spring day, happy that she was going to work, excited as a child because she would see *him*.

On the frequent occasions when Tony Bridgeman came into the main office he would thrill her with discreet, suggestive glances. At lunchtime they would get into their cars and drive away in different directions, to meet a few moments later in Aspley Woods. In his roomy Jaguar they would sit and talk and kiss, making plans for a future together. And often, when there were no walkers around, they would get into the back and make love. To her it was wonderful. To him it was all part of a greater plan.

Right from the first she hated all the secrecy, but he was adamant. It was 'a necessary, but temporary, arrangement', he said. 'No one must know, not until I've made the break with Celia and we're free to spend the rest of our lives together.'

He had promised her the world. And, like a fool, she had believed him. After all, this was his child growing inside her.

She'd desperately needed to believe in him. But on reflection, there had been many times when she'd felt misgivings. Doubting his word. Doubting his love. Little things had made her insecure. Like the time she discovered by chance that he'd ordered two dozen red roses to be delivered to his wife on their anniversary. Another time she had taken her Aunt Martha out for a birthday meal, only to see Tony and his wife hidden away in a corner, enjoying a candlelit dinner and looking for all the world like a couple madly in love. Little things. None of them betraying a deeper madness.

As the shock began to subside and the truth dawned at last, she felt incredibly weary. Sinking into the arm-chair by the fireside she leaned her head into her hands and closed her eyes, trying to shut out the truth, trying to decide what to do.

Desperate for Martha to come home, she went to the window and looked out. The evening was sultry. The small garden that she adored was filled with blossom; the roses intermingled, creating a breathtaking array of colour. The hydrangeas bowed beneath the weight of huge pink flowers. Two greenfinches fluttered on to the cherry tree, softly chattering to each other.

Entranced, she opened the window. The heady scent from the nicotianas filled the room. She leaned out, enjoying the late sun on her face. Startled, the greenfinches flew away. Alone again, she closed the window. The familiar cottage felt eerie and deserted. Night was closing in fast.

Agitated, she paced the floor, back and forth. Coming into the hallway she glanced at the grandfather clock. It was ten minutes past nine. 'She should have been home by now!'

In a moment Sonny was outside, walking down the path to the white-painted gate. Her anxious eyes scoured the street. Still no sign of that homely little woman who, since her parents' death, had been like a mother to her.

Suddenly there she was, waddling up the lane, a familiar figure in a blue linen coat and red-patterned neckerchief. The colours clashed blindingly, but Martha was never one to be bothered about style or fashion. When Sonny had once tried to persuade her into something more fashionable, Martha had put her well and truly in her place. 'I'll wear what's comfortable, and that's that!' she'd declared firmly, and experience showed she would not change her mind.

Sonny was greatly relieved to see her. A small round body with flyaway brown curls, Martha Moon was well known hereabouts. Outspoken to a fault, but with a warm, generous heart, she was loved by all who knew her. Sixty-eight years of age, she still had a naughty twinkle in her bright blue eyes and a zest for life that left others breathless.

As she approached her beloved cottage, Martha chatted to the big ginger cat strolling by her feet. 'Come to meet me, have you?' she asked, touching his ear with the tips of her podgy fingers. 'I ain't brought you nothing, so you needn't roll your saucy eyes at me,' she teased.

Calmed by the sight of her aunt, Sonny turned away. Leaning on the gate, she looked back at the cottage. It was a picture-postcard place, with crooked chimneys and leaning walls, lead-light windows and pretty floral curtains. Filled with old oak beams that sagged in the middle, it had been in the family for generations. Aunt Martha and her own dear mother had grown up in it. Now it was stamped with Martha's cheerful personality and Sonny had found contentment in it. She had come to love it, just as she had come to love Martha.

A thought struck her. It would be too dangerous to stay here now and, knowing Martha, that dear soul would probably insist on coming with her. 'It's no good,' she decided with a sinking heart. Much as she needed to confide in someone, she realised now it could not be Martha. 'I can't tell her,' she muttered aloud. 'I can't ask Martha to shoulder such a responsibility.'

She was startled when a familiar voice chided, 'Talking to yourself is a sign of madness.'

Sonny opened the gate to let her aunt in. 'That's not true, is it?' She needed reassurance. Maybe it wasn't Tony Bridgeman who was mad. Maybe it was her.

Martha's homely face crinkled into a smile. "Course it ain't true!' she scolded. 'If it were, I'd be mad as a hatter. I'm always chattering to myself.' She came through the gate. 'Old Lizzie Trent's been making remarks about my surname again,' she revealed impatiently. 'Wants to know how I came by such an unusual name as "Moon". Says the only person she's ever heard called Moon was hanged twenty years ago for murder, and she wouldn't be surprised if it was a relative of mine!'

'You two always seem to rub each other up the wrong way.'

Martha chuckled. 'She'll think twice in future,' she announced proudly. 'I told her straight . . . *you're* more suited to the name than I am, Lizzie Trent, on account of you having a backside the size of a full moon!'

Happy to be home, delighted because she had dealt with the interfering busybody who wouldn't leave her alone, and tickled pink because she'd won five pounds at bingo, she erupted in a fit of giggles. She giggled while she waddled up the path; she giggled as they went into the house; and she was still giggling while Sonny made the tea.

When, a short time later, they were seated at the old oak table in the kitchen, she told Sonny, 'I think I'll give up the bingo.'

Sonny argued that she said the same thing every week, and every week she went back. 'You meet your friends there,' she reminded her. 'With me at work all day it's the only chance you get for a good old chinwag.' That was another reason why she couldn't tell Martha the truth. If that dear soul insisted on moving from here, it would be a terrible wrench.

Martha regarded her discreetly. 'Is everything all right?' she asked. Like an old fox, she could smell trouble.

'Everything's fine,' Sonny lied, but she felt the flush of guilt creep up her neck.

'That's good.' Sensing Sonny's anxiety, but waiting for

her to confide in her own good time, Martha talked about this and that, none of it important. 'Did you have a good day at work?' she asked eventually.

'Busy.'

'You like your work, don't you?' Martha had an idea what was worrying her niece. In fact she'd noticed it for some time now.

'It's a job, that's all.'

Martha wisely made no reply. Instead she sipped her tea, observing Sonny through worried blue eyes. 'A penny for them,' she said cheerfully.

Sonny painted on a smile. If she thought it hid the heartache beneath, she was wrong.

While Martha chatted, Sonny's thoughts were back in Tony Bridgeman's house. In her mind's eye she could see herself crouching beneath the window, peering in, unable to come to terms with what she was hearing.

Martha watched, and wondered. She suspected Sonny was pregnant, but sensed there was more to her unease than that. There was something more disturbing here than having a child out of wedlock – though that was trouble enough.

Martha looked at her niece straight in the eye. 'You seem worried, my dear. It's nothing to do with John Chapman, is it?'

Visibly shaken, Sonny reminded her, 'That was a long time ago. John Chapman is a happily married man now, with two young babies.' She laughed scornfully. 'I was never very good at choosing the right men.'

Martha wasn't being cruel. She was gently reminding Sonny how easily relationships could go wrong. John

Chapman had hurt her, yes. But that was water under the bridge – a girlish fling that was never meant to be serious. *This* was serious. She and Tony. Sonny tried to shut out reality. 'I see John in the street quite often,' she informed Martha. 'We pass the time of day. There's nothing there. There never really was.'

'And now?'

'What do you mean?'

'I mean ... is there a boyfriend?' She didn't really need to ask. She had seen Sonny blossom over the past year. Lately she had heard her being sick in the mornings. And now she saw the little tell-tale signs in those pretty green eyes. Something bad had happened. Something worse than before.

Blushing to the roots of her hair, Sonny avoided the question. 'I'll be twenty-five soon ... a bit too old to have a boyfriend.' Many times she'd wanted to tell Martha about him, but he wouldn't let her.

Martha was not so easily distracted. 'You would tell me if there was anything worrying you?' she asked anxiously.

'I always have.' At least that was the truth. Until now.

Sensing that she had pressed far enough, Martha collected her crossword book from the drawer. Returning to her chair, she perched her spectacles on the end of her nose and pretended to concentrate on the clues.

Pouring them each another cup of tea, Sonny switched on the radio. Maybe he had been arrested. Maybe they had found him out and he was locked away. Don't be stupid! she told herself. How could anyone else know? The realisation rose like a black cloud inside her.

There was no help coming.

The Nine o'clock News began with protests by the USSR about US aircraft overflying their territory.

'When will they learn to trust each other?' Sonny muttered, switching the radio off.

'When will we all learn to trust each other?' Martha asked without looking up.

Sonny knew what she was getting at and felt ashamed. 'I think I'll go up to bed soon,' she said, clearing away the empty teacups. 'I've a feeling tomorrow will be a heavy day.' She still didn't know what to do. She certainly couldn't go into work, and she couldn't stay here. Like it or not, she had to consider Martha in all of this. She had to make plans. And quickly.

For a while each woman was lost in her own thoughts. Ten minutes passed. Twenty.

Sonny washed the teacups and kissed her aunt goodnight. 'Are you sure you don't want anything before I go?'

'I don't think so,' Martha answered. Catching hold of Sonny's hand as she walked away, she said softly, 'I'm here if you want me. You know that, don't you?'

Sonny lovingly squeezed her hand. 'I know,' she answered affectionately. 'But you mustn't worry. I'm fine. Really.'

Martha nodded, but made no reply. She was not convinced.

'I'll lock up, then I'll be off.'

Martha was astonished. 'You don't have to do that.' Locking up was her job. 'I can do that when I've finished my crossword. Good heavens! I've locked up this house every night for the past forty years.'

'Then it's time you had a night off.' Sonny's remark was casual, but her intent was deadly serious.

She had to secure the house against intruders.

It was hot and humid. The sheets clung to her skin and made her itch. She couldn't sleep. She couldn't even think straight any more.

The reverberating sound of the grandfather clock invaded her room, its deep musical tones striking the hours ... *one* ... *two* ... *three*. There was a time when the pleasant sounds were merely part of the house's heartbeat – a background noise, comforting, never intrusive. Now, though, for the first time, they echoed inside her head, lingering long after the chimes had died in the air.

For what seemed an age Sonny tried to sleep, but her mind was too active, the same awful dread too alive inside her. Was Tony thinking of her? she wondered. Was his heart so black there had never been a moment when he truly loved her? Did his wife go along with him out of loyalty, or love ... or was it a strange kind of revenge? She recalled that last glimpse of her face. Celia Bridgeman had a hauntingly beautiful face, a face both intelligent and cunning. And evil. *Both of them were evil!*

Raising herself up on one elbow, Sonny stretched out her arm and switched on the bedside lamp. Peering at the small porcelain clock she gave the merest whisper of a smile – the pretty timepiece was a Christmas present from her friend Patricia Burton. 'Half-past three,' she

14

groaned, sinking back into the pillows. She had been awake for hours. It seemed like a lifetime.

Getting out of bed, she put on her high-wedge slippers and dressing gown. Leisurely fastening the belt, she went to the window and looked out. The sky was a strange mixture of light and dark, with the merest hint of dawn. Everywhere was quiet. She opened the window and breathed deeply. Resting on her hands, she leaned forward, observant green eyes searching the lane. Below her a rat scuttled across the lawn; farther away in the valley an owl hooted. 'Everything looks normal,' she breathed. 'Have I imagined it?' But no, she had not.

Leaving the window open she went downstairs, tiptoeing past Martha's room so as not to wake her. She wondered what it would be like leaving Martha behind. Moreover, what would it be like, leaving here and starting a new life? The prospect of going away was daunting. The prospect of staying even more so.

In the sitting room she went straight to the mantelpiece, where she took down the cigarettes and matches. 'Must give up this filthy habit,' she muttered as she blew the smoke from her nostrils. 'Especially now, with the baby and all.'

She was still pacing the floor when Martha came down. For a few moments the little woman stayed in the doorway unobserved, watching and worrying. After a while she gave a little tap on the door. 'All right if I come in?' she asked, entering anyway.

Sonny swung round, momentarily startled. 'It's your home,' she answered, resenting the intrusion, resenting herself for making such an unfeeling remark.

15

'Your home too, I hope?' Martha retorted.

'Sorry. I didn't mean to be rude.'

Martha seated herself in the big old armchair by the empty firegrate. When the chair had been handed down from her grandmother it was past its best. Restored now, and bedecked in new floral-patterned covers made by Martha herself, it was a lovely thing. With short chubby legs, arms sturdy enough to hold a cup and plate, and offering much comfort, it resembled Martha in many ways. She had lovingly sited the chair in her favourite place. Set at an angle between the fireplace and the corner wall, it was positioned so she could see through the french doors to the pretty garden. She spent many a pleasant hour resting in the old chair, watching Nature weave its magic spell outside.

Now she made herself comfortable, intending to get to the root of her niece's problem, because she was certain it must be bad. At the same time she didn't want to be too pressing, preferring Sonny to confide in her without persuasion. So she merely observed, 'You still haven't managed to give up the cigarettes then?'

'I've only ever smoked twenty a day and I've managed to cut back to ten. That's a start.' Impatiently Sonny stubbed her cigarette out in the grate. 'I used to enjoy a cigarette, but I know I'll have to pack it in.'

'Why?' But Martha already knew the reason.

The abruptness of her aunt's question threw Sonny for a moment. 'No real reason,' she answered, fobbing her off.

Martha smiled knowingly. 'Not because you're pregnant then?'

Sonny stared at her. Then, as though a great weight had dropped from her shoulders, she almost fell into the chair opposite Martha's. A sense of relief washed over her. The truth was out. She didn't have to deceive Martha any longer. With the relief came a pressing sense of weariness. It wasn't just the pregnancy, though that was bad enough. There were things more terrible. Dare she confide? Dare she draw Martha into such a thing?

Resting her elbows on her knees, she dropped her face into the palms of her hands, her voice emerging muffled as she asked, 'How did you know?'

Martha shook her head and smiled. 'I don't know from personal experience, more's the pity,' she sighed. 'I may be a spinster and old in the tooth, but I do know when a woman's pregnant... the blossoming... the morning sickness. I've watched you these past weeks, and now I'm sure.' She reached out and took hold of Sonny's hand. 'I've always found that when you're troubled it helps to talk about it.'

Sonny looked up. 'I should have told you,' she admitted. 'It's just that—' She hesitated. '*He* asked me not to.'

Martha had already guessed. '*He* being your boss, Mr Tony Bridgeman?'

Even in her dilemma Sonny couldn't help but laugh. 'I never could keep anything from you!'

'That's because I'm an old witch,' Martha teased. Quite suddenly her tone changed to one of disapproval. 'He's married, isn't he?'

'Yes.' There was no point in lying.

'Does he intend to get a divorce?'

Sonny had to smile at that. 'I don't think so.'

Martha nodded her head. 'I see!' Anger flashed in her bright blue eyes. 'Now the bugger's got you pregnant, he wants nothing to do with you, is that it?'

It was on the tip of her tongue to spill out the truth. Instead Sonny answered quietly, 'Something like that.'

Martha detected her reluctance to confide more. She also detected something else. Fear! Just then, when Sonny glanced at her, she thought she had seen a flicker of horror in her eyes. 'Tell me, sweetheart,' she urged, moving to the edge of her seat. 'Tell me everything.'

Uncomfortable beneath Martha's curious gaze, Sonny got up and went to the fireplace, where she stretched out her arms and leaned against the mantelpiece, her every instinct telling her it would be all right to tell. Martha would understand. She would know how to deal with it. But how to start? That was the difficult bit. At the beginning, she decided firmly. That was best.

And so she began. 'Tony and I have been seeing each other for over a year.' Her smile was bitter-sweet. 'I loved him so much.' All that was over now, she told herself. It was no good letting regrets flood in. 'He told me it had been over with his wife for a very long time ... "She leads her life and I lead mine," he said.'

Martha did understand. 'All lies, was it?'

Sonny turned to face her. She was eager now, anxious to confess what was troubling her. 'Like a stupid idiot, I believed everything he told me!' she said scornfully. 'Lately, though, I was beginning to wonder. Little things he did or said played on my mind. Things that told me he wasn't being altogether truthful.' She hung her

18

head. 'Oh, Aunt Martha, how could I have let myself be taken in like that?'

'We all make mistakes.' Martha tried hard never to sit in judgement. She didn't do so now. 'Go on, dear.'

'Whenever I had any doubts, he was quick to reassure me. It was over between him and his wife, he said, and they were both wanting a divorce. Because she was a vindictive woman he asked me to keep our affair secret.' She lowered her voice. 'I never told anyone.'

Deeply agitated, she plucked the cigarettes and matches from the mantelpiece. She struck a match, blew it out, and replaced both the matchbox and the cigarette packet. 'I should have told you, though,' she said forlornly.

'And I'd have told you to drop him like a hot potato!' Martha declared.

Sonny wondered if that was the real reason why she had never said anything. 'All the same, I should have confided in you.'

'Well, you're confiding in me now, thank goodness, so go on.' Martha folded her chubby arms and sat back in the chair. 'You were saying?'

'He promised we'd get married as soon as possible.' Sonny touched her stomach and smiled. 'We planned to have lots of children. He said part of the reason why he and Celia had grown apart was because she didn't want children and he did. You know I've always wanted a family, so it seemed we were the perfect match,' she said bitterly.

'Does he know you're expecting his child?'

Sonny felt the colour drain from her face. 'I meant to

tell him today,' she murmured. 'I didn't get the chance, thank God.' Relief rushed through her. The things she had heard . . . Tony and Celia.

'Something bad happened, didn't it?' Martha queried. 'That's why you didn't tell him?'

Sonny smiled at her. 'You're so perceptive,' she said gratefully. 'The truth is, I'd decided not to involve you, but now I hope you can advise me. You see . . . it isn't as simple as you might think.'

'Nothing ever is.'

'He was out of the office all day today, attending business meetings, that kind of thing. I missed him, like I always do.' Flushed with guilt, she lowered her gaze. 'But I kept myself busy enough, what with trade orders and paperwork for the new housing development. Then there's the purchase of two hundred acres of land he's in the process of buying, and the ongoing negotiations for the shopping precinct.' She grimaced. 'Everything the evil bastard touches turns to gold.'

A hard, disapproving look from Martha was enough to make her feel ten years old again. 'Sorry, but he *is* an evil bugger!' She went on, 'Because of the extra administration, and a great pile of correspondence that needed getting away, I intended working through until eight. So when he phoned at half-past six he knew I'd still be there. He needed some important documents and wanted me to take them to his house.'

Being old fashioned, Martha didn't agree with women taking too much responsibility on themselves. 'What was wrong with Jack Metcalf taking the papers? He's the officeboy, the one who's supposed to do the running, isn't he?' Naturally curious, she had been kept well informed over the years about life in the office.

'Tony did ask for Jack, but, like everyone else, he'd been gone some time. I offered to take the papers, and he seemed delighted. We had a short, intimate conversation, and it was arranged that I should drop them off on my way home.' She took a moment to recall his exact words. 'I wondered if his wife would be out, and he'd planned it so we could spend some time together.'

Smiling nervously, she swung away and again took down the cigarettes and matches. She lit a cigarette and took a puff. Then almost immediately she angrily stubbed it out. Still plagued with doubts about involving Martha, she suggested, 'We can talk about it tomorrow if you like?'

'No time like the present,' Martha said firmly. And it was obvious she meant to stay put until she'd heard it all.

'He said he wouldn't need the documents until seven-thirty. But I was so excited at the prospect of seeing him that I got finished early.' Sonny smiled ruefully. 'I called in at the surgery this morning to collect my test results. I'm pregnant.' She grimaced. 'I can't really believe it.' Nothing in the world, not even Tony Bridgeman, could make her regret having this child. 'I knew he'd be thrilled,' she said regretfully, 'and I couldn't wait to tell him the wonderful news.' In her mind's eye she pictured his face and loathed him.

'I went to the house, just as he'd asked,' she continued softly. 'I rang the doorbell a few times but couldn't seem to make him hear me.'

Overwhelmed, she sat down and took a moment to think. 'The lights were on,' she recalled. 'Music softly playing.' Her voice shook. 'I thought he might be in the bathroom, or out the back ... so I went round the side of the house.' Tears misted her eyes and she had to look away. 'The curtains were open in the lounge and the window wide open. You could see right in ...'

Martha guessed. 'He was there, wasn't he? With his wife?'

Sonny nodded, her voice falling to a whisper. 'They were naked ... writhing about on the floor.' She would never forget what she had seen. Every detail was imprinted on her mind for all time: the cream-coloured carpet; the television flickering in the background; that new singer, Elvis Presley, singing 'Heartbreak Hotel'. Tony and Celia, bare as the day they were born, him beneath, her on top, ecstatic in the throes of pleasure. 'Blatant they were,' she said bitterly. 'Not seeming to care who saw them.'

'They are man and wife, dear,' Martha gently reminded her.

Suffused with shame, but needing to talk, Sonny described what she had seen. 'I turned away and suddenly they were laughing. When I looked back, they were just lying there, holding each other.' Spent of passion, she thought enviously. 'They looked so right with each other, so much in love. I couldn't believe it ...' She glanced up, her face wrung with sadness. 'Oh, Aunt Martha! What a fool I've been!'

'You weren't the first to be fooled by a smooth tongue and I dare say you won't be the last.' Always the practical one, Martha told her, 'Whatever you decide to do, you know I'll be behind you all the way. You and the baby will live here, of course. You mustn't worry about money. I have enough tucked away to keep the three of us if need be. But when you're able, and if you want to, you can return to work. I'm not so ancient that I can't look after the infant.' Her old face crinkled into a grin. 'Matter of fact, I'd love it.'

She chatted on, delighted to think she might be of use, already aching to hold the child in her arms. 'And I don't want you worrying your head about what the neighbours might say. The nearest one hasn't spoken to me in years, and the others are too far away to worry about.' She giggled. 'Just think . . . I'll be a great-Aunt.' She would have gone on chattering, but the look in Sonny's eyes made her stop. 'Tell me,' she urged. 'Whatever it is, you can tell me.'

Raising her face to the ceiling, Sonny groaned. 'Bless you,' she murmured gratefully. 'But you don't understand. He will move heaven and earth to take the baby from me.'

Martha was horrified. 'You wouldn't let that happen, would you? I mean . . . you're the mother. And what about his wife? My God! She'd throw the bugger out if she knew what he'd been up to. You could cause havoc in that house if you wanted. Talk to him. Threaten him if you have to. If all else fails, you must appeal to his better nature. Explain how the child will have a better home with us.' She tutted impatiently, 'Tony Bridgeman might be wealthy, and a pillar of society, but that doesn't mean to say he'll be a good father.' Wagging a chubby finger, she declared angrily, 'No court in the land will take a child away from its mother, especially when the father's marriage has broken up.' She actually chuckled. 'By! His feet won't touch the ground when his wife knows about the child.'

Torn by love for Martha, and fear for herself and the unborn child, and knowing she had gone too far not to tell the whole story, Sonny dropped to her knees before the little woman. Startled, Martha would have protested, but she was stopped by the gentlest finger pressed against her lips. 'Listen to me,' Sonny pleaded. 'Let me finish.'

Wide-eyed, Martha nodded.

Taking a deep breath, Sonny explained, 'I said he used me, and he did.' The shame was red hot inside her. 'But I wasn't just his bit on the side.' Her eyes grew moist, her mouth trembling as she went on. 'I told you how I saw them . . . him and his wife? You remember what I said, how after they had . . .' Her voice dropped to a whisper. 'Afterwards, they sat on the floor, holding each other and talking?'

Martha nodded, concentrating on Sonny's every word. 'I remember,' she said. 'You heard them talking. Yes. Go on, dear.'

'They were talking about me. He was saying how he suspected I might be pregnant. *She was so thrilled, she threw her arms round his neck and hugged him.*'

Martha's face crumpled. 'What do you mean? Wasn't she angry? Didn't she threaten to throw him out? I don't understand. What are you saying?'

Reaching out, Sonny took her aunt's chubby hands in

her own. 'His wife won't throw him out because she wants the baby too. It was all planned.' Sarcasm and self-loathing hardened her voice. 'Apparently his wife can't have children. I was healthy and available, so it was decided that he and I would make the baby and the two of them would lay claim to it.'

'Good God! What kind of monsters are they?'

'The worst kind.'

'But they can't do it! We won't let them.'

'*Listen to me!*' Desperate for Martha to see how futile it was, she quickly went on, 'Tony Bridgeman never gives up. I know him well enough to realise he usually gets what he wants. His wife is made out of the same mould. I can't fight the two of them.' The whisper of a smile lit her face. 'But there is a way. You see, he still doesn't know I'm pregnant, so if I move from here the chances are he will never know. I can just leave and not say anything. Or I can send him a letter . . . friendly and apologetic. Let him believe his awful secret is safe. I'll tell him I've been offered a post with an international corporation, and have to leave for France immediately. He knows my French is good enough to get me such a position. I expect he'll be angry because he's wasted time and money on me. But he'll accept it, because he won't suspect I'll be taking his child with me.'

The idea that he should ever find out made her go cold inside. 'There's little he can do. After I'm gone, he'll probably shift his "affections" to someone else. Though, I tell you—' Her fists clenched and her expression hardened as she promised, 'If I ever found out he and his wife used another woman the way they used me, I'd make sure that woman heard about it before it was too late.'

Falling back into her chair she felt spent of all energy. Her gaze dwelt on Martha. 'I'm sorry to have involved you like this,' she said. 'But now you can see why I have to get away. Far enough so that he'll never find me.'

Martha shook her head. 'I can't let you do that,' she said softly. 'These people are wicked. You must fight them. Go to the police. Tell them what you've told me. If it means a court case, we can find the money. Like I said, I have enough.' She glanced round, her heart aching. 'I'll sell this cottage if I have to.'

Sonny had never loved her more than she did in that moment. 'I couldn't let you sell your lovely home,' she assured her. 'But I'll never be able to thank you enough for making such an offer.' Seated on the edge of the chair now, she was looking straight into Martha's worried blue eyes, aware that what she was about to reveal would hurt her badly. 'The truth is, I've already started making plans. By this time tomorrow night, I mean to be well on my way.'

Martha shook her head. 'You'll do no such thing! This is your home, my girl, and I won't let him or anyone else drive you away.'

'I have to go.'

'Why?' Martha was fighting fit. 'Why do you have to go? And don't give me the argument that he'll have the baby away from you, because, I swear to God, if he tries he'll rue the day.'

'It isn't just the baby.'

'What is it, then? What else can he do to you?'

'He can kill me.'

The fight went out of the old woman. '*Kill you?*' she asked, her face grey with shock. 'You'd better tell me exactly what you mean by that.'

'I heard it all . . . when the two of them were talking.' Sonny paused before speaking more softly, letting the words sink in. 'At first it was just about the baby, and what they would do if and when he got me pregnant.' She heard their voices in her head. 'Celia asked how he would deal with it if I refused to hand over the baby.' She smiled, a hard smile that spoke volumes. 'Tony told her not to worry, that the baby would be theirs. "When the time comes, Sonny will be sensible," he said. "And if she isn't . . . I'll just have to kill her." '

A long silence followed, during which Martha stared disbelievingly at her niece. Her voice came in a strange guttural croak. 'You have to go to the police.'

Springing from the chair, Sonny argued, 'I can't!' She began pacing the room again, more afraid than ever. 'It would be their word against mine. I wouldn't stand a chance. The eminent Tony Bridgeman and his wife on the one hand and me on the other . . . a nobody who answers his phone, and files his letters, and has a crush on the poor man. Oh, yes! I can just imagine what it would be like being cross-examined.'

Hooking her two thumbs into imaginary lapels, she barked out angrily: 'What evidence do you have? All you heard was a conversation between man and wife.

27

And can you explain why you were listening in the first place? What were you doing creeping round the back of your employer's house? Oh? You were asked to take some papers? And is there anyone who can corroborate your story?'

Seeming to shrink as she relaxed, she said hopelessly, 'They'd tear me to shreds. They would never believe me over them.' She threw her arms up in frustration. 'You know what I'm saying is true, Aunt Martha. Those two evil devils are prominent and respected members of society. They collect for needy children every Christmas, they buy new buses for various charities and thanks to their generosity last year, a sick child was flown out to Canada for treatment.'

Martha was only now beginning to realise the enormity of the situation. 'But that's all show,' she protested lamely. 'Camouflage to hide his true nature.'

'You know that, and I know it. But no one else has a bad word to say about them. If I accused them of planning to murder me, *I'd* be the one they'd hang by the neck!'

'There must be some way you can prove that he's the father.'

'I've already considered that,' Sonny said. 'But then he'd have an even greater claim on my baby.' In her heart she knew there was only one solution. Tony Bridgeman must never know she was pregnant with his child.

Grateful that she had an ally in Martha, she felt as though a weight had been lifted from her shoulders.

Martha knew all there was to know and now, after vowing not to let her emotions get the better of her, Sonny broke down. 'I don't want to leave you,' she told her. 'But what else can I do?'

'Come here, child.' Martha stretched out her arms.

With a sob Sonny sank to the floor and laid her head on the old woman's knee. 'I can't fight him,' she said wearily. 'He's made himself untouchable.'

She felt a warm hand on her face, gently stroking her temple. 'I know, dear,' a soft voice told her. 'And you're right. Hard though it is, I do believe it might be better for you to go away.'

'But where?' She shuddered. 'I never dreamed it would come to this.'

Martha was quiet for a moment, assailed by an unspeakable rage against the Bridgemans, and against the utter futility of the situation. Sonny was right. They could never fight the Bridgemans, and even if they did it might prove to be a disaster, with Sonny robbed of her child and maybe even imprisoned for slander. It was a risk Martha would not let her take.

Torn between her lovely old cottage and her beloved niece, she knew there were sacrifices to be made. Presently she said softly, 'You won't be leaving here alone, because I'm coming too.'

When Sonny began to protest, Martha wagged a finger and silenced her with, 'Don't argue now! We'll go north. I lived there for some time when I was in service, and they're good, kind folk.' Already a plan was taking shape in her mind.

'What about your home?' A little ray of brightness

appeared in Sonny's heart. The thing she had feared
most was being alone in a strange place. With Martha
there it would be so much easier. All the same, she
chided herself for being selfish.

'The cottage will be safe,' Martha assured her. 'Leave
that to me.' She smiled lovingly. 'You and the baby are
far more important than bricks and mortar.' Wiping a
thumb over Sonny's tears, she said, 'Go and put the
kettle on, there's a dear. I can't think straight without a
sup or two of strong tea.'

She clenched her fists. 'I ought to go round and see
him. I ought to let him know he's the one who should
be on the run.'

'If I thought it would do any good, I'd have confronted
him myself,' Sonny declared. 'But he's a clever
man, with influential people behind him.' Oh, if only
she could instil the same fear in him that he had put
into her!

Martha watched as Sonny went through to the tiny
kitchen. She reflected on Sonny's words and, in a
brighter voice, called out, 'You and I have things to talk
about, my dear. A new baby. A new life to plan.' Her
voice fell to a whisper. 'It's an upheaval, though. And
I'm not really sure where to start.'

She thought about leaving her lovely home. Her gaze
was drawn to the ceiling, and in her mind's eye beyond,
to the sky above. 'I'll be starting all over again,' she
murmured. 'At a time in my life when I would be content
to end my days quietly.'

A wave of sadness flowed through her. For the briefest
moment her blue eyes were shadowed over. But when

Sonny returned she was smiling.

Like the old fox she was, Martha knew how to hide her deeper feelings.

Chapter Two

Following a week of frenzied activity, Sonny and her aunt were almost at the end of their tether. Martha had interviewed no less than eight prospective tenants for the cottage, and, as she indignantly announced when the last one departed, 'I wouldn't let that lot live in the shed, let alone the cottage!'

'You'll be lucky to find anyone who comes up to your impossibly high standards.' Sonny was worried but amused. 'It's a wonder you've let *me* live here, because there were at least two women who had a far better pedigree than I have.'

'I won't argue with that,' Martha said, looking away and smiling to herself. 'I suppose I should have thrown you out years ago, but unfortunately a body has to make allowances for family.'

Laughing, Sonny took no notice. She was used to Martha's cheeky ways, and loved her all the more for them. 'If we're leaving on Friday, that only gives us tomorrow.' Friday couldn't come quickly enough for her. With Tony unexpectedly called away on business, things seemed to be working in her favour.

'We will manage to get away on Friday, won't we?' He was due back on Saturday morning. She meant to be long gone by then.

'That's what we've planned, and that's what we'll do,' Martha answered assertively. A little humility crept into her voice as she added, 'With the help of the Lord.'

'That's all I want to hear,' Sonny said, greatly relieved.

Already she was beginning to feel better, lighter inside; although it was early days, she was almost convinced she'd felt the baby move this morning. Martha dismissed it. 'By! It's nothing but wind,' she said, and Sonny had to agree.

During this past week, when they'd been too busy to stop and think, Sonny had fleetingly wondered if she had dreamed the whole dreadful episode with regard to Tony and his wife. But no! she reminded herself. It was true enough, and if she was to travel the world twice over and die a very old and lonely woman, she would never forget the danger she had been in.

The hard work had already been done. After searching through umpteen brochures, and making lengthy telephone calls that would swell the bill to twice its normal size, Sonny had finally managed to secure rooms in what seemed to be a respectable boarding house in Samlesbury, Lancashire.

According to the brochure, the property, Sefton House, had been a gentleman's residence. The house was surrounded by its own land; the sizeable orchard and kitchen gardens provided fruit and vegetables for the tables. The many greenhouses produced enough blooms to decorate the house all year round, and from the dining room, you could see the grand sweep of the moors.

It was run by a Miss Sefton. 'I wonder if she's related to the original owner?' Sonny mused aloud when Martha brought the brochure home.

Martha said it was a pity if she was, for it would mean she had come down in the world. 'From being served to serving.' She could be very philosophical when the mood took her, could Martha.

Shaking her head with wonder, Sonny had finished reading the description: 'Situated close to the countryside yet only a short distance from the busy town of Blackburn.' It sounded ideal.

'The hamlet of Samlesbury, Lancashire.' Martha was pleasantly surprised.

Between packing the best china into small cardboard boxes (and Martha calling out a warning every few minutes to 'Be careful with that, my girl!') the two of them chatted about how they would live. Martha said she would stroll the countryside. Sonny was full of her intention to find a job of sorts, 'Until it's time to have the baby.' There was then a heated discussion about how Martha didn't agree with her working until after the baby came. Sonny refused to talk about it. And, for a while, the packing continued in silence.

Now most of it was done, and all that remained was for the delicate china to be collected and stored until they found a house to rent in Lancashire. Neither of them knew how long they would be there. 'We may never be able to come home,' Martha said sadly. 'But if I have you and the baby, I'll be happy enough.'

Sonny silently vowed to return the old lady to her cottage as soon as was humanly possible. But it would not be easy. Martha was a very stubborn woman. As for Sonny herself, she must stay away at least until the danger to herself and the baby was over.

'I think we've earned a cup of tea.' Clambering up from the floor, where she had been kneeling to sort the china, Sonny made her way to the kitchen. 'What time are they coming for the boxes?' she called from the sink.

'Any minute now,' Martha answered. 'I hope I've done the right thing. Oh, I know the firm came highly recommended. Mrs Percival has nothing but praise for them. When she and her husband returned from Australia after two years there wasn't a mark or a scratch on her beautiful furniture.'

'There you are then,' Sonny said. 'That was a whole houseful of furniture and china. All you've got to be stored are three small boxes.'

'I know that, but each of those china pieces carries a memory. Irreplaceable, they are.'

Sonny came in with the tray. 'Why don't you take them to Samlesbury?'

Martha shook her head. 'No, I'm sure they'll be safe in storage. Anyway, I hope it won't be too long before we find a place to rent in the north, then I can have my own china in my own display cabinet.'

After pouring the tea, Sonny looked around the tiny room. The window was open and the sun poured in, bathing the items of furniture that were as much a part of Martha's life as was the china. There was the old walnut sideboard, and the pretty cabinet situated by the window; a jardinière that had stood by the door for as long as Sonny could recall, with the same old cactus plant drooping towards the carpet. Against the wall, between the fireplace and the window, stood a small piano, its surface polished like a mirror. Martha played beautifully, but not so much these days, since her fingers had begun to stiffen.

'What about your furniture?' Sonny asked for the umpteenth time. 'It still isn't too late to put it in storage.'

Sipping her tea, Martha gave her an old-fashioned glance. 'The furniture stays in the cottage, where it belongs,' she answered quietly. 'It's been here longer than I have, and I have no intention of uprooting it.' She paused, taking a deep breath to disguise the catch in her voice.

After a moment she went on, 'Just because I'm leaving for a while doesn't mean to say the furniture has to leave as well.' Suddenly she smiled, her old face beaming. 'I'll feel much better knowing it's here, looking after the cottage, so to speak.'

Sonny's heart was in her boots. 'Oh, Martha! There's no need for you to leave here at all. I'm a grown woman. I can take care of myself.'

Martha was adamant. 'If it's a choice between staying here to look after the furniture and living away for a time to look after you, then there's no choice at all.' Her mood softened. 'If this tea is anything to go by, it's a good job I'm going with you, my girl. It's stone cold!'

Sonny was used to her little ploys. 'Now I know why you've been so impossible about the people who want to rent this cottage. Tell the truth, Martha. You don't even want to find a tenant, do you?'

Martha was caught out. 'Now that's nonsense and you know it,' she declared in a fluster. 'The money from the cottage will pay for our lodgings in the north.' Anticipating Sonny's argument, she said, 'And, no, I do not want your savings. I've got more than enough money in the bank, put away over the years for such an emergency – though I never in my life dreamed we'd be going into hiding.' She still felt an urge to confront the man. But, as Sonny had so rightly pointed out, the best course was to go away, have the baby, and, God willing, Tony Bridgeman would never be any the wiser.

Sonny brought Martha a fresh-brewed cup of tea before going upstairs to sort out her wardrobe. She sat on the bed awhile, staring out of the window and wondering if she or Martha would ever come back to this lovely place.

All week she'd been going through her belongings, deciding what to keep and what to discard. This past year she'd bought some stylish things – glamorous expensive articles. There was a black evening gown, bought for a night at the opera; a red cocktail dress she had worn to the office party; tight-fitting things that showed off her curves and earned Tony's admiring glances; ridiculously high-heeled shoes that nearly crippled her; and flimsy delicate undergarments, bought for the stolen weekends when he'd told her she was the most beautiful woman he had ever seen.

Disgusted with herself, she wrenched them out of the wardrobe. One by one she threw them into a rubbish bag. 'I wish I could tell you,' she muttered through clenched teeth, 'I wish I could say, "look at me, Tony . . . you got me pregnant. You had me, but you can't have the child." ' She laughed out loud. Feeling cheap. Feeling jubilant. Tears welled up and the sobs broke through.

Taking a moment, she let him come into her mind, deeply shocked when she still seemed to feel the faintest stirring of love.

No! The sound of her own voice echoed in her head. Pressing her two hands to her temples she sat on the bed, assailed by frightening and confusing emotions. Suddenly she was at the rubbish bag, tearing the clothes to shreds, rage driving her on. 'You can't love him!' she cried. 'You can despise him. You can want to kill him . . . kill them both. But . . . you . . . must . . . not . . . love . . . him!' She spat out the words slowly, deliberately, as though trying to convince herself. Yet she *had* loved him. Loved him with heart and soul. Dear God! How could she have done such a thing? Why didn't she see him for what he was? She knew now, though. And she wanted to punish him.

Raising her voice, she called out, *'It's not me who's the loser. It's you! Do you hear what I'm saying?'* She ran her hands over her stomach. 'This is your child, Tony,' she said rebelliously. 'But it's my child too. That's why, for as long as you live, you will never see it!'

It was half-past-two. Martha glanced up from reading the church magazine: 'What time is Miss Lorrimer arriving?'

'Three o'clock, and I hope she's suitable because she's

the last.' The woman had answered the advertisement in the most beautiful handwriting.

Martha read the advertisement out now, her face glowing with a mixture of sadness and pride:

The prettiest cottage to be let.
Situated in the old village of Woburn Sands, and set in delightful gardens, the property has close access to ancient woods.
This lovely period cottage has three double bedrooms, a large refurbished bathroom, spacious sitting room, and pine fitted kitchen.
Only serious-minded and respectable people need apply.

The advertisement betrayed Martha's emotions when she had written it out. Firstly, the description showed her deep attachment to the cottage and, secondly, it left no doubt as to the kind of person she would allow through her front door.

Her determination to attract only the 'right' sort of tenant had been revealed two days ago. 'Tell him it's been let already,' she urged Sonny when a tall scruffy man approached them in the garden, grinning at them through yellowing teeth. 'And don't take no nonsense from the bugger!' she called out as Sonny went to meet him.

When he appeared to be arguing, Martha charged down the path like a bull elephant. Thrusting herself between the bemused Sonny and the terrified man, she whacked him with a raspberry cane and sent him running down the lane with a look of sheer horror on his face. 'That'll teach the blighter!' she said, rolling up her sleeves as if ready to have another go. 'He'll not be in a hurry to visit this house again!'

'What a pity,' Sonny said, trying not to giggle. 'Because that was the new church warden. The vicar sent him to ask if you'd kindly arrange the flowers for tomorrow's christening.'

Momentarily taken aback, Martha was lost for words.

Regaining her composure, she squared her shoulders and marched off to the vegetable patch. 'I can't!' she declared huffily. 'I'm interviewing Miss Lorrimer.'

She gave a sideways glance at the man, who was still running down the lane. 'Serves him right, too. If the vicar wants me to arrange flowers, he should at least have the decency to ask me himself!' She dug her hand-fork into the ground and drew out a plump carrot. 'There's never been anybody who can grow early carrots like me,' she announced proudly. 'Won prizes, I have.'

As she worked her way along the row of green tops, there was no doubt that the matter of the church and the flowers was well and truly closed.

At ten minutes to three the man from Clayton's Removers arrived. With long unkempt hair, and dressed in a blue boiler suit, he was bound to get off on the wrong foot with Martha. 'Three boxes to collect,' he announced, checking his job sheet. 'Martha Moon . . . that you, is it?' Taking the pencil from behind his ear, he licked the end and made a note.

When Martha gave no reply but scrutinised him from head to foot he was so unnerved he dropped his job sheet on the step. The breeze picked it up and blew it across the lawn. 'By!' Martha was on the warpath. 'If you can't even take care of a piece of paper, how can I trust you to take care of my best china?' Her blue eyes drilled holes through him.

It took a moment for him to gather his wits. 'Because there ain't nobody better,' he said sharply. 'Clayton's have looked after china belonging to royalty, an' we ain't never had no complaints.'

They stared at each other, eyeball to eyeball, each convinced that the other was in the wrong. 'Inside!' Stepping back, Martha let him pass. 'And less of your bloody cheek!'

He was so astonished to hear her swear he laughed out loud. 'I'm glad it's china we're looking after,' he chuckled, ''Cause we ain't got no facilities for tough old birds like you, missus.'

The ice was broken and soon the two of them were exchanging pleasantries. Sonny watched from the kitchen doorway. He was right, she thought. Martha *was* a tough old bird. She was also the dearest, warmest creature on God's earth.

Ten minutes later he was gone, having suffered Martha's telling him how to carry the boxes, how to load them, and where to place them in the warehouse: 'So they're not buried under other people's paraphernalia,' she told the exasperated fellow.

No sooner had he left than the florist's van drew up. 'For Miss Sonny Fareham,' the driver said with a cheeky wink. It was the largest bouquet of red roses Sonny had ever seen.

With mixed emotions, she carried them into the house and read the card. 'They're from him,' she confirmed, dropping the card as if it had burned a hole in her hand. But then, who else could they be from? For over a year Tony had been the only man in her life.

Martha said nothing. She trusted her niece to do the right thing.

'We could drop them off at the church,' Sonny suggested.

Martha laughed. 'By way of apology to the vicar, you mean?'

Sonny was laughing too. It felt good. 'Something like that,' she said, and so it was agreed. Meanwhile the roses were despatched outside, to the garden.

The next visitor was the prospective tenant for the cottage, Miss Lorrimer.

Martha got straight to the interview, and when it was over they both came up to Sonny's bedroom. 'This is my niece, Sonny,' Martha informed Miss Lorrimer, her face shining with pride. 'As I believe I told you, the girl is very dear to me.'

Sonny shook hands with the young woman. 'Aunt Martha still insists on calling me a girl,' she said with a grin. 'I can see from the surprise on your face you expected a child, not a woman.'

She took an immediate liking to Miss Lorrimer, who was about her own age, with soft brown eyes and long hair tied into a bun at the neck. She was not quite as tall as Sonny, but was slim and very pretty.

'Miss Lorrimer is an artist,' Martha explained. 'She fell in love with the cottage rightaway.' Her chest visibly swelled. 'Would you believe, she wants to paint it in oils?'

One look at Martha's face told Sonny that at long last they had a tenant for the cottage. That was another problem solved.

At nine o'clock Sonny made the cocoa and the two of them sat and talked. 'Well, that's that,' Martha observed. 'My best china is in safe hands, we've found a good place to stay, and the cottage has a suitable tenant at last.'

Sonny grew silent, her gaze falling to the carpet, her mind going over all that had happened.

'Sonny, dear?' Martha was watching her, aware that this awful business had gone very deep. She suspected too that, in spite of herself, Sonny still felt a semblance of affection towards the creature who had fathered her child.

'Yes, Aunt?'

'You mustn't blame yourself . . . about Tony Bridgeman and the baby.' She regarded Sonny through worried blue eyes. 'I'm sure you know what I mean.'

'I know. But, yes, I do blame myself.'

'It won't help.'

'I know that too.'

Martha sighed. 'What about your friend . . . Patricia, isn't it? The one who's been calling to see how you are. What have you told her?'

'Only what I've told everyone else . . . that I've had a bad dose of 'flu.'

'Will you tell her the truth?'

'I'm not sure. She's a good soul, and I know she won't

tell anyone.' Yesterday Patricia had called to chat and Sonny had been tempted to tell her then. Now she wondered if it would have been wise. 'It might be safer if only you and I know the truth.'

'Will you see her again before we go?'

Sonny nodded. It was good to chat to someone her own age. 'I thought I might go tonight.' She glanced at the mantelpiece clock. It was nine-thirty. 'It's late though. By the time I get to Bletchley it'll be ten o'clock.'

'I thought you said she never went to bed early.'

'She doesn't, but I don't know if she'll thank me for turning up at such a late hour.' She considered it for a minute. It would be a real tonic to see her old friend again. 'I'll go!' she declared. 'If it's too late she can always turn me away.' But she knew Patricia would never do that. 'You don't mind, do you?'

'Mind!' Martha gave her a stern little look. 'Get off with you, and don't hurry back on my account, because I'm away to my bed.' To be honest she felt a little lost. Parting with the cottage, even, hopefully, for a short time, was a terrible wrench. But she didn't regret it. There were more important things at stake here.

Sonny had seen the sorrow in Martha's eyes, and the guilt was unbearable. 'It's not too late to change your mind,' she said softly. 'You really don't have to come with me, you know. Let me contact Miss Lorrimer. I'm sure she'll understand.' Funny thing, though. At first she didn't want to uproot Martha. Now, if Martha should change her mind it would make leaving that much harder.

Martha spoke sharply. 'That's enough of that kind of talk, my girl!' she said. 'When I close this cottage door there won't be me on one side and you on the other. We'll be leaving together, and that's an end to it.' Bristling with annoyance, she urged, 'Now, get off and see your friend. It'll do you good.'

But Sonny had changed her mind. 'Tomorrow,' she declared, 'when I've decided what I'll say to her.'

Long after Martha had gone to bed, Sonny lingered downstairs, curled up in her chair, loth to end the day. She felt afraid and rebellious at the same time. Confused and anxious, she wanted to run, and she wanted to stay. She loved him and she hated him. She craved his affection, yet feared it more. Strong emotions, all of them created by him; the child in her body . . . created by him. What now? She daren't think ahead more than one day at a time.

When the turmoil inside her got too much, when she felt as though the very walls were closing in on her, she went outside. The night was clear and beautiful. The gentle late-spring breeze bathed her face. Looking up at a peaceful sky she murmured a prayer. 'I know I did wrong,' she confessed. 'I knew he was married and I didn't care.'

A sudden chill came on her. Fastening her cardigan tighter about her, she returned to the cottage. Before closing the door on the night she glanced up at the sky once more. 'I deserve to be punished,' she whispered. 'But not the child. And not Martha.' That was her greatest fear now; that either of those innocents should be hurt. 'I have to trust you,' she told the quiet sky. 'Punish me if you must, but please don't hurt them.'

An hour later she crept up to bed. She could hear Martha gently snoring. It made her smile. This little cottage wouldn't be the same when it didn't reverberate to Martha's rhythmic snoring. 'Goodnight, Martha,' she whispered. 'And thank you.'

Sliding between the sheets, she lay awake for a time. When at last her eyes closed, she laid her two hands across the mound of her stomach, and was soon asleep.

It was a fitful, tormented sleep. But through it all shone the smallest glimmer of hope. Hope that the worst would soon be over. The day after tomorrow was the start of a new future. With God's help, they would find the contentment they sought.

And a safe haven. Where Tony Bridgeman would never find them.

It was eight o'clock when Sonny woke. She might have slept on, if it hadn't been for the postman whistling as he dropped a pile of mail through the door. 'Life goes on,' she muttered, peering through one tired eye at the chink of sunshine filtering in through the half-open curtains.

Reluctantly she threw off the blankets and sat, shivering, on the edge of the bed. 'It might be warm outside,' she said through chattering teeth, 'but it's bloody freezing in here!'

Crossing her arms over her body, she glanced at the pretty Victorian fireplace and the scuttle of logs close by. For one delicious minute she was tempted to light a fire. 'Better not,' she grumbled. 'I'll only have to clear the ashes afterwards, and what with so much else to do, there won't be time.'

She stretched out a goose-pimpled leg, feeling with her toes for her fleecy-lined slippers. Like a monkey she grabbed the edge of the slipper between her toes, but then, just as she had it almost to the edge of the bed, it slithered out of sight. 'Sod it!' In a minute she was on her knees, the cold lino sending a shock through her system as she searched for the slipper. When that one was found, she put it on and hopped about, searching for the other. 'How on earth did that get there?' The slipper was wedged beneath the dressing table.

Wearing slippers and dressing gown, she made her way to the bathroom. Here she quickly bathed, then scrubbed her teeth before returning to the bedroom, where she flung open the window. Immediately the sun poured in and the room was degrees warmer. She took clean undies from the drawer, slacks and jumper from the wardrobe, and a minute to dress. Next she brushed her short brown hair, and examined herself in the mirror. 'You look ready to fight the world,' she told herself. 'But not *him*,' she whispered as she departed for the kitchen. 'You couldn't fight *him*.'

Martha was already up. As always, she was bustling about in the kitchen. 'I thought I'd bake a cake for the vicar and his wife,' she said. 'By way of apology.'

Sonny couldn't help but smile. 'Oh? I thought the roses were "by way of an apology"?' She came to the table and sat down, getting a firm slap on the hand when she ran her finger round the rim of the mixing bowl. She licked it anyway, and the mixture was delicious. 'Walnut and raisin loaf,' she commented, sniffing the air and sighing. The kitchen was filled with the wonderful aroma. 'I hope you're keeping a slice or two for us.'

'I might,' Martha answered cunningly, 'if I were to get a fresh cup of tea.' She cocked her head to one side. 'You'll find an opened bottle of milk in the sink, but I've a feeling that one's gone off. You might have to get the other out of the bucket in the shed.'

She was right. As soon as Sonny drew the bottle out of the water, she could see the congealed milk settling in great clumps at the top. 'Hasn't the milkman been yet?' she asked, tipping the entire contents down the sink.

Lining the loaf-tin with greaseproof paper, Martha shook her head. 'Nope. The new fella started yesterday, an' he's got as much go in him as a breeze in a colander!' Quietly tutting, she scooped up the cake mix and dropped it into the tin. 'The one in the shed should be all right though.' Crossing to the old fire range, she put the cake in the oven. 'Get a move on then,' she said impatiently. 'I've a thirst on me like a navvy.'

'No sooner said than done.' Now it was Sonny bustling about, putting on the kettle, slicing the bread for toast, and generally preparing a quick breakfast for the pair of them. 'Keep your eye on this, will you?' she asked, placing the bread on the grill and sliding it under. 'I won't be a minute.'

And that was all it took. Before the toast was even

browning, she was back, carrying a bottle of milk. 'It's a lovely day,' she commented.

Wiping her hands, Martha came to the table. She looked round her little kitchen. 'It won't be long before we're back home,' she said wistfully.

Sonny's spirits dipped. 'I'm sure you're right,' she said, buttering the toast and arranging it on the plates. She wasn't as convinced as Martha, especially since, on the few occasions he'd been crossed in business, Tony Bridgeman had proved to be a very vindictive man.

After breakfast, Sonny offered to take the cake and the roses to the vicar. 'It'll save us precious time tomorrow,' she said.

Martha agreed. Slicing off two-thirds of the walnut and raisin loaf she carefully wrapped it in muslin. 'That'll keep it moist,' she explained. She put it into a brown leather bag and gave it into Sonny's keeping. 'Lay it on the floor of your car,' she insisted. 'It'll be safer there.'

Sonny didn't protest, not even when Martha watched while she placed it very tenderly on the rubber mat. 'Oh, and on your way back, call in at the post office and get me some stamps,' Martha said. 'I've a few letters to post before we leave.'

At last, Sonny was on her way. Settling into the leather seat, she slammed shut the car door and switched on the engine. The gear was shifted into first, the brake released, clutch out, and the black Morris Minor moved away at a respectable speed.

At the bottom of the lane, Sonny flicked up the indicator to turn left, into the village. Behind her Martha called out, 'Be careful now! And try not to be too long. We've a mountain of things to do if we're to be away first thing.'

Some people said the vicar resembled an ageing sheep-dog. Others insisted he was more like a decrepit bear. Martha argued that he had a mane of hair any self-respecting lion would be proud of. Sonny thought him a comical creature, with his big square teeth, perpetual smile and starched white dog collar that seemed always to be choking him.

He was delighted with Martha's olive branch. 'What a kind gesture,' he gushed. 'I'll see the flowers get pride of place in the church. As for the cake, that will make the best part of my tea for a week.' He argued that Martha need not have worried about insulting the new church warden. 'Insults roll off his back like water off a duck's!' he said, grinning so wide he almost choked on his teeth.

Sonny left him clutching the cake as though protecting it from the devil. She might have chuckled at the sight he made, but as she got into the car, her gaze fell on the roses at his side and her mood darkened. As she drove away, all she could think of was how she and her aunt were due to leave tomorrow. 'I hope to God we're doing the right thing,' she murmured, turning into the village square. 'But what else is there? Stay here? Lose my baby?' Possibly her life? There was no choice. Except the one she had already made.

Mrs Louis had been the head postmistress for the past

twenty years. Forty-five years old, with a belly the size of a hot-air balloon and eyes that could see round corners, she put the fear of God into the children. But despite her fearsome appearance she was a kind enough soul. 'I heard you'd got a bad attack of 'flu,' she said, counting the change with enormous care. Since mistakenly giving an extra shilling to old Mr Barns she was irritatingly vigilant. 'Nasty thing, 'flu. Mr Benson the butcher went down with it last week.'

'Saps your strength,' remarked Sonny.

'Hmm!' With small suspicious eyes Mrs Louis stared Sonny up and down. 'I must say you don't look ill. As a matter of fact you look glowing.' With her next remark she made herself blush. 'If I didn't know better, I'd say you were pregnant.'

Lost for words, Sonny made a hasty departure.

Calling in at the confectioner's she bought herself a quarter of liquorice allsorts, for which she had developed an insatiable craving.

On the way home, feeling the need for silence and privacy, she parked the car on the fringe of the woods, leaving the doors wide open so the air would rush through. She got out and, taking her liquorice allsorts with her, climbed to the top of the bank, a place of wild natural beauty, inaccessible to cars and rarely visited by people. 'Oh, it's so special here,' she whispered.

Right at the top she drew in a long invigorating breath of pure clean air. The silence was eerie, touching the soul. All around her Mother Nature wove a magic spell. Birdsong filled the skies; busy little creatures foraged in the roots of the wild rhododendrons; curious grey squir-rels chased each other up the tree trunks. One cheeky little fieldmouse peered at her through bright beady eyes, scuttling away when she reached out to touch.

Sitting on the grass, she surveyed the scene below. From here she could see right across the valley to the village. The skyline was comfortably familiar: three church spires, two green silo-columns at nearby farms, four rows of houses and two giant strings of pylons across the fields. Farmhouses were scattered haphazardly about, white and rambling against the green grass, and on the far hills dozens of grazing sheep resembled little piles of snow. 'Nothing can harm me here,' she whispered. 'Here, I could be safe forever.'

Her heart hardened. 'But not from him,' she said bitterly. 'I could never be safe if he knew about the baby!'

She seemed to be there an age, eating her liquorice allsorts, dreaming and wishing, filled with regrets. And hope. And doubts. The sun beat down and warmed her face, but the breeze was wonderfully cool. Leaning back against an old oak tree, she thought there could be no more beautiful place on God's earth. 'I wish I could stay forever and ever,' she sighed. But she couldn't. Time was precious, and with every minute Tony was closer to returning home. When he got back, he must not find her. More than that, he must not have cause to be suspicious. 'Buck up, Sonny girl,' she chided herself. 'Best get home now. Martha's bound to be wondering where you've got to.'

Reluctantly she stood up, amazed that she'd finished off the whole quarter pound of liquorice allsorts. 'You deserve to get fat!' she said, running briskly down the hill. 'And not because you're pregnant either.'

She was right. Martha was worried. 'I bet you've been sitting up the top of Gypsy Lane,' she chided.

'I needed to think,' Sonny said. 'I need to work out what to do next.'

'I can tell you what to do next!' Martha said, leading her through the cottage. 'You can help me tidy the shed. I wouldn't want Miss Lorrimer to think we had dirty habits.'

Sonny followed her. 'You can't really mean you want us to clean out the *shed*?' she asked incredulously. The last time she went in there it had seemed respectable enough.

'I do.' Martha was adamant. 'That place is a disgrace. There's all manner of old tack in there, and I'm determined to leave it spick and span for our new tenant.'

'Everybody's shed is full of old tack,' Sonny argued. 'That's what sheds are for.'

Martha's shoulders squared. That was always a sign she was fighting fit. 'No arguments, my girl!' she declared. 'And that's an end to it. I will not have it said that Martha Moon left her shed like a pigsty.'

Sonny gave up. When Martha was in that kind of mood there was nothing to be done but humour her.

A short while later the two of them headed for the shed, armed with brushes, mops, buckets of water and even a polishing cloth or two. 'No cutting corners, mind,' Martha warned. 'Else we'll have to do it all over again.'

* * *

By half-past eight the work was done. Every cupboard in the cottage was washed and polished; every pot, pan and ornament scrubbed and gleaming. Wardrobe tops were dusted. The windows sparkled. There wasn't a speck of dust above or below any piece of furniture and the shed? Well . . . the shed was a showpiece.

When they had washed the dust and dirt off themselves, Sonny and her aunt fell into the armchairs, bone tired but immensely satisfied. 'I'm ready for my cocoa now,' Martha said, legs akimbo and a little grin on her face.

It took five minutes for Sonny to make the cocoa, fifteen minutes for Martha to drink it, and five minutes more before she began to yawn. 'I'm off to my bed,' she declared lazily. 'If you want to get away at eight in the morning, you'd better get a good night's sleep an' all.'

Still unsure, Sonny asked thoughtfully, 'Am I doing the right thing? Instead of running away, should I face him? Should I tell him how I heard what he and his wife were planning?' But she had considered it from every angle, and each time she came to the same conclusion. Like it or not, she had been caught up in a devious and dangerous plan. Now she was cornered.

Martha had no doubts. 'This man has already said he'll harm you, and that's enough for me. You can't stand up against him, and you certainly can't give the baby to him. No. We'll go away for a while. At least until the baby's born. Then we'll see.' She gathered her spectacles and magazine. 'Goodnight, dear.' Turning her face, she waited for Sonny to kiss her.

Sonny obliged. 'Goodnight, Aunt.' She had made up her mind on another matter. 'I won't be coming to bed for a while. I'm going to see Patricia.'

Martha nodded. 'I thought you might.'

As she went out of the room she said over her shoulder, 'You shouldn't be too late coming in, dear, not if you want to be away early in the morning.'

'I shouldn't be gone above an hour,' Sonny told her. Though with Patricia you never could tell.

Some time later, when the house was quiet and she was in the right frame of mind, Sonny got her coat, a loose pink-linen garment with deep lapels and a stand-up collar. A quick check in the mirror, a comb run through her short brown hair, and she was ready. 'Now, where are the car keys!' She began to panic when they weren't in the usual place. It took a lot of upturned cushions, a grope round the carpet on all fours and a frantic search of the kitchen before she finally found them in the washbucket. 'I must be cracking up,' she joked, making her way to the front door.

She was standing outside on the step, ready to close the door, when the phone rang. 'Damn!' Afraid Martha would be woken, she dashed back into the house and grabbed the receiver.

When he murmured her name she could feel the colour ebb from her face. '*Tony!*' She was shocked, but not really surprised. He often rang her when he was away on a trip.

He commented that she didn't seem pleased to hear from him. Was she angry because he hadn't rung before? It was only because he had been kept busy from morning to night. 'Yesterday was the first chance I've had to ring the office. They told me you were away ill. I've been longing to speak to you ever since, but trying to get past that aunt of yours is like trying to get past the palace guard.' He laughed. 'I'm sure she disapproves of me . . . married man and all that . . . trying to take advantage of you.' His voice hardened. 'What she thinks doesn't bother me. As long as you know the truth, that's all I care.'

'What *is* the truth, Tony?' For one brief mad moment she wondered if he might confess.

'I'm surprised you have to ask, sweetheart!' He sounded appalled. 'I love you. As soon as I can get Celia to agree to a divorce, I want us to get married.' There was a smile in his voice. 'Now it's your turn.'

Momentarily taken aback, she asked, 'What do you mean, my turn?'

'I mean, are you keeping things from me?'

Her heart almost stopped. 'What things?'

'Hey! Don't sound so worried.' His voice dropped to a whisper. 'I was hoping you might have some good news for me,' he said persuasively. 'When they said you were ill, I wondered . . . you're not pregnant, are you?' He gave a small embarrassed laugh. 'It's the best present you could ever give me, you know that, don't you?'

Forcing herself to laugh with him, she dashed his hopes. 'Sorry to disappoint you,' she said, 'but I've been laid up with the 'flu.' She was trembling with fear. And love. And loathing.

'That's a pity, sweetheart, but never mind.' His breathing grew erratic, as though he was in a passion – or a foul temper. 'We'll have to try harder, eh?'

She could hear herself agreeing. Whatever she felt, however much she wanted to scream down the phone at him, she had to keep calm. 'And anyway, I'm feeling much better now.' He hadn't even asked after her health. He didn't care. Why had she never seen him for what he was? Her loathing turned on herself.

'I'll have to go, sweetheart. Take care now ... love you. See you soon.'

She heard someone call out his name. ''Bye,' she said. She got the feeling he was waiting for her to say she loved him. A moment, then the receiver was put down and the line went dead. 'Goodbye, you bastard!' she said through gritted teeth. 'Don't expect to see me again.'

A few minutes later she quietly closed the door. The cool night air had a sobering effect on her. In fact as she got into her car she was smiling, then softly chuckling. 'Don't let him get to you,' she told herself in the mirror. 'Keep calm. Make your plans wisely, and you'll be all right.' She flicked back her hair and glanced at her smiling face in the mirror. 'That's right,' she murmured. 'Keep smiling, and to hell with him!' The smile was defiant. But her eyes were haunted.

There wasn't much traffic about. At the junction for Woburn Sands she had to wait for a pair of drunken men to make their way across the road. 'Hello, darling!' shouted one. 'Don't suppose you'd give us a lift home, would yer?' His companion grabbed him by the scruff of the collar and yanked him on to the pavement. 'He's pissed!' he giggled as she drove off. 'He's always the same when he's pissed.'

Sonny didn't turn round. She had more important things on her mind than a couple of drunks.

It took her fifteen minutes to get to Patricia's place. She wasted another ten minutes sitting in the car, trying to decide whether or not she dare confide in her.

Patricia rented a small one-bedroom flat in a large house that had seen better times. Situated in a pleasant part of old Bletchley, the house had once been home to gentry. Now it was home to people like Patricia, young men and women just starting out, with limited money but unlimited ambition.

The front door was always on the latch. Pushing into the big hallway, Sonny skipped up three flights of stairs then hurried along the corridor to Patricia's flat. As she raised her fist to knock, the door was flung open. 'Saw your car out front,' Patricia said brightly. She was a small, strikingly pretty thing, with big freckles, eyes the same colour, and red hair to her waist.

Now that she was face to face with her, Sonny wasn't at all sure she had done the right thing in coming. 'I'm sorry, it's late,' she apologised, uncertain whether she should go or stay.

Patricia's smile was warm, her manner welcoming. 'You can stand out there admiring the door if you like,' she declared. 'Or are you hoping to catch a glimpse of my handsome neighbour?'

'Don't start all that again.' Sonny's glance went instinctively to the next door. 'Lonnie's a good-looking bloke, but he certainly isn't interested in me.'

'Oh?' Patricia gave a saucy wink. 'And I suppose you're not interested in him?'

'I might have been once,' Sonny admitted. But that was before Tony, she added silently.

'Hmm! I'll believe you, but thousands wouldn't.' Swinging away, Patricia said, 'Anyway, we're safe. He won't be home for a while. He's working late. Now, are you coming in or what?' With that she swung away and disappeared inside.

Sonny followed. Going into the tiny kitchen where Patricia was already boiling the kettle, she stood feeling awkward and looking anxious. The whole sordid story was on the tip of her tongue, waiting to be spilled out. Instead, she choked it back to make inane conversation. 'Mike Pearson,' she began. 'What's he like to work with?'

Patricia bustled about. 'He's a good bloke. Keeps his paperwork in order and stays one step ahead of the job. He's a great improvement on the last fork-lift driver. That silly bugger was always having accidents. In less than a year he managed to smash two bathroom suites and an entire kitchen.' She made a gesture with her hands, showing how he scooped the articles on to the prongs of his fork-lift and dropped them to the ground from a great height. 'Mangled they were. To be honest, I'm not surprised Bridgeman fired him. In fact, I've wondered since whether there was some kind of a feud going on there, because word has it that the fella's gone to work for another property developer. Now, I ask you . . . would any self-respecting employer take on someone like that? And what about references? Bridgeman would have slated him.'

'Hmm.' Sonny wasn't really listening. 'You've painted

the kitchen since I was last here.' Roving her gaze round the tiny room, she remembered the walls had been a lovely shade of rose pink. Now they were bright green, with vivid yellow flowers stencilled around the doorway.

'A change is as good as a rest, they say.' Looking at Sonny out of the corner of her eye, Patricia took a moment to study her. She observed the gaunt face, the wide troubled eyes, and the way in which Sonny was winding her fingers round and round, as though wringing out a wet rag. 'Well?' she said. 'Are yer going to tell me, or what?'

Taken unawares, Sonny blurted out the first thing that came into her head. 'Well, it's . . . different anyway,' she said, blinded by the vivid colours, but not wanting to offend. 'Very colourful.'

Patricia chuckled. The kettle boiled and she made the tea. When it was brewing, she led Sonny into the sitting room. 'Sit yourself down.' Indicating the bigger of two armchairs, she waited for Sonny to be seated, then perched on the arm of the other. There wasn't much space in the room, so there wasn't much furniture, just the two wooden-frame chairs, a chest of drawers and a table with a radio on top. But it was homely enough, and it gave Patricia independence from her widowed mother, a hard-hearted woman who was never happier than when interfering in other people's lives.

Sonny sat in her chair, quiet and sad, wanting to go, needing to stay. She didn't speak. Instead she waited for Patricia to say her piece.

'I wasn't asking your opinion of my colour scheme,'

Patricia said. 'What I meant was, are you going to tell me what's troubling you?'

'What makes you think I'm troubled?'

Patricia cocked her head to one side as though concentrating. 'Because it's not like you to turn up here late at night. Then you loiter outside the door like the landlord when I'm late with the rent. When finally you decide to come in, you stand in the kitchen like a spare part, staring at the walls and pretending to be interested, when it's plain as a pikestaff you've summat more important on yer mind.' She raised her eyebrows. 'Want me to go on?'

'You're a canny devil.'

'That's right. And that's why I know you're not interested in the colour of my kitchen walls.' Her elfin face crinkled with laughter. 'Jesus, I must have been going through a crisis when I chose those colours,' she admitted. 'It's bloody awful . . . looks like somebody spewed up fried eggs.'

Patricia's laughter was infectious. Sonny found herself laughing too. 'You're right,' she said. 'It is bloody awful.'

Serious now, Patricia pressed for an answer. 'I'm right about you too, aren't I? You are in trouble?' Because she cared for Sonny she dared to say it: 'It's a fella, ain't it? What's he done? Thrown you over? Got you pregnant?'

The look on Sonny's face convinced her she was right. 'I knew it!' she cried, banging her fist against the arm of the chair. 'Men! Aren't they all the same? Horny bastards who don't care what trouble they cause so long as they get their pleasure.' Her next remark was gentler.

'I'm sorry. You love him, don't you?'

'You're halfway right,' Sonny admitted.

Concerned but inquisitive, Patricia asked, 'Is it someone I know?'

Sonny took a deep breath. 'Oh, yes, you know him,' she said wryly. 'He pays both our wages.'

Patricia was frowning. 'Pays our wages?' Suddenly the frown was gone and in its place was a look of astonishment. 'Good God almighty! You're telling me you've been having an affair with Tony Bridgeman?' With each word she slid closer to the chair's edge. 'Are you out of your mind?'

Sonny's face told it all.

More sympathetic now, Patricia asked, 'You're pregnant, aren't you?'

Sonny nodded, eyes downcast.

Lost for words, Patricia continued to look at her in disbelief. After a moment she came and sat on the arm of Sonny's chair. With her hand on her friend's shoulder she said, 'I know you probably won't thank me for saying it, but he's a bad lot. There's rumours that it was him who had Bob Coleman beaten up. The two of 'em were fighting over a piece of land, like a dog over a bone. The other fella got the land, and Bridgeman took his pound of flesh.'

Sonny remembered. 'When I heard the rumours I tackled him about it. He told me there was nothing to it, and much to my shame I believed him.' Now she had seen his true nature she could believe anything of him.

'How long have you and Bridgeman been ... you know?'

Sonny looked up. 'You can say it,' she urged. 'How long have we been having it off in the back of his car?' She laughed, a dry hard sound. 'Over a year.'

'And you never said a word, not even to me!'

'I never said a word to anyone. He wanted it that way.'

'Well, he would, wouldn't he? What did he promise? To divorce his wife? To rush to the altar as soon as he could be rid of her? Anything to get his leg over!'

In spite of herself, Sonny had to chuckle. 'You have a wonderful way of stating the obvious.'

'What now?' Patricia was angry and it showed in her voice. 'He's thrown you over because you're pregnant, is that it?'

Sonny had not lifted her face until now. Her eyes glittered. 'He doesn't know I'm pregnant. He must never know.'

Patricia was puzzled. 'Then you're a bigger fool than I took you for,' she declared. 'Make the bugger pay! There'll be a time when you won't be able to work. It costs money to bring up a kiddie. Fleece him, why don't you? I know I would.'

'I'm going away.' The statement stopped Patricia in full flow. 'I'm going into hiding.'

Patricia was on her feet now, staring down at Sonny. 'The minute I clapped eyes on you I knew there was something terribly wrong. It's more than having an affair, isn't it? More than being pregnant?' She looked at Sonny in a new light. 'You're frightened, aren't you? What is it? And what do you mean . . . you're going into hiding?'

Sonny told her everything. About how he'd led her to believe they had a future together. How she had planned her life round his every word, hating the deception, hating not being able to tell Patricia, or her aunt. She explained how much she had come to love him, and how excited she was when she discovered she was carrying his child.

She explained about the phone call and how he'd asked her to take some documents to the house at a particular time. But, because she was eager to tell him the news about the baby, she had gone early. 'I couldn't make him hear, so I went round the side. You see, I've done that before . . . when his wife was away and he was waiting for me.' She drew in a great gulp of air. 'I saw them through the window. They were rolling about on the carpet . . . him and his wife . . . stark naked, going at it like a pair of animals. Wild they were . . .' She paused, taking a moment to compose herself.

Patricia waited. She made no comment, but her angry expression told its own story.

Sonny went on. 'I would have left, but suddenly they were finished and laughing, talking . . . about me.' She raised her eyes again, her every limb trembling as she revealed the awful truth. 'She knew! All the time . . . his wife knew we were seeing each other!'

'What? She knew you and her husband were having an affair, and she didn't care?'

'Oh, she cared all right.' Sonny laughed harshly. 'She cared, because she was in on it. The whole thing was planned.'

'What are you saying? That she *wanted* you to have

an affair with her husband? That she encouraged it?'

'That's exactly what I'm saying.' Now Sonny had an ally. It was a good feeling. 'He never had any intention of leaving her . . . he loves her, but she can't have children. Apparently neither of them will even consider adoption, but they're desperate for a child . . . *his* child.'

She paused to let the truth sink in. 'I was to bear that child for them.'

'I don't believe I'm hearing this!'

'It's true, Patricia. I heard it with my own ears. They chose me to provide them with an heir. Remember the annual party? How she stared at me all evening, and he was extra-attentive? They must have been looking me over then . . . wondering what kind of surrogate mother I'd make. They obviously liked what they saw, because soon after that he made a play for me, and I fell hook, line and sinker.'

'What a pair of bastards!' Patricia was horrified, but her first reaction was to fight. 'Confront him,' she urged. 'Tell him you know what they were up to, and that you'll stand against him in court. When it comes right down to it, what can they do? Do you really think any court would give him the child over you?'

'Think about it, Patricia. Me against Tony Bridgeman? He's a powerful man. I'm his dogsbody – filing his letters, answering his phone calls. Who would take my word against his? No, I wouldn't stand a chance. If I took him to court, what then? I'd only end up fighting for my own baby. And even if the court allowed me to keep the baby, which I don't think it would, he wouldn't let it rest there.'

'He wouldn't be able to do a thing about it. The best he could hope for would be visiting rights.'

Sonny looked her in the eyes, her voice soft and deliberate. 'If I were to die, he would have every right to take the child, wouldn't he?'

'As the father, of course he would, yes.' Patricia chuckled. 'But he'd have to wait a long time 'cause you're so disgustingly healthy you'll outlive the lot of us.'

There was an unsettling span of silence during which Sonny looked at Patricia, and Patricia began to realise what was meant. 'My God!' She leaped out of the chair. 'You can't really think ... no!' She shook her head vehemently, a disbelieving smile lifting the corners of her mouth, but in her eyes the truth was already dawning. 'I'm not denying he's capable of it, but no ... things like that just don't happen.'

Sonny bowed her head. 'I heard them discussing it. She teased him about making love to me ... warned him to remember it was only a means to an end.' His answer still burned in her mind. 'He told her I meant nothing to him, that making love with me was no more important to him than a business meeting.' She visibly shivered, forcing herself to reveal every shocking detail. 'She asked what would happen if I became pregnant and refused to hand over the baby.'

'And?'

Sonny's voice faltered. 'He said in that case he would have to kill me.'

Speechless, Patricia fell back into her chair, her mouth hanging open and her eyes intent on Sonny's face.

Sonny continued softly, 'I think he's insane enough to do it. Now you know why I have to leave the area. Why he must never know I'm pregnant.'

Patricia took a moment to consider and then remarked with awe, 'He's a bad lot. I wouldn't be surprised if he's already had people done away with.'

'Maybe he wouldn't do it,' Sonny offered. 'Maybe it was just words.' A deep shiver rippled through her. 'But it was the way he said it. The look on his face as he smiled at her.'

'Oh, he'd do it all right! If he wants something badly enough, that man would move heaven and earth.' Patricia sat upright in her chair. 'Who else have you told?'

'One other person.'

'Your Aunt Martha?'

'Yes, and I wish I hadn't.' She still felt immensely guilty about involving that dear old woman. 'At first she wanted to strangle him with her own two hands. Later, when she'd calmed down, she realised that it would only make matters worse if I was to go against him.'

'Hmm.' The two of them lapsed into deep thought, until Patricia came up with an idea. 'So far you've told your fears to an old woman and a dizzy bugger like me. I wonder if you should confide in a man ... someone who could put the fear of God into Bridgeman?'

'It wouldn't do any good,' Sonny said. 'Giving him a good hiding wouldn't solve anything.'

Patricia wasn't listening. 'What about Lonnie? He's just the fella, I reckon.'

'To rip out Bridgeman's heart, you mean?'

'Yes. Why not?'

'Because I'd rather deal with it myself. I don't want Tony to know I'm pregnant. I need to be free of him.' She cut the air with the edge of her hand. 'A clean break. No ties, and no reason for him to come after me . . . I hope.'

'So you don't want Lonnie to know?'

'For God's sake, Patricia! *No!* I do not want him to know. I don't want anyone else to know.' Had she done wrong in telling Patricia? she wondered. 'Lonnie's got a temper that could only make matters worse, for him and for me,' she argued. 'Surely you can see that?'

'Yes, you're right.'

'So you won't say anything to him?'

'You can trust me.'

'I hope so.'

Mortified that she'd said all the wrong things, Patricia assured her, 'Your secret's safe with me. Cross my heart.' She made the sign of the cross on her breast. 'Wild horses wouldn't drag it out of me.'

Sonny glanced at her wristwatch. 'I'll need to be up early in the morning. There's a good deal to do before I set off.'

'Where will you go?'

'North.'

'Will you come back once you've had the baby?'

'I haven't planned that far ahead.' Getting up from her chair Sonny went to the fireplace, where she stood for a while, her back to Patricia and her mind spinning. Eventually she turned, asking, 'Knowing what I've told you . . . the way things are . . . do you think I'm doing the right thing?' She chided herself for needing constant reassurance.

Patricia nodded her head decisively. 'You can't take any risks,' she confirmed. 'You've got more to lose if you stay here, so go north like you said. Put him behind you and make a new life.'

'Will you do me a favour?'

'Don't be bloody daft! Of course I will.'

'I intend to write to him . . . saying I've been offered a job overseas and am taking it for a year. He knows we're friends, so he might question you. Everyone in the office thinks I've been away with the 'flu.' Feeling small, she apologised, 'I'm sorry I had to let you think the same, but I wasn't sure whether or not to confide in you.'

'I'd have been hurt if you hadn't. I know you work upstairs in the posh end and I'm only a stores clerk, but you know I'd do anything for you.'

'So, if he asks, you will back me up? Say you know all about the overseas job . . . a secretarial post with an international company. Say you're not sure about all the details, but that I'm going to write to you when I'm settled. Whatever else, he mustn't get suspicious. I want him to think things are still the same, that I'm only taking a year out.'

'Do it then,' Patricia urged. 'If it were me I'd already be down the road.' Clenching her fist, she hissed, 'I'd like to see the pair of them rotting in jail where they belong. But don't worry, I'll keep my mouth shut. For your sake and the baby's, I'll lie through my teeth if needs be.'

On the doorstep they hugged each other. 'You're a good friend,' Sonny said. 'I won't forget.'

The grandfather clock was striking eleven as Sonny let herself into the cottage. As she made her way upstairs she trod softly, carrying her shoes, so as not to wake her aunt.

She thought she heard a sound as she came to Martha's room, and as she went along the landing she heard it again. Pausing, she listened hard and was shocked. Aunt Martha ... crying? The last and only time Sonny had heard Martha cry was years ago, when Sonny's parents had been killed in a boating accident.

She crept back to the door. There was no mistaking the sound now. Martha *was* crying, softly, as though her tears were almost spent.

Concerned, Sonny raised her hand to tap on the door, but stopped her fist in mid-air when she heard Martha talking, as though to herself. Instinctively, she pressed her ear closer to the door, intent on hearing every word.

'Dear Lord, I'm a silly old woman, too old to be uprooting myself, travelling from one end of the country to the other, setting up with strangers and hiding like a thief in the night. It'll break my heart to leave this little cottage where I've lived all my life ... I'll miss everything about it. I'll miss watching the paper boy come down the path of a morning. I'll miss old Widow March when she goes by every evening with her two mongrel dogs. Last week she only had one with her. When I asked what had happened to the other, she said the silly creature had chased a rabbit down a ditch and ended up with a nasty thorn in his paw. The wound turned septic and he wasn't allowed to walk out until it was healed over. I'll miss my little chats with her. I'll miss Barney the postman, cussed old fool, and, most of all, I'll miss my feathered friends perching on the cherry tree and whistling for their breakfast.'

Martha chuckled and sighed, and Sonny was torn between going in and creeping softly away. But she stayed, and the tears rolled down her face as she realised how desperately unhappy Martha really was.

'So you see, Lord, I'm just an old fool. But I can't let her down, can I? She's all I've got in the world. I made a promise on her parents' grave that I'd look after her as long as I were able.

'I'll not go back on that promise, and I'll not let the lass down now. She needs me, you see. Oh, I know it ain't us as should be running away, but sometimes you have to do what you know is for the best. I don't really like the idea of that young Lorrimer woman setting foot in my home, but what else can I do? Time were running out, and she were the best of a bad lot.

'Goodnight, Lord. Take care of us, won't you?'

There was a groan and a long-drawn-out sigh, as though Martha had been on her knees and was clambering up.

Mortified, Sonny made her way along the landing to her room. Once there she closed the door and sat on the bed, rehearing Martha's every word. What have I done? she asked herself. How could I have been so blind?

She had to think, had to reshape her plans. But her mind was racing and her heart was weary. Her own troubles seemed unimportant compared to that dear old woman's despair. Keep a clear head, she told herself. You'll have to work out a way to leave her behind, without hurting her even more. Easier said than done, she thought. Martha was a stubborn old bugger, wily as a fox and twice as quick.

Confused and more troubled than ever, Sonny undressed, put on her towelling robe and tiptoed to the bathroom, where she ran a hot bath. Soaking in the bubbles, she lay there for what seemed an age, letting the silky water run over her skin, and in her mind going backwards and forwards over recent events. What a mess she had made of her life. 'There's only you can put it right, my girl,' she murmured. But how? What if it was all too late? Her heart echoed.

After her bath she made her way back to her bedroom. She dried and brushed her hair, put on her blue silk pyjamas and turned back the bedcovers.

Before climbing between the sheets she had two letters to write – one to the office, giving notice, and the other to Tony.

The letter giving notice was brief and to the point, taking up only one side of a sheet of paper.

The letter to Tony was far more difficult. After three attempts she settled for a friendly but objective message, outlining her plans and asking him to understand.

Dear Tony,
  Welcome back! I've missed you as always. I'm sorry, but I won't be here when you return.
  During the past week, with you away and me

down with the 'flu, I've had plenty of time to think. I've thought about you and me, and the future, and I've thought about your wife, Celia. You know I've never been happy deceiving her. And, to tell you the truth, I'm not altogether convinced you will ever be ready to leave her.

Sweetheart, I've come to a decision . . .

Even writing the word 'Sweetheart' made her feel sick, but she forced herself to finish the letter.

You know I've loved you from the start, but we seem to be going nowhere. I hope you'll agree that we need some time apart from each other, time for us both to decide what we really want.

As you know I've always had a hankering to work overseas. Suddenly I've been given the opportunity and I've thought about it long and hard. I believe the time is right.

It's only for a year. I'm sure the time will pass all too quickly. It might be best if I don't write, because then we can really see how we feel about spending the rest of our lives together. It's bound to be hard for both of us, but it will be a good trial of our commitment, don't you think?

I meant to tell you when you rang the other night, but you were in such a hurry, and it didn't seem right to say it over the phone.

I'll be thinking of you every day until we see each other again. If by that time you've decided to stay with Celia, I'll understand.

All my love,
Sonny
XX

P.S. The other thing that crossed my mind was the fact that I'm not yet pregnant, especially when we've been trying so hard. I think we'll have to consider the possibility that I may be barren.

After reading the letter through several times she slipped it into an envelope. 'That should give him food for thought,' she considered aloud. 'No hostility; no clue that I'm on to him. The right amount of love and pain, and a little hint that I may not be able to bear his precious heir after all.' She felt satisfied she could do no better.

Sealing both envelopes, she took two stamps from her bag and stuck them down. 'Goodbye, Mr Tony Bridgeman,' she muttered icily, placing the envelopes on the dresser. 'Let's hope you can't see through the lies.'

She didn't get straight into bed. The weariness that had dogged her all day seemed to have drained away with the bath water. Now she was sharper of mind, able to focus on the problem of Martha. 'You're an old sweetheart.' She smiled towards the door. 'And I know you feel duty bound to stand by me, but you needn't worry. I promise I won't take you from your hearth and home.' She must have been half out of her mind even to let Martha consider such a drastic move. But then, she reminded herself, 'half out of her mind' was exactly what she had been.

Now she felt good, more relaxed, able to face the

future with a degree of confidence. 'Tomorrow I'm off to a new life,' she said, slithering between the sheets. 'Though I pray to God I won't need to spend the rest of my life looking over my shoulder.'

In the morning Martha was suspicious. 'Yesterday it was all settled and now you say you want to go away on your own?' She was in the middle of packing a bag when Sonny came into her room, and what her niece had to say took her completely by surprise. 'I don't understand it.' But she couldn't hide her relief altogether. 'What's made you change your mind all of a sudden?' Absentmindedly toying with her best hat, she sat on the bed, her eyebrows cocked inquisitively while she waited for an explanation.

Sonny sat beside her, one arm draped affectionately round her shoulders. 'I know how much you want to come with me,' she started craftily, 'but I'm asking if you wouldn't mind me taking off on my own.' She hurried on before Martha could stop her. 'You see, I would really like to see some of the places I've always wanted to visit but never had the time.'

Valiant as ever, Martha suggested half-heartedly, 'Then we'll see them together.'

Frustrated, Sonny gently shook the old woman, tugging her closer as she pleaded, 'Please, Aunt Martha. I know you want to come with me, but I'd be grateful if you'd let me do this by myself.'

'Go travelling on your own ... pregnant an' all?' Martha shook her head. 'I don't know as I'd be able to sleep at night.'

Sonny persisted. 'I'm quite able to take care of myself, you know. I'm twenty-four years old and I do know the ways of the world.' She smiled. 'I can promise you, I will never be taken in so easily again.' Her face hardened. 'Tony Bridgeman has done me that favour at least. He's taught me a lesson I'll never forget.'

Martha chastised her. 'You never told me about these places you've always wanted to see.'

Winking cheekily, Sonny asked, 'I don't have to tell you everything, do I?'

'No, you don't,' Martha said knowingly. 'And you don't have to tell me why you've suddenly changed your mind about me coming with you neither! You're doing this because you think I'll be desperately unhappy away from what I know best.'

Realising she would have to play this very carefully, Sonny assured her, 'No, sweetheart. This is for *me*. Once I've had the baby I won't be able to take off whenever I feel like it. In the past I've been too tied up with making a career for myself, and in the future I'll have another little person to think about. This will be the first time I'll be doing what I really want, and it might be the last. I'm excited about the idea of going where I want, when I want.'

She was very convincing. 'There's no need for you to worry. I've got enough money saved to get me decent board and lodgings. The car's taxed and insured for nearly a year. It's still not obvious that I'm pregnant, so, if the worst comes to the worst, I might even take up a little job now and then . . . just to keep my hand in, so to speak.'

Martha considered. 'Hmm! And how will I know you're all right?'

'I'll phone or write at least once a week.'

'Promise?'

'I promise.'

Martha gazed at her, thinking how she would like to be young again, if only to share an adventure or two. But she wasn't young any more. She was old, and set in her ways, and this was her place until she was brought to face the Almighty. 'God bless you then,' she said softly. 'If it's what you've really set your heart on, I won't stand in your way.'

With that they hugged each other, and Martha cried. But in no time at all the two of them were down in the kitchen, and the tears were washed away with a good strong cup of tea.

There was a lot to do before Sonny could get away. She helped Martha to unpack, then she phoned to have the china returned. There was the larder to restock. 'Miss Lorrimer will have to be told,' Martha said with a happy little smile. They rushed around and got everything in order, until at last Sonny was taking her own things to the car.

Martha carried the smaller bag and placed it on the passenger seat. While Sonny loaded the two cases into the boot, Martha fussed and fretted and dabbed at her eyes with her pretty floral hankie. 'It won't be the same without you here,' she moaned.

Sonny replied by throwing her arms round that dear soul. 'Now stop worrying,' she told her. 'I've said I'll be okay and I will.'

'Good grief!' Martha threw her arms out wide, so agitated she almost danced on the spot. 'Whatever will I tell the vicar?' she cried. 'He's bound to question me about being rude to the church warden.'

Sonny laughed out loud. 'Tell him you wondered how any self-respecting vicar could have employed such a scruffy fella,' she suggested cheekily. 'Explain how he came nosying into the garden and gave you a fright . . . that for one awful minute you thought he was a maniac escaped from the asylum.'

Martha made a face. 'Or a scarecrow out of the fields,' she giggled.

'I don't think I've ever seen anyone run so fast,' Sonny roared. 'His feet hardly touched the ground. Oh, and did you see the look on his face when he glanced back? He must have thought you were a right tyrant!'

For one precious minute Tony Bridgeman and the reason for Sonny's departure were forgotten in laughter.

But all too soon the moment of parting arrived.

'Mind you take care of yourself . . . and drive carefully,' Martha urged. Her old heart was in tatters as she watched the car move out of the lane, taking her beloved Sonny with it. 'Love you!' she shouted, running after the car and waving her hankie in the air. When Sonny waved back, she blew a kiss. 'God go with you,' she murmured, before making her way back to the cottage. Here she sat for a while, in her favourite chair, wondering whether she would ever see her niece again.

As she drove away Sonny continued to wave until the little woman was out of sight. The tears rolled down her face until she couldn't even see the road in front.

When she reached the end of the lane she stopped the car and dried her eyes. 'I'll miss you, sweetheart,' she murmured, gazing longingly up the lane. 'I know you would have come with me, and that would have been fine for me ... but not for you. At your age you deserve a bit of peace and contentment.'

Before leaving the village she posted the letters and bought herself a quarter of liquorice allsorts. It was a long journey to Samlesbury. She would need a bit of sustenance on the way.

She had been driving for about twenty minutes when the traffic began to thicken – people on their way to work, people out shopping, all impatient, all in a hurry. Looking down, she noticed the petrol gauge was reading low. 'Damn!' The first garage was on the A5. 'I should just about make it,' Sonny reasoned aloud.

As it was she drove into the forecourt just as the fuel indicator moved into the red. The attendant was a friendly little man with a cheery grin and legs bowed enough to drive a bus through. 'Fill 'er up, eh?' he acknowledged. 'Off on a long trip, are you?'

'North.' Sonny said it without thinking. Giving herself a mental kick, she realised she shouldn't have revealed her destination. Not to anyone.

'Oh? I've got relatives living in the north,' he said. 'Out Preston way ... got a farm ... raise turkeys, they do.' He grinned from ear to ear while he vigorously shook petrol drips from the nozzle. 'I ain't gone short of a fat Christmas turkey in over twenty years.'

While Sonny waited in the car he fetched her change,

grinning widely when she slid a silver shilling into his hand. 'That's very kind,' he said, stepping back as though afraid she might run over his toes. Truth was, he never did trust women drivers. 'Off you go, miss,' he urged kindly. 'Have a safe journey.'

A few minutes later Sonny was parked in a layby, eating her liquorice allsorts and wondering whether she should go in a different direction. Consulting the map, she ran her finger east and west. 'I don't have to go up north,' she said aloud. 'I don't know anybody there.' Scrutinising the map, she gauged the mileage to Samlesbury. It was quite a stretch. 'I could just as well go to Yarmouth, or Bridport,' she mused. 'Enjoy the sea air . . . maybe get a job as a hotel clerk.'

Leaning back in the seat she chewed on her allsorts and gave the matter some thought. After a while she folded the map and edged the car out on the road again. 'North it is,' she decided. 'If Aunt Martha still has a fondness for it after all these years it must have something special.'

As she drove along the A5, she chuckled. 'Mind you, there are any number of things we don't agree on.' Coming up to the traffic lights she dropped into a lower gear. 'Samlesbury might suit one but not another.' The lights changed and she sped off again. 'Anyway, it's too late now,' she mumbled, shaking her fist at a cyclist who swerved towards her. 'For good or bad, I'm on my way to Samlesbury. And, whatever situation I find myself in, it can't be as bad as the one I'm leaving.'

Chapter Three

The drive had been long and tiring. There was a heavy flow of traffic northwards and, with a half-hour stop for refreshments, the journey had taken all of six hours.

After twice losing her way, Sonny had at last found the place she was looking for. Now though, as she sat parked in her car on the drive, staring up at the house, she found herself wondering whether she should have gone to Yarmouth after all. 'It's not a bit like I imagined,' she murmured, getting out of the car to study the rambling place before her. 'More like a mausoleum than a boarding house.'

The house was huge; a great rambling place in yellow stone and dark wood. Thick drab curtains shrouded the long narrow windows; the closed french doors had two enormous potted palms standing guard outside. From where she stood, Sonny sensed a terrible desolation around the once grand house. Though there was no breeze and the sun was still quite warm, all the windows were tightly shut; some even had blinds drawn across to keep out the sun. There was a little flower bed to one side of the drive, and to the other a big flagged area with two upright wooden benches. 'Aunt Martha wouldn't have liked this at all,' Sonny thought aloud. She didn't think much of it herself.

A noise from behind made her turn. Some short distance away there was a big old barn. The noise was coming from inside. She waited, not wanting to investigate, not even wanting to stay. From the barn a man appeared. In his late twenties, he was tall, wide of shoulder, and walked with an easy stride. His dark hair was tousled and his face wet with sweat. She noticed he was wearing a work-apron of sorts and that, when he raised his arms to wipe away the sweat from his face, the palms of his hands were stained with what looked like earth.

A large brown dog bounded out of the barn, leaping at him and wanting to play. Falling to his knees, he wrapped his arms round its neck, roughing its fur and softly talking. The dog gazed at him adoringly.

For no apparent reason he glanced up and saw Sonny watching.

Visibly startled, he demanded, 'Are you lost?' His voice was deep and resonant, his manner tinged with a coldness that took her unawares.

'Sonny Fareham.' Making her way towards him, she held out her hand in greeting. 'I've just driven up from the south.' She waited for him to shake hands with her. When he didn't she dropped her hand to her side and stared at him with the same coldness he had offered her. 'I see I've made you angry.'

Wagging its tail, the dog made a move as if to welcome her, but was stopped by a sharp click of the man's fingers. It sat down obediently by his side. Looking down, he reassured it by rubbing his hand over its head. The love between these two was a pleasure to see and, for a moment, the man seemed to have forgotten she was there.

Inclining her head to one side, Sonny quietly regarded him. He was incredibly handsome and if she was looking for a relationship – which she wasn't and wouldn't be for some considerable time, if ever – she might have twinkled her green eyes at him. Instead she said in clipped tones, 'Don't let me keep you from your work.'

His slow smile turned her heart over. 'You won't,' he answered, regarding her with equal intensity.

Self-conscious beneath his gaze, she blurted out the first thing that came to mind. 'Do you belong to the house?' she asked. 'Are you one of the family?'

His reaction was surprising. He looked up at the sky, then bowed his head, ran his hands through his tousled black hair and laughed aloud, a warm heartening sound that restored her confidence. 'One of the family?' he muttered. 'What makes you think that?'

When he raised his head the sunlight glinted in his eyes and their beauty took her breath away. Darkest blue, and fringed with short black lashes, they seemed to speak a language all their own. First they smiled, and then they scowled. Now they were studying her with rekindled interest. 'Sonny Fareham, you say?'

'That's right.' She was astonished he'd remembered.

'Odd name ... Sonny.' For the briefest moment his eyes softened.

'People think it's short for Sonia, but it isn't. Apparently the midwife told my mother I had a smile like a sunny day. Hence the name.'

He made no remark, but the corners of his mouth lifted just a little.

'And I really didn't mean to keep you from your work,' she said lamely.

In spite of his original surly attitude, she liked him, liked his smile and that spontaneous burst of laughter just now. Her instincts told her he could be a good friend. But something else, something in his cold, sad manner, warned her to keep her distance.

'No matter.' He squared his shoulders, looking at her with a kind of regret. 'I answer to no one, so I can stay at my work for as long as it suits me.'

'All the same, I'm sorry to have bothered you, Mr . . .' She realised, with some embarrassment, that she didn't know his name.

His dark blue eyes burned into hers. There was the merest hint of curiosity before he looked beyond her, to the car. 'I wouldn't leave that parked there if I were you,' he advised. 'She'll be back soon.' His voice hardened. 'You wouldn't want to get off on the wrong foot with her.'

'With who?' Sonny found herself talking to fresh air as he briskly turned and strode away. 'Rude bugger!' she mumbled. 'Whoever *she* is, I'm sure she can't be more hostile than you!'

For some odd reason she lingered awhile. Against her better judgement she found herself wondering about him, repeating what he had said: 'I answer to no one.'

She half smiled. 'In that case you're either a very

fortunate man,' she mumbled, 'or a very lonely one.'

As she was looking towards the barn he emerged again, this time leading the most beautiful white stallion she had ever seen. With its ears pricked and head high, it was a spirited beast. Suddenly it bent its neck and nuzzled the man, and he stroked it lovingly. There was a unique and unforgettable moment when man and beast were as one.

Unaware that she was watching, the man continued towards a five-barred gate. He opened it, slipped off the horse's halter and turned the beast loose in the field beyond.

From her vantage point, Sonny watched, fascinated, as the beautiful creature sped around the paddock, kicking and rearing. The man was also watching, leaning over the gate, his dark hair blown by the breeze and his face wreathed in smiles. When the horse fell to the ground and rolled over and over like a great kitten, he laughed out loud.

Sonny felt strange, like an outsider watching something very private and very special. 'I was wrong,' she muttered. 'You're not a lonely man.' In fact she envied him. His seemed to be a simple existence. He had his work, and he had the love of that magnificent beast. Any man might settle for less.

In a moment he returned to the barn.

She stayed rooted to the spot, more intrigued than ever. She might have made her way up to the house, but curiosity got the better of her. Glancing round to make certain no one was looking, she went over to the barn.

As she drew closer she saw another building, situated to the rear of the barn and looking over a small courtyard. It was a stable, a spacious place with split doors and a high roof, positioned to face west and take advantage of the sun all day.

Feeling like an intruder, not wanting the man to see her, Sonny crept to the door of the barn and peered cautiously in. Her eyes widened in surprise as she gazed round.

The barn was divided by a high timber arch. The rear area was like a great storeroom. On one side were lengths of timber in various sizes. On the other stood a row of large cardboard boxes, some closed, some open. There were tools hanging on the wall.

But it was the area immediately next to her that fascinated Sonny, for that was where he was. He was so engrossed in his work that he had no idea she was there. Seated on a high stool, he was bent over a bench, his long strong fingers working with a gouge or chisel on a block of wood. As she watched, the wood began to change shape. It became the bust of a woman, with delicate features and long flowing hair. She could see the square line of shoulders, and the subtle rise of a breast.

While he worked, even his own face seemed to be chiselled out of wood – the hard straight line of his nose, the full, wide lips, and the firm set of his square chin. Only the eyes were alive, dark and brooding, filled with immense pleasure.

Her gaze moved along the bench. It was littered with other carvings in various stages of creation. Bowls of fruit were coloured so realistically you could imagine yourself sinking your teeth into them. There were any number of animals – an otter climbing out of rushes, a stag standing proud, kittens, birds – and figures of men, women and children, with the most lifelike features and faces that seemed to come alive as you gazed. All exquisite. All so beautiful it made her feel humble.

Suddenly she had the feeling that she too was being watched. Swinging round, she came face to face with a young woman. Tall and attractive, with long auburn hair and rather small brown eyes, she demanded, 'Who the hell are you? And what do you think you're doing parking your car on my drive? Move it, before I get the tractor and tow the bloody thing off!'

'I'm sorry,' Sonny began. 'I didn't realise ... but that's still no reason for you to screech at me like a fish-wife!' She'd had a long day. She was tired, and she'd been caught snooping. And now her hackles were well and truly up. To make matters worse, as she stepped forward her high heel sank into a rut and no matter how she tried she couldn't pull it out.

Suddenly he was there, reaching down, gently raising the shoe and her ankle out of the mud. While Sonny could only shrink with embarrassment, he addressed the young woman. 'I think your guest would appreciate a hot meal and a warmer welcome,' he suggested quietly. Looking at Sonny, he said, 'You've bruised your ankle. I find witch hazel is as good as anything.' With that he went back inside the barn.

The young woman glared at the doors, then at Sonny.

'I'm sorry,' she said grudgingly. 'You must be Sonny Fareham?'

When Sonny nodded, she sighed aloud, feeling regret. 'Whatever must you think of me?'

'Not a lot, to be honest,' Sonny replied. Her ankle was caked in mud and beginning to hurt. 'But like the man said, I'm hungry and in need of a bath.'

Grabbing Sonny's hand the woman shook it too vigorously. 'I'm Cathy Sefton. Sorry I wasn't here to meet you. I expected to be back before now, but you know how things are.' She glanced towards the house. 'I suppose you couldn't get an answer?'

Following her gaze, Sonny explained, 'I haven't been to the house yet. I was talking to Mr . . .' She shifted her gaze to the barn, waiting for Cathy Sefton to satisfy her curiosity.

The young woman laughed, and Sonny thought she detected a note of satisfaction. 'He didn't introduce himself, then? But I wouldn't have expected him to. He's notoriously unsociable. A bit of a hermit. Doesn't take kindly to strangers . . . especially when they creep up and spy on him.'

Mortified, Sonny protested, 'I wasn't spying on him.'

'Oh? Then what were you doing just now, when I caught you red-handed?'

'I was curious, that's all.' She would have taken great delight in wiping the smug expression off that pretty painted face.

However, the smugness fell away when the young woman's mood quickly changed. 'He does that to women,' she said in a quieter voice. 'Makes them curious.' She stared at the barn doors again and her gaze hardened. 'Makes them want him!'

A strange kind of pleasure flitted over her face. 'One of these days some woman will get through to that hard heart of his.' She smiled. 'Then it'll be his turn, and I won't be sorry.'

Taken aback by the bitterness in her voice, Sonny didn't know what to say. More than ever she wished she hadn't come here. What she was looking for was peace and quiet, a safe hiding place. Instead she seemed to have happened on a kind of rats' nest, where everything rotten festered below the surface.

As they came to the drive, Cathy Sefton realised she had betrayed her feelings too openly to the stranger. To compensate, she laughed a little. 'He's too good-looking, that's the trouble. He's also the most unapproachable man I've ever met! That's always a dangerous combination. When a man like David Langden isn't interested in women, it only encourages them to go after him.'

Sonny thought on that for a minute, finding it easy to believe. Certainly he had been difficult to approach, and yes, he was too handsome. He was also aloof enough to draw any woman's interest – not hers though, because she was not looking for any involvement. Not now, and not at any time that she could foresee.

However, understandably enough after meeting the obnoxious Miss Cathy Sefton, she found herself on the man's side. If she was ever made to choose between the hostile David Langden and this arrogant young woman, Sonny knew instinctively whom she would prefer.

With that in mind, she replied pointedly, 'Everyone's entitled to their privacy.'

'Meaning you?'

'Meaning anyone.'

'Is that why you're here? To get some privacy?'

'Maybe.'

Cathy Sefton glanced ahead, craning her neck to see inside the car. 'I was under the impression there would be two of you?'

'My aunt changed her mind at the last minute.' Feeling at a disadvantage for the second time in a matter of minutes, Sonny mentally kicked herself. 'I'm sorry, I should have let you know.'

'It would have been polite to say the least.'

'There wasn't really time.' That was true enough. What with everything else, the last thing on her mind had been calling to tell Miss Sefton it would be only one guest and not two. Good God! Rude it may have been, or maybe just thoughtless, but it didn't warrant a full-scale investigation, which was what seemed to be developing. 'All I can do is apologise. Now can we leave it?' Sonny stared at the Sefton woman, her ankle throbbing and her hackles rising again.

Cathy Sefton gave a sly irritating grin. 'Of course. Whatever you say.'

By the time she returned to her car, Sonny's ankle was so swollen it hurt to drive. But she wasn't about to admit it and so drove the car to the house and followed the girl inside. As they came into the foyer a man appeared. He looked old and weary; his face was long and narrow, his complexion sallow. He studied Sonny and asked, 'Who's this?'

The young woman stepped forward. 'This is our guest, Miss Fareham,' she answered. 'There were supposed to be two, but apparently the aunt has decided not to come.'

The man shrugged his shoulders as though wanting to be rid of something troublesome. 'Might have told us,' he muttered. 'I've got two rooms ready now.'

Cathy Sefton's smile was more like a stab of hatred. 'It isn't your problem.'

He shrugged his shoulders again, this time bending his head as though supporting a great weight. 'It's me who has to do all the work.' The hatred was returned tenfold.

Darting forward, Cathy pushed him with the flat of her hand. 'A bit of hard work won't hurt you.' When he reeled backwards she pursued, pushing him again. Losing his balance, he fell heavily against a hall table. While he struggled to recover she bent to smell his breath. Now it was her turn to reel back. 'Have you been drinking?'

He looked like a scared rabbit. 'No! Honest to God!'

Cathy stared at him with disgust, and something Sonny could not recognise – a kind of envy perhaps. 'See the water's hot, you lazy old bugger,' she hissed, pursuing and pushing him all the way out of the door. 'Our guest would like a bath. And when you've done that, you'd better take her luggage up.'

As he scurried away, she swung round. 'The silly old fool's drawn all the curtains again!' she snarled.

Crossing to the window, she snatched two handfuls of the thick tapestry curtains. Yanking them back to let the evening light filter in, she pronounced, 'There! That's better.'

'You were a bit harsh on that poor soul, weren't you?' Disgusted, Sonny let her feelings show.

Cathy's smile was devastatingly pleasant. 'Oh, dear! I am sorry you had to witness that.' She inclined her head towards the door. 'I don't mean to be hard on him, but there are times when he drives me to the edge.' She clenched her fists. 'Sometimes I wonder why I keep him on. He's more trouble than he's worth.'

'Then why *do* you keep him on?' It was more of a challenge than a question.

Momentarily lost for words, the other woman turned away and began to fuss with the curtains. After a short, embarrassed silence she came back across the room. 'I suppose he has his good points,' she admitted grudgingly. 'Mainly, he's honest.'

She clapped her hands together as though indicating the subject was closed, adding as an afterthought, 'Honest labour is hard to find these days, don't you think?'

Sonny disliked her more by the minute. 'I wouldn't know,' she replied frostily. 'Never having been in the position where I needed to hire it.'

'It isn't easy, I can tell you.'

Sonny returned a smile as false as Cathy's had been. 'Oh, I'm sure!'

Detecting a sly innuendo, Cathy Sefton bristled. 'We'll go up, if you're ready?'

'Please.' Anything to be rid of her!

As they mounted the stairs, Cathy explained, 'I've put you in the main bedroom. It has its own bathroom, and a lovely view across the valley.'

'Thank you.' The thought of a long soak in a hot bath made Sonny feel better. 'I won't come down to eat,' she said. 'Tea and a couple of rounds of ham sandwiches in my room will be fine.'

'Before or after your bath?'

'Before, I think.' She tried hard not to be rude, but it wasn't easy. 'I really am starving.'

'Tired as well, I shouldn't wonder. After all, you've driven a long way.' Pushing open the bedroom door, Cathy allowed Sonny to walk in first.

'Something to eat, a hot bath and a good night's sleep.' Shaking her head with pleasure, Sonny gave out a long soft sigh. 'Wonderful!'

'I'll have a tray sent up.' Everything Cathy said was uttered with resentment.

When the door was closed and she was alone at last, Sonny sat on the edge of the bed. A tickle of dust made her sneeze. While rummaging in her bag for a hankie, she came across a photograph of her and Martha in the garden of the cottage.

The photograph brought a smile to her face as she recalled how reluctant Martha had been to have it taken. It was early summer and Martha was excitedly pointing to a rhododendron she'd planted just the year before and which was now smothered in huge purple blooms. Since then the shrub had gone from strength to strength, and was Martha's pride and joy.

The picture made Sonny feel a little nostalgic. Already she was missing Martha. If there was an easier way of dealing with the frightening situation forced on to her by the man she had loved and trusted she would have been on her way home right this minute. But there was no easy way. Not if she wanted to keep her child, and herself, out of Tony Bridgeman's clutches.

She glanced round the room. It was beautifully furnished – chic but not pretentious. Sonny was impressed. 'Whoever chose the furnishings has a wonderful eye for detail,' she thought, smiling with appreciation as she directed a critical eye from one part of the room to another. The walls were painted in a dusky shade of pink; the carpet was a soft silver-grey colour, richly piled and laid wall to wall. 'Must have cost an absolute fortune!' she breathed. The rug by the bed was oval, patterned with slender green leaves and tiny rosebuds. Slipping off her shoe, she stretched out her toes to feel the softness through her stockings.

The charming walnut furniture was simply designed. It had obviously been loved in its time, for every curve, every line, even the tiny carved feet, were polished and shone in the warmest hues.

Here the curtains were bright and floral, reflecting the welcoming atmosphere of the room. The wide panoramic window had a seat that ran all the way round the bay; it was dressed with frilled fabrics and big floppy cushions that seemed to invite 'Sit here, relax, and let me coddle you'.

And that was just what Sonny did. Sinking gratefully into the cushions, she lay back and closed her tired green eyes. She felt warm and comfortable – almost as comfortable as when Martha was with her. She felt her presence now. So strong was the feeling that she found herself talking aloud. 'Well, Aunt Martha, here I am. A stranger in a strange place . . . aching in every bone, and so ravenous I could eat the bedstead.' She chuckled at the idea. 'I've met two men who've already fired my curiosity . . . one of them a strong silent type who, the awful Cathy Sefton rightly thinks, is "too good-looking".'

A strange restlessness came over her. Sitting upright, she stared down at Martha's photograph. 'His name is David Langden,' she said softly. 'And he's a very talented man . . . a wood-carver.'

Angry with herself for letting him dwell in her mind, she turned the photograph over and over in her hand, until after a while she addressed it once more. 'The other man must be . . . what? Sixty or so? Or maybe he just looks that old. The way she nags him, I wouldn't be surprised if he's aged before his time. He looks so unhappy too, and lonely, like he hasn't a friend in the world. Poor soul . . . fancy having to answer to a creature like Cathy Sefton. Any other man would have packed his bags and disappeared long ago. But, to be honest, he didn't seem to take her spiteful comments too much to heart. Hmm!' She giggled with satisfaction. 'Come to think of it, I reckon I was more offended than he was!'

She slipped her shoe back on and stood by the window. 'I have to admit she was right about one thing,' she murmured. 'The view from here is absolutely lovely.' The twilight made the land look even more beautiful, mysterious and aloof. 'A bit like David Langden himself.' She smiled. He was creeping into her mind again. With grim determination, she pushed him out and concentrated on the view. Even as she watched, the daylight was dimming. Soon it would be too dark to see beyond the windowsill.

Raising her eyes, she could see the whole of the grounds. She could see the stable where David Langden kept that magnificent stallion, and the place where he worked. Now the horse was grazing in the field, and the man was in the barn, creating his own special beauty.

Sonny could see into the barn. A shaft of daylight picked its way through the far window and silhouetted him, a busy figure, bent to his labours. It made a comforting, humbling sight. Deliberately shifting her gaze, she roved her attention over the land.

The grounds were vast, laid mostly to lawn, with great spreading oak trees touching branches here and there, like friends or lovers or lonely souls needing to communicate.

There were surprisingly few flowers or shrubs, and hardly any colour at all. Beyond she had a clear view of the valleys, dipping and rising, green and satisfying, making the heart feel free. Making it whole.

A slight movement caught her attention. Shifting her gaze to the barn, she saw David Langden emerge, leaning on the door jamb to smoke his pipe, and following the upward trail of smoke with his dark moody eyes. 'Are you lonely too?' she whispered, pressing her face to the window and letting her imagination run riot.

There was something splendid about him, she thought,

a kind of strength and calm that she had never seen in any man before. Certainly not in Tony Bridgeman. Not even when she was looking at him through rose-coloured spectacles.

'So you don't want a relationship either, eh?' she asked softly. 'I wonder . . . is it because you've been hurt, like me?' She felt herself sympathising with him, without even knowing why.

As though he could hear her, he suddenly glanced up, his dark eyes searching her out. Blushing profusely, she swiftly drew away, her heart doing little somersaults as she pressed herself against the wall.

It was a full minute before she dared move. When she did, it was to sneak a look out of the window. He wasn't there any more, and she couldn't see inside the barn because the doors were firmly closed.

Embarrassed, she hurried from the window, picked up her handbag and slid the photograph inside. It's no business of mine, she thought. I've got more than enough of my own problems. She felt irritated. For some reason Cathy Sefton had taken an instant dislike to her. But after a moment she shrugged her shoulders and smiled. 'Oh, well! There's no love lost, because I don't like her either.'

In fact, if her ankle wasn't swollen like two, and hurting like it was severed at the bone, she'd be down the road right now. Oh, she could get a taxi, but it was getting late and she didn't want the hassle of searching for another place at this time of an evening.

More than that, she was starving hungry and so weary she could hardly keep her eyes open. All in all, it seemed far easier and more sensible to stay where she was, at least until the morning. She consulted Martha in her mind. 'I don't think one night under the same roof as the sharp-tongued Miss Sefton is too much to pay for the prospect of a hot bath, some freshly made sandwiches, a welcome cup of tea . . . and a good night's sleep.' She considered the deal and came back with an answer much as Martha might have given. 'It's a fair swap and not to be sniffed at!'

A sharp tap on the door made her jump. 'All right,' she called out, brushing herself down and making sure she was presentable. 'Just a minute, please.'

She had thought a waitress might have brought the tray, but when she opened the door it was to see the old fellow standing there, a polite smile on his face and a look of disinterest in his sad eyes. 'Refreshments,' he said. Walking past her into the room, he placed the tray on the table, straightened his back with a groan and turned to leave. 'If there's anything else, you just have to pick that up.' He pointed to the bedside cabinet, and the large black telephone there. 'It's connected directly to the desk.'

He would have left then, but she called him back. After placing a half-crown into his hand, she asked, 'I don't suppose you've had time to fetch up my luggage, have you?'

He touched his nose with a finger. 'Now that's where you're wrong, miss,' he said mischievously. 'Your bags are right outside the door.' He returned to get them. 'I'd have brought them up sooner,' he apologised, 'only I got called away on another job.'

'A man's work is never done, eh?'

'Nary a truer word, miss.'

'Have you been here long?'

His eyes lit up and his face broke into a warm smile. 'Oh, I've been here a long time, miss.' The smile slid away as he went on in a softer voice, 'Sometimes I wonder if I've been here too long.'

'Why's that?'

'Oh, I don't know. Things change. Sometimes for the worse.' Instinctively his gaze went to the door.

Sonny got the feeling he had Cathy Sefton in mind. 'I saw how she treated you just now.'

Straightaway he was wary. 'Oh?' Taking a step towards the door he suddenly turned to warn in a whisper, 'Don't get on the wrong side of that one, will you?'

There was a twinkle in her eye as she replied reassuringly, 'I think it's "that one" who shouldn't get on the wrong side of me!'

He chuckled, and she chuckled, and soon they were laughing together. 'I can see she's met her match,' he said.

'You can depend on it,' she replied.

He became serious. 'She can be a bad 'un, though.'

'Don't worry.'

Pointing to the tray, he urged, 'Don't let your tea grow cold.'

Sonny was interested. 'What exactly is your job here? I mean . . . I thought a waitress would bring up the tray.'

He chuckled again. 'I *am* the waitress . . . and the porter, and the gardener, and the cook. I clean and do repairs and generally run about.'

Sonny was horrified. 'That's awful!'

He shook his head, saying philosophically, 'It might be "awful", but it's better than being out on the street with no money in your trouser pocket.'

'Does she pay you well?'

There was a moment before he answered and when he did it was with a sigh. 'I'm fed and housed, and I have my ounce of baccy a week. I can't grumble.'

Pressing the point because she felt sorry for him, Sonny asked angrily, 'Why does she talk to you like that?'

He smiled wryly. 'I'd better go.'

The tone of his voice warned her she'd pried too far. 'I'm sorry,' she apologised. 'I've no right to ask you such personal questions.'

'It's all right,' he answered. 'No doubt you mean well.'

'Thank you for the tray.'

'They're good sandwiches . . . fresh ham and home-made pickle. You enjoy them.'

'I will,' she promised.

He was about to leave the room when suddenly he turned and leaned towards her. 'Be careful,' he whispered, 'she's got it in for you.' He glanced at the window. 'David Langden's a good man . . . too good for her by half. But she's got her sights set on him, and she usually gets what she wants.' His old face crinkled into a friendly smile. 'He won't look at her twice and that riles her. But he'd look at you, I reckon. In fact, I saw him just now, gazing up at this window.'

Sonny blushed. If David Langden was gazing up at this window it was only because he suspected she was spying on him again. He was right too, and she felt ashamed. 'I'm sure you were mistaken,' she said.

He smiled again. 'Aye. If you say so.' With that he closed the door, leaving her alone with her guilt, and a persistent feeling that she was getting in over her head. 'Keep to yourself, my girl,' she said in Martha's tone of voice. 'That way you'll stay out of trouble.'

An hour later, fed, rested and about to take a long-awaited bath, she heard Cathy Sefton's voice carrying up from downstairs. 'You lying old bastard! I heard you with my own ears . . . the two of you . . . were you laughing at me? Were you? Answer me, you old fool!'

There was a pause, during which time Sonny imagined someone else must be talking in a softer voice. But then Cathy Sefton screeched out, 'You know you did wrong or you wouldn't have hid from me. I've spent a whole hour searching the house for you. Where were you hiding, eh? Tell me that.'

Again there was a pause.

Then she was yelling, 'I'm not interested in your lies and excuses. In future, you'll just get on with your work and keep your mouth shut. Do you understand? No fraternising with the guests. No chatting and laughing or creeping about as if you own the place. You are an employee in my house, and not a very satisfactory one at that.'

There was a pause while the man answered softly.

Whatever he said must have rankled, because now her voice was harder. 'I'm warning you, old man . . . don't overstep the mark. You'll do as I say, and if you can't accept that, you'd better pack your bags right now and get out. Do you hear?'

Another pause.

There was a noisy scuffle, followed by a sharp sound, like the crack of a whip. '*Get out of my sight!*'

There came the sound of footsteps walking on a tiled floor. Then the sharp click of a door being closed. And then silence.

For a long moment Sonny wasn't sure what to do. 'I blame myself,' she muttered, pacing the floor. 'It was me who got him talking . . . me who asked the questions and got him laughing. And now he's the one paying for it.'

There was only one thing to do. When the yelling started she had been lying on the bed, having eaten the sandwiches and rested her throbbing ankle. Now, though, she was pacing the floor in stockinged feet, her ankle hurting more than ever. But she didn't give it a thought as she hurried to the bed and took up her slippers. Sitting on the edge of the bed she pushed one foot into a slipper, but, try as she might, the other would not go on. The ankle was far too swollen.

Undeterred, she dropped the slipper to the floor and hobbled to the door, then out on to the landing and down the stairs. 'Spiteful bugger!' she muttered as she went. '*She*'s the one who wants throwing out!'

A door in the hall was open. Through it she could see the tiled floor of what was obviously the kitchen. Hurrying through, she came face to face with the old man. He looked like a startled rabbit, his whole body visibly shaking. There was a vivid red mark running from the top of his right temple to the side of his neck, where the skin was broken and bleeding.

Realising she had seen the mark, he brought up his hand to hide it, and she saw that the same wicked mark was imprinted on the back of his hand. 'My God!' So, it had been the crack of a whip she'd heard. 'Did she do that?' Sonny demanded.

'Don't interfere,' he begged in a trembling voice. 'When she's in that kind of a mood it's best to leave her be.' He had a bowl of steaming water on the table and a wad of cotton wool close by. His right eye was oozing and his lip was swelling even as she watched.

'She can wait,' Sonny decided. 'You can't.' Momentarily suppressing the fury inside her, she gently bathed and treated the wound. Once or twice he winced, but said nothing throughout. Even when she asked him if it was comfortable now, he remained silent. It was only when she was heading for the door that he called out, 'I'm sorry. She can be a bad 'un when she takes a mind.'

Pausing, but not looking round, Sonny informed him quietly, 'Sometimes, through no fault of your own and because of the situation you find yourself in, it's imposs-ible to face up to the bad 'uns.' She had Tony Bridgeman in mind.

'I know what you're saying.' He had his own reasons for not wanting to stand up to the woman of this house.

Sonny appeared not to have heard. She was still think-ing of her own dilemma. 'But there are other times when you have to face up to them.' Now she was talking about Cathy Sefton. 'I think it's time this one was told a few home truths.'

She turned then, her eyes pleading with him.

When he looked down uncertainly she was riddled with doubts. What right did she have to interfere? After all she was a stranger in this house. Yet she would be less of a human being if she stood aside and saw this kindly soul being beaten and humiliated. Even so, she did harbour doubts. Was it her place to confront Cathy Sefton? Or was it better to let the old man deal with it in his own way? Her instincts drew her one way. The old man's wishes drew her another.

But then he spoke again, this time with grim determination. 'You'll find her in the lounge, across the hall,' he said softly.

Sonny gave a half-smile and went out of the door, across the hall and straight into the lounge without knocking. 'I'd like a word,' she said angrily, closing the door behind her.

Cathy Sefton had been watching television. On Sonny's arrival she jumped out of the chair, ran to the TV set and switched it off. 'What the hell do you mean by barging in here?' Her eyes were no longer pretty. Instead they were hard and glittering, staring and hating. But showing just the smallest hint of fear. Yet for all that she was fighting mad. 'These are my private quarters. Please leave. *Now*!'

Sonny was not intimidated. 'I'll leave when I've had my say.' Taking a step forward, she braced herself. 'Perhaps I should call the police and be done with it?'

Cathy was still arrogant, but again that little flicker of fear showed through. 'What's all this about calling the police?'

'Well now, let's see. For starters we could mention working an old man into the ground. Then there's the little matter of taking a whip to him, when his only crime is to talk with another human being.'

Cathy's face was set like granite. 'Did he tell you he was whipped?'

'He didn't have to.' Sonny gave her a knowing look. 'I imagine my room is right over the kitchen?'

'You imagine a lot of things. Like you've imagined he was beaten. Don't believe anything he tells you. The man has no brains. You saw for yourself what an old fool he is. He's also a liar, and a thief. Time and again he's stolen from me . . . oh, of course he always denies it.' She snorted. 'It's *me* who should be calling the police.'

'I'll say it again! He didn't have to tell me anything, because I heard it all.' Sonny's voice dropped to a harsh whisper. 'I know what you did, you wicked bitch! I've seen the marks with my own eyes.' When she took another step forward, Cathy Sefton took a step back, and when Sonny spoke again the colour drained from the other woman's face. 'Is that what you used? Is it?' Her green eyes flicked towards the fireplace, where an evil-looking leather whip stood propped in the corner. 'I've a good mind to use it on you . . . give you the beating you deserve. See if you can take as well as give.'

'He's a liar, I tell you!'

'It's you that's the liar.'

Shaking uncontrollably, Cathy Sefton recoiled to press herself against the chair, her eyes wide with terror as she screamed defiantly, 'You're mad! Get out! I want you out of my house, *now*! Is that clear?'

'Oh, I'm going,' Sonny told her in a brighter voice. 'But before I go I want you to know I won't be so far away that I can't keep an eye on you. So if I hear you've been beating that old man – or making his life a misery in any other way – I'll be back.' Pressing her face close to the other woman's, she demanded quietly, 'Now have you got that clear?'

Only when the other woman nodded did she leave. She hobbled upstairs and packed her bags, and hobbled down again. By now the night was closing in. She threw her bags inside the car, then herself. She started the engine and switched on the headlights, but when she tried to drive away her ankle refused to bend and she cried out in agony. 'Damn and bugger it, I won't give her the satisfaction!' Sonny exclaimed.

Silhouetted by the soft light behind her, Cathy Sefton watched from the lounge window. Sonny couldn't see her face, nor her expression, except in her mind's eye. 'If you're waiting for me to grovel for help, you're in for a disappointment,' she declared.

She massaged the ankle and tried again.

Racked with pain, she managed to drive out on to the road, but she had not gone more than a hundred yards from the house before she was forced to a stop to take account of her situation. It was hopeless. 'That's it!' she moaned. 'I can't drive and it hurts to walk, but I'm blowed if I'll stay here in the dark, on a lonely road, all by myself.' She wondered what Martha would say, and vowed never to tell her.

After clambering out of the car, she locked the door

and went at a slow painful limp in the opposite direction, away from the house.

It began to rain, soft wet sploshes comforting against her face. She limped a little further, occasionally resting against a tree, or simply standing by the side of the road, hoping a car might come along and take her into Blackburn town. But there was no sign of life anywhere. She was alone. The darkness engulfed her and the rain became a downpour, wetting her to the skin. 'And there's Aunt Martha tucked up in a warm bed,' she laughed. And with the laughter came a sense of the ridiculous. 'She always said I was impetuous,' she recalled, not minding if anyone should hear her talking to herself – at least it would prove she wasn't the only soul on the planet. 'If I hadn't lost my temper I'd be lying in a warm bed too, instead of being lost in the dark, tramping the road on a bad ankle, with the rain driving right through to my knickers.'

She shuddered. 'Truth is, I'd rather be wet to the skin and lost for a week than stay in that woman's house.' The knowledge that she had done right was compensation for her present discomfort.

The road was badly lit, though she could make out the divide between the bank and the road itself, and so was able to keep a true path. She was surprised and disappointed when only one vehicle passed, and that was a big white van that went by at such a speed that it kicked up the puddles and sprayed her with a fresh shower of water.

It seemed like an age before she saw the lights of Blackburn town. Stretching out before her like twinkling stars on the horizon, they made a welcome sight. How far? she wondered. Six miles? Seven? Her heart sank. She didn't know if she could make it that far.

Weary and hurting all over, and with her ankle feeling like a lead weight at the end of her leg, she paused to rest. The rain had stopped and the air was warmer, but she was soaked to the skin, and racked with pain. When she saw a bench beneath a tree she hobbled thankfully towards it. 'A minute,' she sighed, leaning her aching body against the hard wood. 'Then I'll be on my way.'

Weariness overwhelmed her. Closing her eyes, she thought of the innocent inside her, and inevitably her thoughts turned to the child's father. She had loved him so much. Now she feared him. In truth, he had never been hers to love.

Convinced that what she was suffering now was a punishment for her sins, she began to laugh. The laughter turned to tears, and her heart ached.

'God! It's so cold.' She drew her jacket tighter around her, but it was sodden, sending a chill through her bones. She tried to stand but the pain in her ankle sent a shock through her body, making her cry out. 'Another minute,' she told herself, falling back to the bench. 'Get my breath and I'll be all right.'

But she wasn't all right. Her mind was strong but her body was drained. The rain started again. The skies opened and it poured down. She struggled up, peering through the driving sheets, the raindrops cascading down her face and blinding her. She dragged herself on, in agony.

She couldn't stop shivering and, oh, she was so tired! The tiredness swept through her like a tidal wave, momentarily carrying her senses away. She felt herself slipping, crumpling to the road. As her face scraped the hard ground, she felt her strength drain away.

In a moment she was unconscious and knew nothing.

She didn't know that David Langden had worked late, or that when he saw her car abandoned he realised she might be in trouble. She couldn't know that he kept his eyes peeled all the way from the big house, and that he was going by her at a crawl when he saw her lying in the road. She couldn't feel him lift her into his arms and carry her to the Land Rover, where he gently laid her on his outstretched coat.

Nor did she realise that he had been drawn to her that very first moment when he had seen her outside the barn.

Sonny knew nothing of the journey into Blackburn, or of how, once there, he lifted her tenderly into his arms again.

Fate had brought them together, forged a bond between them – a deep abiding bond that would not be easily broken.

Chapter Four

Ellie Kenny was the salt of the earth. A big Irish woman with auburn hair and plain features, she knew her own limitations. She seemed almost proud of the fact that she was neither rich nor a beauty. 'As long as I've got me health and strength and a fella on me arm now and then, sure I'll want for nothing,' she'd say. 'And so long as the coalman doesn't mind exchanging a cuddle and a warm bed for half a sack o' best nuts, ye'll not hear me complaining.'

Down-to-earth and loved by everyone, Ellie had a heart of gold, two children by different fathers and a house that looked like a bombsite the morning after.

She also had a mangy black cat. As a kitten he'd cocked his leg over her plant pot, killing a white chrysanthemum she'd raised from a cutting. On the very same day he'd climbed on to the kitchen sink and cocked his leg over her best pint mug. Ellie caught him red-handed and christened him Pisspot. The name had stuck ever since.

'Get up outta that bed, you two!' she yelled up the stairs. 'I swear to God, if yer late for school again, I'll tan yer arses till yer can't sit down!'

Seated on the settee, Sonny had to smile. In the three weeks she'd been here she had come to love this big warm woman. 'They're not upstairs, Ellie,' she chuckled. 'Mick's in the back yard, cleaning his bike, and Kathleen's under the table feeding the cat.'

Ellie swung round. 'Why, the little sods!' she declared. 'When did they steal by me, eh? Tell me that!' With two great strides she was across the room and peering under the table. 'Are you in there, our Kathleen?'

The pretty blonde girl stared up at her mother. For a moment she looked startled. Ellie had the tablecloth over her head and looked like a banshee. 'I'm not coming out,' said the child, backing away. 'I'm not going to school neither.'

'Oh, yer not, eh?' Ellie mimicked. 'Well now, sure you've got another think coming, my girl . . . because if yer ain't outta there by the time I count to five I'll be off to the kitchen and fetch a bucket o' water to throw over yer!' She laughed. 'That'll have yer out, I'll be bound.'

'All right, I'll come out,' the girl replied sulkily. 'But I'm not going to school.'

'Yer are!'

'I'm not!'

Turning to Sonny, Ellie gave a wry little smile. 'Here's a young madam who says she won't go to school. What shall we do, eh? I'm at me wit's end, sure I am.'

Sonny had seen the same scene enacted several times since the night David had brought her to this lovely warm woman. Kathleen would hide under the table and Ellie would threaten to throw a bucket of water over her. Kathleen would threaten not to go to school, and Ellie would turn to Sonny and pretend to be at her wit's end. And each time Sonny would make the same suggestion. She made it now. 'Won't go to school? Oh, that's a pity, especially when *you*'ve already bought her a bag of sweeties for her lunch-box.' A big sigh, then, 'Never mind. *We*'ll share them, shall we, Ellie?'

Ellie would get up, as she did now, saying excitedly, 'Now why didn't I think of that?'

The two of them continued the little farce, with Sonny remarking, 'I think Kathleen's very brave, though.'

Ellie gave her a crafty wink. 'Brave, eh?' With one eye on the table and the other on Sonny, she said in a serious voice, 'An' why would yer think that?'

'Well, I mean, who'd want to be stuck under a table all day long? Crouched double, all alone, and getting hungrier by the minute. Oh, I could never be that brave.'

'Me neither!' Ellie declared with horror. 'Still, if that's what the lass wants, I'll not stand in her way. So when her friends come calling to walk with her to school I'll have to send them away.' She raised her voice just a little. 'An' what about cookery class? When they're all making them lovely little scones to take home to their mams, our Kathleen will still be here, under the table.' She smacked her lips loudly. 'Shame though, because I do love them little scones... all golden brown and crumbly they are. Spread with best butter and a generous helping of me homemade jam, they're a real treat.'

'Oh, I'd forgotten it was Friday!' Sonny exclaimed. 'Isn't the geography teacher planning to take the children up to Corporation Park?'

'Well now!' Ellie gave her a wink of approval. 'I'd forgotten all about that. I expect they'll be going to the sandpit, and they'll sit on the old cannons at the top of the hill, and d'yer know ... it wouldn't surprise me if they were allowed to feed the ducks in the lake because, from what I've been told, there'll be four teachers going along, and an army of mams to help keep an eye on the children.'

Suddenly a little voice piped up. 'We're not going to the lake, and that's why I'm not going to school!'

Ellie returned to the table and peered beneath the tablecloth. The girl's eyes were red from crying. 'Who says you're not going to the lake?' Ellie asked gently.

'Susie Beale, that's who! She says we'll be marched round and we won't be able to stop anywhere. She says I'll have to stay right at the back of the line and I can't walk with Amy.' She sniffled and wiped her nose with the back of her hand. 'Amy's my best friend. If I can't walk with her, I don't want to go.'

Ellie stiffened. 'You're going to school, my girl! And I haven't got time to argue.'

'I'll run away!'

'Get outta there, yer little bugger!'

'No!'

Torn between love and duty, Ellie straightened up to cast a pleading look at Sonny. 'I've never known her as bad as this. I can't seem to get through to her,' she said quietly. In a harder voice meant for the girl's ears, she declared, 'An' I'm losing patience.' She'd suffered a bad night, and it showed in her face.

Just then the doorbell rang. 'I expect it's the milkman

for his money.' Ellie went at a run down the hall. 'You's best be outta there when I get back, or you'll know it!' she called over her shoulder.

'I won't!' Kathleen was as stubborn as her mother when she thought she was in the right.

Sonny got out of the chair. Going to the table, she crouched down, then crawled beneath and sat beside the surprised girl. 'You don't mind, do you, Kathleen?' she asked softly.

'No.'

'You don't like Susie Beale, do you?'

'She's a bully.'

'What makes you think she knows the teacher's plans?'

Kathleen stared at her as if she had said something very silly. 'She knows everything.'

Reaching out to thumb a tear from the girl's face, Sonny replied softly, 'Are you going to let Susie Beale get your mam in trouble?'

Taken by surprise, Kathleen stared at her. 'She can't get our mam in trouble . . . can she?'

'If you let her, yes. You see, if you stay away from school for no good reason, the authorities might come and see your mother. If they're not satisfied, they can take her to court . . . fine her a lot of money, which she can't afford to pay. She'd be worried and upset. You wouldn't want that, would you, Kathleen?'

'No.' The tears were falling down her face. 'But I want to walk with Amy . . . and I really want to feed the ducks.'

'Do you always walk with Amy on other outings?'

117

'Every time, because we're the littlest and the teacher puts us at the front.'

'And she will this time, you'll see. What's more, I'll bet you do feed the ducks, and even if the teacher doesn't take you to the lake, I will. We can all go ... you and Mick and me and your mam. We'll go on Sunday, take a picnic.'

The girl's face brightened. 'Honest?'

'Honest.'

'And do you really think I can walk with Amy?'

'If you don't, I'll eat this tablecloth.'

'You won't?'

'I will!'

When Ellie came back it was to the sound of laughter emanating from under the table. 'Be Jaysus!' she exclaimed, peeking under the cloth. 'There's two of the buggers under there now!'

Ten minutes later, dry-eyed and happier, Kathleen went away down the road, with her friend Amy on one arm and her schoolbag on the other. Mick kept a respectable distance. After all, he didn't want to be seen walking to school with two silly young girls. A tall, gangly twelve-year-old, he considered himself to be a man in the making.

'However did yer persuade the lass to come out?' Ellie asked, switching on the kettle.

Sonny explained how she'd promised that Kathleen would walk with Amy on the trip, and that the teacher would be taking them to the lake ... otherwise Ellie would be short of a tablecloth because Sonny had promised to eat it!

Grim-faced, Ellie was indignant. 'Yer should never have done that!' she chided. 'Sure that's me best bloody tablecloth.' Then she fell into the chair, helpless with laughter. Soon the two of them were in hysterics; the kettle rose to the boil and its persistent shrilling screams mingled with the laughter. The postman dropped the mail through the letterbox and went away thinking the world had gone mad.

Eager to repay Ellie's kindness now that she had regained her strength, Sonny made herself busy. While Ellie washed up, she hoovered, and when Ellie collected the week's wash and got the boiler going in the kitchen, Sonny went upstairs and flung open the windows to let the glorious July sunshine flood in. She dusted round, hung all of Mick's discarded garments in the wardrobe, then made all the beds. When that was done, she returned downstairs to help Ellie hang out the wash. 'Put me drawers in the middle, me darling, where folk can't see 'em,' Ellie chuckled. 'Else they'll think we're hanging tents out to dry.'

Sonny did as she was told, and couldn't hide her amusement as she hid the great white bloomers amongst the other washing.

When the line was filled from one end to the other they went back to the kitchen and Sonny made a pot of coffee. 'Nice and milky, mind,' Ellie reminded her. 'Can't drink coffee that looks like bull's blood!'

They sat round the kitchen table and talked of everything in general – the children, the price of milk and the irritating habits of the new postman. 'I wish to God

119

he'd stop picking his nose,' Ellie groaned. 'He'll get the street a bad name.'

Sonny asked about the neighbours. Ellie gave her a long and colourful account of every soul that had ever lived in Penny Street. 'None of us ain't got much money, but we get by – baby-minding, ironing and baking. One way or another the pennies come in. If you've got a strong back and a big heart you'll not starve.' She winked. 'Mind you, I have got a few pounds tucked away for a rainy day. That's summat I can thank my late husband for.'

Just as she started on a lurid account of her neighbour, the late Bert Armitage, who had bedded every woman down the street ('including meself I'm ashamed to say'), the phone rang and saved the day.

Sonny gave a sigh of relief, although she had been riveted by some of the tales Ellie had related – such as the story of Bertha Legg, who 'took a liking to the local bobby and set up a burglary just so she could get him indoors and have his trousers off. Her old man walked in, found 'em naked as the day they were born, and threw the pair of 'em on to the street.'

Sonny was intrigued. 'Did he take her back?'

'Did he buggery!' Ellie laughed out loud. 'He packed up and sailed to foreign parts. The constable lost his job and Bertha took to religion. She went to be a nun, and spent her days collecting money for charity . . . standing on street corners shaking a tin and looking sorry for herself.' A look of regret came over her homely features. 'Last New Year the poor bugger got run over on King Street.'

Now, at the insistent ringing of the phone, she sprang out of her chair. 'Damn and bugger it, who's that?'

Stamping into the hall, she snatched up the receiver, listened attentively for a minute, then lost her temper. 'Don't worry, you'll get your money!' she called out, holding the receiver away from her ear. 'I'll pay the bloody paper bill when you stop putting them dirty books through me door. If I've told yer once, I've told yer a dozen times . . . I've got two young 'uns 'ere an' I don't want them seeing what drops on to me mat. I've asked you afore . . . keep the phonographic stuff under the counter till I come an' get it.'

A pause.

'Sure, isn't that what I said? Yer daft old bugger!'

Another pause, during which Ellie's eyes widened with astonishment. 'Yes! And you!'

She slammed the receiver down with such force that it sprang off the cradle and fell to the floor. 'Be Jaysus! The bloody thing's alive!'

'Pornographic,' Sonny said as she came through the door, red-faced and angry.

Ellie stared at her. 'What?'

'Just now, on the phone, you said "Phonographic".' A smile crept over her face. 'The word is "*Porn*ographic".'

Dropping into the chair, Ellie had to smile, 'It sounds rude, so I won't ask what it means.'

Sonny sipped at her coffee. 'It means I'm a woman of the world,' she said. What she thought was, But I still didn't know better than to get tangled up with a man like Tony Bridgeman.

The thought must have betrayed itself on her face

because now Ellie was saying, 'D'you mind if I say something?'

Sonny put her cup on the fender. 'Go ahead.'

'Only this – troubles are like mushrooms . . . keep 'em in the dark and they'll fester and grow.'

Sonny looked at her with mild surprise before lowering her gaze to the floor. In a quiet voice she said, 'What troubles do you mean, Ellie?'

'Troubles of any kind, that's what I mean. Troubles that can eat away at a body until it might seem like life ain't worth living.' Ellie bent her head so as to look into Sonny's face. 'I've said nothing since the night David brought you to this house, an' I want yer to know I've been grateful to have yer here, for yer a fine young woman, an' good company. But yer not here for my benefit, are yer? Yer here because yer turned up at the Sefton house an' didn't like what yer saw. Yer here because yer had nowhere else to go, an' because David came across yer in the driving rain, when yer were half dead from exposure . . . an' so poorly it took weeks afore yer came alive again.'

Sonny raised her face and smiled at the dear soul. 'I can't thank you enough for having me here, Ellie. You've been like a tonic . . . you and the children. It was just what I needed . . . someone to take me out of myself.' She squared her shoulders, saying staunchly, 'But thanks to you I'm well again, so I'd better soon start looking for a place of my own.'

Ellie regarded her through wise eyes. 'Hmm.' She sucked on her teeth, drummed her fingers on the arm of the chair and in a sombre voice said, 'First of all, yer don't need to be in no hurry to find a place of yer own. And secondly, I don't reckon yer ready to be on yer own just yet.'

'I don't know why you should think that.'

'Call it a woman's intuition if yer like, but I've got the feeling you need to be here with me a while longer...' She carefully considered her next words before saying them aloud. Though they were of a personal nature and might offend she felt they had to be said. 'I may be a nosy old bugger, an' you've every right to tell me I should mind me own business, but, well now... I've come to look on yer as I would me own flesh an' blood, an' I want to help if I can.' Reaching out to touch Sonny on the hand, she asked simply, 'That's if you'll let me help?'

There was no answer Sonny could give. She hadn't wanted to bring her troubles to Ellie's doorstep, so she believed the sooner she found a place of her own the better it would be all round. Deliberately ignoring Ellie's question, she asked brightly, 'Are there any places to rent round here?'

Ellie played along. 'What kind o' place?' she asked. 'Sure, there's allus a few houses to rent on Park Road, but they're big and cold, and they cost the earth. And if yer fancy a cosy little place like mine, here in Penny Street, with enough room to move about but not enough to hold a dance, then I reckon you'd find one easy enough.' She flicked a thumb towards the door. 'Matter o' fact the rentman's due this morning. He'll be the fella to ask, sure he will.' Her eyes lit with a merry twinkle.

Sonny thanked her. 'I'll have a word then,' she said.

'But if I get a place I'll need work in order to pay the rent.' In fact she longed for work. It was the one thing that might stop her from feeling lonely. 'Is there plenty of work in Blackburn?'

Securing a job was an urgent priority, for two reasons: though it wasn't too obvious yet, she was already beginning to show her pregnancy and might not be so easily employed, and the money she'd brought with her wouldn't stretch to renting a house. She needed an income. And a life. That most of all. She needed to make a life, for herself and the child. A good and simple life, where they would be safe.

'Depends on the kind o' work yer used to,' Ellie replied after a little thought. 'There's allus factory work.' She eyed Sonny up and down. 'That's if yer don't mind hard labour an' a speck o' grime under yer nails.'

Sonny laughed. 'I'll sweep the streets if I have to,' she said. 'As long as I get an honest wage for an honest day's work, that's all I'm asking.'

'Then I'd say yer ain't asking much.'

'So, you know of some work then?' Sonny asked. 'I'd like to get straight on to it . . . start as soon as I can.' She felt fitter now, able to make plans. It was a good feeling.

'In a hurry to get from under me feet, are yer?' Ellie sat back in the chair, regarding Sonny a minute longer. When she spoke it was in a warm, caring voice. 'Look 'ere, me darling . . . yer should tek yer time . . . look at the newspapers . . . go round the offices an' see if they've need of clerks an' secretaries.' She nodded her head, agreeing with herself, 'Aye, I reckon that's more what yer want. Yer don't want to be doing no heavy work if yer can help it.' She glanced at the small mound beneath Sonny's skirt. 'Especially not now, eh?'

Her smile said it all.

Sonny was surprised, then relieved, and the look on her face betrayed her affection and gratitude. 'You know, don't you?'

Ellie merely nodded, but there was a look of delight on her homely features.

'How did you guess?' Sonny learned more about this woman by the day, and the more she learned the more she loved her. 'I thought I was hiding it very well.' Being naturally slim and wearing carefully chosen clothes, she had prided herself that the growing mound was hardly detectable.

Ellie laughed then, and it was so infectious that Sonny had to laugh with her. 'Bless yer heart,' Ellie said, 'I might not know much, but yer won't see the day when I can't tell a pregnant woman.' Her gaze lingered on the mound before lifting to Sonny's face. 'I'd say you were, what?' She grimaced, in deep thought, making mental calculations. '. . . Maybe three months?'

Sonny was astonished. 'A little over four,' she confessed. 'But you still haven't told me how you know?'

'Ah, sure it's no great secret to someone who's had two already. I've seen it in yer face . . . a special kind of bloom that comes from inside.' She chuckled. 'Then, o' course, I've heard yer bringing up yer heart of a morning . . . even though you've crept about like a little mouse, hoping it might all go unnoticed.' She tapped her nose. 'Nothing gets by Ellie Kenny, especially when there's a babby on the way.'

'I can see it's no good trying to keep secrets from you,' Sonny said. But she *was* keeping secrets. Secrets of a kind that kept her awake well into the early hours. The secret fear that Tony Bridgeman would somehow discover she was carrying his child would not let her rest. Just thinking about it turned her heart over.

Ellie caught a glimpse of that fear in Sonny's face and in her own way threw her a lifeline: 'There's not a woman alive who hasn't kept a secret at some time or other,' she said. 'Sure, there's no harm in that at all.' Looking Sonny in the eye, she smiled knowingly. 'The harm comes when the secret is so bad it can't be shared with a friend.'

For one desperate minute, Sonny was tempted to tell her about the threat to her baby . . . to her own life if she refused to give up the child to its father. The temptation was so great that she opened her mouth to utter the first words.

They were never spoken, because just then there was a knock on the door. Sonny fell back in the chair with a rush of relief. As Ellie went to answer the door, she chided herself sternly. 'You nearly told her! And what good would it have done? It's enough that you have nightmares about it, without wishing the same on Ellie. In future, keep your mouth shut!' She felt angry with herself; all her emotions knotted up as she thought of Tony and his wife, and of their lovemaking. She recalled the awful things they had planned, and the cold-blooded way he'd said, 'I'll have to kill her.' Even now, hundreds of miles away, she still didn't feel safe.

She heard voices at the door – Ellie's voice and a man's. Fear rose in her. 'I know that voice.' On tiptoe she crept across the room to press her ear to the door. The voices were low. Still she felt she knew the man. Tony Bridgeman flashed through her mind. Had he come to find her? No! How could he know where she was? Martha would never tell, and no one else knew. Even Patricia didn't yet know the address.

Quickly now she hurried back to her chair. They were coming down the passage, Ellie and the man. She could hear them chatting as they came nearer, and the hairs on the back of her neck stood up. Was it Tony? Had he found her? As the footsteps came closer she could hardly breathe.

Ellie rushed in. 'We've got a visitor,' she said. 'He's a busy man in a hurry, but I told him how yer needed a word.' She paused, waiting for him to enter the room. 'So he's spared yer a minute or two.'

David Langden's imposing frame filled the doorway. It seemed like an age before he spoke. Instead he gazed at her through dark serious eyes. When, embarrassed by his scrutiny, Sonny felt the urge to open the conversation, he suddenly smiled. His eyes grew softer and there was a warmth in his voice that touched her deeply. 'You look very well,' he said. 'I'm glad to see you've recovered.'

'Thanks to Ellie,' she answered. 'Oh, and you.' If he hadn't found her she might have died out there on the road. 'Did you get my note?' she asked lamely. 'I would have preferred to thank you in person, but you're a very elusive man.'

'*Busy*,' he corrected. 'I'm a very busy man. But yes, I got your note, thank you. Though I only did what any decent person would have done.'

Sonny stood up. Only now did she realise how small she was against him. Dressed in easy-fitting jeans and a white open-neck shirt, he was as handsome as ever, comfortingly tall and broad of shoulder. When his gaze fell on her as it did now she felt like a child, helpless and acutely embarrassed.

But she didn't let her emotions show. Her voice was strong and confident as she went on, 'All the same, I'll never be able to thank you enough ... especially for bringing me to Ellie.' Her glance shifted to the other woman, who stood there, arms folded, smiling broadly, enjoying the fact that these two were talking together. 'I'm not the easiest patient in the world,' Sonny confessed. 'There must have been times when I drove her to distraction, but Ellie's been wonderful. Nothing is ever too much trouble for her.'

At this praise of Ellie, David's smile widened, showing wonderful white teeth in a suntanned face. 'So now you know why I love her,' he said simply. 'God never made them any better than Ellie Kenny.' He glanced at Ellie who, blushing and red-faced, ran off, saying, 'I'll put the kettle on ... I'm sure ye'll have time for a cup o' strong tea and a slice of me homemade fruit cake.'

'Sorry,' he replied regretfully. 'Much as I'd love to, I've a million and one things to do.'

'Let the buggers wait,' she yelled from the kitchen.

'You work too hard, that ye do.'

He returned his attention to Sonny, who was smiling at Ellie's antics. 'Has she been bullying you, too?' he asked.

'Not so you'd notice,' she replied, tongue in cheek.

Sonny really liked him. She was sure that behind that hard barrier he raised around himself he was a good man, the kind you could always rely on. Not like the kind she usually picked.

'You mustn't let her bully you,' he said. 'Ellie has a way of persuading you to do things against your better instincts.'

'You mean, like sparing me a minute or two of your time?' she asked pointedly.

The smile fell away. 'I'm sorry,' he said genuinely. 'I didn't mean it to sound as though I was impatient to get away, but I really can't stay long.' He stepped further into the room. 'What is it you want to talk about?'

Sonny was confused. 'I'm not sure,' she said. 'What did Ellie say?'

He shrugged his shoulders. 'Nothing much, except that you wanted a word and that it couldn't wait.'

Coming into the room, Ellie put a tray on the table. 'It's urgent, that's what I said,' she informed him. 'Now then, sit yerselves down, the pair of yer. I've some cake and tea here, an' yer neither of yer getting up till you've had yer fill.'

Sighing, David put down the folder he was carrying and sat at the table opposite Sonny. 'See what I mean about being bullied?' he asked with a wink.

The wink became a chuckle when Ellie promptly

placed a plate and a cup in front of him. Then she sliced the fruit cake, gave them each a generous helping and topped up their teacups. 'Get that lot down yer,' she ordered, falling into a chair and helping herself. 'Now,' she said to Sonny, 'ask the man yer business.'

Sonny felt as though she'd missed something. 'What business?'

Now it was Ellie's turn to look astonished. 'Be Jaysus! You've a short memory, that yer have,' she exclaimed. 'Weren't we just now talking about you needing a house?'

'Yes, but . . .' Sonny glanced at David, but he was looking at Ellie, waiting for an explanation. 'I'm sure Mr Langden isn't the slightest bit interested in whether I'm after a house to rent. I thought you said I needed to talk to the rentman?'

Ellie took a great gulp of her tea. 'Well now, sure yer looking at him,' she said. 'This foine gentleman owns half the houses in the street, an' he's the dearest rentman that ever walked the pavement, so he is. If yer should find yerself short o' ready cash through no fault of yer own, this lovely fella never puts the frighteners on yer . . . not like others I can mention.'

It all began to make sense. Staring at David as though seeing him for the first time, Sonny exclaimed, 'Oh, I see! *You*'re the landlord?'

'Ellie's also the best matchmaker there ever was,' he said wryly. 'Who else could get the landlord and the tenant to sit at table ready to thrash out a deal, and neither of them suspecting?' He grimaced at Ellie. 'Nice one, you!'

Ellie watched him drink the dregs of his tea. 'What about next door but one?' she asked, filling his cup again. 'You've been doing it up for weeks now, and it's coming along nicely. Two bedrooms, a newly fitted bathroom and a little garden.' She grinned from one to the other. 'Sounds to me like that place would do Sonny a treat. Neither of 'em are yet in a fit state to be shown in public ... both having fallen apart in their own little way. But, well, I reckon by the time the house is ready for Sonny, she'll be about ready for it.'

David considered for a minute before asking Sonny, 'Is Ellie serious? You really want to move into the street?'

'Is there any reason why I shouldn't?'

'None that I know of.' He regarded her for a minute. 'You won't be going back to Sefton House then?'

'Not unless it's to give Cathy Sefton a taste of her own medicine.'

The corners of his mouth lifted whimsically in the tiniest of smiles as he asked, 'You mean, she needs a thrashing?'

'Something to that effect.'

He nodded. Then turning to Ellie, he said, 'A sharp young lady this. It didn't take her long to see through our little friend.'

'Aye, an' that's because Cath Sefton is transparent as a pane o' glass.' Ellie ambled off to the dresser, where she collected a blue rent book and a brown envelope. Waving the envelope in the air, she told him, 'I'll swap this 'ere money for a signature.' Pushing the book forward, she watched him sign with a flourish. 'Sure it isn't

131

that I don't trust yer,' she added, winking at Sonny.

'Who are you trying to kid, Ellie Kenny?' he laughed. 'We both know you wouldn't trust your own grandmother.'

'Well now, would yer blame me?' she asked wideeyed. 'The randy old sod ran off with the milkman and the pair of 'em took the week's takings an' all!' She roared with laughter. 'Knew a thing or two did my grandmammy.'.

She returned the signed rent book to the dresser and handed David the brown envelope, saying cheekily, 'Don't spend it all on loose women and booze.'

His dark eyes twinkled. 'Shame on you, Ellie,' he chided. 'As if I would.'

'And why wouldn't yer?' she demanded. 'Sure yer a good-looking man, aren't yer? A man any woman would be proud to walk down the street with.' Jaysus! There I go again, she thought, letting me tongue run away with me.

Standing up, David pocketed the envelope. 'I'd best be off before you make me blush,' he told her. Behind his smile lay a restraint that told Ellie she had gone too far.

While these two had been merrily bantering, Sonny had quietly regarded them, listening and drawing her own conclusions. She sensed a tenderness beneath the teasing and an affection that shone through. With a little thrill, she realised that one would risk life and limb should the other be in trouble.

Sonny was drawn to this big quiet man. There was something very sad about him. His smile was warm and wonderful, and very occasionally his eyes sparkled. But the smile was fleeting, and when the dark blue eyes sparkled it was as though the light didn't quite reach the heart.

Now, as he prepared to leave, she reminded him: 'About the house? I really do need a place of my own, and it sounds just right.'

'Hmm.' He drew a long breath, his gaze appraising her. 'It won't be ready for at least a month.'

'That would suit me fine.' By then she hoped to have a job.

He turned to Ellie. 'What do you think?'

'I'd like her to stay with me, but if she's determined to have her own place, then I'd prefer it to be close by, where I can keep an eye on her.'

'You don't think she'd be a troublemaker then?'

'Well, now, she's a bit of a hothead so she is, an' the little bugger won't listen to a word I say. But I promise to keep an eye on her. If she starts having all-night parties, playing loud music an' smashing winders for the hell of it, I'll be the first to let yer know.'

Sonny thought these two were wonderful. 'Do I get first refusal then?' she asked, beaming from ear to ear and thanking her lucky stars she had found a friend like Ellie Kenny.

'If Ellie thinks you'll make a good tenant, who am I to argue?' His gaze lingered on her, as though he was weighing her up in his mind. 'All right. As soon as the work's finished, you can look round . . . see what you think. If you like it, we'll talk rent and terms. If you don't like it, there's nothing lost.'

'If the rent isn't too exorbitant, I shall like it.'

He looked at her with some surprise, but made no comment. Instead, he promised to let her know when the house would be ready for viewing, then said a fond farewell to Ellie and hurried away down the passage and out to his faithful dog, who was sunbathing on the doorstep, waiting for his beloved master.

Ellie and Sonny watched him through the window. 'I think I've hurt his feelings,' Sonny confessed.

'I reckon so,' Ellie remarked truthfully. 'Exorbitant!' She tutted and shook her head. 'That were a harsh word to use.'

'I didn't mean it,' Sonny admitted.

'Then why did yer say it?'

'I don't know. It was his attitude, I suppose. The way he spoke down to me.' She couldn't believe what she was saying. Nor that she was in a little sulk. It had never been in her nature to sulk.

Ellie felt the need to put Sonny right on a thing or two. 'This house should be five pounds a week,' she revealed. 'He lets me have it for thirty bob. I'd hardly call that exorbitant, would you?'

'Why would he do that?' Somehow, though, Sonny was not surprised.

'Because he knows I pay what I can, and because he has a heart of gold, that's why.'

'I can't argue with that when he's already saved my life,' Sonny replied. 'But you have to admit he's not very friendly.'

'Sure, he has his reasons.'

'Oh?' Sonny would have preferred to shut him out of

her mind, but he had intrigued her and now she wanted to know. 'What reasons?'

Ellie pretended not to hear. 'Will yer look at that?' She pointed to David and his dog going down the street. Every now and then David would bend to stroke the dog, which looked up with adoring eyes, occasionally rubbing against David's leg and wagging a short, balding tail. 'David rescued that mangy bugger from under the wheels of a lorry,' Ellie explained. 'It cost a fortune in vet's bills, and months o' nursing before he were well again.' She gave a contented sigh. 'I tell yer, me darling . . . sure there's a queue o' fine handsome women who'd give their right arm to share that man's life, but they've as much chance as a flea in a desert. That great lolloping dog gets more affection than they'll ever see. David Langden is content to live alone in that big old farmhouse . . . end his days the same way, I shouldn't wonder. More's the pity.'

Sonny was curious. 'Why would he want to end his days alone?' She kept her eyes on that tall commanding figure as it strode away and, for one fleeting minute, she felt incredibly lonely.

Ellie smiled, a crafty little smile that put Sonny on her guard. 'Ah! So you're interested in him, eh?'

'Not a bit,' Sonny retorted. 'In fact, I couldn't care less what he does or doesn't do, as long as he rents me a house.'

'Well, anyway, it's a long story,' Ellie persisted. She nudged Sonny in the ribs. 'But it's a long walk to the market, so I'll tell yer on the way.'

About half an hour later the two of them set out,

Ellie looking uncomfortable in a tight-fitting yellow jacket and a straight white skirt that showed her fat knees.

Sonny looked lovely in a calf-length blue paisley dress belted at the waist. Loosely fastened, it cleverly disguised the fact that she was pregnant. Her short-cropped hair shone like melted chocolate in the sunshine and the pretty blue shoes flattered her slim legs. 'I suppose I ought to go and sign on with the doctor?' she said as they crossed the road.

Having seen their reflections in a shop window, Ellie's attention was taken up in comparing herself with Sonny. Though they were different in age and build, and with all the best will in the world would never look the same, Ellie wondered whether, with Sonny's help, she might be able to improve her appearance. With that in mind she asked tentatively, 'Will yer teach me how to dress? Show me what clothes to wear and how to make the best of meself?'

Waiting for a response about her idea of signing on with the doctor, Sonny was taken by surprise. 'Teach you how to dress?' she asked incredulously. 'Whatever for?'

'Because I've just seen meself in that shop winder,' Ellie replied dolefully. 'And I'm ashamed to say, out of the two of us, it's me that looks pregnant!' Her voice flattened with despair. 'It isn't surprising though. I'm fat and clumsy and I haven't got the first idea of how a lady should dress.' She turned to Sonny with a desolate look. 'Oh, me darling, will yer help? It's not something out of the blue, 'cause I've been thinking for a long time

how I might improve meself. I've never had no idea
of how to dress proper, an' since I've had the babbies
I've let meself go.' She sighed so loud a passerby turned
to stare. 'I know I'm an ugly old bugger,' she whispered,
slowing her step until she and Sonny were walking alone.
'But sure to God there must be ways I can make meself
a bit more attractive?'

'You *are* attractive,' Sonny assured her. In fact Ellie
had the most beautiful smile of any woman she had ever
seen. Shining from the eyes, it lit her face with a childlike
beauty.

Ellie blushed carrot red. 'Ah, away with yer!' she
grumbled with pleasure. 'Be honest now, me darling.
Sure, aren't I a sight?'

'I don't know why you should think that.' Ellie sensed
the despair beneath the remark and her heart went out
to this lovely soul. 'There's many a woman who would
give their eye teeth to change places with you.' Sonny
was convinced of that.

Not Ellie though. 'Yer can say what yer like but I
know the truth,' she declared indignantly. 'I need a complete overhaul. Like a beaten-up old car on its last legs,
that's what I am. But it may not be too late, eh? If I get
meself a new outfit an' some different make-up, an' if
you teach me how to hold meself, there's bound to be
an improvement.' Taking a gulp of air, she recovered
her breath and glanced at Sonny with desperate eyes.
Then she rolled her eyes to heaven. 'Jaysus! What am I
saying? I'm forty-five years old. An old dog set in its
ways. I'm kidding meself, that I am. Like it or not, sure
I'm too far gone down the road to ruin.'

Sonny was adamant. 'You're nothing of the sort!' she retorted. 'You've got a lot going for you, Ellie – skin a sixteen-year-old would be proud of, pretty hair and a fine pair of legs. More than that, you've a lovely personality and that's what really counts.'

Ellie's face was a picture. 'Gerraway!' she muttered in embarrassment. 'Yer make me sound like a stranger to meself.'

'I'm telling the truth,' Sonny insisted. 'You only see what you want to see. People who know you see a different person altogether.' She didn't like Ellie putting herself down. 'You're too hard on yourself,' she told her. 'Haven't you heard the saying, "Oh dear God the gift to gi' us, to see ourselves as others see us"?'

'Aye.'

'Well, then?'

'I'll think on it.'

As they went down Penny Street, Ellie lapsed into a deep silence.

When they emerged towards the market place, she announced, 'I'll be a devil, that I will! I'll do the lot and suffer the consequences.' Turning to Sonny she went on excitedly, 'I've been thinking, I should make the best of meself. I ought to get me a nice two-piece an' new shoes . . . an' I might get meself a hat, because they say the hat makes the woman, don't they?' Her face crinkled into a cheeky grin. 'Not a red hat though, because there's an old saying, "red hat, no drawers", an' I don't want folk thinking I walk the streets with a bare arse.'

'Heaven forbid,' laughed Sonny.

'That's it, then. I'll have a whole new look, sure I

will!' Now the decision was made, Ellie beamed from ear to ear. 'An' me fella won't know me.'

'I might have known there was a man behind all this,' Sonny teased.

Ellie's blush reached right up to her ears. 'His name's Arnie Laing.'

'What? The man who serviced my car?'

Ellie nodded. 'Arnie used to live round these parts. When I were sixteen an' he were twenty, we allus said we'd get married one day.' A tone of disappointment crept into her voice. 'We never did, though. When Arnie got the wanderlust and took off I never saw him again until that day when he brought your car back.'

'That must have been a surprise.'

Ellie laughed out loud. 'Gawd Almighty, it were more than a surprise! When I opened the door and saw him standing there, it were a bloody shock, I can tell yer. The bugger hadn't changed a bit. He were allus well built an' good-looking, an' I'd know that mop of hair anywhere . . . though it's a bit thinner on top these days.' She chuckled with pleasure. 'Yer should have seen his face when he realised it were me.'

'A shock for him too, eh?'

'What! The poor sod looked like a goldfish outta water. Anyway, we got talking. Turns out he's a widower now, looking to make a new life.' Her chest swelled with pride. 'The truth is, Arnie's asked me out, an' I want to look me best. What's wrong with that?'

'Nothing at all,' Sonny told her. 'I think it's very romantic.'

There was no holding Ellie now, 'So you'll help me?

Tell me what suits me best, what colour an' style . . . an' what should I do with me hair, an' whether I should change me make-up – I don't want to look naked, mind, 'cause I'm fond o' me lipstick an' rouge, but neither do I want to look like a tart.' She gabbled on, almost tripping over the pavement when she didn't look where she was going. 'I've a little money saved, for a rainy day. But Arnie's special. He might just be the one to make an honest woman of me . . . so I could say this was the rainy day, couldn't I?' Her excitement mounted. 'Oh, me darling, you will help me, won't yer? I don't expect yer to work miracles, but yer might be able to make me more presentable. I'm a terrible woman, so I am. But I've never had any sense of style, y'see? I've known too many men and not one of 'em cared what I looked like. Sure the buggers were too intent on getting their hands up me knicker leg.' She grinned. 'Mind you, I'm not saying I didn't enjoy it, 'cause I did. But, like I say, Arnie Laing is a bit special. When I go on the date with him, sure, I want to look me best.'

She would have gone on, but Sonny calmed her down. 'I don't know if I'm the one you should be asking for advice,' she said. 'I'm no expert, and I'm nothing special myself. But you've been good to me, Ellie, so if you value my opinion on anything I'll be only too glad to give it. In fact, I'll do whatever you want. You can try on all the two-pieces in every fashion shop in Blackburn . . . we'll go to all the shoe shops, we'll visit the best hairdresser in town, and afterwards we'll go to Boots and you can have your face done up by the experts.'

'It'll do me good to be pampered.' Ellie clicked her

tongue. 'What! I'll be that glamorous, me own childer won't recognise me!'

Sonny had a sinking feeling in the pit of her stomach that Ellie might go too far and end up hating what she'd done to herself. But if she were to try and dissuade her Ellie might just take it the wrong way.

Sonny decided a bit of cunning was called for. 'You're right!' she exclaimed. 'You want a new image, so that's what we'll do. Anyway, you deserve a treat. You can lie back in the chair dozing while some young thing works magic on your face. It'll be wonderful! And it won't end there, you can be sure of that.'

Ellie gawped at her. 'What d'yer mean?'

'*Creating* a new image is only half the fun. It's the routine you have to stick to afterwards that will keep you on your toes. Hard work, but enjoyable ... daily cleansing ... skin toning ... your eyebrows will keep on growing, so they'll need to be plucked regularly. Oh, and your facial muscles will have to be exercised ... a twenty-minute daily workout in front of a mirror should do it. And if you have your hair dyed, you won't want the roots to show through too soon, so there'll be regular trips to the hairdresser ... retouching the roots ... trimming and styling, spending hours under the hairdryer and all that. And you'll need to keep an eye on the new fashions. I mean, you don't want to let yourself fall behind.'

'Hmm. Yer saying I'll have to keep a tight check on the purse-strings, eh?'

'Afraid so.' She gave Ellie a sideways glance, hoping her tactics were beginning to work. 'It'll be expensive,

I suppose, but you owe it to yourself to keep up with the latest fashions. Nothing worthwhile ever comes easy,' she added.

'Sounds like fun.'

'You'll come out of the beautician's wondering why you didn't have it done years ago.'

'I didn't need it years ago.' Ellie laughed aloud. 'Besides, I could never have sat still long enough when I were young and randy, because I were allus too busy chasing the fellas.' She frowned, commenting softly, 'To tell yer the God's honest truth, I'm not too sure I've got the time now either.'

Sonny looked suitably horrified. 'You're not backing out, are you?'

Oh, she hoped so, because, when all was said and done, Ellie was Ellie. All the hair dye and expensive make-up in the world would never change her, thank God. Sonny loved Ellie just as she was; though, to be honest, there were a few tiny things that could be improved on – such as the big hooped earrings that made her face look larger than it was, and the skirt which was too tight and short and made her knees look extraordinarily big. Just little things. Nothing too drastic, but enough to make a difference. Sonny hated the idea of Ellie reshaping herself from top to toe.

'Never!' Ellie declared. 'Off with the old and on with the new! And you're not backing out, either. You promised to help and I'm holding yer to it.'

'Right!' Sonny assured her, still hoping Ellie was having doubts. 'So let's get on with it all, and afterwards we can make our way to the cafe where you can tell me all about your boyfriend.'

The next words tripped from her mouth before she could stop them. 'And David Langden. I want to know all about him too.'

'Oh?' Ellie chuckled. 'An' here was me thinking you'd forgotten all about that young man.'

Seeing the look in Ellie's eyes, Sonny said, 'Not that I'm interested in him, you understand. Just curious, that's all.'

'Of course. Sure I never thought anything else.'

'That's all right then.'

Opening the door into a department store, Sonny waited for Ellie to pass through. David Langden indeed! As if she didn't have enough troubles without getting involved with a man like that . . . a man who made her feel deeply uncomfortable – a man who was a law unto himself and didn't want any company but his own.

But then she didn't want company either. At least not of the male variety. She'd had enough of that to last her a lifetime!

Already it was lunchtime, and there was still a great deal to be done. Though she was thoroughly enjoying herself, Sonny felt enough was enough. After traipsing through every clothes shop in town, with Ellie trying on everything in sight, it was time for a breather.

Exhausted, hot and ready to strangle the next crazy bargain hunter who trampled her toes, Sonny was acutely aware of the child inside her. It gave her a good feeling but at the same time seemed to drain every last ounce of her strength.

As she followed Ellie to the next shop, her feet felt like lead balloons and her stomach had a hole in it the size of the Blackwall Tunnel. 'That's it! We're stopping here, at the cafe,' she told Ellie. 'And before you start arguing, no, we're not going for your shoes first. They can wait until I've had six cups of strong tea and a ham-salad sandwich.'

Pushing her way into the cafe, she headed for the only empty table in the place. Throwing her multitude of bags on to the floor, she took her purse from her handbag. 'Right.' She stared at Ellie, who had collapsed into the other chair. 'What do you want?'

'Let me get it.' Ellie began struggling out of her chair. Now that she was sitting down, with the weight off her legs, she looked like a rag doll with the stuffing out.

'Stay where you are,' Sonny said, putting up a restrain-ing hand. It pleased her just the tiniest bit to see that Ellie was as tired as she was. 'It's my treat, so put your money away.'

'Ah, sure, you've spent a small fortune on me,' Ellie protested. 'The least I can do is buy us a snack.'

'I've enjoyed buying you things,' Sonny said. Always in the back of her mind was the fact that she did not have money to squander. 'Anyway, it was hardly a small fortune.' She took a step from the table. 'Now ... are you going to tell me what you want or would you rather see me collapse from exhaustion?' Leaning on a chair, she waited patiently for Ellie's answer.

'What are you having?'

Sonny drew a weary sigh. 'Tea and a ham-salad sandwich.' And bugger the expense, she thought.

'That'll do for me.'

With her feet throbbing, Sonny trudged the length of the crowded cafe to the counter. She gave her order and was quickly served.

As she made her way back to the table she was amused to see Ellie seated on her chair with her legs wide open and the bottoms of her frilly knickers showing to the world – or at least to a couple of goggle-eyed young men at the next table. 'I think you've made their day,' she told the horrified Ellie, who promptly drew the attention of everyone when she yelled at the men, 'Sure yer a pair o' bloody perverts . . . staring at a lady's bare arse when all she's doing is resting from her labours. An' do yer poor wives know what yer get up to, I wonder, eh?' Quickly crossing her legs, she almost fell off the chair. Incensed and embarrassed when a great roar of laughter went up, she bolted out of the chair and made a beeline for the two men, who by this time were sneaking shamefaced out of the door. 'Go on! Away with yer!' she shouted, waving her fist. 'Bugger off and leave a lady in peace, why don't yer?'

By the time she returned to the table most of the laughter had died down, but Sonny was struggling hard to compose herself. 'You'll get us hanged,' she said, pouring the tea.

She was shaking so much from trying to control her laughter that the tea went all over the table. 'Now look what you've made me do!' she said. 'I don't think I'll ever dare show my face in this place again.'

'Shouldn't think you'd want to!' retorted Ellie, taking a great bite out of her sandwich and spitting the food out with her next words. 'Not when they let perverts like that through the door.' With her cheeks filled with ham and lettuce she resembled a hamster. Suddenly her face crinkled in a cheeky grin. 'They may not keep an orderly house,' she said, 'but they do a bloody good sandwich.' Digging Sonny in the ribs, she began to chuckle.

'A good floorshow too,' Sonny joked. And the two of them were soon roaring with laughter.

'You're incorrigible,' Sonny told her.

Ellie said she didn't know what 'incorrigible' meant, but if there was time she'd have another ham-salad sandwich before they set off on their trek again.

The next stop was the shoe shop. After much fussing and fretting, and admiring herself in a dozen pairs of assorted shoes, Ellie insisted on taking two pairs of strappy things with four-inch-high heels – one pair bright red, the other bright green with black stripes along the sides. The high slim heels made her look like a chicken on tiptoe, but Sonny was too considerate to tell her that. Instead she argued diplomatically, 'Honestly, Ellie, they're just not you.'

'They're the new me,' Ellie retorted. Her heart was set on the shoes, and nothing nor no one was going to change her mind.

The next stop was the beautician's. 'We do your face downstairs and hair upstairs,' the young woman receptionist informed them. 'If you'll look through the portfolio and choose a hairstyle, it will help to speed matters along.'

'Which hairstyle do you think?' Ellie asked, pointing to one after another in the portfolio.

'Do you really want my opinion?'

'Well o' course I do.'

'You didn't take my advice on the skirt . . . or the blouses . . . and you bought the two pairs of shoes even after I said they weren't really you.'

'Well, that was then and this is now. Tell me what style suits, and I promise I'll listen.'

'That one.' Sonny had no hesitation in pointing to a soft semi-short style that was both pretty and practical. 'It frames the face and I think it will highlight your best features.'

'Do you think Arnie will like it?'

'I think he'll love it.'

'That's it then!' Ellie almost leaped off the chair and, presenting both herself and the book to the receptionist she told her, 'That's the hairstyle I want.'

The young woman made no comment. Instead she made a grimace and entered the relevant number in her ledger. 'And is it a full facial?' she asked.

Ellie called across to Sonny, 'The young lady needs to know, do I want a full facial?'

Sonny came across the room and addressed the receptionist. 'Not too heavy a treatment, I'd say . . . easy on the eye. Soft pastel colours, I think. Nothing startling.'

'Nothing tarty neither!' Ellie warned.

Satisfied that the young woman understood and that Ellie was happy enough, Sonny returned to her chair, leaving the two women sorting out the formalities.

Ellie asked the receptionist what she thought about the chosen hairstyle, and would it suit her as Sonny thought?

The receptionist replied in hushed tones, occasionally glancing at Sonny, who was absorbed in the letters section of a magazine. 'I wouldn't have chosen that one, madam,' she said. 'You have lovely thick hair and in my opinion it would really suit a bob. And I think it should be coloured too. A colour rinse would bring the richness out.'

'What about the facial?' Ellie was already suffering doubts. 'Do you think pastel?'

Again the receptionist glanced at Sonny, who just then looked up and caught her unawares. The receptionist quickly turned away. 'I'm sure your daughter means well, but really the beautician upstairs will know best how to treat you. After all, it is her profession and she is well trained.'

Ellie was easily convinced. 'I'm sure you know best,' she decided. 'Leave it to the experts, that's what I say.'

After being told she wouldn't be needed for the best part of two hours, Sonny took the opportunity to stroll along the canal bank, where she sat on a wooden bench and watched the ducks.

The July sun was glorious. A light breeze played across the strip of water and in the distance a colourful narrow-boat chugged gently towards her. Contented, she leaned back on the bench and closed her eyes. It's so peaceful here, she thought, and so safe. Suddenly a black cloud rose inside her. Safe? Would she ever be really safe?

In the warm sunshine of a July day, here in a place she considered to be far enough away from the nightmare she had been caught up in, Sonny remembered the way it was, and her heart grew cold.

She raised her eyes to the far bank of the canal and a rush of horror sped through her, bringing her to her feet with a cry. Like a startled creature paralysed in the headlights of a car, she watched a man stroll along the far towpath – a tall, dark-haired man, with an authoritative manner and a swing to his shoulders that struck terror to the roots of her heart. All she could think of was that he had found her. Tony Bridgeman had found her!

Slowly, as though he could sense her watching him, the man turned to stare in her direction. In a panic she fled. Twice she fell and cut herself before she stumbled into the arms of a man walking his dog.

She closed her eyes and screamed. The man took her by the shoulders and gently shook her. 'Hey! It's all right,' he murmured. 'It's all right.'

Recognising his voice, she lifted her gaze and stared into his warm, dark blue eyes. David Langden was unnerving in his own way, but right now she was grateful for his arms about her. 'I'm sorry,' she muttered lamely. 'Sorry.'

For a moment she couldn't think straight. The sight of that figure strolling on the other side of the canal had shattered her composure.

'Are you hurt?' Only a moment before David

Langden had seen her sitting on the bench, eyes closed and face raised to the sun. He had been captivated, thinking that she would make a wonderful subject for his next carving.

'No, I'm fine. Really,' she lied. In fact she hurt all over, her knee was bleeding and her wrist hurt like hell.

Stooping, he raised her skirt to the knee, gently wiping away the trickle of blood with the back of his fingers. 'That's a nasty cut.' His voice was soft and comforting.

'It's okay,' she said gratefully. With a small laugh she recalled, 'This is the second time you've rescued me. You must think I'm a dizzy fool.' Suddenly it was important that he didn't get the wrong impression.

Something in her smile seemed to touch him deeply, cautioning him to keep his distance. This wasn't the first time he'd been drawn to her, and that was dangerous. He wasn't ready for a relationship. Maybe he never would be.

In a colder voice he told her, 'Rats come up from the river and foul the area here. If I were you, I'd get that cut seen to as soon as possible.'

Puzzled but not surprised by his sudden change of manner, she felt a small rush of anger, Mimicking his cold tone of voice, she replied, 'Thank you for the advice, Mr Langden. I'll do that.'

He smiled then, warm and spontaneously, stirring her heart as before. But the smile wasn't for her. It was for the loyal friend by his side. The dog, which had been patiently sitting by his leg, was now eager to be off and was pulling hard on the leash. 'It isn't often I get the time to bring him here for a run,' David explained. 'But I've been in town on business and thought I'd bring him back this way.' He nodded towards the bridge. 'He can run free down there.'

Leaning down, Sonny tickled the dog's ears. 'He's lovely,' she said. 'I might get myself a dog when I'm settled.' When the dog nuzzled up to her she fell to her undamaged knee, wrapping her arms round his neck. 'Animals give you love and loyalty and ask for nothing in return,' she murmured.

David's gaze softened. His heart told him she was something very special. Right from the first he'd thought she was the loveliest creature he had ever seen. Not like the other one! Not like the one who had hardened his heart against all women for all time!

He saw how the dog sensed her gentle nature, how it licked her face and made her laugh. He laughed too. She was getting to him again. He must not let that happen.

In those few moments when they were each thinking of the other, another voice intervened. 'I saw you fall and thought you might be hurt.' The man had run from the other side of the bank and was breathless. 'But I see you're all right.'

Even his voice was authoritative.

Momentarily taken aback, Sonny turned her gaze, taking in a light summerjacket, dark, expensive-looking trousers and polished shoes now covered in dust. 'Thank you,' she said, a little shakily. 'I shouldn't have run like that.' She felt foolish. This man was plain-faced, with a military moustache and small crinkly eyes. He was

151

nothing like Tony Bridgeman. 'But it was kind of you to be concerned.'

The man lingered. 'You're sure there's nothing I can do?'

The answer came from David. 'Yes. You can leave us now.'

Seeing the glint in David's eyes the man believed he was intruding on a lovers' rendezvous. 'Right,' he muttered sheepishly. 'I'll leave you to it.'

Sonny and David watched him walk away.

When Sonny turned to speak with David, he too was gone, a tall lithe figure striding off with the dog straining on the leash. They made a splendid sight.

'Unsociable bugger!' Sonny muttered. Somehow, though, she couldn't tear herself away. Her thoughtful gaze followed David. Soon he was gone, and she quickly started on her way back to the main street. As she went she grumbled about the way he always seemed to turn on her for no reason. 'Makes no difference to me,' she told herself. 'All I want from him is a roof over my head.' All the same, it would have been nice to make a friend of him. Nothing more, just a friend.

'Got a craving for liquorice allsorts, have you?' The shopkeeper knew a pregnant woman when she saw one. 'When I carried my last baby I could never get enough raw onions,' she said with a grin. 'Stank the house out, they did. But they did me a favour, 'cause the stink kept the old man away, so I didn't have to put up with him heaving and grunting on top of me.'

Sonny couldn't help but laugh. 'I'm not partial to

onions,' she confessed with a shudder.

'Just as well we don't all crave the same things or there'd be a dire shortage.' The shopkeeper weighed out the sweets and wondered how a woman bearing a child could seem so disgustingly slim and bright. 'Not showing much yet, are you?' she observed, staring down at Sonny's midriff. 'Give it another couple of months and you'll have a stomach the size of Mount Everest!'

'Well, thank you. I'll look forward to that.' Sonny thought there was a hint of cruelty in the remark.

As she left the woman called out, 'Enjoy your allsorts.' Busying herself tidying the shelves, she grumbled, 'Why is it some of us look like army tanks right from the start, and others, like her, don't even start showing until they're halfway through? Bloody unfair, if you ask me!'

Sonny was fascinated by the market. All around her vendors shouted their wares, winking and joking as she walked by. Stray dogs dodged around her ankles to snatch up any juicy titbit that fell to the ground, and irate children bawled and screamed while their mothers raised eyes to heaven and wondered why they ever came out that morning. 'Little sods!' one poor soul yelled as her three offspring drove her to distraction. 'Just wait till I tell your father what a time you've given me. Your arse will be ringing a tune, I can promise you that!'

Lingering a little longer than she'd anticipated, Sonny bought a beautiful flimsy neckerchief for herself and a pair of comfortable slippers for Ellie. 'She'll need these after hobbling round on four-inch-high heels,' she chuckled, quickening her steps towards the beautician's.

'Wonder what they've done to her,' she mused aloud as she approached the premises. 'Hope she likes it.'

Raised voices greeted her as she opened the door. 'But we only did as you asked!' wailed the manageress. 'A colour rinse, that's what you said. And as for your facial, I can't see why you're complaining. Leave it to the experts, that's what you said to us.'

Wild-eyed, and with her hair hanging wet, Ellie stared at the woman across the counter. 'It wasn't me who suggested a colour rinse. It was your girl there . . . made me look like a bloody firework display she did! And as for you being experts, well now, I'd say that's a matter of opinion.'

'It isn't our fault if you come in not knowing your own mind! You left it to us and we did what we believed to be suitable.' The manageress's voice took on an acid tone. 'I think we did very well, considering your age and the obvious neglect of your hair and skin.' Totally oblivious of the reddening rage that spread over Ellie's features, she foolishly continued, 'But we did make amends after you caused a fuss . . . in front of our regular customers, I might add.'

Ringing open the till, she went on in a sweeter tone, 'I'm well within my rights to charge the full amount. However, in the circumstances I'm prepared to allow a discount.' With her hand stretched out to receive, she said, 'That'll be just ten pounds, please.'

Sonny stood back and waited for the explosion. When it came it was with Ellie's fist banging on the counter, and a roar of anger that gave everyone such a fright that a woman jumped up under the hairdryer and almost knocked herself out, another had her face shampooed when she turned her head at the washbasin, and the poor young thing sweeping the floor ran into the nearest cupboard. 'Ten pounds!' Ellie yelled incredulously. 'You'll want a tip as well, I expect? I mean ... it was unforgivable of me to cause a fuss in front of your regular customers. And how could I ask you to work on an old hag like me ... all them years of neglect, deep tunnels round the eyes and skin like leather, eh? Oh, and however could you have done anything worthwhile with hair like this?' She flicked one hand through her damp hair. With the other she picked up a huge tube of cream from the range displayed on the counter and, without warning, emptied the entire contents into the palm of the manageress's well-manicured hand. Grabbing the woman's other arm, she pressed the two hands together until the cream oozed out between her fingers. 'Keep the change!' she suggested, with a wicked grin.

Turning to go, she caught sight of a bemused Sonny, gave her a beaming smile and said, 'I don't recommend this place.' Then she marched out of the shop and down the street at such a pace that Sonny had to run to keep up.

It was only when they reached the cafe where they'd stopped before that Sonny got a good look at her. Ellie was a mess. Her hair was wet and lank and the make-up had run on her face as though she'd been caught in a thunderstorm. 'What in God's name happened?' she asked.

Ellie dropped her bags on the floor and pulled a chair up to the table. She kept her legs firmly closed because this time she had no intention of showing her knickers to anyone. 'You should have seen what the buggers did,' she replied indignantly. 'My hair came out the colour of rust down a drainpipe, and the make-up they plastered on made me look like a clown. Mud too. Can you believe that? They caked mud all over my face and neck. When I took one look in that mirror I went bloody mad.' Cupping her hands over her mouth, she leaned forward. 'I feel like everybody's staring at me,' she finished with a groan.

'Sounds like you've been through an ordeal.' Secretly Sonny was relieved that Ellie had turned against the idea of revamping herself.

Ellie patted her hair and wiped the tips of her fingers over her skin. 'You're right!' she exclaimed. 'That's exactly what it was – an ordeal. Still, you'd never know, would you?' she asked hopefully. 'Not now I've washed the make-up off and made the girl rinse the hair colour out.' She looked worried. 'I do look all right, don't I? After all, I'm seeing Arnie and I don't want to frighten him off.'

Sonny took a moment to regard her. Ellie's eyes were still blackened by mascara, but now it was thick and runny. Bright crimson lipstick was smeared from one side of her mouth to the other and all the way down her chin. The dark eyeliner had washed all the way up to her eyebrows and left a tidemark on her forehead. It was unnerving, to say the least.

For a moment Sonny didn't know what to say. She certainly didn't want to offend Ellie, yet neither did she want her to walk the streets looking like that. While she searched for the right words a small bubble of laughter rose in her, growing and spreading until she could hardly hold it back. 'After you'd washed your face, did you look in the mirror?' she asked.

Ellie tutted. 'How could I?' she retorted. 'I were too busy searching for a towel. Them buggers wouldn't help me. All they wanted was for me to get out of it.'

'Do you want to visit the loo?'

'No.'

'I think you should.'

'Why?'

'Because they've got a mirror in there, that's why.' Sonny's eyes twinkled.

Ellie was beginning to realise. The tiniest grin lifted the corners of her mouth. 'Bad as that, is it?'

Sonny bit her lip, before the laughter she'd been stifling erupted in a giggle. 'Depends.'

'On what?'

'On whether you like your make-up put on or thrown on.'

Just then the waitress came to the table. 'Yes?' She addressed herself to Sonny. 'What would you like?'

'Tea, I think,' Sonny replied. 'Two cups, please.' Glancing at Ellie she added, tongue in cheek, 'This lady's had a bit of a shock, so you'd better make it very strong.'

The girl's eyes went to Ellie and opened wide. 'Oh! I am sorry,' she said. She saw the crimson-smudged mouth, the black eyes and the dark-washed forehead and her face paled. 'Oh, I really am so sorry.'

'Don't be sorry,' Ellie said. 'Just bring the tea, please . . . and a helping of that chocolate fudge cake.'

She pointed to the counter and the display there. 'I'm that hungry I could eat a scabby donkey!'

The poor girl looked worried. 'I'm sorry, but I'm not supposed to serve you just tea. It's waitress service now and we're only taking orders for hot meals.'

Sonny gave her her most endearing smile. 'Can't you make this an exception?' she asked hopefully.

The girl shrugged nervously, looking around and returned a feeble smile as she got out her notepad. 'The owner's a stickler for rules,' she explained. 'But he's not in today, so what he doesn't know won't hurt him.'

While she went to get their order, Ellie went to the toilet. A few moments later she came out chuckling. 'You might have told me I looked like a disaster area,' she laughed. 'All right now?' Her face was scrubbed shiny clean, with just the faintest trace of freshly applied make-up. 'Sure it serves me right for wanting to change the face God gave me,' she remarked, throwing herself into the chair.

'You look like the woman we all know and love,' Sonny told her fondly.

'From now on, I'll stick with the crow's feet and the straggly eyebrows, and if the colour of my hair is good enough for Arnie then it's good enough for me!'

'What about the four-inch heels and the skin-tight skirt?' Sonny asked, glancing at the shopping bags at Ellie's feet.

Ellie sighed. 'A woman's dreams will be the ruin of her. All right then. We've got time before picking the kids up. So if you'll help me choose something more suitable – classy like – I'll take this lot back.' She sighed again. 'It would have saved a lot of grief if I'd listened to you in the first place.'

'I can't disagree with that,' Sonny chuckled.

Tea was served, and the conversation took a fresh turn. 'While you were in the beautician's I went for a walk down by the canal,' Sonny began. 'David Langden was there, walking his dog.'

Ellie was all ears, 'Oh? And did he speak to you?'

'We kind of bumped into each other.'

'How's that?'

'I stumbled and he caught me.'

Ellie gave a low whistle. 'Caught you, eh?' she said mischievously. 'Held you in his arms, did he?'

Sonny found herself blushing. 'Sort of.'

'In that case you've got nearer to him than any woman in many a long while. Nice, was it? Smell his aftershave could you? An' don't yer think he's got the most lovely blue eyes?' She gave a cheeky wink.

'It was nothing like that, so don't let your imagination run away with you.'

'Oh. Shame!' A look of disappointment clouded Ellie's features. 'What was it like then?'

'I slipped. He caught me. That's all there was to it,' Sonny lied. In fact she had felt the hard muscles beneath his shirt and, though she had not been aware of any aftershave, she had smelt the earthy sweat he'd worked up while playing with the dog. But Ellie was right in one thing – she had been wonderfully shocked by those dark blue eyes. And now she couldn't get him out of her mind.

'And how did you come to slip?'

'I was sitting on the seat, low down on the bank. Something startled me. I turned and ran ... stumbling into his arms the way I told you.'

Ellie took a sip of her tea, blowing on it when it almost scalded her. She had the feeling there was more to the incident than Sonny was admitting. 'What startled yer?' she asked quietly.

Sonny shrugged her shoulders. 'Something and nothing. A rat maybe.' Though it hadn't been the rat she was afraid of, thank God.

She could feel Ellie staring at her and knew that the other woman was wise enough to perceive that she wasn't telling the whole truth. But then, how could she tell the truth? How could she confess that she had fled hundreds of miles from her work and home because she'd been duped by a handsome charmer and his wife? How could she let anyone know what a fool she'd been? How could she reveal what she had seen and heard that night, when the two of them had spoken about her as if she was a commodity and not a person, to be discarded if things didn't go their way?

Even now, Sonny could not forget their laughter and every word of their intimate conversation was burned inside her brain. Since that night there was hardly a moment when she didn't hear his voice – the voice that had murmured in her ear, the voice that had promised they would be married as soon as he and his wife were divorced – promising 'I'll just have to kill her'.

Seated here, with the delightful Ellie, in this ordinary cafe, surrounded by ordinary down-to-earth people, the awful truth of why she had run away seemed unreal.

And yet it *was* chillingly real. Real as every breath she took. As real as Ellie, staggering about on high-heeled shoes and sipping her tea as though it was the most pleasurable thing in the world.

Sonny feared that life would never be ordinary again, that she would have to look over her shoulder everywhere she went for as long as she lived. It was a frightening prospect. Certainly she would never again look at a man with the same trusting eyes. What was her future, then? What did life have in store for her and her child?

Even though she was drawn to David Langden, Sonny was instinctively afraid. The only man she had loved had proved to be dangerously insane. A shiver ran through her. Suppose he were to find her? Suppose he were to discover she was carrying the child he would gladly kill for?

When Sonny shivered, Ellie laid her big hand over Sonny's small clenched fist. 'Cold, are yer?' she asked affectionately. 'Drink yer tea, me darling. It'll warm the cockles of yer heart.' She felt the tension in Sonny's fist, and was convinced that here was a young woman with a secret. A secret that would be better shared. But it was for Sonny to open her heart. Brash and loud though she was, Ellie was not the sort to pry where she wasn't wanted.

Sonny did as she was told, and just as Ellie had predicted the tea warmed her through, relaxing, comforting. But the fear lingered. She shivered again. 'Someone must be walking over my grave,' she laughed.

'Oh? Is that what it is?' Ellie commented.

'What do you mean?' Sonny realised she would have

to be careful. Ellie had a canny way of getting to the root of things.

'Yer seem a bit unsettled, that's what I mean,' the older woman said. And, in a softer voice, 'If there's something bothering yer, I'm known to be a good listener.' She cocked her head to one side, quietly regarding Sonny's troubled face. 'Whenever yer ready, that is,' she added gently.

Sonny was on her guard. 'Must have been that rat from the canal bank,' she answered with a deliberate shudder. She hated lying, but daren't admit that for one awful minute down by the canal she'd thought she'd seen a ghost from the past. 'Rats give me the creeps,' she said, cringing exaggeratedly. At least that wasn't a lie.

'Did David have much to say for himself?'

'Not a great deal.'

'Ah, now, he always was a very private man.' Ellie wondered how she might get these two together. Whether they knew it or not, they were well suited. 'Walk with you, did he?'

'No. He went his way and I went mine.' That was how it should be, Sonny mused. Much safer that way.

'Pity you couldn't share a few minutes of each other's company,' Ellie murmured. 'Because, however much the pair of you deny it, you could each do with a friend.'

'Haven't we got one in you?'

'Aw, me darling, o' course yer have!' Ellie was mortified. 'What I meant was . . . you need young folk to go about with, not an old trout like meself. An' sure it grieves me to see a fine handsome young man like that going to waste. What David Langden needs is someone to take him in hand. Some able young thing like yerself, to make him see life can be worth living again. Sure, he's a good fella. It's a great pity there's no good woman for him to come home to.'

Now that they had embarked on the subject of David Langden, Sonny made the most of the opportunity. 'Has he never married?' she asked.

Ellie's sadness showed in her eyes. 'Aw, sure.' She took a sip of her tea. 'David had a wife so he did. Oh, and a wonderful baby girl.' She paused and stared into her teacup. 'It's a sorry tale, though.'

Sonny recalled how David had looked by the canal, when, not for the first time, she had sensed the loneliness beneath that harsh and cold exterior. 'I'd like to know what happened,' she told Ellie now. 'If I'm going to rent one of his properties, it would help to know about the man.'

'Then I'll tell yer,' Ellie declared. And what she went on to say was astonishing.

Lowering her voice, she began, 'David was married to Cathy Sefton's older sister. Alice, her name was. She was lovely-looking, with dark hair and a fiery temperament, though the marriage seemed content enough. Sure it was even better when Alice gave birth to a beautiful baby girl whom they called Charlene.'

Sonny's feelings were a mingling of pleasure and envy. 'Why isn't he with them now?' she asked, puzzled. 'Are he and his wife divorced?'

Ellie put up her hand. 'All in good time,' she insisted. 'There are other things yer need to know first.' When

Sonny looked as if she might interrupt again, Ellie said sternly, 'Sit still an' listen now, or you'll put me off me stride.'

Settling comfortably in her chair, Sonny apologised. 'Sorry. Go on.' Catching the eye of the waitress, she surreptitiously ordered two more cups of tea.

Having taken to Sonny's warm, friendly nature, the waitress quickly served her. 'If you need any more, just ask,' she said softly, seeing that these two were waiting to resume their conversation. She would have given anything to know what they were talking about. Sometimes, when people talked loudly, she did manage to pick up a snippet or two of interesting gossip, but she had no chance of that with these two. When she got close they stopped talking, and when she moved off the older one lowered her voice and the other bent her head and paid serious attention. One thing was for sure, she thought, whatever they had to chat about must be very interesting. And she couldn't hear a word, more was the pity! All the same, hopeful as ever, she lingered by the table a moment longer than was necessary.

Suspecting the girl of eavesdropping, Sonny thanked her and told her they didn't want anything else just yet.

'David and his family lived at the big house,' Ellie went on when they were alone again. 'The mother was alive then . . . a pathetic, timid soul who was abused and bullied by her younger daughter. Time and again David tried to change things for the better, but it had gone too far and there was little he could do other than to take young Cathy and turn her over his knee – which he did once or twice, before she became a young woman, too grown up for a spanking and too selfish to reason with. The truth was, the older she got the more of a bully she became.'

'What about the father? Surely he should have stood up to Cathy?'

'Tom Sefton? You'd think so. But he was even more of a coward than she was a bully.' She sipped her tea and studied Sonny's response as she told her in deliberate tones, 'You've met him.'

Sonny shook her head. 'I don't think so.'

'Yes, yer have, me darling,' Ellie insisted. 'He'd be the man who carried your bags in.'

Sonny was shocked. 'I can't believe it!' She recalled how Cathy had taken pleasure in humiliating him. 'Are you telling me that poor man is her father?'

'I am that. She treats him like the dirt under her pretty feet. Leads him a dog's life so she does, God forgive her!'

'Why does he stay?'

'Where else would the poor bugger go, eh? That house has been his home for many years. It belonged to his father before him, when the family were prosperous farmers, respected and looked up to by the townspeople. He took his new bride there. Oh, yes, he's lived in that house since a young man, long before he took a wife and she bore him two daughters.' She smiled with pleasure. 'When Alice was born he wrote a fourth part of the land over to his wife as a thank you. He did the same when she gave him a second child, Cathy.' She lowered her head. 'They were blessed with one daughter and cursed with the other. Cathy was never any good, the

165

bad apple in the barrel yer might say. By! If she were mine I'd horsewhip her, that I would!'

Sonny gave a wry little smile. 'You couldn't horsewhip anybody.'

Ellie's face hardened. 'Then you've not known me long enough,' she said grimly. 'To punish the likes of Cathy Sefton, I'd willingly swing from the end of a rope.'

In that moment Sonny saw another side to Ellie, and it was frightening. Yet she could also see her point. She recalled too the harsh things David had had to say about the young woman they were discussing. 'You're right,' she agreed, 'I saw how cruel she was towards her own father and, yes, I can see why you and David feel so strongly.' In fact she too had been sorely tempted to give Cathy Sefton a good hiding!

'You don't know half,' Ellie told her.

'I hope you're about to tell me?' Sonny had this feeling in the pit of her stomach that David was also a victim, though she couldn't see how.

Ellie went on, 'The Seftons thought the world of David. They were delighted when he and Alice announced the date of their wedding.' She paused, grinning. 'Cathy wasn't too pleased, mind yer, because now she was older and feeling like a woman, wanting a young man of her own. She could have had any man she wanted, but she wanted none, because now she was eaten up with desire for her sister's young man.'

'She wanted David?' Then she remembered, and it all fell into place. 'Of course! I saw the way she looked at him that first day I arrived. I really thought there was something between them.'

'Oh, no! She might wish it were so, but it's never likely to happen, I can assure yer of that.' Ellie narrowed her eyes and focused them on Sonny's face. 'Did yer not see how he can hardly bear to look at her?'

Sonny shook her head. 'He's such a difficult man to read.'

'You asked about his wife and baby girl.'

'Yes.' Sonny felt uneasy. 'And you said it was a sorry tale.'

'So it is!' Ellie took another sip of her tea and swallowed the last bit of her cake. 'It happened on a Sunday... the same day the new baby girl was christened. Oh, it were a beautiful day, much like today, with the sun beaming down and a gentle breeze wafting over yer. The Seftons held the reception in the big house and invited all and sundry. They were that proud of their little grand-daughter, they wanted to show her off to the world.'

She paused, the tears brimming in her eyes. 'The only sour face was Cathy's. She stayed well away, sulking at the back of the room, or wandering the grounds, childishly kicking the earth beneath her feet and occasionally giving bitter glances towards her sister and baby. She even made a blatant play for David. Well, he soon put her in her place. I saw it all.'

'Did anyone else see?' Sonny was thinking of David's wife.

'I don't think so. I'd wandered away to sit with me feet in the brook when I saw David come down the bank to swill his face in the cool water. Before I could let meself be known, Cathy crept up on him from behind and pressed her hands over his eyes. I reckon he must have thought it was his wife, because he swung round and grabbed her by the waist. Before he knew what was happening she kissed him full on the mouth. He pushed her away, but she got a bit overwrought, clinging to him, asking him to kiss her again. When he wouldn't, she laid into him like a wildcat, kicking and fighting and scratching his face. He stood enough, then picked her up like she was a rag doll and dropped her in the water. "You'd better cool off," he told her angrily. She swore and called him all the names under the sun, but he took no notice. He just strode off, leaving her there.' Ellie laughed. 'I can tell you, I were enjoying every minute. I watched her get out of the brook and shake herself like the bitch she was. Afterwards she sneaked into the house by the back way. Good Lord, she was furious! Muttering under her breath, saying how she'd make him regret treating her like that.'

As vividly as if she'd been there herself, Sonny could see the whole thing in her mind. Her admiration for David soared. 'Good for him,' she laughed. 'But what did she mean, she'd make him regret treating her like that?'

Ellie gave her a strange look. 'Your guess is as good as mine,' she replied. 'But a few days later something happened that will prey on my mind till the day I die.' She took a deep breath before going on. 'Mr Sefton was never up to much, so David took the family responsibilities on to himself, working from dawn to dusk, farming the land, breeding horses and earning every penny that came into the house. The harder he worked the more the family leaned on him. But he didn't mind. Hard work comes as second nature to a man like David Langden.'

'What did he do before he got married?'

'David was an only child. When he was eighteen his parents died within a year of each other. Any other young fella on the brink of his education might have fallen apart, but not David. Like the man he is, he did his grieving privately and began to take control of his life. He gave up the idea of going to art school and decided to start dealing in property, then found he had a talent for it. Now he owns three houses and gets a nice little income from them. The house he's renovating is the latest addition. Then of course he has his art. Even as a lad he'd go into Corporation Park and collect the fallen twigs and branches. He'd spend hours chipping away at the wood with his pen-knife, carving birds and creatures from the wild.' Ellie beamed with pride. 'Oh, aye! David is a very talented young man. A real catch for any woman.'

Sensing that Ellie was matchmaking again, Sonny reminded her, 'You said something happened that would prey on your mind?'

Ellie pressed on, the tone of her voice softening. 'It was four years ago, another much like today, with the sun beating down. David was working in the fields when a policeman came to tell him there had been a terrible car accident. Three people had been killed outright . . . his wife and baby, and his mother-in-law.'

Sonny gasped. 'Dear God! That's awful!'

'David was devastated,' Ellie revealed. 'But he's got

a strong heart. And time is a great healer.'

'Something puzzles me.' It didn't make sense to Sonny. 'If he dislikes Cathy so much, and he has a good income from his own property, why doesn't he stay well away from the place? I can understand why he would still want to keep his horses and I'm sure he needs to work on his carvings. But wouldn't it be better all round if he bought land and outbuildings elsewhere?'

'He has his reasons. And besides, do you remember I told you how Mr Sefton settled half the land on his wife as thanksgiving for the births of their two children?'

'Yes.'

'Well, in her will, she left everything she owned to her baby grand-daughter. Consequently, when the child was killed, half the land passed to David.'

'That must be a real thorn in Cathy's side?'

'Cathy Sefton has her own plans and they include David Langden. Since her mother's untimely death, her father is a shadow of his former self, not seeming to care what happens to him anymore. Cathy's managed to bully him into handing over to her the remainder of his land and property. Now she wants the rest . . . and David Langden with it.'

'And he's determined not to sell it to her?'

Ellie gave her that strange look again. 'It goes deeper than that, I think.'

'Oh?' Sonny could see why David would want to keep the land, because it had been left to his daughter and he might see himself as its keeper. 'But surely it must be a painful reminder of what might have been?'

'He means to find out the truth of what happened when his family was killed.'

'What are you saying, Ellie?' Again she had that churning feeling in the pit of her stomach.

'I'm saying this an' no more. There was one survivor from that car accident. And that was Cathy Sefton herself.'

Something in Ellie's eyes told Sonny. 'You think she killed them, don't you?'

Ellie leaned forward, lowering her voice to a whisper. 'I'm saying there are questions still unanswered, that's all.'

Sonny knew what Ellie was afraid to say. Without realising it, she said it herself. 'My God! You think that's what she meant when she said David would be made to regret treating her like that?' She slowly shook her head from side to side, unable to come to terms with what Ellie was implying, 'My God! You think she killed them, don't you? You think she killed her own family!'

Swiftly, Ellie stretched out her hand and put a silencing finger over Sonny's lips. 'We can think it,' she whispered. 'There's little danger in that. But saying it out loud is dangerous talk.'

For a full minute they were both silent. Then Ellie looked up at the cafe clock. 'Jesus, Mary and Joseph!' she exclaimed. 'Look at the time! We'd best get back to the shops and change the things we've bought. After that we'll make our way home. I should think Old Rose has had enough of the kids by now.' Old Rose was a kindly neighbour. With no children of her own, she always jumped at the chance to look after anybody else's.

On the way down the street, Ellie turned to Sonny with a worried little glance. 'I don't want you reading things into what I've told you,' she said. 'Cathy Sefton's a bad lot, so you'd do well to stay away from her. David Langden is his own master and, whether she likes it or not, he'll do whatever he puts his mind to.'

She began singing an Irish ditty, then stopped just as quickly. Drawing Sonny to a halt at a pedestrian crossing, she said anxiously, 'Yer know me well enough to know me tongue runs away before me brain starts thinking, so, for both our sakes, it might be as well if you forget what I said . . . if yer know what I mean?'

Sonny knew well enough what Ellie meant, and put her mind at rest by telling her so. She also promised never to raise that particular subject again because, as Ellie rightly warned, it was dangerous talk.

With Ellie's words echoing in her ears, Sonny wondered about Cathy Sefton. A cold, hard creature. She and Tony Bridgeman were peas out of the same pod, she thought. But Cathy Sefton couldn't hurt her. Nor could Tony Bridgeman. Not now. Not here.

As Ellie's children ran to meet her, Sonny smiled at their comical antics and the endless questions. 'What did you buy today, Mam?' asked Kathleen, tugging at the shopping bags.

'Never you mind!' Ellie teased. 'Behave yerself, an' I might give you a fashion parade. I'll not charge yer a penny neither,' she chuckled. When she pretended to chase them, they ran down the street squealing with delight.

That night, after the children were in bed, Ellie and Sonny sat chatting as usual. 'What will you do after the baby comes?' Ellie wanted to know.

'Work,' Sonny replied without hesitation. 'Like it or not, I'm the only provider. Come rain or shine I mean to find some kind of a job in the next few days. I don't mind what it is, as long as it pays enough for my rent and food, with a bit left over for a rainy day.'

'You're a determined bugger, I'll give yer that!' Ellie declared with a snort. 'Anyway, if it'll help, I'll be happy to mind the baby while yer at work.'

'That's very generous,' Sonny said. She knew her baby would be safe enough with Ellie. Besides, she didn't intend working long hours. For now she'd be happy working only as many hours as would keep her head above water. It would be hard though, going out to work and leaving her baby behind. The thought saddened her.

The next morning they had a visitor. David Langden brought news that gave Sonny a new lease of life. 'I've bought a shop in town,' he told them. 'Nothing grand. It's a little place between the railway station and the Boulevard.'

At first Ellie was amused. 'What in God's name d'yer want a shop for?'

'To sell my carvings,' he told her patiently. When he saw her face sag with astonishment, he added, 'You know I've been bringing on a gelding for Jimmy Long from the antiques shop?'

Ellie frowned. 'Aye, I know that. But what's that got

to do with selling yer carvings?'

'It's Jimmy who's been worrying me to go into it in a businesslike way. I wasn't too keen on the idea at first, because you know how I am with my carvings – sell one here, sell one there, when the mood takes me.' He smiled at Sonny and she melted inside. 'I need someone to run the shop,' he said. 'Someone trustworthy. There'll be a flat above. Whoever takes the job will get a sensible wage. Also the flat, furnished and decorated to their own taste, rent free.'

Sonny was astounded. 'Are you offering it to me?'

'If you want it.'

'But, why?' After all she was little more than a stranger, and now that she was beginning to show, even he must have seen she was pregnant.

'Because you're intelligent, and you have a certain style.' His tone became more businesslike. 'I feel you're the right person for the job, that's all. Besides, you need work, and you need somewhere to live. What I'm offering you is the best of both worlds.'

He might have said, 'Because I trust you, and because I know you would appreciate the love that's gone into every piece of my work.' He might have said, 'Because I know you're having a child and you have no man to care for you. Because, like me, you're lonely and afraid and, for whatever reason, unable to reach out.' He might have said all of that. Instead, he sat silently and waited for her answer.

When Sonny hesitated, Ellie cried out, 'It's ideal!' Prodding Sonny on the shoulder, she urged, 'Tell the man yes!'

Still amazed at her good fortune, Sonny thanked him. Now she would be able to keep her baby with her and earn a living at the same time. It all seemed too good to be true. 'I'll work hard,' she assured him. 'And I want no favours.'

'You'll get none,' he replied.

Taking a piece of paper from his pocket he scribbled on it, laid it on the table and placed a key alongside. 'You'll need to see it,' he told her, standing up and making ready to leave. 'I'd like the whole thing to be up and running inside a month.' He kissed Ellie on the cheek and by the time Sonny had gathered her wits he was gone.

Sonny was thrilled. Ellie was jubilant. Getting out two glasses and the bottle of wine she'd been keeping for a special occasion, she gave Sonny a big hug. 'Let's drink to your future,' she said. And that's just what they did.

Later that night, Sonny's heart was warmed as she stood at the bedroom door and watched Ellie kiss her sleeping children. Her eyes misted with joy. 'You and the baby will be safe now,' she softly assured herself. 'No one will find you here.'

As she snuggled into bed, she had no way of knowing. But danger was not far away.

PART TWO

1956–7

Friendship

Chapter Five

Martha rushed to answer the phone. 'Yes?' She always greeted the caller with the same question. 'This is Martha Moon. Who's that?' She listened for a moment, a smile creasing her old face. 'Oh, hello. What can I do for you?' There followed a short conversation during which Martha's smile became a frown. 'Yes, of course you can,' she concluded. 'I'll look forward to it.' She replaced the receiver and turned the conversation over in her mind. 'Hmm!' Martha didn't much care for secrets.

To the cat, which was fussing round her ankles, she murmured absent-mindedly, 'That was Sonny's friend Patricia Burton. She wants to know if it's all right for her to pop round during her lunch break. Of course I said yes.' Scooping the cat into her arms she tickled its ears. 'And anyway it sounded very important.'

Ten minutes later she had the kettle boiling and the coffee table laid with her best china. 'Oh dear! When I think how I packed all this away and was on the point of leaving it behind,' she recalled with a sigh. 'I should have known better. However much I love my niece and want to keep her safe, I'm just too old to be useful. Sonny's young and healthy. She's doing fine, just like I knew she would.'

She regarded the table with a critical eye: the rose-patterned china teaset; the dainty sandwiches on the dainty plates; and the three-tiered cakestand, set with some of her homemade apple scones and succulent jam tarts. 'That's what I call civilised,' she exclaimed, wagging a gnarled finger at the cat. 'You won't see the day when Martha Moon's visitors have to eat out of their sandwich boxes.' Her lips tightened into a sharp hard line. 'Except for the devil who meant to harm my Sonny,' she muttered. 'A man like that isn't fit to grace anyone's table.'

Pushing him to the back of her mind, she spun round on the spot. 'Now then, what was I doing?' She had become a little absent-minded lately and it irritated her. 'I know!' she exclaimed with relief. 'I was just about to get the sugar spoon from the kitchen.'

She started towards the kitchen and paused again, lapsing into deep thought and scratching her chin as she recalled the brief conversation over the phone. 'Sonny's friend didn't have much to say,' she mused aloud. 'But she did seem worried.' A thought had crept into her mind and it wouldn't go away. She voiced it now. 'I hope it's nothing to do with our Sonny. I hope that evil man hasn't found out where she is.'

A smile flitted over her homely features. 'Of course he hasn't!' she chided herself. 'How could he? No one knows where Sonny is except me and Patricia.' Martha had confided in her some time back, when the secret had become too heavy a burden.

She went to get the spoon, still muttering and reassuring herself. 'So you can rest easy in your bed, Martha Moon, because even when he's been round here asking his impertinent questions he's got nothing out of you.' Returning with the spoon, she placed it in the sugar bowl. 'He's clever though, and cunning,' she reminded herself warily. 'A man like that will never give up easily.'

In fact Tony Bridgeman had been irritatingly persistent. He had been round to see Martha several times. He was never made welcome, but stayed all the same. Always asking after Sonny, always probing, frighteningly dogged in his determination to know when she would be back.

Martha's answer was always the same. 'She's working abroad,' she'd tell him impatiently. 'And no, I don't have an address for her. Sonny's always on the move, so she never gives me an address. I'm sure she'll contact you, all in good time.'

Martha thought about that now, about how he was, never satisfied with her answers, and how he seemed to sense that she was keeping Sonny's address from him. Martha hated his visits. His very presence seemed to taint her lovely cottage. The minute he left she would run to throw open the windows and let the air rush through.

She thought him a strange man, yet she could see how Sonny might have fallen for him. Tony Bridgeman was intelligent and highly successful, smart to a fault, and handsome in his own way. All the same, he unsettled her. Busying herself ready for Patricia Burton's visit, she tried hard not to dwell too much on him.

When the doorbell rang she almost jumped out of her skin. Hurrying to the door, she was relieved to see the familiar small figure of Patricia, with its pointed face and big freckles, hair tumbling from beneath the hood of her gabardine mac, and boots wet where she'd kicked her way through the snow along the cottage path. 'Look at you!' Martha exclaimed. 'You look frozen.'

'I've never known it so cold.' Patricia's lips were blue. 'To make matters worse the heater in the car has just packed up.'

Glancing scathingly at the little red car by the kerbside, Martha tutted. 'I prefer Shanks's pony,' she said. 'But then I never learned to drive, so I don't know what I'm missing.' Opening the door wider, she urged Patricia to come in out of the cold.

Waiting for Patricia to shake the snow from her boots Martha began to feel chilled. 'Hurry up, dear,' she urged. 'Or we'll both catch our deaths.'

'Sorry.' Somehow, Martha always made Patricia feel like a little girl being scolded.

As Patricia came up the steps, Martha continued to mutter. 'I think my nerves must be going,' she said. 'When you rang the bell just now, I was afraid it might be him.'

When Patricia foolishly paused on the step, Martha caught hold of her by the arm. 'You're letting the heat out!' she grumbled. Ushering her inside, she glanced down at her boots. 'You'd best take them off, dear. I'm sorry the path is in such a state, but I'll sweep it clear when I get a minute.' Hugging herself, she gave a little self-satisfied grin. 'On second thoughts, I might leave it until the postman's been. He'll be furious if he has to wade through a carpet of snow.'

Patricia had seen that look in Martha's eyes before. 'Don't tell me you're at each other's throats again?' she queried with a smile.

'Well, he's such a cantankerous old devil,' Martha replied. 'Lately he's impossible. Try and hold a sensible conversation with him and he'll fly off the handle and sulk for a week.'

Patricia thought the description fitted Martha just as well. 'Why would he do that, I wonder?' she teased.

Martha feigned astonishment. 'I have no idea!' she retorted. 'I do my best to be civil, but he's up in arms and wanting to fight the minute I open my mouth. It's his age, I expect . . . he must be pushing sixty.' Indignant now, she flung the door shut. 'All I can say is, some people don't know how to grow old gracefully!'

It was common knowledge that Martha had a long-running feud with the postman, who at times could be as crotchety and impatient as she herself. The root of their differences lay in the stray cat that Martha had found along the lane, which had taken a fierce dislike to anyone in uniform. Martha had explained to the postman that she suspected the cat had been ill treated by the man who lived at the end of the lane, who worked on the buses as a conductor. 'It's obvious that's why the cat hates you,' she told him. Unfortunately the hatred was mutual. The postman despised cats of every shape, size and description, so it didn't help when the cat threw itself at him and clung to his trouser leg the minute he set foot on the path. To make matters worse, he and Martha disagreed on virtually every other topic under the sun, including the building of the first nuclear power station at Calder Hall. Martha thought it was the beginning of the end of the coal industry. 'Utter rubbish,' he retorted.

As she closed the door Martha peered out. 'I honestly didn't realise it had been snowing that hard,' she apologised. 'I'm so nice and cosy in the cottage I hardly know what's going on outside.' The snow was a good two inches thick on the ground, and it looked as though the heavens were about to open again. 'Slippers, slippers,' she murmured, looking from Patricia to the hall cupboard. 'Yes, of course. Now then, take off those wet clothes.'

She bustled about, helping Patricia take off her coat and boots, afterwards going to the cupboard and taking out an old pair of slippers. Dropping them at Patricia's feet, she told her, 'I know they're past their best, but they'll serve a purpose.'

Patricia gaped down at the slippers with awe. They were ragged and misshapen, and when she put them on it felt as if she was standing on a tray of hard-boiled eggs. 'I really don't mind walking about in my stockinged feet,' she protested.

'Nonsense!' argued Martha. 'I know they're not much to look at, but they'll keep your feet warm.' Satisfied, she gave Patricia an encouraging shove towards the living room. 'Stop fussing and go on through, dear.'

Without further ado she led the way through to the

living room. 'Sit yourself down,' she ordered, 'while I get the tea.'

Digging into her bag, Patricia took out a plastic lunch-box. 'Is it all right if I eat my lunch while we talk?' she asked.

'Of course it's all right,' Martha told her. 'But I'll not have you eating out of that carton.' Gently easing the offending article from Patricia's hands she placed it back in the bag. 'I've already made lunch,' she said, indicating the lovely spread on the coffee table and adding point-edly, 'for the two of us.'

Patricia had already seen the food, and it made her mouth water. 'Oh! Is that for me?' She laughed. 'And here I was thinking you must be expecting the vicar.'

'The vicar!' It was Martha's turn to laugh. 'That's hardly likely,' she said. 'He still hasn't forgiven me for letting him down the day Sonny left.' She hurried into the kitchen, returning a moment later with the tray. 'Tuck in,' she told Patricia. 'We can talk as we eat.'

Patricia wasn't sure she'd done the right thing in coming here. After all, Martha was old, and the last thing she needed was to have trouble brought to her doorstep.

Playing for time, she chewed her food longer than was necessary, taking the opportunity to study her generous hostess. Martha had grown stouter these past months. Her hair was almost white now, and her step just that little bit slower. Yet she was full of energy, witty, well read, and possessed of an opinion on every facet of life. She knew the name of every politician in every party. She knew their policies and didn't hesitate to run them down if she thought they deserved it. She regularly wrote to her Member of Parliament on particular issues that riled her, sending newspaper cuttings to support her cause, and writing again and again if he chose not to reply. She was wonderfully irritating, outspoken and cranky, and there were those of a retiring nature who would walk on the other side of the road or hide in doorways when they saw her coming.

Yet she was kind and considerate and would never turn away anyone in need. Her still-pretty face was wrinkled and sagging, but the deep laughter lines and the bright blue eyes betrayed a generosity of heart that shone through.

Next year, God willing, Martha would be sixty-nine. There might be a few more wrinkles and a few more grey hairs, but the blue eyes would continue to twinkle. Martha would go on being Martha, a lovable sergeant-major, fiercely protective of those she loved.

Suddenly she looked up and, as though reading Patricia's thoughts, said softly, 'If it's to do with Sonny, you mustn't be afraid to tell me, dear.'

'I know.'

'Well then?'

'It's Tony Bridgeman,' Patricia confessed, replacing a sandwich on the place. 'I really think he means to find Sonny.'

The smile slid from Martha's face. Her voice took on a sharper edge. 'What makes you say that?'

'Yesterday he called me into the office. It isn't the first time he's asked me if I know where she is, but this time he went on and on, saying he owed her a lot of back wages and didn't want to give them to anyone else. He said if I knew where she was, I owed it to Sonny to tell him.'

Martha's face dropped. 'You didn't tell him, did you?'

Patricia was upset. 'I wouldn't do that!'

Cursing herself for ever doubting, Martha was quick to apologise. 'I know you wouldn't,' she affirmed. 'It's just that he's such a persuasive creature.'

'I'm up to his tricks. After I saw him leave I went to have a word with a mate of mine in accounts. She said there was no money owing to Sonny. She said it was all sent to this address soon after they got her letter of resignation.'

'This mate, she doesn't suspect anything, does she?'

'Not a thing. I slipped it in casually, while we were discussing all the people who'd left in the past year. Nobody stays long. The pay's not wonderful, but it suits me.'

'Hmm!' Martha's thoughts ran ahead. 'What else did Tony Bridgeman say?'

Having just taken a huge bite out of a scone, Patricia took a moment to answer. 'I told him I had no idea where Sonny was. He asked me if I liked working for him.' She became embarrassed. 'You know how I feel about him, Martha,' she said, seeking reassurance. 'He frightens me. But the truth is, I do enjoy my job. I told him that much, and he seemed satisfied, but then he said he might have to think twice about keeping an employee who was not loyal to him.'

'What did you say to that?'

'I said I was loyal, but that I really didn't know where

Sonny was. I told him we'd been friends while she was working there, but that we'd lost touch after she left.'

'Did he believe you?'

'I'm not sure. It's hard to know what he's thinking.' She looked at Martha through scared eyes. 'He's not going to give up, is he? One way or another he's bound to find her.'

Martha shook her head. 'He won't. Sonny's far enough away, thank goodness.'

'There's something else. I didn't want to say it over the phone because you never know who's listening in.'

'What is it?' Martha braced herself.

'He said he was getting very worried about Sonny, and that he'd really thought she would have been in touch by now. He said that if he didn't hear from her soon he might bring in a private detective. He didn't want to, he said, because they cost money and he was not a man to waste resources. But that if he was left with no choice, that's what he would do.'

'He's cunning, I'll give him that.' Getting out of the chair, Martha began pacing the floor. This wasn't Patricia's problem. It was hers. And it was up to her to find a way of dealing with it. 'Finish your lunch,' she suggested, 'or you'll be going back to work starving hungry.'

'I am right though, aren't I?' Patricia insisted. 'He will find her, won't he?'

Martha appeared not to have heard. 'Why won't he let Sonny be?' she mused aloud. 'It's been months and still he's hankering after her. What is it he wants from her? He can have any woman he wants, so why Sonny? He can't know she's having his child.'

A horrible thought occurred to her. 'You don't think he's found out she's expecting? Or that she was at the house that night? That she saw him and his wife . . . heard how they'd been using her?'

Patricia shook her head decisively. 'No, I don't.'

'From what Sonny told us, all he wanted was for her to bear him a child. As far as he's concerned it didn't happen with Sonny, so why isn't he casting his net elsewhere?'

'Maybe he is.'

'So why is he so determined to find Sonny?'

'Men like that hate a woman breaking off the relationship. It hurts their pride. And Sonny did leave him licking his wounds.'

'By rights he should be behind bars!' At times Martha was still tempted to report the whole thing to the police. Only the fact that it might make things worse for Sonny stopped her from doing that.

'However much you'd like to put him there, you have to think of Sonny first,' Patricia reminded her.

'I know. More's the pity.'

'Do you think we should warn Sonny he might set a detective on to her?'

That was the last thing Martha wanted. 'I don't really believe he would,' she decided. 'Besides, I won't let him ruin things for Sonny. Since she took over the running of the craft shop and got herself a nice little flat over it, she's been so happy.' The gentlest smile lit her face. 'I suppose you know the baby's due any day now.' She went to the dresser and opened a drawer. 'I had a letter from her the other day.'

Handing Patricia the letter she said fondly, 'She sounds so happy it does my heart good.'

While Patricia read the letter, Martha went to the window. Here she stood for a while, watching a robin in the snow and wondering whether or not she should warn Sonny that Tony Bridgeman was thinking of employing a private detective. 'I think he only mentioned getting a detective to make you tell him where Sonny was,' she told Patricia. 'Detectives must cost a fortune, and he's too much of a miser to spend his money that way.'

Patricia glanced up. 'That's what I think too,' she confessed.

Bending her head to read on, she commented with a grin, 'This David Langden doesn't sound too friendly, does he? Last time Sonny wrote to me she said he hardly ever spoke, and then only to complain.' For a second or two she laid the letter on her lap and dreamed aloud. 'Bet he's dishy,' she sighed. Not a day passed when she didn't wish for a knight in shining armour to rescue her from a dreary life. It hadn't happened yet, but there was no harm in living in hope. 'If I were Sonny, I'd grab him with both hands. Property and land, and earning a fortune from his wood-carvings by all accounts. Ooh! I bet he's rolling in money.' She clapped her hands together in delight.

'Money isn't everything,' Martha remarked. 'All I know is that David Langden has given Sonny a job and a home, and I'm eternally grateful to him for that.'

'Still, I wonder why he's so stand-offish? Sonny says here that she hardly ever sees him. He makes a delivery every third Wednesday, when the shop's closed and she's at the clinic, or on Friday evening while she's visiting Ellie Kenny.' She grimaced. 'What's wrong with the bloke? Can't he see what a good-looking lady he's got there?'

'Stop trying to matchmake,' Martha told her. 'David Langden is a very private man, that's all. It's his shop, and he has every right to conduct his business the way he sees fit. And you know very well that Sonny is perfectly content the way things are. She's also heavily pregnant, and the last thing she wants right now is any kind of relationship.'

'You're right. It's just me and my imagination. I have a habit of putting two and two together and coming up with five.'

Martha was not impressed. 'It can be dangerous to let your imagination run away with you.'

'Talks a lot about him though, doesn't she?' Patricia just had to have the last word.

Martha gave her a silent, withering glance. It did the trick, because Patricia quickly changed the subject. 'When Sonny wrote to me a couple of weeks ago she mentioned she might be staying with Ellie Kenny for Christmas. With the baby so close, I think that's a good idea, don't you?' Me and my big mouth, she thought. It was obvious from the look on Martha's face that Sonny had not mentioned it to her.

Disappointed but not surprised, Martha glanced out of the window. Somehow the cat had sneaked out and was crouching down by the hedge. Sensing trouble, the robin flew away. 'Mrs Kenny's been a wonderful friend to Sonny,' she said presently. 'And the way things are, I'm sure it's better for Sonny to stay up north. She'll be in good hands, I'm sure.'

'Mrs Kenny sounds very nice. It's a shame you two have never spoken.'

'That's because Sonny doesn't want anyone knowing her past. You and I both know why.' Martha's gaze fell as she lapsed into deep thought. 'To tell you the truth, I had been toying with the idea of spending Christmas with Sonny.' When she smiled her face crinkled into a multitude of wrinkles. 'Wouldn't it be wonderful if the baby was born while I was there?'

Patricia's mouth fell open. 'How can you even think of going all that way!' she demanded. 'It's a long journey and the weather up north is nearly always worse than here.'

Martha smiled. 'What you mean is . . . I'm too old for such a journey?' When, embarrassed, Patricia looked away, she added reluctantly, 'You're right though. I am old. The truth is, what with Sonny about to become a mother for the first time, I expect I'm feeling a bit sorry for myself.'

'Feeling a bit lonely too, eh?'

Martha nodded, grinned too widely and put on a brave front. 'I'm a silly old fool!'

'You're not the only one who's lonely,' Patricia admitted. 'I'm missing Sonny too, you know. I don't make friends easily, and I'm not the kind of woman men swoon over, so it looks like I'll be spending Christmas alone . . . unless you want to come and share my Christmas dinner?' The invitation hadn't been planned, but now that it had been given she warmed to the idea. 'I'd really like that,' she said eagerly. 'We could break open a few crackers and after dinner we could play Scrabble or something, and you could bring some of your home-made wine.'

'I've got a better idea.' Martha preferred her own home comforts. 'You could come to me.'

'Ah! Don't fancy my cooking, is that it?'

'I'm sure your cooking's wonderful,' Martha said. 'It's just that I would love to have you here.' The idea grew on her. 'Do you know, I haven't entertained anyone in a long time.'

'Not even the vicar?'

'Especially not the vicar.'

Patricia thought about the invitation for a moment before giving her answer. 'Yes, why not?' she declared defiantly. She had nothing else to look foward to. 'Thank you very much. But I insist on doing my share of the cooking.'

'We'll see.' Martha didn't share her kitchen easily.

Glancing at the clock, Patricia almost leaped out of the chair. 'I don't want to be late,' she explained. 'I'll help you with the dishes, then I'd better get going.' She bent to collect the tray but Martha beat her to it.

'I'll do that. You get back to work.' Martha gave Patricia an odd little look, her voice falling to a whisper as she added, 'And don't worry. I'm sure everything will be all right.'

While Patricia prepared herself for the outdoors, Martha took the tray into the kitchen. A moment later she came to see Patricia off.

The two of them watched astonished as Tony Bridgeman's car drew up. They watched in horror as he got out of the car and began to walk towards the cottage.

'I wish he hadn't caught me here,' Patricia wailed as he made his way up the path.

'Nonsense! You're entitled to visit an old lady,' Martha said sternly. 'Off you go now.' She gave her a little push. 'Leave him to me.'

'What will you tell him?'

'Nothing.' Martha thrust her arms into the deep pockets of her skirt. 'I shall say very little. I shall treat him the same as I would treat any other guest. No better, and no worse.'

Which was what she did now, as he came up to them. He seemed pleasantly surprised to see Patricia there. 'Keeping up with old friends?' he asked.

There was something about him that made Patricia want to run and hide, yet he had a dark charm that was almost irresistible. 'I thought what I did in my lunch-break was my own business.'

His hard grey gaze bored into her eyes. 'And so it is,' he said, with a quick, disarming smile. 'But hadn't you better get back?' He tapped his expensive wristwatch.

Hoping to allay his suspicions and at the same time give Patricia a chance to make her escape, Martha intervened. 'Thank you for calling,' she told Patricia in a formal voice. 'It was very kind of you. If I do hear from Sonny, I'll be in touch.'

Taking her cue, Patricia thanked her and hurried down the path. When she glanced back from the gate, Martha and her visitor were disappearing into the cottage. 'Be careful what you say in front of him,' Patricia muttered. Then she got into her little red car and drove up the snow-filled lane, following the deep wide tracks that Tony Bridgeman's wheels had created.

The more she thought about Tony Bridgeman turning up while she was there, the more suspicious she became. 'Did he follow me?' she asked herself in the mirror. 'Has he been watching where I go, hoping I'll lead him to Sonny?' She laughed nervously. 'Don't be a stupid cow!' she decided. 'He's got more important things to do than follow you around.'

All the same, the idea of being watched wherever she went was nerve-wracking. She thought of the look on his face when he saw her just now, and she was convinced that she had seen madness in those hard grey eyes!

Martha ushered Tony into the sitting room. 'You've caught me at a bad moment,' she explained charmingly. 'I have to take the cat to the vet's.' She remained standing and he did the same.

'Can I offer you a lift?' His smile deepened. 'It's no trouble.'

Martha was equally polite. 'Thank you all the same, but I have a friend picking me up. I'm sorry I can't offer you a drink, but I don't have much time. That nice young Patricia Burton stayed a bit longer than I would have liked.' She made a face, indicating that it had been a rather tiresome visit: 'But then she used to be a friend of Sonny's, so it's understandable that she should ask after her.'

Hopeful that her comment would put Patricia in the clear, she gave him her best smile. 'And how can I help *you*?'

Arrogant as ever, he rested one hand on the back of her sofa. 'I'm afraid I've come on the same errand as your previous visitor,' he said charmingly. 'Anxious for news of Sonny.'

'Then I'll have to disappoint you as well.'

His brows furrowed as he stared at her. 'You mean she still hasn't contacted you?'

'Not since the last time you were here, no.' God forgive me for lying, she prayed.

'And you're not worried?'

'Not really. Sonny is a grown woman and well able to take care of herself. As I told you before, she'll be in touch when the mood takes her.' Impatient to be rid of him, and hoping he might betray himself, she suggested, 'You seem very determined, Mr Bridgeman. What exactly is it you want from Sonny?'

For the briefest moment he was a little flustered. 'Just interested,' he said, with a calmness he wasn't feeling. 'Your niece was the best secretary I've ever had. Of course I've taken on a new woman, but to be honest, she's not a patch on Sonny. I just want her to know that her job will be waiting for her whenever she wants it.'

'Well, if that's all, I could pass the message on when she does contact me.' Martha was enjoying putting him on the spot.

'Oh, it isn't just that,' he was quick to inform her. 'She left in such a hurry that there are other matters left unfinished – important matters we need to discuss.'

'Then I'll pass on your message when I can. Whether she gets in touch is entirely up to her. But is it a good idea for you to be seen to take such an interest in an ex-employee? People will begin to think you and she were having an affair.' She said it light-heartedly and was delighted when he looked taken aback.

The doorbell rang, startling Martha. As she glanced out of the window, seeing a delivery man at the door, her eyes fell on Sonny's letter lying on the dresser where she'd put it. Her heart turned over. If Tony were to set eyes on that letter it would undo everything. 'That must be the friend I was telling you about,' she said, thinking quickly.

When, instinctively, he too glanced out the window, she snatched up Sonny's letter and crumpled it into the palm of her hand. 'I really must go,' she said. 'But then, I believe we have finished our little conversation.'

Although convinced that she was lying, he smiled. 'The main reason I came was to deliver this to you.' He handed her a long brown envelope. 'It's a cheque for your niece. Money owed to her.'

When, reluctantly, Martha took possession of the envelope, he was thrilled. If the old biddy sent that cheque to Sonny, and she cashed it anywhere in the world, he would have no difficulty in tracking her down.

'A parcel,' the delivery man said. 'Weighs a bit.' He seemed bow-legged beneath the big square box. 'Where do you want it, missus?'

Keen to get himself in Martha's good books, Tony Bridgeman stepped forward. 'I'll take it inside,' he offered, easing it to himself. While Martha signed for the delivery he returned to the sitting room, where he placed the box on the coffee table.

'He's right.' He laughed falsely. 'It is heavy.'

Eager to be rid of him, Martha walked to the door and swung it open. 'Goodbye, Mr Bridgeman.'

After he had gone, she fell into a chair. 'Thank God he didn't see Sonny's letter,' she exclaimed, feeling drained. 'If he should ever find her, I would never forgive myself.'

Once away from the lane, Tony Bridgeman stopped the car. 'She's lying!' he muttered. 'They're both lying.' He felt so close. It was infuriating.

As he drove away, he realised he would have to think it through rather more carefully. I must be cleverer than the pair of them, he thought. And that shouldn't be hard. Martha Moon is an old woman and the other one should be putty in my hands. His smile was ugly. 'Softly, softly, catchee monkey,' he reminded himself. There was no reason to feel down-hearted.

By the time he reached his office he was feeling very pleased with himself. He parked the car and got out with a jaunty air, stretching his legs and congratulating himself. Patricia Burton! That empty-headed little nothing might prove to be useful after all.

With a certain idea in mind and a smile on his face like that of the cat who got the cream, he ran up the steps and into the building.

Not for one moment was he aware that he had been followed.

Chapter Six

Ellie was frantic. 'I knew it would be here in good time for Christmas,' she cried, helping Sonny out of the taxi. 'I saw it when yer called round last night. Yer face were a bright shade of scarlet, and yer could hardly put one foot before the other.'

Doubled up in pain, Sonny was glad to have Ellie close. But she could see young Mick was not enjoying the situation, and in a low voice she told Ellie, 'Take the children home. I'll be all right now.'

Ellie wouldn't hear of it. 'I'll do no such thing, my girl! Not till I've seen yer safely inside and know what's happening.' She had one arm around Sonny's swollen midriff and the other around her son's shoulders. 'Yer want to stay with yer mam, don't yer?' she insisted, giving him a little prod.

Just as Sonny thought, young Mick was deeply embarrassed. He would rather have been any place in the world but here at the hospital. Yet he worshipped the ground his mam walked on. Besides, he had come to recognise Sonny as a real friend, and hated seeing her in so much pain. Now, when he answered Ellie, he looked at Sonny. 'Me and Kathleen are staying with you,' he answered, wincing when Sonny's smile crumpled beneath a spasm of pain.

'Tell 'em, Kathleen!' Ellie called out to her daughter. 'Tell the buggers to hurry up.'

Even in the throes of labour, Sonny had to chuckle when she saw young Kathleen running in front, clapping her hands and yelling at the nurses, 'Bring a stretcher. Sonny's having her baby!'

A big rosy-faced nurse came rushing towards the little group. 'It's all right,' she told Sonny. 'We'll soon have you comfortable.'

She was as good as her word. One minute Sonny was bent double with pain; the next she was lying in bed being examined. And then, after a short rest and a few wise words from the doctor, she was on her way out. 'Well, I'll be buggered!' Ellie declared in the taxi. 'We're no better off than we were before.'

With the pain gone, Sonny could laugh. 'That's the third false alarm in as many weeks,' she said. 'If I have any more I'll begin to think I'm not having a baby at all.'

Sitting opposite, with Mick on one side and Kathleen on the other, Ellie tutted loudly. 'It has to be a boy,' she said, exasperated. 'Only a fella would cause so much panic.'

Kathleen tugged her mam's arm. 'How do you know it's a boy?' she asked innocently.

Ellie gave her a cuddle. 'Sure I *don't* know, me darling,' she confessed. 'But I'll tell yer what, though. I'll be glad when this baby comes, 'cause the little sod's wearing me out.'

The taxi driver happened to be the same one who had delivered them to the hospital not two hours before. Listening intently to their conversation, he had his own point of view. 'You women have your fun, and you pay the price,' he commented wryly, swearing at a cyclist who suddenly shot across the path.

Ellie was bristling with indignation. 'Oh, and what about you men, eh?'

His attention was momentarily caught by a leggy blonde waiting on the pavement. He gave her a cheeky wink, before remembering Ellie's question. 'What about us men?' he asked.

'You said women "have their fun" and "pay the price". What about you men . . . don't yer reckon you should have a price to pay?' Ellie had experience of men, but she had never learned to respect them. With the exception of just one, and that was David Langden.

The taxi driver smiled at her in her mirror. 'All right, I admit it, lady. The fella gets the pleasure and the woman gets the pain. I just thank God I'm a fella!'

She returned his stare in the mirror. He had a straggly beard and a shaggy ginger fringe. 'Yer remind me of our cat,' she said. 'I bet you've got the same name too.'

'Go on,' he said, egging her on. 'What's its name, then?'

'Pisspot,' she replied. 'Suits yer to a tee, don't it?'

They got out of the taxi and he drove off, laughing fit to bust. 'Bet she was a raver in her time,' he chuckled, turning his taxi round and heading to the spot where he'd seen the leggy blonde. ' I like mine tall, slim and blue-eyed,' he drooled. 'If I get a move on I might just be in with a chance.'

Insisting that Sonny should sit down and take things easy, Ellie delegated the tea-making to Kathleen and the fire-raising to Mick. 'Build it up now,' she told him. 'It's freezing out there, and we don't want Sonny catching cold.'

'Don't treat me like an invalid,' Sonny protested. Ellie was wonderful, but she could be hard work sometimes.

'Sit there and do as you're told,' Ellie ordered. 'You forget I've had two of my own, so I know how tough it is.' Bringing a blanket, she tucked it round Sonny's legs and fussed over her like an old mother hen. 'After you've had a hot drink inside you, I'm marching you up them stairs and I don't want to hear another peep out of you till morning.' The fire was beginning to roar away and already she could hear the kettle on the boil. 'I've got two good kids,' she said proudly, adding in a softer voice, 'They've turned out grand, considering they've never had a father to guide them.'

'They've had you,' Sonny reminded her. 'The best father and mother both.'

'Bless yer heart.'

'I'm not staying, Ellie.'

The smile faded from Ellie's bright blue eyes. 'What d'yer mean, yer not staying?'

Not wanting to hurt her feelings, but protective of her own independence, Sonny tried to let her down graciously. 'You're the best friend I've ever had,' she murmured. 'And, to tell the truth, I don't know what I'd do without you.'

'But you don't want me fussing over you, is that it?'

'Not exactly,' Sonny replied. 'It's just that I've never had my own place before. I'm my own boss now, and I cherish my independence. I know I have to leave the flat and go into hospital for a week, but I've been given a reprieve, and I mean to make the most of it.'

'Yer really love that little flat, don't yer?'

The sound of the letterbox being rattled interrupted them. 'Mick! See who that is,' Ellie shouted. 'If it's the insuranceman, tell him I'll see him next week.' Turning to Sonny she explained, 'I've a bone to pick with him. Kathleen broke my best vase and they won't pay out. They better had, or I'll take my custom elsewhere.' Scratching her head, she muttered vaguely, 'Now then, where were we?'

'We were talking about the flat,' Sonny reminded her. 'And I wanted to say that it's not so much the flat itself I love.' She struggled to find the right words, words that Ellie could understand and accept. 'It's more because it's my own place. I've made it mine, chosen the curtains and the furniture, helped to paint the walls and lay the carpet. It's the first place I've ever had that I can call my own. Well, almost my own,' she corrected herself. 'The building belongs to David, but it's my home.'

'But it's not wise to be there on yer own,' Ellie insisted. 'Not when yer on the verge of dropping that lump.' She flattened her hand on the bulge beneath Sonny's skirt. 'I know it's not due for another fortnight, and I know the midwife said there were no panic.' She tapped the table hard. 'Midwives are a blessing, but they're not always right. I've got a nose for these things, and I say it'll be here for Christmas.'

Kathleen had been listening from the doorway, her blue eyes as bright as Ellie's and her face lit like a beacon. 'Jesus was here for Christmas,' she announced grandly, 'but he had to sleep in a stable because he didn't have a proper cot.' Her face fell. 'I don't want Sonny's baby to sleep in a stable.'

Sonny opened her arms. 'Come here, sweetheart,' she invited. When the child came and pressed herself up to her, she asked softly, 'What makes you think the baby might have to sleep in a stable?'

'Because he hasn't got a proper cot either.' Like her mam she was convinced it would be a boy.

When a man's voice interrupted, everyone looked up. Sonny's heart skipped a beat when David Langden stepped into the room. 'Will this do?' he enquired, smiling first at Kathleen, then at Sonny. His smile lingered longest on Sonny's surprised face. 'I called at the flat. When I realised you weren't there, I thought you would either be at the hospital or here. Ellie told me that you're coming here with the baby for a few days after you leave the hospital, so I suppose this is the best place to bring it anyway.' He rubbed his chin with the tips of his fingers, his face thoughtful as he went on, 'I know I should have asked you first, but I won't be offended if you don't want it.'

Kathleen screeched out, 'Look, Sonny! It's a cradle!' She ran to Ellie and hugged her with delight. 'Look, Mam, it's a cradle. David's made the baby a cradle!'

Sonny was thrilled. 'It's beautiful.' The cradle was made out of light-coloured wood, lovingly festooned with delicate carvings – birds at the top and wild flowers at the bottom. The whole thing rested on two long rockers, and there was even a hood, made from a flowered linen and finished with a pretty frill.

'You can thank Ellie for that bit,' David confessed. 'I wouldn't have know where to start without her.'

Raising her eyes to Ellie, Sonny accused, 'And you never said a word!' With great difficulty she got out of the chair and dropped to her knees. Stroking her two hands over the cradle, she felt emotionally overwhelmed. 'Thank you, both,' she whispered. 'It's the loveliest thing I've ever seen.'

'See, I told yer,' Ellie said to David, who was deeply touched by Sonny's joy. 'And you said she'd think it were summat out of the ark.' She grinned at Sonny. 'David here thought you'd rather have a modern cot, all in white, with a side that dropped down. I convinced him you'd love this one, that yer like beautiful things.'

'I love it,' Sonny murmured, trying to get up but falling sideways. Suddenly she was giggling. 'I feel like a beached whale,' she laughed, struggling to right herself.

Ellie wasn't amused. 'Yer won't be told, will yer?' she accused, coming out of her chair to give Sonny a helping hand. 'You'll hurt yerself, that's what you'll do.' She looked at David, who was already on his way across the room. 'Would yer believe she means to stay by herself in that flat?' Reaching down, she slid her hands beneath Sonny's armpits. 'Difficult, that's what yer are, Sonny Fareham. A stubborn, difficult woman!'

'Here, let me.' Waiting for Ellie to stand away, David stooped down. Putting one arm underneath Sonny's knees and the other around her shoulders, he took her weight, carried her to the chair and set her down. 'I must weigh a ton,' she murmured, blushing with embarrassment. Right now she would have settled for the earth to open and swallow her up.

'You're no weight at all,' he said. His dark blue eyes lingered on her face, and for one special moment, softened. Then, as quickly as he had warmed to her, his manner changed and he grew cold. Straightening up, he backed away.

'He's used to dealing with mares in foal,' Ellie declared in her usual down-to-earth fashion. 'Compared to them yer must be light as a feather.'

Everyone laughed and the spell was broken.

'Are yer having a drink or what?' Ellie was addressing David now. 'These days yer never stay more than two minutes at a time.'

'Things to do,' he said, leaning on the door jamb. 'But I'll take you up on that Christmas invitation, if I may.'

Ellie clapped her hands. 'Wonderful!' she cried.

Both children echoed her excitement, with Kathleen running to be swung into his strong arms and Mick remarking that it would be 'like a real family Christmas.' He lowered his gaze when Ellie gave him a peculiar look. But the damage was done, and for the first time she realised how Mick missed having a father.

'You'll be here too, won't you, Sonny?' Kathleen wanted to satisfy herself that they would all be together.

'I can't promise, sweetheart,' Sonny told her. 'It all depends on when the baby wants to arrive.'

She didn't see the fleeting expression of disappointment on David's face. Ellie saw it and was secretly glad. There was a fire kindling between these two, though they didn't seem to realise it themselves, and it did her old heart good to see it.

Sweeping Kathleen into her arms, Ellie promised, 'If Sonny's in hospital on Christmas morning we'll postpone Christmas till she comes out. What d'yer say to that?'

Her suggestion was greeted with shocked silence. It was Sonny who answered. 'You'll do no such thing,' she said firmly, seeing how Kathleen was torn two ways. 'I've got a better suggestion. If I'm in hospital over Christmas we'll have another Christmas after I bring the baby home.' Grimacing at Kathleen, she pretended to dismiss the thought. 'I don't suppose you like that idea either, do you?'

'I *do*! I *do*!' Thrilled, Kathleen twirled on the spot. Realising how she had saved the situation, Mick returned Sonny's knowing wink, and Ellie greeted the suggestion by mischievously declaring she would have to think about it.

David remained silent, but yet again he was surprised by Sonny's warm, bright spirit. 'I'll have to love you and leave you,' he said regretfully. 'Like I said . . . things to do.'

Striding across the room, he gave Ellie his usual kiss on the cheek. 'Christmas Day then?' he confirmed.

Grabbing the lapels of his jacket, she kept him close. 'The whole day, mind?'

'I promise.'

'Go on then,' she said, releasing him. 'And don't you

dare think you've to come loaded with presents. Friends don't need that.'

'I do!' Kathleen yelled, to Ellie's embarrassment and everyone else's amusement. 'I need a present.'

David chuckled. 'And you shall have one,' he promised, swinging her to the ceiling.

As he prepared to leave, Sonny asked, 'You wouldn't be going by way of the flat, would you?'

'As a matter of fact, yes, I am.' The dark eyes were kinder now. 'If there's something you want, I won't be able to bring it back until much later, though.'

Ellie's voice cut across his. 'What she wants is for you to give her a lift home.' She peeped at Sonny from beneath frowning brows. 'Sure I'm right, aren't I?'

''Fraid so,' The last thing Sonny wanted was to hurt Ellie's feelings. 'Oh, Ellie, you know I'm grateful for your offer to keep me here until I'm ready for hospital, but you know the reasons why I want to stay at the flat.' She didn't want to repeat them in front of David.

'Because yer a stubborn, difficult woman, that's why!'

Sonny turned to David once more. 'If you're not going that way, I can always get a taxi.'

He glanced at Ellie with a twinkle in his eye. 'You're right. She really is stubborn.'

'She'll not listen to reason, so what can I do?'

'Get her coat,' he suggested. 'It's bitter cold outside.'

A few moments later he was helping Sonny into the front seat of his car. 'I'm not an invalid,' she told him. 'I'm pregnant, that's all.'

Ignoring her protests, he asked, 'You're sure you'll be all right at the flat?'

'Why shouldn't I be?'

'Because Ellie does have a point, and there aren't any neighbours to speak of.'

Ellie was more direct. 'If yer waters break, phone for an ambulance first, then phone me. Keep the phone by yer bed. When it happens, it's nearly always in the early hours of the morning.'

'Will you stop worrying?' Sonny pleaded. 'You heard what the midwife said. The baby's not due for another fortnight.'

'Aye, but yer know what *I* think, sure yer do, an' I'll not let yer go until yer promise me.' Her face lit up with an idea. 'In fact, I think I'll come with yer.'

'No, you won't!'

'Then I'll send our Mick. He's got a good head on his shoulders. He'll know what to do if the baby starts.'

'No, he won't.' Reaching out to hug her, Sonny affirmed, 'I'm going home on my own, and I'll be fine. Now, will you please shut the door because my teeth are chattering.'

Horrified, Ellie slammed shut the door. 'Jesus, Mary and Joseph!' she was heard to cry as the car moved off. 'Sonny Fareham, you'll be the death of me!'

At the corner, David stopped the car. Reaching behind, he took his overcoat from the back seat. 'Here, drape that across you,' he told Sonny. 'If you catch cold on top of everything else, I'll never hear the last of it.'

Taking the coat, she did as she was told. The soft lining brushed her face. It smelled warm and earthy. Like him, she thought, when he had put his arms around her.

Easing the car into gear, he turned to her. 'All right now?'

'I was all right before,' she answered with a sly little grin. 'I only said my teeth were chattering to make Ellie close the door, so we could escape.'

He turned to smile at her. 'Shame on you.'

Suddenly she was having a fit of the giggles. 'Did you hear her as we drove away? It's a wonder she didn't have the whole street out.'

Her laughter was infectious and soon he too was chuckling. 'You've got a wicked sense of humour,' he said.

'Ellie finds it difficult to accept that I would rather be at home just now,' she said. 'And I can understand why she's feeling just a little rejected.' In fact there was no way to let Ellie down gently on the issue. Sonny desperately needed these next two weeks to get her house in order. She had a great deal of thinking to do, and that was best done when she was quiet and alone. 'I'll make it up to her,' she promised now. 'The last thing I want to do is hurt Ellie's feelings.'

'She's as tough as old boots,' David declared, turning the corner into Ainsworth Street. 'With a heart of gold. They broke the mould when they made her.'

Sensing the affection in his remarks, Sonny asked, 'You've known her a long time, haven't you?'

Giving her a sideways glance, he remarked, 'That was very clever.'

'What was?'

The laughter had gone from his eyes. Instead they

were darkly accusing. 'Just now. The way you turned
the conversation round.'

'I didn't mean to pry.' Ellie had told her he was a
private man, but she couldn't help being curious. Had
he got over the tragedy of losing his wife and child? No.
How could anyone ever get over such a thing? What
about Cathy Sefton? Did he believe, like Ellie, that she
might have had something to do with the accident? And,
if so, was he clinging to the land and buildings as a kind
of revenge, or was he staying there to watch and listen,
hoping there would come a day when he could prove
Cathy Sefton to be a murderer? Most of all, would he
ever fall in love again? Could he put the past behind
him and start afresh? She took a crafty glance at him –
at the dark tousled hair and the strong square chin,
those wonderful blue eyes and the wide manly mouth.

He turned unexpectedly. 'Sorry,' he murmured. 'And,
yes, me and Ellie go back a long way.'

She took that to be a statement needing no comment
from her. In fact she was a little afraid to make any
comment, in case she said the wrong thing. Ellie was
right. He was a very private man.

She sneaked another look at him. Right from the first
time she had seen him, she thought there was a loneliness about him, a sadness that touched his eyes. She'd
seen it just now when he smiled at her. Beneath the
prickly veneer he was a good man, hard-working and
ambitious. It would be a great pity if he spent his life
lonely and embittered. Certainly any woman could be
swept off her feet by him. But not her, she told herself.
Not her!

'You do know Ellie would walk on coals for you?' she said with a smile.

'I'd do the same for her,' he said, keeping his attention on the road. 'When I needed a friend, Ellie was there.'

Not for the first time Sonny acknowledged her deep debt to Ellie. 'I know exactly what you mean,' she replied softly. 'I don't know what I would have done without her.'

There was a pause before he asked hesitantly, 'Are you happy running the shop?'

Startled, she sat up in the seat, groaning when her back felt stiff. 'Of course I'm happy running the shop. Why? Are you thinking of getting someone else in? Do you think I won't be able to do my job after I've had the baby? Well, I can assure you, I will. I have it all planned. And Ellie has offered to help if needs be. Your shop will open as usual . . . even if I have to pay a girl to help out.'

Desperately afraid she might lose her home and work, she would have gone on, but his hand stretched out to touch hers. 'Ssh!' he murmured reassuringly. 'Don't get yourself in a state. It's just that I thought you might be returning south once the baby's born.'

She breathed a sigh of relief. 'No,' she said firmly. 'I won't be returning south or anywhere else. Blackburn is my home now, and this is where I intend to stay.' She wondered at the determination in her voice. Tony Bridgeman really had turned her life upside down. Did she honestly intend to stay here for the rest of her life? It suddenly occurred to her that she belonged nowhere. She had left behind a good friend in Patricia Burton, and never a day went by when she didn't miss Aunt Martha.

Patricia. Aunt Martha. All part of Sonny's life in the south. Lost to her now. But not forever, she hoped. Surely it would not be forever? A great sadness engulfed her.

David's voice interrupted her thoughts. 'Little Kathleen idolises you.'

Sonny laughed. 'Kathleen is her mother in the making.' Thoughts of the little girl warmed her heart. 'She soon put Ellie right when you were told not to bring presents at Christmas. Little monkey.'

Talking of Kathleen made her feel better. It was true she had become separated from one family, but thankfully she had found another. Instead of feeling sorry for herself she should be counting her blessings. 'Ellie's done a good job of raising her children,' she murmured.

'Without a man, you mean?'

'I didn't say that.'

'She was never the marrying kind.' He wasn't sure how much Ellie had told her. 'There was one man ... name of Arnie if I remember right. Seemed a nice enough bloke.'

Sonny recalled the name. 'Arnie, eh?' She couldn't help but smile.

'It was a long time ago. I can't be certain, but I think his name was Arnie.' He shrugged his shoulders. 'But he didn't hang around long enough to propose. If he had I think Ellie might have said yes. Mick was born eight months after he went. He looks very much like him.'

Sonny was murmuring beneath her breath, '*Arnie* is Mick's father!'

Stopping the car to let a pedestrian cross the road, David turned to look at her. 'Did you say something?'

'No! No!' Obviously Ellie hadn't told him that Arnie was back in her life. He was the man she had gone to so much trouble for, the man for whom she had been prepared to create a new image and spend money she could ill afford on new clothes.

'This Arnie,' she asked, 'is he Kathleen's father as well?'

'I thought women talked about these things.'

'We do.'

'And she hasn't told you about the men in her life?'

'Not really.'

'Then it's not for me to say.'

'How old were you when Arnie went away?'

He smiled. 'Young and foolish.'

'I can't imagine you were ever foolish.'

'Then you'd be wrong.' He was foolish now, feeling her presence beside him, doting on her every word, wanting to hold her, to kiss her, to ask if she could be patient with him. He was foolish even to be thinking these things.

'Ellie deserves to be loved,' she said impetuously.

He smiled at that. 'Don't we all?'

She closed her eyes. 'It must have been awful when he left her. He probably didn't even know she was pregnant.'

'Maybe not.' His quiet voice gentled into her mind. 'I'd be grateful for your help.'

'Oh? In what way?'

Worried, he glanced at her. 'I'm not very good on presents. I was wondering whether you might advise me on what to get for Kathleen.'

Sonny thought for a minute, trying to remember what kind of things she had liked when she was Kathleen's age. 'A party dress. She's just at that age.'

'Not a doll, then?'

'Kathleen considers herself too old to play with dolls.'

'A bike?'

'I've bought her a bike. They're keeping it in the shop until Christmas Eve.'

'Hmm! Has it got a bell . . . pump . . . basket for the front?'

'Ellie's bought all the accessories. They're hidden behind the wardrobe. She's also got Kathleen a new pair of shoes and a pretty silver locket.'

'But no party dress?'

Laughing, Sonny shook her head. 'No party dress.'

'That settles it, then.' Still worried, he half turned to look at her. 'You're sure?'

'Positive.'

'There's no problem with Mick's present. I've made him a dartboard.'

'A dartboard, eh?' She raised her eyebrows in amusement. 'Ellie *will* be pleased.'

He frowned. 'Wrong choice?'

'No. It's perfect.'

'Good.' You're perfect too, he thought. But you've come into my life too late.

'You're wrong, by the way,' Sonny said.

'But you just said a party dress!'

'No, not that. You said just now that you weren't very good at presents. That beautiful cradle is the best present I've ever had.' She could say that without the slightest hesitation.

'I'm glad you like it.'

A silence followed, during which David thought about his late wife and the daughter he would never see grow up. A tide of bitterness engulfed him. He would have given almost anything to be able to forgive. But there was such resentment in him. Such a deep sense of tragedy. He had tried so hard to forget but he couldn't. In the four years since that shocking day he had deliberately avoided women – unable to trust, unable to love again. But then Sonny had entered his life, bringing sunshine to dispel the shadows. It would be so easy to fall in love with her, he knew. But he mustn't let that happen. Not only for his sake, but for Sonny's too.

Now, when she laid her head back and closed her eyes, he took the briefest moment to glance at her. Even in the heaviness of pregnancy she was lovely, with skin that shone like dew, long dark lashes resting on high cheekbones and short brown shining hair framing her face like a pretty picture. In his dreams, he could see the smiling green eyes looking up at him and hear the soft laughter in her voice. There was no doubt in his mind: Sonny Fareham was very special. One day, she would make some man a wonderful wife. Some very lucky man. Some other man.

He let his thoughts be drawn to the child soon to be born. He had wondered time and again about that. And now, as before, he believed the man who had let Sonny go must be all kinds of a fool.

When they arrived at the shop, David insisted on accompanying Sonny upstairs to her flat. 'You've done wonders with this place,' he told her as they came into the living room.

The room was small and cosy, yet tasteful. Along the back wall was a long cream sofa with a round table and lamp at either end. There was room only for one chair to match; scattered with big squashy cushions and set at an angle near the fireplace, this was where Sonny gratefully collapsed every night after the shop was closed.

The curtains were bright and cheerful, and the carpet was the softest shade of pink. There was a semi-circular cream rug in front of the fireplace. The fire-surround was made of iron and decorated with ceramic tiles. Its mantel shelf was filled with bric-à-brac bought in Blackburn's second-hand shops, and on the wall above there was the prettiest old mirror, framed in black wrought iron.

'Did you know the fireplace is Victorian?' Sonny queried now. 'Pretty, don't you think?'

'I'll tell you what I think,' he answered, when a sudden twinge in her lower back made Sonny gasp. 'I think you should have stayed with Ellie. I was wrong to bring you back here.'

Taking off his coat, which he insisted she wear all the way up to the flat, she handed it to him. 'Thank you for the loan of your coat.' The tone of her voice told him she thought it was time for him to leave. 'I know you have things to do,' she said, 'so I won't keep you.' She resented the way he could create these unpredictable mood swings in her.

Taking the coat, he laid it on the sofa. 'It strikes cold in here,' he said, glancing at the empty fireplace – there was paper and kindling wood in the hearth and a heap of small coals in the scuttle. 'It'll only take me a minute to get the fire going.'

'Thanks all the same, but I really am capable of doing it myself.' As if to prove she was right, she went over to the fireplace where, going down on stiff legs, she managed to lay the fire in a matter of minutes. 'There!' she said. 'Nothing to it.' Going to the sideboard, she took a box of matches from the drawer, holding her breath to ease the pain in her back.

Exasperated, he shook his head. 'Stubborn and difficult,' he muttered. 'Ellie knows you better than I realised.' He turned to go. 'You have my phone number,' he said, 'in case of emergency.'

When she didn't answer he turned again, to see her standing by the sideboard, bent almost double and with her hands gripping the small of her back. Her face was grey with pain. 'I'm sorry,' she said. 'I think it's the real thing this time.'

In two strides he was across the room. 'What do I do?' he pleaded, his face contorted as if he too was suffering the pangs of labour.

Even in the throes of agony, Sonny could smile. 'Unless you want to deliver the baby right here,' she grunted, 'I think you should get me to hospital, as quick as you can!'

Chapter Seven

'You're a liar!' As she confronted her husband, Celia Bridgeman's sapphire-blue eyes flamed with anger. 'I saw you go into the cottage,' she accused. 'It isn't the first time either, is it?' When he didn't answer she yelled louder, *'Damn you! I said, it isn't the first time, is it?'* With her fleshy lips stretched thin and her teeth bared, she resembled a wild dog.

He had never seen her like this before and it frightened him – because, when all was said and done, it was Celia's money that had started his business and it was her money that allowed him to keep expanding. 'I don't know what you're getting at,' he lied. 'But if you think there was anything sinister about my visit to the cottage, then you couldn't be more wrong.'

Agitated, she stared at him for a moment. 'How can I be sure of that?' she demanded. Loving him so much, the idea of him wanting anyone but her was more than she could bear.

'What's this . . . a bloody inquisition?' When she had started her questioning he had been preparing for a shower. Now, in bare feet, with his trousers partway off and the tail of his shirt hanging to his knees, he looked a little comical. 'Come here,' he commanded softly.

From the other side of the bed, she glared at him.

He took a step forward. 'You're getting yourself all worked up for nothing.'

Putting up her hand, she hissed, 'Stay away!'

'For God's sake!'

'Stay away!' Tears sprang to her eyes. Taking a long slow drag on her cigarette, she blew the smoke out of her nostrils. 'Why did you go to the cottage?'

'We're due at the party in an hour,' he reminded her. Anger tinged his voice. Lately she had been driving him crazy.

'Bugger the party! Answer the question.'

Thinking fast, he played the old cat and mouse game. He had played it so often he was a master at it. 'No! If you can't trust me there's nothing I can say or do that will convince you the visit was in all innocence.' He turned away, secretly smiling, confident that she would come to him as she always did.

This time, though, she surprised him by staying at the other side of the room. For an endless moment he was shocked, confused, not knowing how to react. He wanted to turn and look at her, to study her face, to see what she might be thinking. But he daren't turn round. If he did, she would see that as a sign of weakness, a sign that he really was guilty of something.

He would have to brave it out, let her make the next move. '*You* can miss the party if you like,' he said. 'But the workforce will expect *me* to be there.'

Throwing off his clothes, he walked towards her. Her

eyes roved his naked body, igniting with passion as he stood before her. He didn't speak. Instead he smiled provocatively, touching her shoulder where her dressing gown had slid down. Then still without a word, he left her there.

She screamed after him, 'I need to know why you were there!'

The only answer was the sound of water running.

While she remained in the bedroom, he stood beneath the shower, soaping his body and wondering whether he had judged her wrongly this time. 'She's not as naive as I thought,' he muttered. 'But she'll come round.' His smile was evil. 'She still needs me more than I need her.'

He paused, twisting the shower to a higher angle, his eyes widening with fear when a very unpleasant fact came to mind. 'Face it, Bridgeman! The truth is, you still need her. You need her money, and you need her continuing support. You'll go on needing her until the day the business is making more money than it spends.' His heart filled with loathing. 'As long as she's a sleeping partner, you're a prisoner here.'

He could see only two feasible ways of being rid of her. Murder was one, but he had dismissed that as being too much of a threat to his own freedom.

The second choice was his favourite. 'She can't give you the child you want,' he said bitterly. 'But if you can keep her sweet on the idea of an heir, you'll find no difficulty in persuading her to sign over her business interests to the child – girl or boy, it won't matter either way.'

He congratulated himself on his plan. 'When you've got what you want you can file for divorce. No court in the land would refuse you custody of your own child. Especially if you have the real mother standing beside you, waiting to offer the child a secure home and loving parents.'

His smug expression slipped into an ugly frown. Clenching his fist, he pounded the wall. 'You had it all in your grasp!' he snarled. 'And you let it go!'

Sonny came to mind then, attractive, intelligent, funny and warm. She would have charmed the judge. He would have seen how she was everything a child could want in a mother. In fact everything a *man* could want. 'Oh, Sonny! Sonny! I had you right here in the palms of my hands,' he murmured. 'A way to be rid of her. A way to have it all. And have you.' Closing his eyes, he moaned with anguish. 'I could have had you.'

He had been so intent on his plan to secure an heir that he hadn't realised he was falling in love. Not a gentle, easy kind of love, not one that would give and protect and share. He was incapable of that kind of love. No, his kind of love was possessive and brutal. It would smother and destroy. It filled him now, and the need to find Sonny throbbed through his veins.

He was startled when groping fingers touched his private parts. 'Jesus!' Momentarily blinded by the spray of water, he spun round to see his wife peering at him through the shower curtain. 'What the hell did you do that for?' he demanded. 'You gave me a fright!'

'Didn't mean to,' she said, staying out of his reach

beyond the curtain. 'But you still haven't answered my question.'

Ducking out of the spray, he shook his damp hair from his eyes and wiped the palms of his hands over his face. Seeing more clearly now, he stared at her, wondering how he could overcome her suspicions. She was very attractive, he thought with her baby-doll eyes and the skin of a child. Up until now he had thought her gullible. He could always win her over – though not this time, it seemed. That disturbed him. In his black heart he didn't care, but in his head he knew he had to keep her sweet.

Celia was a business asset, an attractive decoration on a man's arm. That was all. Pretty though she was, he could never love her. It had been her money that attracted him to her in the first place, and it was her money that kept him with her.

It was also her money that made him soften his voice and say, more gently, 'Come here.' He held out his arms. 'I don't like you thinking bad things of me.'

She hesitated.

'I would never hurt you,' he murmured, reaching out to touch her face. 'You know that, don't you?'

Still she hesitated, her eyes downcast, sadness flooding her soul.

'We want the same things,' he lied. 'Nothing's changed.'

Raising her eyes, she silently pleaded. Tears began to fall.

He saw her weakness and was jubilant. 'Come here,' he whispered. Damn it all! He wanted her. Wanted to hurt her. To punish her for disbelieving. For being alive!

'Why did you go to the cottage?'

'Business.'

'You wouldn't lie to me?'

'I never have.' He hung his head. 'I never would.' Beneath his breath he cursed her to hell.

'What business?' She wound her arms round him.

Pleasantly shocked, he realised she was naked too. 'There was money still owing to Sonny Fareham. I delivered it to her aunt.'

'Why couldn't the wages clerk post it?'

'It seemed more correct to take it to the aunt.' God! She was touching him below again. Driving him crazy. Damn her! Damn her!

'It would have been more "correct" to post it.'

'I didn't think so.'

'Were you hoping she would be at the cottage?' As she spoke her fingers squeezed ever so gently.

He winced but couldn't move. In a hard, threatening voice he told her, 'Take your hand away.'

The look in his eyes was warning enough. Subdued, she stepped inside the cubicle where, falling to her knees, she kissed his thigh. 'You haven't been silly, have you?'

Passion rising, he stroked her hair with the flat of his hands, longing to strangle her there and then. Pushing her head down towards his throbbing penis, he said innocently, 'I don't know what you mean.'

Looking up, she waited for his gaze to fall on her. When it did, she held it. 'You don't miss her, do you?'

Water ran down his shoulders and trickled over her face. 'Who?'

'Sonny Fareham.'

'Why would I miss her?' Water cascaded down, glue-ing his hair to his forehead.

'You would miss her if you had fallen in love with her.'

He laughed. 'Is that what you've been thinking?'

'It's what I've been afraid of.' She buried her head between his thighs. 'Sonny was very attractive.' Sinking her teeth into his skin, she excited him by drawing blood.

Unable to control himself any longer, he took her by the shoulders and raised her to him. 'She could never be as beautiful as you,' he said. 'And anyway, beauty isn't everything. What we have is far more important.'

She rubbed herself against him. 'But we don't have a child,' she reminded him. 'The only reason I said yes to the arrangement between you and her was because I couldn't give you an heir and she could.'

'And that's all you need to remember,' he said, cup-ping her breasts in the curve of his hands. 'It was just an arrangement. Sonny Fareham would provide us with an heir. Afterwards, we'd have no further use for her.'

That appeased her a little. 'And you didn't fall in love along the way?'

'She was purely and simply a means to an end.' Press-ing her to the shower wall, he took up the soap and began rubbing it into her skin. 'Besides, I'm in love with my beautiful wife, and I'm not the kind of man to love more than one woman at a time.' At least that much was true. But it was Sonny he craved. And only her.

Smiling and reassured, Celia said, 'You're right. I'm

being silly. She didn't get pregnant, and anyway, she's gone. Hopefully we'll never set eyes on her again.'

'Hopefully.' The urge to strangle her grew almost irresistible.

She was all over him now. 'If you had got her pregnant and she refused to hand over the child, would you really have killed her?'

The idea of murder was vividly attractive to him at that moment. 'Of course.' His hands stroked her neck. It would be so easy.

Her hands caressed his erect penis. 'Love me,' she pleaded, pushing against him.

With the water flowing over them and her skin like silk against his, he could wait no longer. Shaping his hands round her buttocks, he forced her legs open and, with a mighty push, drove himself into her. When she cried out, raising her face for a kiss, he turned away, pretending it was Sonny he was holding, aching for it to be her.

Sensing his need to be finished, Celia incensed him by drawing away. Surprised, he looked at her, eyes half-closed with passion. 'Want me, do you?' she teased, winding her arms round his neck. Grabbing two hanks of his hair, she forced his head down. He shuddered. 'Witch!' Desperate, he clasped her to him.

Resisting, she insisted, 'Kiss me.' This time she wanted it to be different. Instead of him having it all his own way and leaving her dissatisfied, she needed to share with him. She needed to feel wanted. And reassured.

Grudgingly he kissed her, digging the tips of his fingers into her soft skin until they drew blood.

Again and again he drove into her, spurred on by a wild and furious desperation to see Sonny again, to hold her and make her his. Closing his eyes, he pretended he was with her. The long savage kisses he gave his wife were for Sonny. Every time he pushed into her he was pushing into Sonny, hurting and bruising and soaring to ever greater heights. With Sonny . . .

His wife's cries of exquisite sensation were Sonny's cries. When the tide of passion burst through him, anger flowed too. And bitterness. And a great crippling fear that he might never find her. In that moment of fulfilment, it was all he could do not to call out her name.

Celia probed his mouth with her tongue and they climaxed in a kiss. For the first time in ages, she was deeply satisfied.

Drenched through and exhausted to the point of collapse, Tony fell against the wall. Switching the water to 'Cool', he let it wash over his burning body. He rolled his head in pleasure. 'Get out;' he told her. 'Leave me be.'

'Was I good?' she asked, infuriatingly.

'Yes. Now get out!'

'We'll have to do it in the shower more often,' she teased afterwards.

'Whatever pleases you,' he agreed. He was almost dressed now, and eager to be gone from the house. Knotting his tie, he looked in the mirror. 'Damn!' His fingers were wooden.

'Here. Let me do it.' She sidled up behind him, her arms outstretched.

'I'm not helpless!' The taste of her kisses lingered, made him sick to his stomach.

Rebuffed, but not hurt, she turned away. 'If you want me, I'll be downstairs.'

He watched her go. As always she cut a dashing figure. Her shoulder-length hair shone like ripe corn. The straight blue dress accentuated her curves and high-heeled shoes set off her pretty ankles. 'You've got more than enough money, fancy hairstylists and beauty coun-sellors,' he whispered bitterly. 'You spend a fortune and half your life on looking good for me. And I won't deny you'll turn every head tonight.' Strange how he didn't seem to mind that any more. 'But you will never have her style, nor her looks. Nor her sparkling freshness.'

Leaning over the dressing table, he raised his eyes to regard himself in the mirror. For one awful minute he looked haggard, old. 'You shouldn't have waited . . . day after day, hoping she'd get in touch, being sure she would have to come home, that she was missing you as much as you were beginning to miss her.'

He began to panic. 'You were too arrogant. Too sure of yourself,' he cursed. 'Months have gone by and still she hasn't been in touch. You're a bloody fool! What if you've waited too long? What if she doesn't want you any more?'

Because of her he couldn't think straight any more. But what to do next? He couldn't go on like this. Then a quick, sly grin lit his eyes, as he recalled seeing Patricia Burton at Martha's cottage.

Patricia Burton might well be the key. And if tradition held, she would be at the party tonight. Convinced now that she knew more than she was telling, he decided he would have to be very, very cunning. But, that wouldn't be too hard. Being cunning was second nature to him.

An hour later he ushered Celia into his expensive car. 'I'm sorry if I've made us late,' she apologised, settling into the leather seat and touching his knee in a suggestive manner. 'Worth it though, don't you think?'

'If you say so.'

'Oh, I do.'

'I don't like being late.' He pushed her hand away.

'I'm sure they won't mind.' She began to sulk, just a little.

'They'd better not mind,' he retorted, thrusting the key into the ignition. 'It's my money that's paying for the party, so I'm entitled to be late if I choose.' He felt better, now that he had half convinced himself that Patricia might even tell him where Sonny was.

'I think you mean *ours.*'

'What did you say?' His eyes were on the road ahead. His mind on Sonny.

'You said just now that your money had paid for the party,' she reminded him. 'It isn't your money, darling. It's ours.'

He half turned, staring disbelievingly at her for a long hard minute. Then, deliberately, he returned his attention to the road ahead. She knew how to get at him, the bitch!

Aware she had riled him, Celia grew afraid. 'Sorry,' she fawned. 'I shouldn't have said that.'

'It's the truth,' Tony grudgingly admitted. How he loathed her!

'All the same, I shouldn't have said it.'

'For Chrissake, let it drop!' Her voice was monotonous, and he needed to clear his mind. He needed to think of Sonny. Of how it would be when he found her. They would make love in every way, at every opportunity. Eventually they would make a child, and through that child, they would get rid of the woman sitting next to him. With Sonny at his side life would be better. He would be a rich man, with no one to answer to, and no one to hold the purse-strings.

His need for Sonny was becoming an obsession. He was angry when she went away. Then worried. When the weeks ran into months he began imagining all sorts of horrors.

Had she grown tired of him?

Did she believe he would never leave Celia for her?

Certainly she had every right to be restless. Maybe he had played her along until she began to have doubts. He didn't blame her. Sonny was a strong-minded woman.

Was she concerned, as he was, about her being slow to conceive?

Sonny knew how much he wanted a child. She wanted it too, but for different reasons – for love and the secure future he had promised.

He still wanted the child, but he wanted the mother too. And he intended to have both.

But was she really working abroad? Or had she gone

away to lick her wounds and make a new life with someone else?

He couldn't bear the thought of that! Imagining her in someone else's arms was his worst nightmare. The idea raised murderous thoughts in him.

If only he could find her. If only he could tell her how sorry he was, and how much he wanted her. If only, if only. He was going mad. He had to find her!

Oh, but he would. He wasn't giving up.

He would never give up.

The party was already under way by the time Patricia got there. As she walked across the yard a group of four young men watched from the canteen, where the party was being held.

Jock was a laugh a minute. A fork-lift driver, he was also a comedian in the making. He could stand on his head and turn cartwheels that left you gasping. Once he sprang from a trampoline and did fourteen turns before landing in the branches of a tree. It had taken the fire brigade a full hour to get him down.

Lonnie was the site foreman. After serving a long, hard apprenticeship he had worked his way up until now he was more experienced in the house-building industry than Tony Bridgeman himself. A cheeky charmer, slim and of medium build, he was liked and respected by everyone. His mop of wild blond hair and freckles made him look younger than his thirty-two years, but there was no questioning his ability or his professional judgement.

Lonnie had a heart filled with romance and a way

with the girls that left every other red-blooded male envious. He had eyes that twinkled when he spoke, and a bright wide smile that could light a room. When his lilting voice lifted in song the female workers would dream of knights on white horses, long gentle kisses and love everlasting. Any one of them would have walked over coals for Lonnie. But he only had eyes for one girl, and that girl was Patricia Burton.

The other two men were casuals, brought in when work was plentiful and laid off when the rush was over. They mixed well, enjoying each other's company and laughing at each other's bad jokes. At the end of the day they went their separate ways and lived their separate lives.

Patricia caught sight of them as she came nearer. Wearing her new tight skirt, stiletto heels and red blouse, she knew she looked good. 'Goggle-eyed buggers!' she chuckled, wiggling her bottom and drawing wolf whistles. 'They can look, but they can't touch.'

It was Lonnie who came forward, a smile on his face and a drink in his hand. 'Would you look at you!' he gasped, shaking his head from side to side and wiggling his rear end. 'Anyone would think you were going to a party.'

Patricia played along. 'Are you inviting me?'

He crooked his arm. 'Be my guest,' he said, bowing. 'Slip your dainty little fingers in there and I'll escort you inside.'

While the other men laughed and girls looked on with envy, Lonnie strolled inside with Patricia on his arm. Behind his back he made a rude gesture. 'Eat your heart out,' he whispered to Jock, giving him a devil-may-care glance.

Jock winked and chuckled and gave his approval, and Lonnie returned his attention to the best-looking girl in the room. 'You look good enough to eat,' he murmured in her ear.

'You don't look so bad yourself,' she replied, eyeing him up and down. She never knew whether or not he was being serious. 'But don't get any ideas,' she warned, 'I'm a good girl.' Secretly she hoped he'd get more ideas than she could handle.

Just then the music struck up and they moved naturally on to the dance floor where they gyrated and shook until they were ready to drop. 'You're a bloody good dancer,' Lonnie said admiringly.

Patricia thanked him. 'How about a gentleman getting a lady a drink?' she asked.

He swept an arm towards the makeshift bar. 'This way,' he suggested grandly.

They made their way to the bar, where they sat and talked and laughed and enjoyed a glass or two, or more of the good stuff. 'I've always liked you,' he said between hiccups, and she confessed 'I've got a soft spot for you too, you crazy bugger.'

Outside, it was beginning to snow. 'We'd better not stay long,' Celia suggested as the car drew to a halt. 'We don't want to get caught in this bad weather.'

Tony got out of his own side and rounded the car. Aware that someone might be watching, he held the door open for her. 'I can take you back now if you're worried,' he said hopefully.

Swinging out her long legs she removed herself gracefully from the Jaguar. 'Are you staying?' she asked pointedly.

'I have to,' he said, shrugging his shoulders and sighing wearily. 'I've got no choice.'

'Then neither have I,' she answered, pecking him lovingly on the cheek.

'Of course you have,' he insisted, looking up at a full sky. 'You could be right about the weather. This snow could set in.'

As she gazed up at his face, the glow from the lighted windows caught her blue eyes. They were filled with adoration. 'Let it snow then,' she murmured. 'My place is with my husband.'

'Have it your own way,' he said sullenly, ushering her inside. 'But don't say I didn't warn you.' He was so incensed at being cheated out of a few hours away from her and with Patricia Burton that he pushed her over the step, feigning horror when she fell into Jock's ready arms.

The party was in full swing, the music loud and exciting. Among the few people not dancing were the bartenders and two ladies who came in twice a week to clean the toilets who had already danced until their legs gave up. 'I have to watch me varicose veins,' one was saying to the other, rubbing her leg and groaning. 'But, oh, if only I were twenty years younger!' The storesmanager was draped on a hard-backed chair, fast asleep and snoring above the music. Two young girls a bit merry on Babychams stood by the door, giggling and pointing.

'Everyone looks like they're having a good time,' Celia commented, her eyes sweeping the room with approval.

'Hmm!' Tony was busy searching for Patricia.

'Get me a drink will you, darling? Bacardi and Coke, I think.'

Among the dancing figures Tony spotted Patricia. Hardly giving his wife a glance, he confirmed, 'Bacardi and Coke.' Already he was leaving her. 'Mingle,' he urged, half turning but not looking at her. 'Enjoy yourself. I'll be as quick as I can.'

As he fought his way across the room he kept his eyes on Patricia, realising with delight that she was already the worse for drink. She had spent too long at the bar and was more than a little unsteady on her feet. As the attentive Lonnie led her to a chair, she laughed and giggled, playfully pushing him away when twice he picked her up from the floor.

Celia watched as her husband went in the opposite direction from the bar. 'Got tangled up with business again, I suppose,' she muttered with frustration. 'So much for my Bacardi and Coke!'

Jock's strong accent was unmistakable. 'Let *me* get you a drink,' he said. 'After all, it were my big feet that sent you flying.'

Celia swung round, relieved when she saw it was the man who had saved her from what could have been a nasty fall. 'It wasn't your fault,' she assured him. 'That was me, being clumsy.'

Jock had a talent for being in the right place at the

right time. A big plain fellow with carefully combed hair, scrubbed white teeth and a soft manner, he had an eye for the women and a nose for a juicy situation. If he was right, and he usually was, the boss's wife was not getting the attention she deserved. Especially if, as a rumour had it, she was disgustingly wealthy.

'Let me get you a drink all the same,' he pleaded. Casting a glance in Tony Bridgeman's direction, he added diplomatically, 'Mr Bridgeman seems to have been called away.'

'I won't see him for hours now,' she groaned.

'Feeling neglected, eh?'

'Something like that.'

Being bold, he thought the drink might wait – 'until we've had a dance?'

Celia shook her head. 'I don't think so,' she said. 'I'm not in the mood for dancing yet.' In fact she would have loved to dance. But with Tony. No one else.

He grinned. 'Whatever you say, Mrs Bridgeman.' It was common knowledge that she worshipped the ground her husband walked on.

With that in mind, together with the instinct that there might be just the tiniest rift appearing in the marriage, he acted shrewdly. 'Bacardi and Coke, then?'

'If you please.' He's harmless enough, she thought, giving him a big smile, and anyway it would serve Tony right if I did dance with another man.

In fact, the only reason Tony Bridgeman might disapprove of his wife dancing with another man, would be the slim chance that she might be lured away, and her money too.

At that moment, though, he was far too preoccupied to worry about his irritating wife. Besides which he was arrogantly certain of her absolute devotion to himself.

With her head lolling back on the chair and a benign smile on her face, Patricia Burton was out of her senses. 'For God's sake, man!' Tony stared accusingly at the downcast Lonnie, seeing a whole evening and his best opportunity wasted. 'What did you do to her . . . slip her a Mickey Finn?'

'She must have had a drink or two before she came to the party,' Lonnie explained woefully. 'I can't believe she's flaked out on just two gin and tonics.' He looked ashamed. 'I've only had a couple of beers meself. If you'll be kind enough to watch her for a minute, I'll call a taxi and get her home.'

Tony was thinking quickly. Now that he was so close he couldn't let the moment go. 'I'll see to Miss Burton,' he promised briskly. 'There's no need for you to go out of your way.'

Surprised, Lonnie answered, 'It won't be out of my way. Didn't you know? We're neighbours.'

Now it was Tony Bridgeman's turn to be surprised. And infuriated. 'You're in no fit state yourself,' he lied. 'Besides, it's my responsibility to see my employee safely home.' He gave the other man a reassuring smile. 'You've done all you can. Thank you.'

While they were talking, Celia had seen the predicament and hurried over. 'I'll come with you,' she offered.

Lonnie had the same idea. 'I'm the one who got her tipsy,' he said regretfully. 'I should be the one taking her home.' Besides, he couldn't quite put his finger on it, and his brain was a bit fuzzed with the drink, but there was something not quite right here.

'There's no need for either of you to leave the party,' Tony said firmly. For what he had in mind an audience was the last thing he wanted. 'All I need is the address and a helping hand to get her to the car, then you can both stay here and enjoy the rest of the evening. As soon as I've delivered her safely home, I'll be back.'

While Celia found herself whisked on to the dance floor by the persistent Jock, the two men got Patricia on her feet. Giggling, she looked from one to the other. 'Are we dancing? she asked, her legs buckling.

'You're a little the worse for drink,' Tony told her in a kind voice. 'I'm taking you home.'

The two men got her outside, into the cold sobering air. 'Are you sure you'll be all right now?' Lonnie persisted. 'It's no trouble at all for me to come along. In fact, I'd like to.'

'I'd appreciate it more if you'd keep an eye on my wife while I'm gone,' came the reply.

'It's as good as done.'

Anxious to get Patricia alone, Tony Bridgeman ascertained her address, bundled her into the passenger seat and asked if she was comfortable.

Opening her eyes, she saw Lonnie. 'I want to go home,' she wailed. She felt tired and sick, and her head was throbbing as if a herd of elephants had stampeded over it.

Seeing the other man start towards him, Tony Bridgeman leaned inside the car. In the dark she couldn't recognise him. 'You are going home,' he told her softly.

'I do like you, Lonnie,' Patricia said, chuckling. 'And I know you fancy me, but I'm not the settling-down type.'

When she started singing, Tony quickly closed the door. 'She's all right,' he observed, keeping Lonnie at bay. 'You can go back inside. I'll have her home in no time.'

Once inside the car he locked all the doors and made a hasty getaway, leaving Lonnie looking regretful and ashamed, wondering why he couldn't have gone along too.

Snow was falling heavily by the time Tony drew up outside Patricia's home. 'Where's the music?' she asked, shivering from the rush of cold air, as he half carried her over the pavement.

'Don't you worry your pretty head about that,' he told her. 'You and I have a little talking to do.'

She snuggled up to him. 'Cuddle up, Lonnie,' she laughed. 'It's bloody freezing!'

It suited his purpose to let her believe he was Lonnie. For the moment anyway.

When they went into her flat, she staggered into the bedroom, fell on to the bed and promptly passed out.

'Oh no, you don't,' he murmured beneath his breath. 'Not until you tell me what I want to know.'

Finding his way to the bathroom, he ran a flannel under the tap and squeezed it out. When he put it on her forehead she stirred. 'Not now, Lonnie. What will the neighbours think?' She burst out laughing, then rolled over and threw her arm across her face. 'I don't feel well.'

'If you're ill, I can bring your friend Sonny to see you.' He stroked her forehead. 'Would you like that? Would you like me to bring her here?'

There was a moment's pause, then in a cracked and weary voice she replied, 'Sonny's not here any more.'

'Where is she then? Tell me where she is and I'll bring her here.'

'No.' Curling her legs, she folded her arms over her head. She gave a muffled laugh. 'You bugger, Lonnie.'

'Sonny's a good friend, isn't she?'

Silence.

'Patricia!' His patience was running out. 'Sonny's your very best friend, isn't she?'

She began to snore.

He wasn't quite so gentle now. 'Where is she?' Grabbing her by the arm, he turned her over. She didn't look at him. Instead she kept her eyes closed and snuggled up. 'Sonny's gone away,' she whispered. 'And she's not coming back.'

'Do you want her to come back?'

'I miss her.'

'Then tell me where she is, and I'll bring her back.'

'Can't tell.'

'But you know!' He was exhilarated. 'You know where she is?'

'Ssh!'

Forgetting the need to be discreet, he began to shake her. 'Tell me where she is. I need to see her.'

'Can't tell!'

'Is she close?'

'Can't tell.' She collapsed in a fit of giggles. Lying on her back, she put her fingers to her lips. 'Secret.'

'Bitch!' His anger knew no bounds. Taking her by the shoulders, he threw her backwards and forwards. 'Where is she, damn you?' As he threw her from him, her head cracked against the wooden headboard. With a long shivering groan she went limp and slithered across the pillow.

Frantic, he examined her. There were no cuts on her head. No blood, and no sign that the knock had damaged her. But she was past conversation. 'Stupid cow!' he shouted at her.

For what seemed an age he stood over her, wondering whether he should try to beat the truth out of her. He decided against it. So far she believed it was Lonnie who had brought her home. Thankfully, she was in no fit state to realise what had gone on, and it was best to leave it that way. 'You've told me one thing, though,' he said aloud. His smile was sinister. 'Just as I suspected, you know where she is.'

A thought struck him. 'She must have an address book . . . a letter . . . something that will lead me to Sonny.'

He snatched Patricia's bag from the floor and was about to go through it when the bedroom door opened and in walked Lonnie. 'You left the flat door ajar,' he said, his concerned gaze falling to the bag.

'She dropped it when we came in,' Tony exclaimed. Putting the bag on the dressing table, he said casually,

'Now that you're here, I'll get back to the party.'

Lonnie nodded. 'Your wife was anxious.'

Even before the flat door had closed and the sound of footsteps had receded, Lonnie was tending Patricia. He laid her more comfortably on the bed and mopped her brow with a fresh wet flannel. 'You stupid little sod,' he said affectionately. 'If you'd told me you weren't used to the drink I'd never have got you those gins. On top of whatever you had before it's no wonder they knocked you out.'

Stirring, Patricia put out her arms. 'I think I could love you.'

He laughed. 'I could love you too,' he told her. 'But I'm not a man to take advantage of a woman when she's the worse for booze.'

All the same, he toyed with the idea of climbing on to the bed beside her. He even stroked his hand down the curve of her throat. 'Shame on you!' he chided himself. 'And the poor lass lying there helpless.'

Dismissing the idea of undressing her, he covered her with a blanket. Kissing her on the forehead, he then undid the neck of her blouse, laughing out loud when she slapped him on the hand. 'Don't you dare take advantage of me, you randy sod!' she warned. Then she fell back and was soon snoring to waken the dead.

'Jesus! I never heard a woman snore like that,' he chuckled as he left. 'It might make a man think twice about marrying.'

The party was over. Celia's mood was sober. 'You

weren't much company,' she complained to Tony as they drove home.

'Sorry.'

The silence was unbearable.

'Tony?'

'What now?'

'Is there something you should be telling me?'

No answer.

'That young woman . . . Patricia Burton?'

'What about her?'

'I hope you're not thinking of using *her* to get us a child.'

'Don't be stupid!'

'It's a shame Sonny Fareham didn't produce a baby for us. At least there would have been a fair chance that it would possess brains and a certain degree of grace – Sonny Fareham was a very sensible, intelligent woman.'

'Must we talk about it?'

'Against my better judgement, I agreed to her. But I don't know if I want you to do it with anyone else.'

'You do still want a child as much as I do, don't you?'

'You know I do. I've always been distraught that I can't give you the son you long for. That's the only reason I've gone along with your idea.' Stretching up, she kissed him on the face. 'It's hard, but I have to trust you.'

'That's right. Trust me. I won't let you down.'

'I know.'

Tony smiled to himself. She didn't know *anything*!

She didn't know that Sonny was the only woman he wanted. She didn't know he had taken Patricia Burton home in order to get Sonny's address. Nor did she know that the moment he got that address – and he sensed it would be soon – Celia would be out of his life forever.

Chapter Eight

'Isn't she beautiful?' The nurse handed the baby to Sonny. 'And wasn't she worth all the effort?' Nurse Armstrong was a sweet blonde thing, stronger than she looked, and a favourite with everyone.

'Yes, she is beautiful,' Sonny agreed, unbuttoning the top of her nightie. Her daughter was small and strong, with a fuzz of golden hair and big round blue eyes. She'd arrived in the world, kicking and screaming, after a long and difficult labour, followed by a frantic rush to the operating theatre, where she was delivered by Caesarean section. 'And yes, she was worth all the effort . . . though I never thought I'd have to go through a Caesarean to get her here.' Easing the nightie open, she bared her nipple and pushed the suckling mouth to it. 'She's got a healthy appetite, that's for sure.'

'And what about her mother?' Nurse Armstrong wagged a reprimanding finger. 'No supper last night and no breakfast again this morning. Carry on like that and we'll have to keep you in.'

'You wouldn't dare!' Sonny was so looking forward to going home.

'Oh, wouldn't I?'

'It's Christmas Eve, and the doctor promised I could go today.'

Nurse Armstrong pushed a trolley to the bed. 'See this?' she asked, pointing to the untouched breakfast tray. 'If that's gone when I get back in half an hour, I'll help you get dressed for going home. But if it's still there, I'm off to see the doctor and tell tales.'

'That's blackmail.' Sonny had a horrible feeling that she meant it.

'Call it what you like, I'll be back in half an hour. And don't try any tricks, because I'll check your rubbish bag and those of your neighbours.' Peeking at the two women on either side of Sonny, she told them with a little smile, 'Don't forget, I know how cunning you lot can be.'

'Might as well be in kindergarten,' the first woman replied with a grin.

The second woman made them all chuckle. 'More like being in bleedin' Colditz!' she said.

'Remember!' the nurse warned as she went about her duties, 'half an hour.'

Sonny looked at the fried eggs and the curly bacon and her stomach turned somersaults. 'I can't eat that,' she groaned. 'It's all greasy.'

'It'll keep the cold out,' said one of her neighbours.

'Put hairs on your chest,' said the other.

The suggestions flowed thick and fast. 'Hide it under your bedclothes till she's gone,' said one of the women. 'Then we can throw it in the rubbish bag. It won't matter if the fat gets on the sheets, 'cause they'll wash 'em anyway once you've left.'

'Scrape the stuff into your pillow-slip,' suggested the other. 'I've seen that done afore.'

Sonny was feeling sick at the thought when a familiar, authoritative voice intervened. '*I've* seen it done before as well.' Nurse Armstrong had been listening from behind the screen. 'I've also seen food thrown out of the window and I've known a mother stuff it down her nightie. Sometimes the porter will do a favour for a few shillings ... and before now the bed pan has had hot dinners dropped in it *before* they were eaten.'

Thoroughly enjoying herself, she laughed out loud. 'So you see, I'm up to all your little tricks.'

'You weren't in the army by any chance, were you?' the first woman asked.

'Happen she were one of them bouncers at the Palais,' the other suggested.

Still laughing, Nurse Armstrong touched the tip of her nose with a finger. 'Twenty minutes now,' she warned. 'Being as you've made me waste my time. And it has to be all gone by the time I get back.'

'What if I can't stomach it?' Sonny wanted to know. And she couldn't. Not even to save her life.

'I'm not forcing you,' Nurse Armstrong said brightly. 'But if it's not all eaten by the time I get back you won't be going home, and that's a promise.' With that she marched away down the ward.

'Bloody hell, gal!' the first woman exclaimed. 'Looks like you'll have to gobble it up after all.'

Sonny stared at the mess on the plate. By this time

the bacon had gone a funny yellow colour and the eggs were curling at the corners. 'Honest to God, I can't,' she said.

'What's it worth?' one of her neighbours asked, leaning across her bed and winking conspiratorially at Sonny.

'What's what worth?' Sonny asked, frowning with puzzlement.

'That there.' The woman pointed to the unappetising breakfast. 'What's it worth if *I* eat it?'

Sonny was astounded. 'Do you mean it?'

'She must be bloody mad,' her other neighbour exclaimed, turning up her nose in disgust. 'I'd rather eat the cat's leftovers.'

'Go on. What's it worth?'

'What do you want?'

'I like that flowered toilet bag your friend brought in.'

'No deal.' Sonny was adamant. 'That was a present. What else?'

'You've got a nice silver hairbrush.'

'Sorry. That was a present from my Aunt Martha.'

'Get a lot o' bleedin' presents, don't you?' the second woman remarked. 'I don't get a present from one year's end to the next.'

'Shut up, you,' the other woman demanded. 'We're talking business here.'

'Some business, I must say!'

'I said, shut up.' Turning to Sonny, she went on, 'What have you got that *isn't* a present?'

'What about the soap dish?' Drawing the woman's attention to the top of the bedside cabinet, Sonny pointed it out. A pretty thing, it was small and shell-like, with a flowered rim and fluted middle. 'I bought that from the trolley lady,' she reminded the woman. 'Cost me half a crown.'

The woman wasn't impressed. 'Got no use for it,' she said, shaking her head. 'I'm not a lover of soap and water. I only wash when I'm in hospital, and only then because I've got no bloody choice!'

'It's no wonder you stink,' laughed the second woman. 'I could smell you a mile away when they first brought you in.'

'I said, shut it!' Returning her attention to Sonny, she asked bluntly, 'Got any money, have you?'

It was all Sonny could do not to burst out laughing. The situation was like nothing she had ever encountered before, and it was tickling her pink. 'How much were you thinking of?' she asked with a straight face.

'Two quid.'

'Too much.' She could buy a lot of baby things with two pounds.

'A quid then?'

'That's bare-faced blackmail!' The second woman gawped at Sonny with a horrified expression. 'I bet she makes a living at it.'

Ignoring her, the woman continued to bargain. 'Ten bob then?'

Sonny felt the baby sag in her arms. Gently she eased her away from her breast, wiped her little mouth with a tissue and proceeded to wind her. 'And you really will eat my breakfast?' she asked disbelievingly. 'Toast, eggs, bacon, the lot?'

'Every morsel.'

'Tea an' all,' added the second woman. 'You'll have to drink the tea an' all.'

'All of it,' she promised. 'Right down to the dregs. When that nurse comes back, she can hunt high and low and she won't find nothing!'

Leaning over, Sonny got out her bag and withdrew a pound note. Handing it to the woman, she told her, 'If you can do that for me, and get me out of here, it's worth a pound.'

Grabbing the note, the woman stuffed it down her nightie. 'Just watch me,' she said proudly.

By this time the bacon was stiff and cold and the eggs had solidified into two hard lumps. The toast was like leather and the tea stone cold. But she tucked in eagerly, as if having breakfast at the Savoy.

'God Almighty!' muttered the second woman, clutching her throat. 'She's making me feel ill.'

She was making Sonny feel ill too. And there was no place else to look.

Undaunted, the woman wolfed down first the eggs then the bacon, crunching it so loudly that Sonny was afraid the nurse might hear and make her way back. Next came the toast. That was the hardest – in the end she had to break it in her hands to make it manageable enough to eat.

The tea washed it all down, and she looked very pleased with herself. 'A quid earned,' she said with a puffed-out chest. 'Can't be bad.'

A moment later she turned an odd shade of green, then ran to the loo and brought it all back.

'Serves her right,' laughed the second woman.

Sonny thought it was a sad situation to laugh at. But she had to laugh all the same, even though the cut on her abdomen hurt like hell. It hurt when she laughed and when she moved. And it hurt now, when she reached over to lay the baby in her cot and change her nappy.

The nurse returned to congratulate Sonny. 'You managed to eat your breakfast then?' she cooed, glancing at the empty plate. 'The doctor makes his rounds at eleven. After that, you should be able to get yourself ready for off.'

'I'm ready now,' Sonny told her. In fact, she'd been ready yesterday, and the day before that.

'Baby fed?' Nurse Armstrong's experienced eyes peered into the cot.

'If she has any more she'll burst.' It was always a relief when the baby had had her fill, because then Sonny's breasts were more comfortable and she could usually sneak a welcome nap. Not today though, she thought jubilantly. Today she was going home.

Glancing at her upside-down watch, Nurse Armstrong tidied the bed. 'Goodness me!' she remarked, looking at the empty bed next door. 'Where's she gone now?'

'She felt a bit queasy,' said the remaining woman, stifling giggles. 'Ate summat that didn't agree with her, I dare say.'

'She's gone looking for the trolley lady,' Sonny fibbed. 'She was asleep when the trolley came round, and they forgot to leave her magazine.' She didn't want the nurse to catch her neighbour being sick in the loo, or she might put two and two together.

Exasperated, Nurse Armstrong hurried away, muttering under her breath. 'She knows perfectly well all wards have to be ready for the doctor.'

Behind her, Sonny and her companion roared with laughter. 'You won't have half as much fun when you get home,' the woman said.

'Don't count on it,' Sonny replied through tears of mirth.

The idea of going home with her new daughter was like a song in her heart. 'Only another couple of hours,' she murmured, 'and we'll be on our way.'

It was strange how she had come to think of Blackburn as home. But maybe it wasn't so strange, she reasoned, when it was the place where she had found a new life, and a measure of peace.

'What have you decided to call the baby?' asked her remaining neighbour.

'Louise,' Sonny answered. 'It's my aunt's second name and I've always loved it.

'Hmh!' Taking a pinch of snuff from her little tin, the woman drew it up her nose and sneezed loudly. 'Louise, eh? Can't say I care for that name meself. I like the old traditional names ... Ada ... Lottie ...' She chuckled. 'Had an Aunt Lottie once. We used to call her Dotty Lottie, 'cause she was daft as a brush ... used to sweep the chimney with a feather duster. One time she poured a full pisspot all over the milkman. After that he'd leave her pint o' milk at the front gate. The birds pecked the top off and drank all the cream. When they were finished the kids down the street would have a go, and by the time Lottie got the bottle in there was hardly enough milk for a cup o' tea.' She chortled at the memory.

'Honest to God, it were like summat out of the Keystone Kops.'

Sonny laughed so much she was in pain.

The other woman returned from the loo and fell into bed. 'That's the hardest pound note I've ever earned,' she groaned. Covering herself up, she rolled over and was soon fast asleep.

Breakfast trays were cleared and soon everyone was dozing.

Sonny sat up for a while, looking round the ward, impatient for the doctor to come and give her the all clear. Entranced, she wound her finger round the tiny hand of her sleeping child. She touched the little face and thanked the good Lord for such a precious gift, and her heart was filled to overflowing.

It was inevitable that she should think of the baby's father. The memory chilled her to the bone. 'He won't find you,' she promised the slumbering child. 'He won't find either of us.'

The fear that he could somehow trace them made her deeply apprehensive. She glanced up and down the ward, as though afraid he might suddenly appear. She tried desperately to keep awake, but tiredness crept up on her. Lying back on her pillow she closed her eyes. 'Less than two hours,' she consoled herself again, 'then I'll be going home.'

Sonny was in a deep sleep when, a short time later, she was gently disturbed.

'You have a visitor,' Nurse Armstrong whispered. 'It's not usual to allow visitors in so close to the doctors' rounds, but in this case we'll make an exception.' Putting her fingers to her lips to enjoin quietness, she ushered the visitor in. 'Five minutes,' she ruled firmly. 'Then you'll have to leave.'

Still not fully awake, and having gone to sleep with Tony Bridgeman on her mind, Sonny sat up with a start, convinced that he had discovered her and the baby.

Thankfully, it was not Tony Bridgeman, but it was someone equally unwelcome.

Cathy Sefton looked stunning. Her slim figure was clothed in the most elegant blue swing coat. On her head she wore the perkiest little hat, and her small hands were covered with the softest leather gloves. 'I gave them a cock-and-bull story about being a long-lost relative and having to travel back to the other side of the world,' she said arrogantly, 'I know it seems rather drastic, but I'm going away for Christmas and I had to talk to you first.'

'I can't see what we would have to talk about.' Sonny could not hide her dislike.

'David Langden, for starters.'

Something in the tone of her voice offended Sonny. 'What about him?'

'I thought *you* might tell *me*.' Cathy looked into the cot, making silly little noises. 'Ah, she's asleep. I heard you had a baby girl. Myself, I want a son first.' Her voice hardened. 'Unlike you, though, I'd prefer to be married when my baby is born.' Staring at Sonny's ringless wedding finger, she went on callously, 'I might be wrong, though. Maybe you are married, and you've dumped him.'

'I think you'd better leave!' Sonny would have taken great pleasure in landing her one. Apart from the anger she felt at being the object of scorn, she hadn't forgotten how harshly this cruel young woman had treated her own father.

'Oh, dear! Now you're upset, and I didn't come here to upset you.'

In spite of herself Sonny was curious. 'What did you come here for?'

Suddenly the smile was gone and Cathy's true colours began to show. 'You and David,' she said, coming straight to the point. 'Are you having a relationship?'

'What if we are?' Annoyed by the intrusion into her privacy, Sonny was in no mood to deny or to confirm.

'I wouldn't like it if you were making a play for him.'

'Is that supposed to worry me?' Sonny had no intention of making a play for David, or anyone else, but she wasn't about to confide in Cathy Sefton.

'I'm here to warn you, that's all.' The smile returned to Cathy's face, a slow sardonic smile that made Sonny's flesh creep. 'Keep away from him.'

'And if I don't?'

'Time will tell.'

'And what is that supposed to mean?'

'It means you'll wish you'd never come to this part of the world.'

'Threats, eh?' Straightening her shoulders, Sonny leaned forward until she and the other woman were eyeball to eyeball. 'If I were you, I'd leave now!'

Choosing to ignore her, Cathy Sefton glanced at the baby. 'I must admit I did have my suspicions . . . about the child, I mean. But I see she's a fully developed little thing, and anyway the time scale doesn't fit. However, if she'd had dark hair and blue eyes, I might be tempted into believing David had created another brat to come between us.'

Sonny shook her head in disbelief. 'You what!' In a swift movement that took Cathy by surprise she grabbed her by the wrist. Holding her in an iron grasp, she drew her closer, saying in a harsh whisper, 'I ought to wring your neck, but then I'd be sinking to your level. Instead, I'll tell you just once and no more ... don't ever come near me or my baby again. *Ever*!' Squeezing Cathy's thin wrist until she cried out in pain, Sonny suggested with feigned politeness, 'And now, I really do think you should leave ... before I forget I'm a lady.' She then released her hold so suddenly that Cathy stumbled backwards, her arms flailing as she lost her balance.

Rubbing her wrist, and wincing with pain, she faced Sonny with a warning. 'He's mine,' she said, her voice threatening. 'You'd better know ... I won't let him go without a fight.'

'I think I asked you to leave.'

'I mean it.' There was no doubting her sinister message. 'I'll see you under the ground before I'll let you take him from me!'

'Get out!'

Seeing that she had outstayed her welcome, and having said what she'd come to say, Cathy Sefton hurried away, regarding Sonny from the doorway, her eyes alight with hatred.

'By! You've made yourself a bad enemy there.' The woman in the next bed had heard and seen everything. 'I'd keep an eye on that bugger if I were you. She's dangerous and no mistake!'

'All talk,' Sonny said, still shaking. 'Nothing to worry about.'

All the same, she *was* worried. Even if she had explained that there was nothing between herself and David, Cathy Sefton was not in the mood to believe her. She was obviously determined to take her late sister's man for herself.

So determined, in fact, that Sonny was tempted to believe, like Ellie, that David's entire family had been murdered, after all. But no! How could anyone be so monstrous?

As always, Tony Bridgeman rose in her thoughts, reminding her that there were such bad people in the world – people who would stop at nothing to get what they wanted.

Cathy Sefton had been Sonny's first surprise that day.

Before the morning was out she would be surprised twice more.

At ten minutes past eleven, Dr Munn gave her the all clear. 'But you must remember to take it easy for a week or two,' he said sternly. 'Give the tummy muscles a chance to heal.'

Sonny promised she would. 'But I'm not an invalid,' she reminded him. 'And I do have a baby to care for.'

'You also have a long deep scar across your abdomen, and beneath that a layer of damaged tissue and muscle.

So do as you're told, or you'll be back in here for repair work.' He admired her fortitude, but insisted on the last word. 'All right?'

'All right,' she answered. 'I'll do as you say.'

The moment he was gone, Sonny asked the nurse if she could use the telephone to order a taxi. 'I don't suppose you know of a reliable firm, do you?' she enquired hopefully. She rarely used the local taxis, and so didn't have any names handy.

'Leave it to me,' Nurse Armstrong said. 'There's one we use all the time.' She left Sonny to dress. 'Don't worry now, I'll let you know the minute he arrives,' she promised. 'But it's chilly outside, so wrap yourself up warm now.'

Ellie had already brought in a pile of suitable outdoor clothing, including Sonny's long coat and beret. She had her stout shoes with her, and a thick shawl for the baby. 'Don't want you to catch cold,' she said, talking to the child while she dressed. 'You're too precious.'

Her mood darkened as she recalled Cathy Sefton's words: 'If she'd had dark hair and blue eyes.' She went to the child and tenderly stroked her forehead. 'Thank God you don't look like your father,' she murmured.

Twenty minutes later she was fully clothed, her bag was packed and all that remained was for the baby to be wrapped up tight and secure in her shawl. 'Over your head and tucked beneath your little feet,' Sonny said, giving her a loving squeeze.

The curtains flicked back to reveal Nurse Armstrong. 'All ready, are we?'

'Ready as we'll ever be.'

'Good, because your taxi's waiting.'

The porter came in and took Sonny's bag, and Nurse Armstrong relieved Sonny of the small bundle in her arms. 'Remember what the doctor said,' she chided. 'No unnecessary lifting, or dancing the night away . . . at least not until the scar is healed.'

'Dancing the night away?' Sonny chuckled. 'I should be so lucky!' In fact she couldn't remember the last time she'd danced. Oh yes, she could! It was last year's Christmas party. Heavens, was it that long ago? When she was in love, and so easily deluded. Well, never again, not now she was wise in the ways of the world.

Nurse Armstrong smiled with her. 'Me too,' she said. 'It's been so long since I went dancing I've forgotten how to do it.'

A voice came from behind a bed-cubicle curtain, making them laugh out loud: 'You put one foot in front of the other. And so long as you don't catch him in the groin with your knee, he might even take you back to his place and make it a night you'll never forget!'

Sonny wished everyone a Happy Christmas and made her way down the ward behind the nurse. 'Wait in the office,' Nurse Armstrong said. 'I'll tell the man you're ready.' She bustled off to summon the taxi driver.

He was Sonny's second surprise of the morning.

She had been standing by the window, watching the cold grey sky and wondering if the snow would come again. The sound of the door opening made her turn. Her heart skipped a beat. '*David*! What are you doing here?'

Dressed against the cold in a brown cable-knit jumper

and blue denims, he looked boyishly handsome. The wind had blown his dark wavy curls over his forehead and his blue eyes sparkled. 'At your service,' he said with a grin.

Sonny didn't know what to think. 'I've ordered a taxi,' she said, thrilled that he was there but afraid also.

'I'm your taxi,' he told her, picking up her bag from the floor and leaning over to peep at the child in her arms. 'So this is the lovely Louise?' He tickled the baby's chin with the tip of his finger. 'She's like you.' The child was still sleeping. 'Has she got your green eyes?'

Sonny's wonderful eyes were the first thing that had caught his attention when she came to the barn. They were not only strikingly beautiful but warm and compassionate. Sometimes, when he was alone in his room at night, he would think of those eyes and feel so desperately lonely that life was almost unbearable.

'No,' Sonny replied. 'Her eyes are cornflower blue. But Nurse Armstrong says a baby's eyes change all the time. She swears Louise's eyes are already tinged the softest shade of green.' Laughing, she added, 'And nobody argues with Nurse Armstrong.'

They followed the porter to the head of the stairs. 'Normally we'd have gone in the lift,' the big fellow explained, 'but it's playing up again. Still, it's only one flight and we can take our time.'

'I'll take the baby,' David offered, handing the bag to the porter. 'As he says, you can take your time.'

'Hold her close,' Sonny told him, unwilling to let the baby go.

'Trust me.' His dark eyes beseeched her, and with a

little shock she saw the pain there.

'Sorry,' she murmured. And she truly was.

The porter walked in front while David remained behind. Holding the baby in the curve of his strong arm, he cupped his other hand beneath Sonny's elbow. 'Gently now.'

She walked slowly. Her instinct was to hurry, but her body said no. Every step pulled at her stomach. 'I feel like an old woman,' she chuckled.

Downstairs, David made sure she was comfortable before he went to get his car. 'Stay right where you are,' he told her. 'I'll be as quick as I can.'

While he was gone Nurse Armstrong came running down the stairs, breathless and apologetic. 'I'm sorry,' she gasped. 'I meant to come down with you, but Mrs Beale was desperate for a bed pan and everyone else was busy.'

She went on to say that Ellie had arranged everything on her visit the day before. 'I was to telephone her this morning and let her know whether you were being allowed home. Then, when you ordered the taxi, I was to ring her and say you were ready.'

'Typical of her.' In fact, Sonny had already put two and two together.

Nurse Armstrong giggled. 'I think it's really romantic. To tell you the truth, I wouldn't mind a handsome bloke like that picking *me* up. Come to think of it, I wouldn't mind any bloke picking me up.'

Sonny smiled at that. 'Don't tell me you're short of boyfriends . . . a pretty thing like you?'

'I work too many hours, that's the trouble. By the

time I get home I'm so tired that if I did have a boyfriend I couldn't do him justice.' She glanced at David, who was striding towards the front entrance. 'Mind you, if I had a boyfriend like him, I'd make an extra special effort!'

Sonny thought it was time she put her right. 'David Langden isn't a boyfriend,' she said quietly so that he should not hear. 'He's my employer. Nothing more.' She tried to harden her heart, but a warm feeling spiralled up inside her.

'Oooh!' Nurse Armstrong was deeply embarrassed. 'And here was I thinking . . .' Lost for words, she pointed to the baby in Sonny's arms. 'I'm sorry. I mean . . . I just assumed . . .'

Sonny's smile put her at ease. 'Well, you assumed wrong.'

'Of course. I should have known, because he never visited that I know of.'

'That's because he had no reason to.' In actual fact Sonny had just been the tiniest bit disappointed when David didn't visit. But then, why should he? And why should she want him to?

Funny though, she thought interestedly, that twice in as many hours David had been virtually accused of being her baby's father. Funny, too, that for a fleeting moment the idea cast a warm glow all over her.

A few moments later the little group made its way to the car.

This time David carried the bag while Nurse Armstrong carried the baby. 'Hope I did right?' she asked Sonny, furtively glancing at David as he rounded the car. 'It was your friend Ellie's idea.'

'It's all right.'

'Really?'

'Really.'

With Sonny settled into the back seat, the nurse handed her the baby. 'It's a good job you're not one of those people who hate surprises.'

Seeing she was still worried, Sonny dispelled her anxiety. 'Mrs Kenny is a born matchmaker, and no, I'm not one of those people who hate surprises. And it's just as well because I've had two already since I woke up this morning.' But now she was going home. At long last, she was finally on her way home!

'You tell Mrs Kenny she can practise her matchmaking on me!' Nurse Armstrong sneaked another admiring glance at David as he climbed into the driving seat. 'He'll do nicely, thank you.'

Sonny laughed. 'You shameless thing! Get back to your bedpans.'

They exchanged hugs. 'Look after yourself,' Nurse Armstrong told her. Sonny said she would, and when the car began moving away she waved until her arm ached.

David was quiet, seemingly lost in thoughts too deep to share. Sonny respected his need for quiet, because she too had things to mull over. She was also entranced with the babe in her arms, a tiny wonderful being who could not know the circumstances surrounding her birth and, if Sonny had her way, never would.

While Sonny tenderly murmured to the child, David listened, his heart touched by the love in Sonny's voice.

The memory of his own little daughter made him hurt. And always, amidst the pain, there was anger. The kind of anger that could tear at a man's soul.

As the minutes passed and the miles shortened, the atmosphere in the car was oddly comforting – as though two old friends had talked themselves out and were now relaxed in each other's company.

The silence was broken when Sonny realised she was not on the route home, but on the way to Ellie's house. 'Where are we going?' Perched on the edge of her seat, she looked out of the window. 'This isn't the way to the shop.'

'We're not going to the shop.' In the mirror his dark blue eyes smiled at her. 'We're going to Ellie's house.'

'No,' she protested. 'You've got it wrong. Ellie wanted me to stay with her for a week or so – she thought I'd be too weak to take care of myself and Louise. But we came to a compromise. She and the kids are coming to stay with me for Christmas. That way I get to stay in my own home and Ellie gets to bully me.' She couldn't understand it. 'She can't have forgotten our arrangement. We only spoke about it the day before yesterday.'

'Sorry.' Again the dark eyes were smiling.

'What are you up to?'

'I'm not up to anything,' he said innocently. 'I was told to take you straight to Ellie's house, and that's what I'm doing. When you get there the two of you can argue it out between yourselves. Afterwards, if you still want me to take you home, then I will.'

'Right!' Sonny hated being made to feel so useless. 'I love her to bits,' she muttered, 'and I know she means well, but she can't do this! We talked it through, and she agreed. And I was so looking forward to going home with Louise . . . to our own fireside. And to sleep in my own bed! Sheer bliss.'

He appraised her through the mirror, thinking how lovely she was. 'Ellie's got no right trying to run your life,' he said sternly, though there was a twinkle in his eyes. 'You'll just have to tell her.'

'Oh, I will!' she replied. 'I will!'

But she didn't.

And for a very good reason.

As they rounded the corner and came into Ellie's street, Sonny leaned towards David. 'I don't want to upset her,' she said woefully. 'Ellie is my very best friend and I owe her everything. But I do so want to go home.'

'Of course you do.'

There was something about his manner that worried her. Something about the easy way in which he'd sided with her against Ellie. It didn't seem right.

They were outside the house now, and he was helping her from the car. 'Will you wait for me?' she pleaded. 'After I've spoken with Ellie, I'd appreciate a lift home.' She added confidently, 'Once she realises her mistake, Ellie and the kids will be coming too. Can you squeeze them all in?'

'Sure, we can squeeze them in.' David took the baby from her and slammed shut the car door. 'Watch your step now,' he warned. 'It's still slippery underfoot.'

Indicating the front door, which was open and attended by a beaming Ellie, he helped Sonny along. 'No bad language now,' he whispered. 'And no fighting.'

'Don't be silly.' Astonished she glanced up at him.

Unable to hide the pleasure that sparkled in his eyes, he avoided her quizzical glance. 'Only I'm not in the mood to referee,' he told her. 'Besides, I've got a party to go to, and I don't want to arrive all bloodied and dishevelled.'

'You're laughing at me, aren't you?'

'Maybe. Just a little.'

She tried to suppress her own laughter, but it bubbled up and broke loose. 'All right,' she said through the laughter. 'Point taken. I'll count to ten before I say anything.'

'Promise?'

'Promise.'

Ellie was like a mother hen. 'Hurry up! Get in out of the cold! Straight out of hospital and there youse both are ... lingering on the pavement, like you've all the time in the world!'

Inside the house, in the living room, the little waiting group chuckled at Ellie's bossy ways. 'Ssh!' Young Mick shook his sister. 'Mam said to keep quiet or she'd skin us alive.'

'But I want to see the baby.'

'Well, you'll just have to wait.'

Kathleen stole a peek at the two visitors waiting to surprise Sonny. 'How long are they staying?' she whispered.

'As long as Mam wants them to, I suppose.'

'Do you think Sonny will be pleased to see them?' Ever since Martha and Patricia had arrived early yesterday morning Kathleen had been thinking about what Sonny would say, and she had come to a conclusion. She told Mick now: 'I think she'll be pleased about the one called Patricia, because she's her friend. But I don't think she'll be pleased to see the one called Martha, because she's her auntie.'

'So?' Mick was far too grown up for all these games.

'So!' She put her fists on her hips and gave him one of her most disapproving stares. 'Boys are so silly,' she said. 'Don't you know that aunties can be even more bossy than our mam?'

'How would you know?' he asked impatiently. 'We haven't got any aunties.' He wished he had. And uncles. And a dad. Oh, how he wished he had a dad!

'Peggy Edwards from Brown Street told me, and she ought to know, because she's got four aunties!'

Together they looked at their visitors, not sure what to make of them. They had taken an instant liking to Patricia, but it had taken a little longer with Martha, who seemed ill at ease with children.

She was standing now by the fireplace, where Ellie had positioned her.

Patricia was pressed against the wall, her face alight with excitement.

All of them were ready to pounce the minute Sonny showed her face.

'She'll see you straightaway,' Kathleen told her brother. 'You'd better get back.'

'Be quiet!'

'Stop arguing,' Patricia commanded.

'Do you want the surprise to be ruined?' Martha's

stern whisper stopped them all dead.

"Course not.' The answer came in unison.

'Then, all of you, be quiet!'

It seemed to take an age for Sonny and the others to make their way down the passage towards the living room. First, David took Sonny's coat and hung it up. She protested a little, saying that she would soon be on her way home.

Ellie scolded David for keeping his own coat on. 'Anybody would think yer can't wait to get away!' she cried, making such a fuss that he was obliged to hand the baby to her while he took off his coat and hung it alongside Sonny's.

Satisfied, Ellie took charge of the baby, billing and cooing as she led them down the passage.

'Why did you tell David to bring me here?' Sonny asked. 'I thought we'd agreed ... you and the children would have Christmas with me, then I'd come back here for a few days?'

'God love us! I completely forgot,' Ellie lied. More to the point, she argued, there had been no arrangements made to light a fire and the flat would be cold and damp. 'So you might as well come in and have a cup of tea with me. In a while David can go back to the flat and get it warmed up. There's plenty o' time. Come in, me beauty ... come away inside.'

She winked at David, who promptly winked back, then nuzzled her face to the baby's and was lost in a sea of emotion. Ellie's greatest weakness was babies. When they grew older they learned how to talk back and argue. When they were little, like Sonny's new-born

Louise, they were pink and gurgly and totally dependent.

Sonny was suddenly aware of the silence in the house. 'Where are the children?' she asked, disappointed that they weren't here to see the baby.

For a moment Ellie was thrown. 'Oh! Er ... they've gone into town to buy a little something for the young 'un,' she fibbed. 'Sure, they'll be back in a minute.'

Sonny didn't know why, but she was uneasy. Without being able quite to put her finger on it, she could sense something strange going on. First David's odd manner in the car, and now Ellie lost for words. It was very peculiar.

Then Ellie said, 'Close yer eyes.'

Sonny stared at her, then at David. Neither of them gave anything away. David was whistling and staring up at the ceiling. Ellie was grinning from ear to ear.

Sonny's uneasiness melted. The intrigue was all because Ellie had bought her a surprise. 'Oh, Ellie!' She rolled her eyes in mock anguish. 'You've been spending money you can't afford. And after I told you me and the baby have everything we need.'

'Close yer eyes, I tell yer!'

Obediently, Sonny closed her eyes.

'And no peeking till I tell yer.'

'No peeking.' Sonny felt herself being drawn forward. 'I'm gasping for a drink.' She hadn't enjoyed a proper cup of tea in ages. 'The hospital staff do their best, but the tea tastes like dishwater. Honest, Ellie, I'm so thirsty my tongue feels glued to my throat.'

'Then yer shouldn't be talking so much.'

Ellie guided her forward until they were standing just inside the living room. Silently, she gestured the others to get ready.

As soon as they were gathered around, she told Sonny, 'All right. Yer can open yer eyes now.'

Smiling, Sonny peeked out of one eye. She half expected to see a new blanket for the baby, or a pair of furry slippers for herself – the kind she hated. Instead, she saw a sea of familiar and beloved faces, all smiling at her, all shouting, 'Welcome home!'

Sonny's heart soared with joy. 'I don't believe it!' She was laughing and crying all at the same time, then her arms were round each of them in turn, hugging and laughing, laughing and hugging. 'Oh, Aunt Martha!' she cried. 'And Patricia! Oh! What a Christmas present!'

She had so many questions. 'How did you get here? When? Why didn't you tell me you were coming? Oh, Ellie! You crafty old thing, and you never said a word!' She looked at Martha's old face, and saw the love there. She looked at her friend, and saw something like guilt. She mistook it. Ignored it. They were here and that was all that mattered.

'They're staying for Christmas,' Ellie declared proudly. 'You as well, me beauty. It's all arranged. Yer visitors will sleep in the spare room upstairs ... there's two single beds, and a wardrobe big enough to share. You'll sleep in the front room down here. I've made the bed, and you'll find a fire already alight to warm the room.' She paused for breath, but not long enough for Sonny to get a word in. 'Now yer can't say no, because it's going to be a wonderful Christmas ... one we'll never forget.' She chuckled and sang and tapped her feet in an Irish jig, and David laughed out loud, and the children fought with each other until Ellie clipped their ears.

Sonny thought it was the most wonderful homecoming she could ever have imagined, and she didn't know who to thank first.

In her excitement she forgot she had wanted to keep her old life and her new life apart. She had forgotten Tony Bridgeman, and the reason she had fled. She only knew that her baby was here, with her, safe for the moment, and her family was all around.

The kettle was soon boiling and the tea made and poured. Soon, too, everyone was gathered round the cheery fire, talking and laughing, and catching up on little snippets of news. David, though, remained by the door, embarrassed and overwhelmed by the women and their chatter and seemingly forgotten by them all – except Sonny, who occasionally looked up at him and smiled, filling his heart with secret love.

Seated with her back to David, and so unable to see the looks that passed between him and Sonny, Martha told how the vicar had sacked the organist who, after a blazing row with her husband, had the congregation in fits when she played 'Heartbreak Hotel' during a wedding. The bride apparently ran out crying, and the groom promptly disappeared – some said he was already having second thoughts, so in the uproar he seized the opportunity to make good his escape.

'Cowardly devil!' Ellie remarked indignantly.

Patricia had stronger views. 'If he was having second

thoughts the poor cow's better off without him.'

Sonny felt sorry for the couple and secretly hoped they would get back together.

The baby received a great deal of attention. 'She's a real beauty,' Martha declared. Patricia was just a little envious, and everyone loved the name Sonny had chosen.

'Louise is such a bonny name,' Ellie said, drooling over the child.

Martha, too, thought it a lovely name. 'It suits her perfectly.'

As usual, Ellie took charge. 'Let the little mite sleep for now,' she declared, laying the small bundle carefully down in a corner of the sofa. 'I dare say she'll be wanting her titty soon enough.'

Sonny had been wondering. 'How did you two arrange all this?' she asked, sharing the question between Ellie and Martha. She had not told Ellie about her aunt, and though Martha knew how good Ellie had been to her, Sonny had made a deliberate effort to keep the pair apart, if only to protect her new life from the past.

Ellie wagged a finger. 'You might well ask!' she chided. 'If your aunt hadn't written to me, saying she wanted to surprise you for Christmas, I don't suppose I would ever have known she existed. Are you ashamed of me, or what?'

Sonny was mortified. 'Of course I'm not ashamed of you.'

'Then why didn't you tell me?'

'There are reasons.' Suddenly it all came flooding

back. Her spirits sank. 'I'll tell you one day,' she said, forcing a smile.

Ellie was ashamed. 'Would yer believe it! I've done it again,' she apologised sheepishly. 'When will I ever learn? Oh, look, I'm sorry, me beauty. If I get too nosy again, just tell me to mind me own business and I won't mind a bit.'

The baby's cries got Sonny quickly to her feet. As she passed Ellie, she gave her a kiss and a smile that said all was forgiven.

Relieved, Ellie touched her hand fleetingly, and the love between these two was evident to everyone there.

David, too, saw the gesture, and it did his heart good. His was a lonely and loveless existence and, although they might not be aware of it, these two women had come to mean the world to him.

He stayed long enough to see Sonny gently lift Louise into her arms. He watched her go to the armchair and discreetly open her blouse. He saw the baby snuggling close to her breast and his eyes filled with tenderness. His greatest desire in that moment was to take care of them both. His greatest regret was that he did not have the right.

Sonny was suddenly aware of his gaze. When she looked up, it was to see his eyes smiling into hers. She felt a blush warm her neck and face, and quickly glanced down, self-consciously turning her body so he would not see the baby at her breast.

When she looked up again he was gone.

And she felt incredibly lonely.

* * *

By ten-thirty the children were in bed fast asleep. 'It's all been too exciting for them,' Martha announced, herself settled and comfortable in the cosiest armchair.

By midnight all the presents had been brought out of hiding and placed beneath the tree. With her arm around Sonny's shoulders, Ellie stood back to admire it yet again. 'David wouldn't take a penny for that tree,' she said for the umpteenth time. 'He even helped me and the children to dress it. Pretty, don't yer think?'

'I think it's beautiful,' Sonny answered. And it really was lovely. It took up the entire corner next to the window, its baubles and lights twinkling and the pretty decorations draped from top to toe.

'I can't recall us ever having a Christmas tree at home,' Patricia said. 'But then, it's not surprising . . . considering.'

'Considering what?' Ellie was curious.

Patricia hesitated. 'We never had much of a family life,' she admitted. 'The trouble was, my mother loved her booze more than she loved her family.' She had been happily toying with the tree decorations. Now, though, she moved away, subdued and thoughtful.

Realising she had touched on a sore point, Ellie wrung her hands together. 'There I go again!' she moaned. 'I've upset yer, I can see that.'

Patricia half smiled. 'No, you haven't,' she said. 'It was a long time ago, best forgotten.'

Martha called her over, and the two of them began to chat. Sonny watched and thought it wonderful that each had found a friend, unlikely pair though they might be.

Ellie continued to admire the tree, while Sonny hurried away to check the baby in the next room.

As soon as she had closed the door behind her, Martha addressed Ellie. 'That young man – does he have a soft spot for my Sonny?'

'I'm not sure,' answered Ellie, glancing furtively at the doorway in case Sonny should return.

'I'll go and see if she's all right,' offered Patricia. In fact she would be glad to get away from Ellie, who, though a dear soul, was a bit too fond of asking questions.

'Go on,' Martha urged when Patricia had gone. 'You were saying you weren't sure whether... David, isn't it?... has a soft spot for my Sonny?'

Very briefly, Ellie told her how David's wife and child, along with his mother-in-law, had been tragically killed. 'That was four years ago, but he still hasn't got over it.'

Martha dwelt on that for a while, thinking how life could sometimes take away the reason for living. 'What kind of man is he?' she asked. 'I know how generous he's been to Sonny... giving her a job and a home. But I have to admit I thought he might be looking for a favour of sorts in return, if you know what I mean?' Now it was her turn to glance furtively at the doorway.

'Oh, bless yer heart, no.' Ellie's face told a tale. 'David's a businessman and he's looking after his own business interests. He's a talented wood-carver. He also makes beautiful furniture. Someone suggested he should take it up in a serious way, so he bought a shop, and put the best person in charge. Sonny's done him proud an' all. She's selling the pieces so fast he can hardly keep up.' She chuckled with pleasure. 'Your niece has a clever head on her shoulders. I'm surprised she isn't in some high-flying position in a big firm.'

Something in Martha's expression made her wonder. 'Ah! She did have a good job, didn't she?'

'Yes, she did. But you're not to say I told you.'

'Something bad made her run away, didn't it?'

'You're very perceptive, my dear.'

'She never said.'

'That's why I'm asking you not to repeat our conversation, especially not to Sonny. I'm sure there will be a time when she'll tell you herself. As you say, she's a very strong-minded person and wouldn't thank me for interfering.'

'Me lips are sealed.' Ellie pressed her lips together and gave a small wink.

'I'm trusting you, Mrs Kenny.'

'And you do right to trust me,' Ellie assured her. 'But I'm not a "missus". I'm a silly woman without a man, and thanks to my wayward habits the kids are without a father.'

'They seem happy enough.'

'That's what yer see on top. Underneath it's different. Especially with the lad. He doesn't say much, and he's very fond of David, but deep down he aches for a father.'

'I'm sorry.' And she was.

'So am I.' Ellie thought of Arnie, and grew sad. It seemed as though it wasn't meant to be.

'Is there no man in your life at all?' Martha had known her for only a short time, but because of Ellie's

276

lovely, open nature, she felt she could ask such a question.

'Bless yer heart, there was one man I could have settled down with years ago, but he went away just when I needed him.'

'You mean when you were pregnant?'

'Now *you*'re being perceptive.' The children were safely tucked up in bed, but Ellie lowered her voice all the same. 'The fella's name is Arnie, and he's Mick's father.'

She nearly let another secret slip, but stopped herself just in time.

'Does he know he's Mick's father?'

'No. I never got the chance to tell him.' Ellie's eyes lit up. 'But he came back ... widowed and alone. He hasn't changed all that much, a bit thinner on top and not so tall and masculine as I recall, but he's still the same Arnie to me.'

'Will you tell him he has a son?'

The sparkle faded from Ellie's eyes. 'Ah, sure I were all set to tell the bugger, but he's done it on me again. He made a date to meet me, but never turned up. I haven't seen hide nor hair of him since.' She shrugged her shoulders, pretending it didn't matter, when it clearly mattered desperately.

'Some men are like that, my dear. Here today, gone tomorrow.'

Ellie was momentarily lost in thoughts of Arnie, of how it used to be between them. In her sad heart she felt such times were lost forever. 'I'm too old in the tooth to worry about him now,' she said quietly. 'Sure, a man can please himself when all's said and done.'

Martha was already thinking of another man. 'You said David Langden is a wood-carver?'

'Woodland creatures and things of nature.' Ellie's face was wreathed in wonder. 'He has a genius for it.'

'And he makes furniture?'

'The best.' Ellie could see what the other woman was getting at, so she saved her the trouble of any more questions. 'He also owns a couple of houses and the shop. He owns a large chunk of land and the prettiest cottage you've ever seen. He's not short of a bob or two, if that's what yer after.'

'Hmm!' Martha liked the sound of that. 'And you say there's nothing between him and Sonny?'

'I only wish there were.'

'Oh! Do you now?' Martha seemed surprised.

Ellie explained. 'David is a fine young fella, sure he is. He's had such tragedy in his young life, and now he lives alone, with only a mangy dog for company.' She shook her head and sighed. 'It's no life for a man like that. He needs a family . . . children . . . a wife who he can shower with love and affection. Instead, he's terribly lonely.'

She continued to look Martha in the eye. 'Sonny and David were made for each other. What's more, I've seen the way they peek at one another when they think nobody's looking.' She chuckled. 'I'm telling yer . . . there's a spark between those two, and they don't even know it themselves.'

Ellie had a very special reason for wanting that 'spark' to ignite. But for now, it was her little secret.

* * *

In the other room, Patricia was confiding in Sonny. 'Pissed out of my mind I was,' she groaned. 'Lonnie had to take me home . . .' She giggled. 'At least, I think it was Lonnie.'

'Who else could it have been?'

'No, it was Lonnie, I'm sure.' A flicker of doubt crossed her face. 'But he did seem to ask a lot of questions, as I recall.'

'What kind of questions?'

'About you . . . I think.'

Sonny gulped back the fear. 'What do you mean? Why would Lonnie ask a lot of questions about me?' The fear intensified until she could hardly breathe. 'Patricia! Are you sure it wasn't someone else? Think,' she urged. 'Think hard. Are you sure it wasn't Tony Bridgeman who took you home? Are you sure it wasn't him who asked the questions?'

'It wasn't him, I'm certain,' Patricia said. 'I would have known. I wasn't *that* pissed, for Chrissake!'

'But why would Lonnie want to know about me? Could Tony have bribed him, do you think?' Sonny was grasping at straws. 'Maybe he offered him money to get my address out of you.' The thought made her blood run cold. 'Did Lonnie ask for my address?'

'No! No, he didn't.' Pressing the flat of her hands to her temples, Patricia dropped her gaze and seemed to be in distress. 'You know Lonnie as well as I do. He would never take a bribe.'

This time Sonny spoke more gently. 'Please, Patricia.

I have to know if he's looking for me.'

'I know you do.'

'And you don't think he is?'

'How would I know that?'

Sonny looked her in the eye. 'You would know.' She held Patricia's hands in hers. 'And if you knew he was trying to find me ... I hope, as a friend, you might think to warn me?'

'You know I would. In fact, I've been keeping an ear to the ground, like I promised.'

'I'm sorry. I shouldn't doubt you.' She had to believe. She had to trust.

'No, you shouldn't doubt me. And it was Lonnie who took me home. It was Lonnie who asked the questions, but it was only because he knew I was missing you.'

'You haven't told him anything?'

'I haven't told anyone.' The crisis was over. She had Sonny's trust, though she didn't deserve it. 'I won't let you down,' she said earnestly. 'Before I'd let anyone know where you are, or that you've had Tony's baby, I'd cut off my right arm.' Her eyes brimmed with tears. 'You should know that.'

Sonny wrapped her arms around her. 'I do,' she said. 'And I'm sorry.' All the same, she'd had a terrible fright.

'You're trembling.'

Sonny's laugh was a nervous little sound. 'You had me worried, that's all.'

'Not now, though?'

Sonny shook her head. 'No, not now,' she lied. She went over to the baby's cot. 'This is what it's all about,' she said. 'My baby, my lovely daughter.' She half turned. 'What do you think of her?'

'I'm glad she's not like ... *him*.'

'That was the first thing I looked for. I can't tell you how relieved I was when I saw her little face and it was nothing like his.'

'Sonny?'

'Yes?'

'Suppose he did come looking for you?'

The idea was so horrifying she couldn't speak for a minute.

Patricia suspected that Tony was already trying to find out where Sonny was, but she was too cowardly to say so. 'What would you do?'

'If I thought he might find me here, I'd have to run away.'

'Why don't you run anyway? Now.'

'That's crazy. Why should I?'

'No, you're right.' Patricia knew in her heart that it had not been Lonnie who had taken her home. But he claimed she was imagining things. He said *he* got her home safely. 'Who else but me would have put you in bed and not taken off every stitch and climbed in beside you?' he asked cheekily. She had no choice to believe him. Unless she were to tackle Tony Bridgeman, and she didn't relish the thought of that.

Sonny felt ill just thinking about the possibility that Tony might come looking for her. Determinedly, she pushed him to the back of her mind, asking, 'Is it serious with you and Lonnie?'

'No more than usual.'

'You know he'd marry you tomorrow?'

'I'm not ready for that kind of commitment.'

'Because of the example your parents set?'

'Could be.'

'Marriage isn't always a battleground, Patricia.'

'You seem to have carved out a good life here.'

'I hope so.'

'Are you happy?'

Sonny considered. 'Sort of,' she answered thoughtfully. The question made her examine what she had here.

'That's no answer.'

'I mean . . . I have my baby, a job and a place to live. And I have two very good friends in Ellie and David.'

Patricia sniggered. 'Is that all he is . . . a friend?'

'That's all.' Sonny's voice gave nothing away.

'I saw the way he looked at you, and I saw how you smiled at him.' Nudging Sonny, she asked with a knowing little grin, 'Can you honestly say you don't fancy him?'

'Like I say, he's a very good friend.' Going to the door, she beckoned Patricia out. 'We'd better go, or they'll be sending out the cavalry.'

'Subject closed, eh?'

'Nothing else to be said.' As Patricia came out of the room, Sonny suggested, 'Tomorrow, I'll show you the flat and the shop if you like?'

Patricia liked the idea, and so, when asked, did Martha.

An hour later, tired and talked out, they retired to their various beds. Ellie went to her own; Martha and

Patricia were shown to the spare room; Sonny was despatched to the front room, to the comfortable narrow bed next to the cot placed there for her baby.

But it was a long time before she went to sleep. Instead she lay there, staring at the glowing embers in the little firegrate, and wondering why she suddenly felt so insecure.

After all, Patricia had promised there was nothing to worry about. Tony hadn't even asked after her. He was so busy he was hardly ever in the office.

All the same, Sonny couldn't sleep. She could see him in her mind's eye. And she felt haunted.

On Christmas morning, Sonny woke with a start. The day had already begun. Through the curtains the brightness of a winter sky lit the room, and the excited screams of the children opening their presents told her she had badly overslept. Panic gripped her. 'The baby!' As quickly as her sore tummy would allow she hurried to the cot and looked inside.

When a pair of blue eyes looked up at her, she laughed aloud, filled with immense relief. 'You gave me a fright,' she murmured. 'All night, and not a sound . . . either that or I didn't hear you. No, I would have heard you,' she decided. 'All mothers sleep with one eye open.'

Hurriedly, she put on her dressing gown and slippers, before taking the child into the next room.

She opened the door and there they all were. Martha and Ellie were clearing away the breakfast things and Patricia was on her knees with the children. 'Morning,'

Ellie said, catching sight of Sonny and the baby. 'Rested well, are ye?'

'Why didn't you wake me?' Coming into the room, Sonny gave Martha a kiss. 'You come all this way to spend Christmas with me and here am I lying in.'

Martha took baby Louise while Ellie hurried to get Sonny a cup of tea from the pot. 'It's still hot,' she said. 'Nobody wanted any breakfast, but I'll make yer a slice of toast if yer like.'

Sonny wouldn't hear of it. 'Thanks anyway, but I'm not here to be waited on, Ellie. Anyway, I need to see to the baby.'

Mick and Kathleen rushed to Sonny and kissed her for their presents, which Ellie had kindly wrapped while Sonny was in hospital. Martha had brought for Mick a pair of binoculars and for Kathleen the sweetest little handbag, with a purse containing five shillings. Surrounded by all the coloured paper and mess of a family Christmas morning, the children were laughing and talking happily.

Patricia called out 'Good morning' and carried on playing with the children. She didn't get up. In fact she was still feeling guilty about the conversation she and Sonny had had last night. When she got back she meant to have further words with Lonnie.

When the baby was fed, bathed and dressed, and Sonny was ready to face the world, the adults received their presents. 'The children couldn't wait,' Ellie sighed. 'But we saved ours till you could be here.'

Sonny was astonished when Ellie took two presents from the tree and gave them to Martha and Patricia.

'You crafty thing!' She stared at Ellie with amusement. 'You told me you'd already posted my presents to Aunt Martha and Patricia.'

'Ah, away with yer,' Ellie replied with a little wink. 'Sure, what was the use of posting presents to these lovely people when I knew they were coming here anyway?'

Presents were swapped and greatly appreciated. Ellie got a beautiful scarf, a flower print for her wall and a new snuff-box from Mick – a gift that both delighted and embarrassed her.

Martha got a silver butterfly brooch from Sonny, a small china cat from Patricia, and a pair of fluffy slippers from Ellie. Sonny thanked her lucky stars the slippers weren't for her, because they were outrageous. There was also a huge box of chocolates from the children, which Martha accepted with enthusiasm, hiding the fact that she couldn't eat hard chocolates because they stuck to her false teeth.

Sonny received one gift which was from all of them. When she opened her parcel to reveal a blue silk dressing gown she gasped with pleasure. 'It's just beautiful!' she said, hugging them all in turn. 'You must have known my old one is ready for the scrap heap.'

Everybody was thrilled with their presents, but now the working began – clearing away the paper, hoovering and polishing, washing dishes and preparing food. Everyone helped. Everyone was having such fun. And for Sonny it couldn't have been a more perfect Christmas Day.

The aroma of cooking turkey had filled the house

since early light. It was a tradition with Ellie to rise early and let the turkey cook slowly in its own juices. The mince tarts had been baked the day before and were warming under the grill.

Sonny peeled a mountain of potatoes. 'I feel like I'm on jankers,' she laughed, throwing another into the pot. Martha did the Brussels sprouts. Patricia took care of the children and kept them amused. Ellie took care of everything else.

By midday the meal was ready for serving up. The table was laid, and the children did their bit by fetching and carrying and being generally useful – although Ellie got a bit stern when they argued loudly about which side of the plate the crackers should go. 'Sit yourself down, you two,' she ordered. 'Your Christmas dinner's ready.'

No sooner had she said the words than there was a knock on the door. Mick ran to it and ran back again. 'It's David!' he shouted excitedly. 'And somebody else.'

The 'somebody else' was Arnie.

'He was just leaving when I drew up,' David confided. 'He said he'd been knocking for ages and couldn't make anybody hear.'

Ellie suspected he hadn't knocked at all but had lost his nerve and was making a quick getaway. 'Sit yerselves down,' she told them.

And that was what they did. They each got a cracker to pull and wore silly hats on their heads; Arnie was a policeman and David a sailor.

They shared the most wonderful meal – of tender turkey and vegetables cooked to a turn, roast potatoes

ut of the blue Martha posed a question that put
ny on her guard. 'Is there any chance you and David
ngden might get together?'

'No chance at all.'

'Because of Tony Bridgeman?'

'Maybe.'

'But you mustn't let what happened spoil your chance
of happiness with someone else.'

'I'm not ready for a relationship. You know that.'

'I know, dear, and I do understand. But David Langden seems to be fond of you, and from what Ellie tells
me he is a fine young man who could give you and the
baby a good life.'

'I do like David, and I'll never be able to repay him
for his kindness. But I don't want anything more than
his friendship. He feels the same way, I'm sure. Besides,
he's still grieving for his family.' She studied Martha's
face. 'Did Ellie tell you that?' Her frustration betrayed
itself in her voice and in her eyes.

'Perhaps I've spoken out of turn. Forgive me, my
dear.'

As far as Sonny was concerned the subject was closed.
She was thankful when there came a tap on the door
and Patricia poked her head inside. 'You said you were
going to show us the flat and the shop,' she reminded
Sonny. 'Is it still on?'

'Give me a few minutes.'

Just before she closed the door, Patricia said, 'I mentioned it to David and he said he'd be happy to take
us.' Then she ran upstairs to change.

Martha excused herself. 'I'll go and freshen up,' she

that were brown and crispy on the outside and soft as
butter on the inside, gravy that left a taste on the tongue
that could keep a man going for a week, and mince
tarts that melted in the mouth, covered in smooth cus-
tard and dressed with a drop of brandy.

Throughout the meal the children chatted and Patricia
made them laugh. Martha tucked into her delicious meal
while keeping an eagle but discreet eye on the young
man whom Ellie had said was made for Sonny. Once,
when she had a mouth full of turkey, David smiled at
her, and, though momentarily embarrassed, she could
easily have fallen for him herself.

Ellie kept looking at Arnie, and he kept apologising.
But it didn't matter that he had let her down yet again.
It didn't matter that he had an adventurous and cavalier
streak in him. Nor did it matter that she had been left
to raise his offspring all by herself. That had been a
labour of love. Now he was back, here at her table,
eating the food she had cooked and smiling into her
eyes as though they were two shy, foolish things just
learning about each other.

Excited and content, Ellie relived the emotions that
had stirred her heart when she and Arnie were in love
the first time around.

Now, when he touched her leg under the table, she
blushed so fiercely the children thought she'd choked
on a Brussels sprout.

As for Sonny, she didn't know where to look. With
her usual matchmaking talents, Ellie had seated her
and David directly opposite each other, so their eyes
constantly met across the table.

Acutely aware of Sonny's embarrassment, David talked to everyone but her.

Sonny turned her head this way and that, chatting to the others and avoiding him as best she could, but always ending up gazing straight into his brooding blue eyes.

When that happened the moment was stopped in time, as one lonely heart reached out to another, afraid to touch, desperately afraid of being hurt.

When the meal was over, the children dragged poor Arnie outside to help build a snowman. Patricia commandeered David and Ellie busied herself in the kitchen.

Sonny retired to the front room, where she fed her baby and chatted to Aunt Martha. 'Do you think you'll ever come home?' Martha asked.

'I don't know what the future holds,' Sonny answered, after some thought. 'But I won't leave it so long again before we see each other.'

'That might be difficult, my dear,' Martha warned. 'I don't know if I could make this journey again. To be honest, I did find it quite an ordeal.'

'Then me and Louise will have to come to you.' Sonny reached out to take the old woman's hand. 'I do miss you.'

'I miss you too,' Martha replied softly. 'And I'm thrilled that you've chosen to call the baby after me.' She hesitated to say it, but knew it had to be done. 'As for you coming to me, my dear, I don't think it would be safe. Not yet, anyway.'

Sonny knew her aunt of old. Her voice was harsh. 'He's been round to the cottage, hasn't he?'

Her question was greeted with sile...

'Please, Aunt Martha. I have to know...

'He brought some money he said was...

Martha's face hardened. 'But he really wa...

out where you were.' Before Sonny could ask...

tion, she put her mind at rest. 'Don't worry, ...

He got nothing out of me.'

'Do you think he'll be back?'

'No.' Martha shook her head. 'I made it clear he w...

not welcome in my house. I also made it clear that you

were working away for some long time to come and were

in no hurry to come home.' She puffed out her chest.

'Though I say so myself, I did an excellent job. He won't

be back, you can rest assured.'

'He's very devious.'

'No more than me, my dear.'

Sonny wished she could be as sure as Martha. But it wasn't easy. She knew him. Martha didn't.

'I should have stayed,' she told the old lady. 'It isn't right that you should have to deal with the likes of him.'

Martha smiled patiently. 'Would you want him to take her?' she asked softly, her kind old eyes gazing at the baby.

Instinctively Sonny clutched Louise to her. 'No, God forbid!'

'Then you had no choice.'

Sonny looked into the tiny face of her baby and knew Martha was right. If she had stayed, Tony Bridgeman would have fought her tooth and nail for his child, and resistance would have been futile. She had no choice but do as she had.

said, following Patricia up the stairs, one slow step at a time. 'My days of running are over,' she mused wryly.

Alone now, Sonny gave thought to what Martha had said. 'She's a lovely, kind old soul,' she told Louise, 'but I wish people would stop trying to put me and David Langden together.' A sad, faraway look came into her green eyes. 'If only it could be possible for David and me. If only the past had been kind to us.' A wistful smile touched the corners of her mouth. 'Things might have been different,' she murmured. 'We might have been free to dream.'

A few moments later, when Louise was contentedly sleeping in her cot, Sonny crept out of the room. 'Sleep tight,' she whispered. 'I'll be back in a minute.'

As she went towards the living room she heard David and Ellie speaking quietly. 'I know you mean well,' he was saying, 'and I have great regard for Sonny, but only as a friend.'

'Ah, now, that's a real shame,' came the reply. 'Because the two of you would make a perfect match.' Ellie lowered her voice. 'Don't yer think she's the love-liest creature?'

'I can't deny that.'

'And hasn't she got the kindest nature?'

'You obviously haven't seen the other side to her.'

'Oh? And what side is that?'

'The side that sells my carvings. The side that strikes a hard deal with the most difficult customers and always seems to come off best.'

'That's her good business sense.' Ellie laughed. 'See what a catch she'd be.'

His voice was tender. 'You like her a lot, don't you, Ellie?'

'I've come to love her,' Ellie said. 'I know there's a little love deep down inside of you, too,' she went on, 'if only you'd let it out. Oh, look, me darling . . . the lass is lonely, and so are you. I know in me heart you'd be good for each other.'

There followed a deep silence, as though he was turning her words over in his mind. Presently he answered, 'You're right, Ellie, I *am* lonely, and if I was looking for someone to share my life, I can think of no one I'd rather share it with than Sonny.'

When it seemed Ellie was about to say something, he put up his hand and carried on. 'And you're right, she does seem lonely . . . sad too . . . and maybe I wish there was something I could do about that. But it isn't my place and what's more I don't think she would thank me for interfering. So, yes, you're right, Ellie. Sonny and I are both lonely people. But it doesn't follow that I need her to make my life complete, nor that she needs me. Life is hard, you should know that. We all have our trials, and we deal with them the best way we know how.' His eyes appealed to her for understanding. 'You're a good woman, Ellie,' he said softly. 'But your match-making talents are wasted on me. And on Sonny too, I dare say.'

Ellie was saddened by his answer. 'I know you won't thank me for saying this, but I will anyway.' She took a deep breath. 'I know your world fell apart when you lost your family, but you can't go on grieving forever.'

'I know that.'

'Then why won't you let yourself think of the future? It can be long and lonely all by yourself.'

'I know that too, and I expect one day my thoughts will turn to marriage and family, but not yet. I have too much on my mind right now. Too much to do. Too many things to put right.'

Ellie sensed the agony behind his words. 'You mean Cathy Sefton, don't you?'

'Maybe.'

'You can never be sure of her part in it.'

'Maybe not.'

'Revenge is a bad thing. It can destroy you.'

The back door was flung open, bringing in the children and a blast of cold air. 'The snowman's crumbling,' they called out from the kitchen.

'He's not the only one,' Arnie complained, coming into the warm. 'My hands are frozen solid, and I reckon my nose fell off about ten minutes since.'

In the hallway, Sonny had stayed pressed to the wall, hating herself for listening but wanting to know what David thought about her. Now, though, her feelings were strangely mixed.

She was relieved when David told Ellie what she had already told Martha – that there could be nothing between them. But, conversely, she felt a deep aching regret that she and David were not meant for each other. He was a good man, the kind of man a woman would wait a lifetime for. You can't have it both ways, she told herself, preparing to go inside with a bright smile. You don't want him and he doesn't want you. And that's an end to it.

When she walked into the living room, David stood up to greet her. 'I understand you'd like to go to the flat?'

'I was going to call for a taxi.'

Before he could answer, Patricia came rushing in, followed more sedately by Martha.

'Don't ring for a taxi,' David told Sonny. 'I can take you. It's no bother.' Just to be near her for a while longer, that was all he wanted.

'Are you sure?'

'Why not?' he asked with a twinkle in his eye. 'I've got nothing else to do.'

Ellie insisted on remaining behind to mind the baby and Arnie seized the opportunity to be with her. The children were hell-bent on restoring their snowman, rushing to it the minute David closed the car doors.

Patricia parked herself in the front seat next to David, while Sonny sat behind with Martha. 'She's got her cap set at that young man,' Martha told Sonny disapprovingly.

'She's every right,' Sonny replied. Inside, though, she was just the teeniest bit resentful.

When they got to the shop, Patricia lingered outside, staring at the bow windows and small crooked door. 'It's like something out of the dark ages,' she said scornfully.

'Suits me then,' David answered with a little grin.

'And me,' Sonny added. 'The customers aren't buying the shop,' she pointed out, 'they're buying what's on the shelves.' Turning the key in the lock, she urged Patricia and Martha to 'come and see'.

'Maybe your friend's got a point,' David said, looking

up at the shop's frontage. 'Perhaps it could do with a facial.'

Sonny left him to it. As she brought the little party into the shop, the cold struck bitterly. 'Jesus! It's bloody freezing!' Patricia exclaimed. 'Haven't you got any heating?'

Sonny laughed. 'There,' she said, pointing to an oil heater in the hearth. 'It gives out a good heat, but when we're closed we just keep it on very low, to stop the pipes from freezing.'

'Turn the bugger up, then!' Patricia cried. 'Or it won't only be the pipes that freeze.' She hugged herself and shivered theatrically.

Martha reproved her. 'You're getting soft in your old age,' she said, head up and shoulders squared. 'If you lived a winter in my cottage you'd soon be hardened to the cold.'

'I'd soon have it on the market, you mean,' Patricia rejoined. Turning to Sonny, she pleaded, 'Turn the fire up, eh? You know what a cold-blooded sort I am.'

Sonny turned up the heater, then took them through the shop. She showed them David's wonderful wood-carvings. 'Oh! They're just beautiful!' breathed Patricia, gazing with admiration at a woodland scene with squir-rels and voles and a robin perched on a twig. 'How can a man carve such tiny delicate things? I mean . . . men have got such big hands, haven't they?'

Sonny caressed the robin and said softly, 'It's the heart that carves them, not the hands.'

Martha loved the furniture, with its bold carved decorations. 'I wouldn't mind that for my cottage,' she said, selecting David's latest piece of work, a four-drawer chest in polished pine, with strong, curved feet, big round knobs and a garland of raised daisies etched into the top rim. 'You're right,' she told Sonny, 'David is a very talented man.'

David came in and, hearing his name, grew embarrassed. Having taken the keys out of the lock, where Sonny had left them, he made his way upstairs to the flat.

Here he assembled newspaper and, from the scuttle, kindling wood and a few small lumps of coal. Taking matches from the mantelshelf, he knelt on the rug and began to light a fire. Having looked after the flat while Sonny was in hospital, he was familiar with everything.

By the time the others arrived he had the fire nicely blazing and four cups of tea poured out. 'Sorry, all out of cakes,' he joked as they came in.

Then he saw Sonny, who, white as a sheet, was clinging to the door handle, and the laughter fled from his face. 'Ellie was right,' he chided gently, leading her to a chair. 'You shouldn't have come here. This place isn't properly aired, and you're only just out of hospital.'

'I'm all right,' she insisted. 'I've just got a stitch, that's all.' She bravely sat up straight, though she felt more like keeling over.

Martha, too, was worried. 'You're not all right,' she declared. 'You're as headstrong as ever. Trying to do too much too soon.' She gave Sonny her tea. 'Drink that, then we're going straight back.'

'I'm not an invalid.'

'Are you going to argue with me?'

'No.' She hadn't got the strength to argue. In fact she was forced to admit that Ellie had been right after all, and Martha was right now. Just as the doctor had warned, her body would set the pace for her recovery, and there was little she could do about it.

Patricia looked at Sonny, at Martha, and at Sonny again. 'You look bloody awful!' she said, frightened by Sonny's pinched and grey face. 'Your aunt's right. I think we should go straight back.'

Sonny gave a little laugh. 'Is it all right if I have my tea first?'

That gave time for the others to look around her little flat. Martha and Patricia were thrilled with the way Sonny had furnished her home. 'Such pretty little curtains,' Martha beamed. Patricia liked the colour combinations and the choice of furniture, and said she thought Sonny was fortunate to have a job and a home 'all rolled into one'.

Before checking through the shop, David secured the fire, placing a guard round it. 'I'll come back later and make sure it's out,' he promised.

In no time at all they were on their way back to Ellie's. 'If you need me to run you to the station tomorrow, give me a ring at home,' David told Martha. 'Don't go paying for a taxi when I can do the job for nothing.'

Both Martha and Sonny thought he had done enough, but Patricia said that was very kind and they would be glad of a lift. 'The train leaves at midday,' she informed him, looking away when Martha gave her a severe, disapproving glance.

Sonny remained quiet throughout the short journey. She didn't want her aunt to leave so soon, and she still had much to say to Patricia. She felt ill, and cold, and angry with herself for not being strong and having to rely on others. That was what she hated most of all, having to rely on others.

Impulsively she slid her hand into Martha's. 'I do miss you,' she whispered, squeezing the gnarled old fingers.

'I know . . . I know.' Martha's tear-brimmed eyes told the same tale. 'But it won't be forever. Things will come right, I'm sure. We'll just have to trust in the good Lord.'

Later that evening, when she believed everyone else to be asleep, Sonny sat by the cot, gazing at her baby and thinking about the twists and turns of her life. 'Patricia's right,' she murmured. 'Even though I've lost the only home I've ever known, and I'm miles away from everything that was familiar, I'm lucky to have landed on my feet here.'

She stroked the head of her sleeping baby, enjoying the sensation of downy hair beneath her fingertips. 'I'm lucky to have you,' she mused. 'And I've got friends here. David, too. I don't know what I would have done without him.'

But when he seemed likely to fill her mind and creep into her heart she pushed him away. 'Goodnight, sweetheart,' she whispered to Louise. 'Tomorrow Martha and Patricia will be gone, and it'll be just you and me and our newfound friends.' Tears glistened in her eyes. 'Martha says she may not be able to make another journey north. I wonder if that means we'll never see her again.' But she couldn't bear that thought, so she didn't dwell on it for too long.

A few moments later she lay in her bed, with only the bedside lamp to light the dark corners of the room. She felt too emotional for sleep. She got out of bed and went to the window, where she gazed out at the dark night. The view was very different to that from her bedroom at Martha's cottage. There the scene was of dark fields and silhouetted trees, with the occasional glimpse of nocturnal creatures foraging for food. Here, from Ellie's house, it was of terraced houses, pavements and lamp-posts, with cats fighting and occasionally a happy drunkard singing his heart out after a bevy too many. 'This is home now,' Sonny murmured, returning to her baby. 'This is where Fate has brought us.' She wasn't sorry about that in itself. She was only sorry that the future was so uncertain. 'I wonder if we're meant to end our days here?'

She closed her eyes and shook her head and, after pondering on that prospect for a minute, walked across the room and was about to climb into bed when a knock on the door startled her. 'Who's there?'

'It's me . . . Patricia. Can I come in?'

'Come in. It's not locked.' There was no one in this house she needed to keep out.

'I can't sleep.' Patricia made herself comfortable in a wicker chair. 'My conscience won't let me.'

Expecting this conversation to last some time, and not wanting the baby to be disturbed, Sonny put on her new dressing gown. 'Do you fancy a mug of Ovaltine? It might help you to sleep.'

'Lead on.' Patricia was on her feet again, and following Sonny to the kitchen.

When the Ovaltine was made and the two of them were settled in the living room, Patricia in Ellie's favourite chair and Sonny seated opposite, there was a short silence while each of them eyed the other.

Sonny stifled a burst of laughter. 'Wherever did you get that dressing gown?' It was of crimson towelling, with big bright sunflowers all over and a stand-up collar.

Patricia giggled. 'You mean you don't like it? And here was I thinking you'd like to keep it, as a memento of my visit.'

'I've got a new one of my own, thank you,' Sonny reminded her. 'And I'll remember your visit without that, so you can take it back where it came from.'

'I can't. I've had it three years and only just plucked up the courage to wear it.'

There was a little more laughter, then they sat in silence sipping their Ovaltine, during which time Sonny took the opportunity to observe her friend. She thought Patricia seemed on edge. 'You said you couldn't sleep,' she reminded her, 'that your conscience wouldn't let you.'

Patricia's face fell. 'I owe you an apology.'

Sonny immediately thought the worst. 'You weren't lying, about Tony ... what you said?' Her heart turned somersaults.

'It's not about Tony Bridgeman.'

'What then?'

'It's about my behaviour since I've been here. It's about that way I've envied the life you've made ... your

300

friends . . . the baby . . . your job and the flat.'

Sonny realised it was much more than that. 'It's David, isn't it?'

Patricia's gaze dropped to the carpet. 'Are you . . .?' It was a moment before she could bring herself to say it. Even then it stuck in her throat and Sonny had to finish it for her.

'If you're asking whether we're lovers, the answer is no, we're not.'

Relief spread over Patricia's features and a little smile emerged. 'I should have known. Especially after what the other one's done to you.' She gave a sheepish grin. 'I know I'm a silly cow, but I was jealous.'

'Nothing to be jealous about.'

'And you'll forgive me for behaving like a spoilt brat?'

'Is that what you were? I just thought it was a case of bad temper, brought on by three hours of sitting next to Aunt Martha on the train.' Sonny couldn't help but giggle.

'Stop teasing.'

'I will. If you stop apologising.'

'No bad feelings between us?'

'I hope not.'

'Best friends, then?'

Sonny raised her mug of Ovaltine. 'Best friends.'

They drank to friendship and talked a while longer. Afterwards, when the air was cleared between them and they understood each other a little better, they went their separate ways, Sonny to her room and Patricia up the stairs.

Soon the house was quiet while its occupants slumbered. Hours passed and the night sky mingled with the dawn. Soon a new day would begin. A memorable day, when there would be goodbyes, and regrets, and maybe a few tears.

Ready for work, David flung open the stable door. This was the time of day he loved best, when the world was just awakening.

The horse knew his footsteps. Man and beast greeted each other like old friends. 'Ready for your breakfast, eh?' David kept the oats and hay close by. He mixed the right amount, refilled the water bucket and was about to leave for work when a shadow fell across the doorway. The dog at his side growled. He calmed it. 'Easy, boy.'

The visitor was Cathy Sefton. Clad in a long black coat with boots to her knees and her long auburn hair blowing wild, she looked stunningly beautiful. 'I woke early, too,' she said, drawing the coat tighter about her. 'I saw you come across the field and thought we might talk.'

His eyes blazed. 'Are you ready at last to talk about what happened?'

She smiled wickedly. 'You know what happened.'

He shook his head. 'I only know your version of it.'

'What do you want from me?'

In two strides he was before her, towering over her, his face set like stone and his tortured eyes boring into hers. 'I want you to tell the truth – that *you* were driving the car that day, that you deliberately turned it over, that you saved yourself and murdered them. Say it,

Cathy! You murdered my daughter and your own mother and sister. *Say it*!'

She stepped forward, her face uplifted, eyes cunning. 'Why would I do such a terrible thing?'

Gripping her by the shoulders, he bent her away from him. 'For money, and property. For the land we're standing on.' Hatred fired his blood. His voice fell to a harsh whisper. 'You killed so that you could have your own sister's husband!'

'You're mad!' Fear showed in her eyes.

'Yes, I'm mad,' he said. 'Mad enough to break your neck, as you broke hers.'

'No.' She shook her head. 'You need me, as I need you.'

Revulsion coursed through him. 'Get out!' Thrusting her from him, he turned away.

Laughing, she taunted, 'You'll have to throw me out!'

When he spun round he was shocked to see she had flung off her coat and was standing there naked and seductive. 'Make love to me,' she murmured. 'What does it matter about them? They're dead. But we're alive, warm and alive. Love me, David. Please, love me!'

With a cry of rage, he picked her up bodily and threw her out into the cold morning. 'One day . . .' he growled, tossing her coat after her, 'one day I'll see you get the justice you deserve!'

Cathy watched him, evil in her heart, as he strode away with the dog at his heels. 'If I can't have you, she won't either,' she hissed. 'I've killed before, and I can kill again.'

PART THREE

1957

Hope

Chapter Nine

'What do you mean, you can't find her?' Bristling with anger, Tony Bridgeman thumped his fist on the desk. 'You've got all the information. I'm paying you good money, aren't I?' Rounding the desk, he thrust his face into the other man's. 'Or is it that you think I'm not paying you enough? Is that it? Answer me, damn you!'

The private investigator looked at Bridgeman with hard eyes. He had been threatened by better men. This one, for all his mouth and manner, did not intimidate him. In a slow, deliberate voice he answered, 'I've followed every lead, but they all come to a dead end. I think you're wrong about Patricia Burton. If you ask me, she knows nothing about Sonny Fareham's whereabouts. As for Martha Moon, she's a wily old bird. She's not going to tell us anything.'

'Have you searched her cottage? Have you tried roughing her up?'

'If you want that done, you've come to the wrong detective agency. I've got a clean licence, and I mean to keep it that way.'

'Not if I have my way, you won't.'

'There's nothing you can do to me.' The PI could be as hard as the next man when his livelihood was threatened. 'Try harming me and you just might come off worse.'

'So now you're threatening me?'

'No, just giving a warning. I mean, you're an important man . . . thinking of standing for the council if my information is right. You're a big supplier to the building trade and you're making a fortune in property development. On top of all that you're married to a wealthy woman who, I'm given to understand, was the person who got you started and who still finances every venture you undertake.'

Tony Bridgeman was deathly white. 'Go on,' he urged.

The PI did just that. 'Oh, I dare say the day isn't too far away when you'll be a very rich man in your own right, and if Mrs Bridgeman throws you aside you'll probably get a very handsome settlement. But that wouldn't be enough, would it? Not for a man like yourself. I think you want her off your back. I think you want to control your own purse-strings without a woman looking over your shoulder. No man likes to answer to a woman. Degrading, isn't it? Is that how you feel, Mr Bridgeman – degraded?' He saw that the other man was rising to the bait and turned the knife in the wound. 'This other woman, Sonny Fareham . . . nice bit of stuff, is she?' He licked his lips. 'Good in bed? She must have got under your skin or you wouldn't be so anxious to track her down.' He smirked in Tony's face. 'Well now, I wonder what your wife would have to say about that?'

The hard fist that crunched into his face knocked him

clean off his chair. With blood pouring from his mouth, he tried desperately to get up, but Tony was too quick for him. Two vicious kicks caught him full in the face. Then, as he toppled over, he felt himself being snatched by the scruff of the neck and roughly thrown back into his chair.

Tony leaned over him, his voice soft and penetrating. 'Dear me! How easily a man can trip over his own feet! But then it isn't just your feet that are too big, is it? You've got a big mouth as well.' His voice was rasping now, heavy with menace. 'Open it again and I just might have to shut you up for good. Do you hear what I'm saying?'

Even if the other man had wanted to speak, he couldn't. His lips were fat and swollen with blood and his eye was already closing. Sick to his stomach, he merely nodded.

'That's good.'

As he walked away, Tony Bridgeman left another warning. 'Oh, and if you're thinking of blackmail, I would strongly advise against it. Others have made the mistake of underestimating me, and they've been made to regret it.' With that he departed, wincing as he tenderly rubbed his sore fist. In his arrogance, he left the office door wide open.

Behind him he left a man seething with pain and rage.

As he drove back to his office Tony thought what his next move should be. 'The more elusive you get, the more I'm determined to find you, Sonny, my love,' he murmured. 'But we'll have to do it another way. So far your little friend Patricia has been worse than useless to me. But when it comes down to it, she's no different from any other woman, and experience tells me all women can be bought. I just haven't tempted her with the right price.' He grinned. 'I think it's time I upped the stakes.'

As he drove along, he continued to scheme, talking dementedly to himself. 'I'll have to get Lonnie out of the way, though. I can't sack him, because that would be more trouble than it's worth. But the bugger's always there. And I need a clear field with her.'

He drove the car into a petrol station and sat for a moment wondering how he could get Lonnie out of the way for a while. There were any number of ways, but it had to be right. He didn't want suspicions roused.

'How many, guv?' A young attendant in a boiler suit grinned in at the window. 'Daydreaming, eh? Can't blame you in a car like this.' He regarded the white Jaguar with envious eyes and sighed, 'I'd have to win the Pools before I could afford a beauty like this. Or marry a rich widow.' He laughed, rolling his eyes.

Bridgeman didn't know the young man and had never used this out-of-town station before, so he realised the remark was not aimed at him personally. All the same, he took offence. Swinging the door open so that it caught the man hard on the hand, he snarled, 'Fill it up. And don't drip petrol on the bodywork.'

A short time later he continued his journey. He felt better. Some things were going right. Only two days ago he had taken delivery of a new Jaguar, and now he was hoping to duck out of a planned trip with Celia. And in his mind a plan was already coming together. He felt in his bones that everything would turn out just as he wanted. 'I know I should have taken more care of you, Sonny, my love,' he murmured. 'But I promise you it won't be too long before we're together again. And then I'll make it all up to you.'

Exhilarated, he pressed his foot down on the accelerator, surging forward with a thrill. Towards work. And Patricia. And the start of his sly little enterprise.

Tony sauntered into the storeroom. Lonnie was the first to see him. 'Watch out.' He winked at Jock, who was busy unloading a consignment of taps. 'You'd best get that lot stacked away, and quick, or he'll have you on unpaid overtime.'

'Hmm!' Jock had been out with a woman until the early hours and wasn't feeling too sociable. 'With a hangover like I've got, he'll be lucky if I can last the next hour to going-home time, let alone stay on.' All the same, he shoved the fork-lift truck into a lower gear and scooted away.

Patricia had seen the whole thing. 'You're a rotter,' she told the big Irishman. 'Anyway, he'll probably want to know why you're still here. You've been here an hour already.'

'That's because I can't locate the bathroom suites for the Bedford houses.'

'You haven't tried very hard, have you?'

'Hard enough.'

'Come off it! If you take two steps backwards and turn round, you'll find the bathroom suites right there.'

He turned round where he stood and clapped his hand to his mouth in feigned horror. 'You little bugger!' he said. 'You knew where they were all the time.'

'So did you,' she retorted with a grin. 'Because I told you the minute you came in.'

'Well then, I expect I'd better get them into the van.' He bent his head to hers and, with one eye on the approaching figure of their boss, told her, 'You know something? I just might have to wring that man's head off his shoulders.'

'Why's that?'

'Because he's developed a nasty habit of making eyes at my intended bride.'

'I'm not your intended bride.'

'Not yet, maybe. But I'm a stubborn bugger.'

He made her giggle, as always. 'You're also a cheeky bugger,' she said. 'Now sod off!'

Tony Bridgeman got to Lonnie before Lonnie got to the bathroom suites. 'Shouldn't you be at the Bedford site?' he asked, irritated. 'I don't pay you to loiter around the warehouse.'

'Just doing my job,' Lonnie responded uncompromisingly. 'You'll find no one can do it better.' He was proud of his achievements and was not about to let Bridgeman belittle him, boss or no boss, and certainly not in front of Patricia.

Patricia felt a row brewing, and knew it might cost Lonnie his job. 'He came for the bathroom suites,' she interrupted. 'They've only just arrived.'

Tony nodded his head, carefully considering the right way to handle this situation. He knew the value of his foreman, and what he said was right enough. He did do a good job. His three predecessors had been lazy cheating scoundrels who'd had to be got rid of. Since Lonnie had taken it on the job had run like oiled clockwork.

Tony sauntered over to the bathroom suites. 'These the ones, are they?'

Lonnie remained silent. Patricia gave him a sharp dig in the ribs, surreptitiously urging him to make amends to their boss. When he still remained silent she spoke out. 'Like I say, they've only just arrived.'

Tony looked at the pair of them and knew they were lying. But it didn't suit his plan to get rid of either of them just yet. 'You'd better take them and go, hadn't you?' he asked Lonnie.

'That's what I was about to do,' Lonnie replied. What he would have preferred was to swipe that smarmy smile off the bugger's face and put one of the baths over his head!

With Lonnie out of the way, Tony stayed to talk to Patricia. 'He's a good man.'

'The best there is.'

'I wouldn't want you to think I don't appreciate him.' He looked around. The place could have been neater, he thought, and a number of invoices were mixed up with delivery notes. She was getting sloppy. The time would soon come when he would have to get rid of her, but not yet. Not until he'd got Sonny's whereabouts out of her. 'I appreciate you, too,' he lied. 'You're a good despatch clerk, but you're wasted here.'

'Oh! Does that mean you're about to sack me?'

'On the contrary. It means I'm offering you a better position, with a higher salary.'

Patricia was visibly surprised. 'What better position?'

'You know we've just finished the show house on the new site at Woburn?'

'I should do. I've just finished despatching the last lampshade.'

'These are the most prestigious houses we've built so far, and the most expensive. I've been thinking for some time that we should have a representative at the show house. Nothing strenuous. Just someone who can show the customers round. Make the old ones a cup of tea . . . be polite and friendly. Hand out brochures, that sort of thing.'

'You wouldn't want me to sell the places, would you? I'm no good at that sort of thing.' Unlike Sonny, she had no heart for selling.

'No. There'll be an agent on site and he'll do the selling and the serious stuff. But I thought we should have our own person there. Someone attractive and smart, like yourself.' He wasn't lying, because Patricia did have a certain naivety that was in itself attractive, although her looks were a little too vulgar for his taste. 'Of course, you'll have your own desk, and a uniform.'

The offer was tempting, but . . . 'What's the catch?'

'No catch. This is a simple business proposition.'

'I hope you don't think you can buy your way into getting Sonny's address out of me?' Panic rushed through her. 'You'd be wasting your time because I've no idea where she is.'

'I'm not interested in Sonny Fareham's address,' he

314

lied convincingly. 'That's all water under the bridge.'
Dismissing the subject as though it meant nothing to
him, he persisted impatiently, 'Well, do you want the
job or don't you?'

'What about my job here?'

'You can't be in two places at once, but your job
here will be waiting for you when you want it. We'll get
someone in temporarily.'

'And when all the houses are sold and I want to come
back here, will I stay on the new salary?'

'I think we can arrange that.'

'All right. Yes, I'd like to work at the new site.'

Unfortunately, Lonnie didn't get to see Patricia take up
her new job.

That same evening, just before the daylight began to
fade, Tony drove away from the office and, instead of
making his way home, travelled to the site at Bedford.
He knew Lonnie's work habits, and calculated that by
the time he got there it would be turning dusk and
Lonnie would be the only man left on site. He had a
strict routine of going in and out of every house, making
sure the buildings were safe and the materials securely
locked away.

Tonight Lonnie had an unwanted, unseen visitor.

While Lonnie was starting his rounds, Tony was parking his car out of sight. When he came on to the main
site, he saw Lonnie going into one of the houses. Soon
it would be dark and the automatic security lights would
come on. Before that happened, Tony wanted to be
safely out of sight.

Swiftly, silently, he made his way along the row of partially built houses until he came to one that suited his purpose.

The house was finished on the ground floor only, with a ladder serving the upper floor, which was open to the elements. Resting on the chimney-stub immediately in front of the ladder was a square wooden platform. On it were stacked a large number of neatly piled bricks awaiting the bricklayers.

Tony crept up the ladder. Hiding behind a large barrel used for mixing, he waited. It wasn't long before he heard Lonnie on the ground floor. He crouched lower, pressing his body to the barrel, hardly daring to breathe. He stayed like that for what seemed an age, while Lonnie climbed up and then stood at the head of the ladder, looking around, making sure everything was as it should be. Seeing a length of cable lying close to the edge, he swore beneath his breath. 'I'll have a few words to say in the morning! Some poor sod could trip over that and go over the top.' Bending to secure the cable, he kicked a small pile of rubble over the side, leaning forward as he watched it fall on to some debris below. 'Careless buggers, so they are!'

For one excited moment the watching man was tempted to sneak out and send Lonnie over the side the same way. But he decided against it. Firstly, because it might not do the damage he hoped for, and secondly because there was just a chance Lonnie might catch sight of him, or feel the push from behind. The incident had to be accepted as a tragic accident. What he wanted was to hurt Lonnie so badly that he would be out of action for some time; it wouldn't even matter if he was killed. In fact that might be preferable.

Whatever the outcome of tonight's little escapade, Tony did not want to risk being seen. So he stuck to his original plan and patiently waited, pressed flat behind the barrel.

There was one anxious moment when Lonnie leaned on the barrel to make a few notes. But then he turned and made his way back to the ladder.

Lonnie had just begun his descent when Tony made his move. Like a cat in the night, he slid stealthily to the top of the ladder. Peeping over, he saw that Lonnie was already halfway down. Quickly now, he put his whole weight behind the platform of bricks and sent them hurtling downwards.

For a split second Lonnie looked up, his eyes filled with terror as the avalanche rained down on him. There was a cry of 'Jesus!' and then only an eerie silence.

Tony peered cautiously over the edge. All that could be seen beneath the mountain of bricks was one broken, upturned arm and a bloodied face.

With the bricks covering the bottom half of the ladder, it was difficult for Tony to make it to the ground. At the foot of the ladder he didn't hesitate to step on Lonnie's crushed body in order to get to the door.

Once outside, he brushed himself down and ran to his car. Within minutes he was making his getaway, satisfied that no one had seen him, and hoping that Lonnie would be dead before help came.

As he travelled between the lighted lamps lining the long driveway to his house he could see Celia at the window. 'She's always watching!' he moaned, gritting his teeth. 'Watching and waiting, like a big spider.'

When she waved to him he waved back, smiling, playing the part of the loving husband. As he locked the garage door he congratulated himself. 'One down, one to go. All you have to do is bide your time.'

Celia was waiting for him. He had his shower. They made love. Afterwards he ate a meal of steamed fish and baby peas with new potatoes, followed by raspberry pavlova and a glass of bubbly. 'You know how to look after a man,' he complimented her.

'And I intend to look after you on our trip to Jersey,' she said, pulling him on to the carpet before the fire. 'We are still going, aren't we?' She could never be sure. He made promises and hardly ever kept them. But that was the pressure of his work and she had to accept that. This time, though, she was certain he meant to take her away.

'Of course we're going,' lied Tony, his eyes half closing in the heat from the fire. 'I'm looking forward to having you all to myself.' He bit her neck and made her squeal with delight.

When a few moments later she went into the kitchen to get more chilled bubbly he called after her, 'I'll be able to have my wicked way with you twice a day and all night long.'

'Can't wait,' she whispered.

Under his breath he hissed, 'I'm afraid you'll have to, my sweetie. You see, there's been a terrible accident, and I can't leave after all.' He began laughing softly. Soon he was roaring with laughter.

'What's so funny?' She playfully threatened to tip the bubbly all over him.

'Just thinking,' he said.

'About what?'

He had to think fast. He couldn't say he was laughing because tomorrow morning Lonnie was be discovered and he would use that as an excuse to send her away, alone. 'I was thinking of the money,' he answered. 'All that money we're making.'

'You're right,' she said. 'I think we should celebrate.'

He filled the glasses. 'To money,' he said.

She raised her glass, her adoring gaze on his face. 'And here's to the wonderful time we'll have in Jersey,' she murmured.

When he laughed again, she laughed with him.

It was two o'clock in the morning when the knock came on the door. 'I'm sorry to get you out of bed,' the policeman said, taking his helmet off as he came into the sitting room, 'only there's been a bad accident...' Catching sight of Celia in her dressing gown, looking confused and worried, he told Tony quietly, 'There's really no need for your wife to be here, sir.'

'Thank you, officer.' Turning to Celia, Tony suggested, 'Wouldn't you rather go back to bed?' He held his breath, hoping she would insist on staying. He wanted her beside him. He wanted her to hear everything. He knew why the officer had come, although he couldn't understand how they had found Lonnie so quickly.

'I'm staying with you,' she said, nestling up to him. 'I want to know what's happened.'

When the news was broken that Lonnie had been found by an old tramp, who had been using the partially built house as a base, and had been rushed to hospital, Tony did his best to look appalled. 'My God!' He looked at Celia and held her close. 'Is he badly injured?' he asked the officer. 'Will he be all right?'

'I'm told the young man is in a bad way, but you'll need to talk to the doctor about that.'

'I'll have to go to him.' Tony appeared shocked and puzzled. 'I can't understand it. He's always so careful.'

'I'll accompany you to the hospital,' the officer said. 'There'll be a few questions, of course. We'll also need to be satisfied about site security.'

White as a ghost, Celia offered to go to the hospital with her husband. It took Tony a moment to dissuade her. 'I'd rather you didn't,' he said. 'You'll be better off here.'

A short time later, with Celia installed in the kitchen sipping a hot drink and looking more composed, he told her, 'I'll ring the minute I know what's going on. And don't worry. He's a strong, healthy young man. He'll be fine, I'm sure.' More's the pity, he thought bitterly. But he'd got him out of the way.

For the first twenty-four hours, while Lonnie was unconscious, Patricia hardly left his bedside. Now he was awake and she was still with him, holding his hand and gently chiding. 'You're a bloody fool. Why didn't you get out of the way? And why didn't you check the bricks were safe in the first place?'

Wincing as he turned his head, Lonnie croaked, 'Stop

nagging, woman.' His hand tightened over hers and the two of them were closer than they had ever been. 'I could murder a drink.'

'I'll ask the doctor.'

He gave a painful grin. 'Bugger the doctor, he can get his own.'

In a burst of laughter she told him, 'You're as daft as ever.'

A nurse came. Then the doctor. 'You can have a drink,' he said, after examining Lonnie. 'Not coffee, though. Maybe a glass of milk, or cordial.' He also told Lonnie that he was likely to stay in hospital for some weeks – he had two broken ribs, a broken arm and a right leg fractured in two places.

'What about this blinding headache?' Lonnie asked. He closed his eyes. 'Jesus! It's worse than the morning after.'

'The side of your head took a battering,' the doctor told him. 'We still have more tests to do, and you'll be going down for X-ray shortly. You're lucky not to have been killed.'

'Can you patch me up all right, doc?' Lonnie's worst fear was that he might be unable to work. Work, Patricia, and the raising of a good pint were all he lived for.

'That's my job,' the doctor replied. 'You just have to do as you're told.' He looked worried, but only the nurse noticed.

When the doctor and nurse had left them alone, Patricia asked Lonnie, 'Are you sure you don't want me to contact anybody?'

'No.'

'What about your mother? You must have family who would want to know if you were in hospital?'

'I cut my ties with them years ago. If I died tomorrow none of them would care.' He took his hand away from hers. 'There's nobody, so let it be, eh?'

'Let me ring them, Lonnie. I'm sure they would want to know.'

'Why can't you mind your own bloody business?' Closing his eyes, he turned his head. 'I'm tired,' he muttered. 'You'd better go now.'

He had never spoken to her like that before, and she was momentarily shocked. Tight-mouthed, she got up and stared at him for a moment. 'Do you really want me to go?'

He made no response so she hurried away, a little angry and more than a little hurt. 'Sod off, then!' she grumbled when she turned at the door and he was still looking away. 'If that's the way you want it, then sod you!'

Opening one eye he saw her flounce out. 'Oh, Lonnie! You and your quick temper,' he sighed. 'You never did learn how to handle women. It'll serve you right if she doesn't come back.'

He could have taken a lesson from Tony Bridgeman, who was a master at 'handling' women.

After a frustrating day of meetings with the local council he came into his house and went straight to the drinks cabinet. 'Bloody bureaucrats!' he fumed at his wife. 'All day I've been stuck in that dingy office, stupid arguments going backwards and forwards . . . don't want this, don't want that. Christ Almighty! All I want is permission to put up that block of flats. I've revised the plans three times and still they won't budge!' He paced the floor like a wounded cat. 'It's like banging my head against a brick wall. Why won't they listen to reason?'

'They will.' Celia's voice was sugar-sweet as always. 'I'm sure you'll persuade them to your way of thinking.'

'Don't patronise me. It only makes me angry.' Giving her a scathing glance he brushed past her to the living room.

Coming up behind his chair, she gently massaged his temples. 'Have you been to see him?'

Irritated, he got up. 'Who are we talking about now?'

She followed him. 'The foreman . . . the one who was rushed to hospital the night before last. I just wondered if you'd been to see him today?'

Slamming his glass on to the coffee table, Tony laughed. 'Are you deaf or something?' he demanded. 'Haven't I just said I've been tied up all bloody day with the council do-gooders.' He crossed the room in two strides, his eyes glaring into hers. 'You haven't disobeyed me, have you?'

'If you mean have I been to the hospital, no, I haven't.' Guilt flooded her features. 'But I should. You're his employer, and I'm your wife. It's my place to pay a visit.' She hoped he wouldn't press her further, but knew he would. She was right.

He regarded her suspiciously for a moment, realisation dawning. 'Damn your eyes, you've been to that school again, haven't you?'

A little afraid, she turned away.

Grabbing her by the shoulders, he swung her around. 'Answer me, bitch! You've been watching her again, haven't you? Hiding around corners and trailing her, after you promised you wouldn't go anywhere near.'

The tears fell. 'She's my daughter, Tony . . . my own flesh and blood.'

Incensed, he shook her so hard that she stumbled backwards, her spine slamming the wall with such force that she fell forward against him. Taking hold of her, he lowered his voice. 'That girl is not your daughter any more. Do you hear me? You were fourteen years old when she was adopted. You had no right tracking her down. God Almighty! She doesn't even know you. You're strangers to each other. Are you listening to what I'm saying? That girl would look at you and see a stranger.'

'Don't, Tony. Please don't!'

His lips stretched into a thin hard line, hatred darkening his eyes. 'No! *You* don't! Don't play games with me. Don't go behind my back. And most of all, don't take me for a bloody fool.'

'I wouldn't do that.'

'Oh?' Cunning now, he persisted. 'So you haven't made a fool of me by writing out a will where everything, even your half of the business, would be left to this stranger?'

'To my daughter. I abandoned her all those years ago, and I owe her something. I can't give her a mother's love, but I can make sure she always has the best of everything.'

'Oh, I see! As long as the stranger is all right, it

doesn't matter about your husband.'

Her smile was more revealing than she realised. She knew the kind of man she was married to, but she loved him so much she was prepared to do almost anything for him. 'I hope we grow very old together,' she whispered. 'Then, if I die, you'll be so rich it won't matter that all *my* wealth goes to the girl.'

His manner changed, growing kinder, growing more cunning. 'Of course we'll grow old together,' he promised. 'But I'd be much happier if only you'd trust me.'

'But I do trust you.'

'Then prove it. Change your will. If, God forbid, anything was to happen to you, I swear I would take care of the girl.'

She kissed him. 'That's sweet of you,' she said. 'But we've been through all this before, time and again.' Twining her fingers in his hair, she went on, 'If things had worked out with Sonny Fareham, if we had a child we could call our own, things would be different, you know that. Oh, it's true, I would still want to make sure my daughter would be taken care of if anything should happen to me, but nearly everything I own would go to *our* child.'

He liked the sound of that. Even better he liked the idea that she should sign over her entire interests to their child. His child. Sonny's child. It had to happen. If he had his way it still would.

Almost as though she could read his mind she laid her head on his chest and sighed regretfully. 'I'm sorry it didn't work out, Tony. I know how much you wanted a child of your own.'

'Nothing's changed,' he answered. The plan was still the same. Sonny would have his child and Celia would turn over her holdings to it. At long last he would be in control. He would have Sonny, a child of his own, and almost everything Celia owned. How could he lose sight of that goal? He couldn't. Wouldn't!

'I never wanted you to make love with another woman.' Dark envy coloured Celia's voice. 'I'm glad she's gone. I really thought you were beginning to fall in love with her.'

'About the will . . . the girl. I want you to change your mind.'

When she hesitated for a moment he really thought he'd won her over, that she would alter the will in his favour. All he had to do was wait a few months, then he could do away with her. She liked the idea of a cruise, and for once he might indulge her. It would be so easy, and no one would be any the wiser. He tried a different tact, 'How would you feel if I was to leave everything to someone you didn't even know?'

'I never thought of it like that.'

'There you are then. Do you want me to come and see the solicitor with you?'

Her answer was devastatingly final. 'Please, Tony, I won't change my mind. If you had made Sonny Fareham pregnant I would have loved your child as my own, but things haven't turned out the way we planned. It's just you and me. I've set you up in business and given you access to my bank account. Now you're beginning to make it on your own, and I'm very proud of you. Soon, I expect, you won't need my help.' A passion came into

326

her then, a fierce and proud passion he had never seen before. 'But my daughter does. And please don't say she isn't my daughter, because she always will be. She was created by my own father's abuse of me. Because I was so young, and my mother so blind with hatred, that innocent child spent four years in an institution.'

Her voice trembled. 'Because of what my father did to me I'll never be able to give you the children you so desperately want. That's my greatest regret.'

'And mine.' He tried hard not to blame her, but it was difficult. He couldn't even love her. He had never been able to love her.

'We have so much,' Celia said. 'She has so little. When she was adopted, I thought I could forget her. I was wrong. Oh, don't worry, I know she's happy enough, and I won't interfere in her life. I won't cause her more pain. But I mean to repay my debt to her.' Her voice shook with emotion.

He loathed her, but he had to play along. 'You must realise I haven't given up hope of having my own child . . . our child?'

'I was afraid of that.'

'But I love you.'

'And I love you.' Anguish filled her eyes. 'I wouldn't want to live without you.'

'I won't adopt, you know that too, don't you? A man wants to father his own child.'

'Yes.'

'Sonny Fareham was the one we chose to give us a child.'

'But she's gone.'

'Suppose she came back?'

'Do you want her to?'

'Do you want me to stay with you?'

She shook her head, eyes wide as she whispered, 'I won't let you leave me.'

'So, if she came back, things could be as before?' He kissed her on the mouth. 'Until I made her pregnant and we had no further use for her.'

There was a long moment, during which she seemed to be thinking it over and he was mortally afraid that her jealousy might be stronger than her love for him. He need not have worried. Though, when she answered, there was murder in her eyes. 'If that's what it takes to keep you.'

His whole body relaxed. Above her head he raised his eyes to the ceiling, smiling, knowing he still had her devotion. 'You make me feel ashamed,' he murmured. 'No wonder I love you.'

'And Sonny means nothing to you?'

'Only to bear us the child we want.'

'I believe you.'

'And so you should.'

'Do you really think she'll come back?'

'Who knows?' His answer was casual, but Sonny's image burned in his mind as he vowed to get her back if he had to search the world for her from one end to the other.

'If she does come back, yes, things will be the same as before, because I want our child as much as you do.' But she, like him, had her own secret thoughts and as she looked up at the face she adored she prayed with all her heart that they would never see Sonny again.

Satisfied that she was as naive as ever, he declared jauntily, 'I'll go and get freshened up. I'm starving hungry.' He kissed her lips. 'After dinner there's something very important I need you to do for me.'

'What is it?'

'Dinner first, then we'll see.'

After dinner they sat by the roaring fire, enjoying a glass of fine wine. 'You've kept me waiting long enough,' Celia complained. 'What is it you want me to do for you?'

Tony looked at her with admiring eyes. 'You're very beautiful,' he murmured, slyly preparing her for the shock that was to come – though it was true she did look attractive, in cream trousers and a black velour sweater and with pearls at the throat. Her fair hair was newly styled and she had taken a great deal of trouble with her make-up. 'I'm counting on you to represent me in the Channel Isles. The groundwork is already done. All that remains are the formalities. They're preparing plans, photographs, a breakdown of costings and so on. They know what I want, and it will all be ready. I'll speak to them on the phone. They'll welcome you with open arms.'

Instantly she was on her feet, almost in tears. 'No! I won't go without you. You want to build a hotel in Jersey, and I want to see the island. It was to be part holiday, part business. We would have some time for ourselves. That was the whole point, that's what we agreed.'

He took her in his arms. 'Don't let me down,' he pleaded. 'Like you, I want us to have more time together. But I can't leave now, with my foreman in hospital. I'm caught up in that new site at Woburn. It's the most expensive project we've ever undertaken, and if all goes well it stands to make hundreds of thousands in clear profit. You must see, it would be stupid for me to take time away from it now.'

'I don't care about the money.'

'Of course you do,' he said, holding her close and nuzzling her ear. 'You know I'm only thinking of you. You've put so much of your own capital into this project, I wouldn't be much of a man if I didn't look after your interests, now would I?'

Too much in love to see his wickedness, Celia looked up appealingly. 'I miss you all day when you're at work and when you come home you're locked in your office doing paperwork. You can't know how much I've been looking forward to having you all to myself.'

'I know, darling.' He gazed down at her, smiling lovingly. 'And we will go away, trust me. But I can't go now.' He wanted her out of the way so badly he couldn't think straight. 'All you have to do is be present at the various meetings, listen to what's being said and report it all back to me. The real work hasn't even started yet, but I have to know what's being said . . . who's for and who's against. The chatter that goes on before and after . . . the names of those who can be bought. Oh, look, darling, can't you see? I need you there. You're the only one I can trust to do this for me.'

'All right.' Celia could never resist him. 'I'll go, but

I'm not worried about losing money. I'll go because I think it's wrong for you to leave when Lonnie is lying in hospital.'

'I knew you wouldn't let me down.' She was so easy to manipulate!

He was sickened when she pawed him, desperate for love. And when they writhed naked on the carpet it was Sonny who filled his mind. Sonny whose slim warm body he caressed. Sonny who fired his blood. And it was Sonny who filled his dreams when afterwards he lay in his bed. 'I have to find you,' he murmured.

Turning over, he gazed at his wife, whose only crime was loving him. Laughing softly, he got out of bed and stared out of the window. 'You're out there somewhere,' he whispered. 'But not too far away. Not now.' With that thought in mind, he returned to his bed and slept like a baby.

The following morning he made a phone call to Jersey. 'My foreman's been badly injured,' he said. 'And I can't leave here. I'm at the hospital now. But my partner is on her way. No, she's merely an observer, but I'm sending certain plans and schedules over. These should be put to the meeting, and hopefully they'll strengthen my application. Of course I'll be there myself in the final stages. For now, I just need to know the mood of the council ... who's on my side and who isn't. I'm sure you know what I mean.'

An hour later he had delivered Celia to the airport. 'Remember now,' he cautioned, 'watch and listen. Deliver the plans as arranged, but don't get drawn into any arguments. You're there as my representative, to observe and carry information back, that's all.'

'I understand.'

'Good girl. Now then, there will be four meetings in all, spread over three days. After that you're free for the rest of the week. You might as well explore the island ... enjoy the scenery, hire a car, take leisurely strolls along the beaches. Go where your instincts take you, and don't worry about hurrying home.'

When her name was called over the Tannoy he urged her aboard. 'We don't want them to leave without you.'

Celia was obviously distressed. 'I don't want to go without you.'

'What nonsense! Look, darling, you and I should be able to take a fortnight away quite soon. We'll go back to Jersey. You can show me the best places to eat, and we'll make love all night long.' He kissed her long and hard, then propelled her towards the desk. 'Remember what I said. You're not expected to make comments. And when the meetings are done, just enjoy yourself.'

She was still blowing kisses as he walked out of sight.

Patricia put down the receiver. 'Everybody wants their deliveries yesterday,' she groaned.

'That's Friday for you,' one of the storekeepers chuckled as he went by.

'Don't I know it?' she sighed.

Friday was the day when all the invoices had to be entered, with deliveries arriving and leaving and paperwork piling up all around. The deliveries had to be checked, then carefully entered into the system. In addition, any item surplus to site requirements was returned to stock and had to be reinstated in the records. It was Patricia's busiest time.

By evening she was exhausted.

'Tired, eh?'

She looked up to see Jock leaning over the counter. 'Knackered more like,' she said, putting down her pen.

'Know what you mean,' he laughed. 'It's been a long day.' Jock had been run off his feet too. 'I'm off to the pub for a pint, then on to see my old mate Lonnie.'

'Hope you find him in a better mood than when I left him,' she retorted.

'Lover's tiff, eh?'

'We're not lovers!'

'Aye, well, it's not for the want of him trying, I'll give him that.'

'Goodnight, Jock.'

'You're soft on him, too, why don't you admit it? I heard you giving a phone order for flowers to be sent, and I know you've rung at least twice today, checking that he's okay.'

'Neighbourly interest, that's all.'

'What about the boss, eh?'

'What about him?'

'Been to see Lonnie twice from what I can gather. Wants to be certain he has everything he needs, at least that's what he told Lonnie. Seems like he's not such a bad sort after all.'

'You reckon?'

'Aye. Happen we've had him wrong all the way down the line. I mean, it can't be easy running a budding empire, even though he's playing with his wife's money.

Still, I reckon he'll double it for her the way he's going.'

'You've changed your tune. It isn't all that long ago when you were moaning about him being a slave driver.'

'That was before I saw the better side to him. Honestly, though, I don't suppose he's all that bad, as bosses go. He pays decent wages, and look at you . . . you're getting a better job, with more money, and a chance to prove yourself.'

'That's because he recognises my talents.' Laughing, she made another entry in the ledger. 'Anyway, clear off, you're stopping me from working.'

'Have you wondered whether there's another reason why he's promoting you?'

She put down her pen, smirking as she urged, 'Go on then, smart arse. No doubt you're itching to tell me.'

'He might fancy you.'

'And pigs might fly.' Secretly she was flattered. Next to Sonny, she was second-hand goods, but Sonny seemed to have landed on her feet -- and, however much she might deny it, the gorgeous David was obviously very keen. All the same, right now Sonny was terribly lonely. But then so was she. She was also just a bit pissed off by Lonnie's treatment of her. Maybe a little attention from the boss might be welcome after all.

'If the horny bugger has got his eyes on you, you'd better both watch out.'

'Oh, and why's that?'

'Because his wife has a possessive streak. She'll likely have your eyes out. And because, if I know Lonnie, he'll choke the life out of him for even looking at you.'

'Lonnie's not my keeper.'

'Oh!' Jock's brows went up in astonishment. 'Sounds to me like you wouldn't say no if the boss were to crook his little finger at you.'

'What I would or wouldn't say is nobody's business but mine.' She surprised herself by wondering what she would do if Tony Bridgeman were to crook his little finger at her.

Jock had been thinking too. 'I'm sorry,' he apologised. 'Sometimes I don't think before I speak. You're right. With a wife like he's got, why would he want to look at any other woman?' He prepared to get on with his work. 'But I still think we misjudged him. The way he's looking out for Lonnie, it seems he's not a bad sort after all.'

'Goodnight, Jock.'

'You're sure you don't want to come with me? We'll have a short at the pub, then on to the hospital?'

'*Goodnight, Jock!*'

He left, bowing and scraping and making her smile. After he'd gone, she thought about what he'd said. I wonder if Tony Bridgeman does fancy me? And if he does why shouldn't I take advantage? she mused. Maybe I could wangle a new wardrobe out of him . . . or a long exotic holiday. She giggled. It might be a laugh. She thought of Sonny, and her face fell. 'Time you went home, you silly cow!' she said aloud, snatching up the keys. 'Have you forgotten what he did to Sonny? Have you forgotten how he threatened to murder her if she didn't hand over the baby?'

She paused in mid-flight. Thank God he doesn't know she's had his child. She gulped hard as she recalled why Sonny had fled from her home and friends. 'He must never know,' she whispered. 'Tony Bridgeman must never know he's fathered Sonny's child. And above all he must not find out where she is.' She laughed out loud. That's it, you stupid mare! He doesn't fancy you. He fancies the information you might give him. Well, he can think again, the crafty bastard!

In a temper now, she rushed around locking all the doors. All the same, I know what kind of man he is, and Sonny didn't. Maybe I could handle him after all. Besides, nobody else seems to take an interest in me, and Lonnie has already shown his true colours. Mind your own business, he said. Well now, I just might do that. It would serve the bugger right if I did have an affair. The way he spoke to me, I might enjoy rubbing his nose in it!

She locked the doors and left. As she drove away in her little white car she was still bubbling with anger.

Forgiving had never been easy for Patricia.

After a long hard day of meetings, Tony Bridgeman was tired and moody. 'Your work isn't over yet,' he told himself, stripping off and stepping into the hot soothing water. 'There's still a lot to do.'

He lazed in the bath for some time, thinking about Sonny – about what he would do and say when he was face to face with her again. He wondered how difficult it would be to persuade her to come back. Until now he hadn't even contemplated the idea that she might not want to return. 'She'll have to come back!' he said, closing his eyes and raising her image to torture himself.

'Oh, Sonny! Sonny! My plan means nothing unless you're part of it.'

But she would be! He had it all worked out.

With Celia out of the way and Lonnie lying disabled in a hospital bed he had overcome the hardest obstacles. By comparison, the prospect of getting what he wanted from Sonny's old friend should be like taking candy from a babe.

An hour later he was bathed and changed and looking relaxed in light-coloured trousers and casual shirt. 'A treat for a treat,' he chuckled, twirling the champagne bottle in the ice-bucket. 'I know you have a weakness for the drink, my beauty, so I've bought only the best.'

There was more booze in the fridge, and food enough to sink an army. 'There isn't a lady alive who doesn't enjoy being wined and dined . . . and made love to,' he laughed. 'And when that lady is a vulgar, empty-headed creature, it should be all the easier.'

He glanced up at the clock. It was eight-thirty. 'She should be at home,' he murmured, confidently lifting the telephone receiver. 'I doubt if she'll be at the hospital after what Lonnie told me.' He laughed out loud. There was no one to hear him. No one to question why he was pleased with himself. 'Told him to sod off, eh?' He laughed again, enjoying the rift between those two. 'Let's hope, for all our sakes, that she doesn't tell me to do the same.'

That sobering thought wiped the smile off his face. Slowly, deliberately, he dialled the number. 'Come on! Come on!' It seemed to be ringing for an age, and still there was no answer.

* * *

Patricia was asleep. After a quick wash and change, and a cheese sandwich, she had settled down to listen to the wireless. It had been a hectic day and no sooner had she settled down in the armchair than she nodded off, snoring so loudly she drowned out the voice of the news announcer.

The phone rang insistently. Still she snored on.

It was only when the news gave way to a pop group that she woke with a start. 'Bloody hell! It's a quarter to nine.' The ringing of the phone had stopped, but now it began again. 'Who the hell's that at this time of night?' she muttered.

Dog tired and unsteady on her feet she hurried across the room. It might be Lonnie! she mused, patting her hair in place as though the caller might be able to see her. I hope he's ready to apologise, because I don't like us being at loggerheads.

Snatching up the receiver she said tentatively, 'Lonnie? Is that you?' She couldn't think who else it would be. She lived a lonely life. Too bloody lonely.

'It's me, Tony Bridgeman. Look, I know it's late in the evening, but I'd like us to have a chat.'

'Mr Bridgeman!' She stiffened. 'A chat?' For one awful minute she thought she'd done something wrong, or forgotten to do something she should have done. Shaking the tiredness from her head she tried hard to get her thoughts together. 'What's it about?'

He was as charming as ever. 'It's nothing for you to worry about,' he assured her. 'It's just that we need to go through your duties with regard to your new position at the show house. I would have come to see you today, but I've been rushed off my feet. I've got a full schedule over the weekend, and you start in the post on Monday morning, so we have to discuss it tonight.'

'I'm not sure. I was planning an early night.' Patricia was not happy about disappointing him. He was her boss, after all. 'What if I get to the show house a bit earlier on Monday morning? We could go through it all before anyone else arrives.'

He held his breath for a second, afraid his plan was about to fall through. Boldly, he overrode her suggestion. 'Sorry. Someone at the door. It's probably the chap from the estate agent's. They're supposed to be sending someone across. That's why I want you here. Got to go. Look, I'll send a taxi to collect you.'

'Mr Bridge—'

'Be ready!' Quickly, before she could argue, he put the receiver down, then took it off the hook in case she should try to ring him back.

Half an hour later Patricia arrived, agitated and nervous. 'Where's the estate agent?' she asked, looking around as he brought her into the sumptuous living room.

'He should be here soon,' he lied.

'But I thought ... when you were on the phone, you said ...'

He shook his head. 'It wasn't him at all. Just a young man wanting to set up on his own and needing some advice.' His smile was disarming. 'I help where I can.'

Feeling more relaxed, she recalled an earlier

discussion that day. 'Jock was telling me how kind you've been to Lonnie.'

'Lonnie's a good man.'

'I think so too.'

He laughed. 'Oh? I heard you told him to sod off.'

She groaned, a little embarrassed, but said firmly, 'He deserved it.'

'That's a bit harsh, isn't it? When the poor man's lying there helpless.' He could feel her warming to him. And his confidence grew in leaps and bounds.

'Lonnie's not all that helpless,' she replied. 'He's capable of picking up a phone. When he has the decency to apologise, I'll be willing to make up.'

'You're a hard woman.' Taking her coat, he gave her an approving glance. 'Lonnie thinks a lot of you, and I can certainly see why.' He was being blatantly flattering but she did look more than presentable, in a black pleated skirt and pale green blouse – though her make-up, he thought, was too heavily plastered on. 'Might as well make ourselves comfortable,' he said, 'while we wait for the estate agent.' A man who excelled in charming the ladies, he prided himself on being a good liar. 'What about a drink?'

'Coffee, please.'

'Surely we can do better than that?' He knew her weakness and was playing on it. 'I have some excellent champagne cooling?'

She hesitated. Booze always brought out the worst in her. 'I'd rather have a cup of coffee.'

'But I refuse to drink alone.'

'Just a small one then.'

Filling two glasses to the brim, he came and sat beside her on the settee. Handing her one of the glasses, he made a toast. 'Here's to your new post,' he said with a grin. 'You've earned it.'

She took a sip.

The liquid was smooth as silk as it slithered down her throat. Keep a level head, she told herself. He's a devious bugger.

'And here's to Lonnie's speedy recovery.' He raised his glass again.

She took another sip.

'He's a very lucky man,' Tony murmured. 'He may be laid up, but he has you to come home to.'

'We're not engaged or anything like that.'

'But you do have an understanding?' He was making small talk, worming his way inside her head, making her trust him. And all he could see when he looked at her was Sonny. He was impatient and had to force himself to take it one step at a time. If he was to find out what she knew he must be very careful not to frighten her away.

Getting up from the settee he looked out of the window. 'Where in God's name is he? He should have been here an hour ago!'

'I can't stay long.' Patricia, seated on the plush settee, glanced about, overawed by the luxury around her. 'I've promised myself an early night.'

His smile was beguiling. 'Are you looking forward to your new post?' he asked interestedly.

'Yes, I am.' In fact she was thrilled. 'I can't believe I've been given the job ... I mean, looking after those people. Rich people who can afford to buy one of your beautiful houses.' Returning his smile, she said softly, 'You know, I really think Jock's right. You're not such a bad sort after all.'

'We'll drink to that,' he said, chinking his glass against hers.

She took a longer sip. It was good. So good she felt brave. 'And here's to every one of those houses being sold in record time,' she giggled, taking a long deep gulp of the potent liquid.

Secretly gloating, he lost no time in filling her glass again. And again. 'I have your uniform here,' he told her. 'I collected it today. Would you like to try it on?'

'You randy bugger,' she laughed. 'You only want to see me in the nude.' She hiccupped. 'Oh, I am sorry,' she said, putting her hand over her mouth. 'It's the booze. It always does that to me.'

He filled her glass once more. 'But I thought you liked the stuff.'

'That's the trouble. I like it too much,' she confessed shamefacedly. Then she took another long gulp. 'Expensive stuff, this.'

'Very expensive.' He almost had her. Soon he would make his first move. 'But then you're a very special lady and this is a very special occasion.'

'You're a liar, Mr Bridgeman.' Falling back against the cushions, she roared with laughter. 'The estate agent isn't coming, is he? You've got me here to have your wicked way with me.'

He gave a sigh of relief. For a minute he'd thought

she'd guessed the real reason why he'd brought her here. 'I won't deny the thought had crossed my mind,' he murmured. 'As I said before, you are a very attractive lady.'

'I'm a drunkard!'

'No! There's no harm in enjoying a drink. We all do.' Taking her glass out of her hand he put it to her lips. She kept her mouth tightly shut for a second, then, to his relief, took another, more genteel sip. 'You're a bugger!' she laughed. 'You want to get me pissed so you can get between my legs. Admit it. You fancy me rotten, don't you?'

'Would you mind if I did?'

She looked at him through an alcoholic haze. 'Or perhaps you don't fancy me at all,' she said with a sad little sigh. 'Perhaps you still fancy Sonny.'

'Forget about her,' he said, feigning impatience. 'Let's talk about you.'

'What's there to say?' He was too close – and she was too lonely.

He kissed her hard on the mouth, making her senses reel. 'What if I said I find you very attractive? That I have an uncontrollable urge to take you to bed?'

She almost collapsed with relief when the phone rang and he had to loosen his hold on her. 'Don't go away,' he said. 'We've still got a lot of talking to do.'

Muddle-headed, she watched him take the phone call. It was his wife. 'Yes, darling, I'm fine,' he answered. 'Working hard as usual. I've brought home a pile of papers to deal with.'

While Celia was speaking he turned to make certain

his guest had not made her escape. When she glanced up he winked intimately, at the same time putting his fingers to his lips, warning her not to speak or make a sound. 'Then it was a good meeting?' he said into the phone. 'Well done, darling. Yes, I love you. I'd better get on with my work, or I won't get a wink of sleep tonight. All right. Yes, of course I love you. I'll call you in the morning. Goodnight, darling.'

Returning to Patricia, he slid his arm around her shoulders. 'You're wrong in thinking I'm interested in Sonny,' he said. 'As far as I'm concerned she never existed.' He shrugged his shoulders as though the matter was an irritant to him. 'I don't even know where she is.'

Patricia giggled drunkenly. '*I* do.'

It was all he could do to make himself sound casual. 'Oh, really?'

'Sonny's my friend.'

'That's good.'

Leaning forward, she whispered in a slurred voice, 'If I tell you a secret, will you promise not to tell anyone else?'

He was so elated he thought his heart would stop. At last! She was going to tell him where Sonny was. 'Not a word, I promise,' he said.

Placing the tips of her fingers across her mouth, she looked all around, then, putting her mouth close to his ear, she confided, 'I've never told anyone else, but I was an alcoholic. I went to special meetings for a whole year. Sonny knew, though. She made me go. She even came with me. Oh, that Sonny! She's a real good friend.' Patricia began to cry. 'I don't deserve a friend like her.'

Tony was wild. Pushing her away, he demanded, 'Is that it? You're an alcoholic? Is that your "secret"?'

She saw his rage and for a minute she was confused. Suddenly realisation dawned. 'You lying bastard! You didn't want to talk about my new job, did you? You only want to know where Sonny is. That's why you've promoted me, isn't it? A sweetener to loosen my tongue! A bribe! Just now, when I told you about my drinking, you thought I was going to give you Sonny's address, didn't you? That's why you've got me pissed!' She scrambled up, steadying herself on the arm of the settee and staring at him through bleary eyes. 'I'm going home, before I tell you what I really think of you.'

Her senses were reeling. She wanted to cry. He had made a fool of her, and she hated him for it. Her pride was hurt, and she wanted to kill him.

His hands were on her now. Not gentle any more, but hard and pressing, bruising her flesh. 'I'm sorry,' he murmured, kissing her neck. 'It's all right, you know. You can tell me where she is.'

Pushing him off, she almost fell over. Filled with a terrible anger she screamed at him, 'Yes, I do know where she is, you bastard! I've known all along what happened between you two – how you wanted to get her pregnant and force her to hand the child over. Well, it's finished, do you hear? That night, when you asked her to bring some documents to this house, Sonny heard what you said – that if she got pregnant and wanted to keep the baby you'd murder her.'

The words fell one over the other, out of her control, telling him things he should never know. 'Well, they're safe from you now. You'll never find them.'

Suddenly he was smiling. ' "Them"?' His eyes narrowed with pleasure. 'So I did make her pregnant! She's had the baby and she's afraid I might take it from her, is that it?'

Patricia's heart sank. 'I didn't mean that,' she whimpered. 'I'm drunk. I don't know what I'm saying when I'm drunk.'

'Where is she?' he demanded. He wasn't smiling any more.

'Sonny's the best friend I've ever had.'

Snarling, Tony struck out with a clenched fist. Blood spurted from Patricia's nose. 'I won't hurt her,' he said, trembling, 'but I have to find her. I love her, don't you see? I know I shouldn't have fallen in love, but I did, and now I can't sleep for thinking about her. I'm going crazy.' His laughter was insane. 'I even paid a private detective to find her, but he was a fool. I knew you were keeping the truth from me, so I decided to work on you. I even put your boyfriend in hospital so he wouldn't be a nuisance.' When her eyes opened wide with horror he laughed again. 'You didn't know that, did you? And you didn't know that I sent Celia away so the two of us could have as much time together as it took.' He looked around, his voice falling to a terrible whisper. 'So, you see, we're alone, just the two of us. I could kill you here and now. I could hide your body underneath one of the buildings, and nobody would ever know.'

Patricia was shaking uncontrollably. She knew now, beyond a shadow of doubt, that Tony Bridgeman was insane. 'Please don't,' she pleaded. 'I can't tell you where

Sonny is. Why don't you leave her alone? She's made a new life.'

'*Bitch!*' He dragged her by the hair into the kitchen. The more she screamed the more he yanked on her hair, until it was almost pulled out by the roots.

In the kitchen he rammed her head under the hot-water tap and turned it on. The water cascaded down her neck, warm at first, then growing hotter, burning her neck. '*Where is she?*' he screamed.

She was sobbing, unable to speak, helpless in his iron grip. Suddenly she was facing him and his eyes put the fear of God in her. She didn't see his fist. She just felt a hard blow against her temple. Swaying, she held on to him, begging, 'Don't hurt me any more. *Please!* Don't hurt me any more!'

His answer was two sharp blows – one to her face, the other to her stomach. She fell to the floor, writhing in agony, and he raised his foot threateningly, his voice grating as he asked again, '*Where is she?*'

Dazed and in pain, she looked at him from a bloody face. For a moment she couldn't speak. He waited. She opened her mouth and he bent closer. Through her fogged mind came a recollection of something that he had said. Slowly, she mouthed the words, 'Sef . . . ton . . . House.'

There was a long, painful pause, during which time he dug her hard in the ribs, 'Sefton House!' he repeated impatiently. '*Where damn you? Where?*'

She saw his fist raised to hit her again. 'No!' She heard her own voice, feeble and small. 'Don't . . . hit me again.'

Falling to his knees he grabbed her by the shoulders and pulled her up. Cradling her as a woman might cradle a child, he said softly, 'Sefton House. Where is it?'

The tears rolled down her face. 'Saml ...' She was choking, hurting all over.

'Go on!' he urged gently, 'Saml ...?'

'Saml ... es ... bury.' She gave a great sigh. 'Please,' she said brokenly, 'don't hurt her.'

'Listen to me, bitch,' Tony murmured. 'Don't try to warn her. And not one word to the police about what happened here, or I swear I'll finish you off. You know I'd do it without a second thought.' He sniggered. 'But you won't tell, will you? Because you know that even if they put me behind bars I'll find you when I get out. I'll search the four corners of the earth if I have to.'

Satisfied that she'd heard every word, he threw her to the floor, grabbed a coat and his wallet and ran from the house.

'Sefton House, Samlesbury,' he wrote on a scrap of paper he found in the glove box. With a low, triumphant chuckle he started the engine and roared away. 'North,' he told the car. 'We're heading north.'

Patricia heard the front door slam. She knew he had gone, but she still lay there, broken and hurting, drifting in and out of consciousness.

It was almost four hours later when the chiming of the grandfather clock stirred her senses. *One ... two ... three.* Almost immediately the telephone started ringing. Persistently, angrily almost. Over and over. She rolled to one side, tried to get up, but fell back again.

For a minute she didn't know where she was, only

that she was badly hurt and that, because of her, Sonny was in great danger.

Slowly, agonisingly, things began to take shape in her mind. Tony's parting threat made her shiver. 'Don't try to warn her . . . not one word to the police or I'll finish you off.'

With agonising slowness, clinging to the kitchen stool, she dragged herself up. Exhausted, she looked around. The telephone was still ringing. It stopped for a short interlude, then started again.

'Sonny.' The name issued from between her bruised and bloody lips. 'What have I done?' For what seemed an age she lay across the stool, trying to gain strength, knowing that somehow she had to warn Sonny.

Over the next few minutes, she found the energy to get to the sink, where she stood doubled over, her every rib feeling as though it was smashed. Crying out, she reached forward and turned on the tap, remembering how he had burned her neck, afraid he might come back and hurt her again.

She splashed cool water over her face and head. When the water ran down the plughole it was red with blood. She kept on until it ran clear.

On leaden feet she made her way to the living room. The sight of her blood on the carpet made her cringe. Taking a moment to lean on the wall and recover herself she went forward. Her handbag was on the settee. She scooped it up and went into the hall. Here she had to sit down to rest, on the chair by the telephone, which began ringing again, startling her. She didn't know whether to pick it up or not. Could it be him? Was he checking whether she was still here? Maybe it was his wife.

Her hand reached out to pick up the receiver. If it was Celia, she should be told what her husband had done. She put the receiver to her ear. The sound of a woman's voice at the other end made her panic. As though it was burning her hand she dropped the phone, leaving it to dangle against the table. The woman's voice was shouting, '*Tony! Tony!*'

Patricia reached out to pick up the receiver again, but stopped. 'I'll search the four corners of the earth if I have to.' His words were etched on her brain. He would kill her. He would find her and kill her. He was completely insane.

As she struggled to stand she caught sight of herself in the hall mirror. 'My God!' Her face was swollen, almost unrecognisable. Her hair was dripping wet, and her clothes torn. 'My God!' And this was only a taste of what he could do to her if she told . . . if she tried to warn Sonny.

Slow step by slow step she went back to the living room and found her coat where Tony had thrown it over a chair. She put it on and left the house. At the foot of the drive she leaned over the wall and brought her heart up. Then she staggered towards the main road.

It was pitch black. She had to get home. She had to think.

The taxi driver laughed. 'Been out on the tiles?' he asked with a wink. 'Lucky sod.'

During the short journey back to her flat she made no conversation. The driver thought she was drunk and left her alone.

When she got out, and almost fell over, he laughed. 'That's what they mean when they say "legless", is it?' he chortled. 'Want me to help you inside, lady?'

She shook her head and he went away, still chuckling. He U-turned in the road and was soon gone from sight.

It took all Patricia's energy to get from the street up to her flat and into the living room. Once there she felt the world coming in on her. Desperately she tried not to lose her senses. Sitting in the chair by the phone, she relived the night in her mind. The pain had gone now, and only a terrible crippling numbness remained.

Slowly it spread all over her, until she could hardly think any more. With trembling fingers she picked up the receiver and dialled Martha's number. It seemed an age before the phone was answered. 'Help me,' Patricia pleaded. 'Please, Martha . . . help me.'

'Patricia, is that you?' Martha was scarcely able to recognise the small, lost voice. 'Are you ill?' An unnerving silence answered her. 'Patricia, are you ill?' More silence. Then, 'I'm coming right over.'

Twenty minutes later, Martha stepped out of a taxi and made her way straight up to Patricia's flat. The door was partway open, so she pushed her head inside and called out, 'Patricia!'

Receiving no answer, she went in – and saw Patricia lying beside the dangling phone, her swollen face looking up to the ceiling and her body as still as death. 'Dear God!' Martha raised Patricia in her arms. 'Patricia! It's Martha. Who's done this to you?' It was like holding a corpse. Gently she laid her down again.

Keeping her gaze on that battered face, Martha rang for an ambulance. 'Please hurry!' she cried. 'She's in a bad way.'

It was only minutes before the ambulance arrived, and only another few moments before it was speeding on its way to hospital.

The baby wouldn't stop crying. 'Missing yer mammy, are yer?' Cradling Louise in her arms, Ellie paced up and down the bedroom. 'Jesus, Mary and Joseph!' Glaring bleary-eyed at the bedside clock, she groaned, 'Here I am walking the floor, instead o' snoring to me heart's content.'

After a while the baby fell asleep. 'Thank the good Lord,' Ellie sighed, tucking the infant into its cot. 'Another minute and I'd be fit for nothing but the knacker's yard.'

She stroked the sleeping face. 'I don't blame yer for missing yer mammy though. She's a ray of sunshine on a wet morning, that's yer mammy.'

She thought about Sonny and a smile rippled over her chubby face. 'Wouldn't it be grand if her and David got together, eh? I don't know who yer real father might be, and it's none of my business, but I'll tell yer this, me beauty . . . you could never get a better daddy than David, and that's for sure.'

Sighing, she gazed towards the window. The curtains were open and outside the sky was already glowing with a new day. 'I know yer mammy will be missing you, too,' she cooed. 'What! I had the devil of a job persuading her to spend a night away from yer.'

She sat by the cot, gently rocking it and dreaming aloud. 'One night, that's all,' she murmured, 'when yer mammy and David could go off together, even if it is only on business.' She wished with all her heart that it had been more than that, but she knew the score and she knew it would be a long time before David wanted another woman.

'It isn't just David,' she told the sleeping child. 'It's yer mammy too. There are things in their lives that won't let them get together the way they should.' She hung her head and thought awhile, then, in a softer voice, she confided, 'Shall I tell yer something, me beauty?' Cocking her head as if waiting for an answer, she continued, 'I think yer mammy's been through a bad relationship – so bad she can't even bring herself to talk about it.'

She gazed at Louise and was struck to the heart by her perfect innocence. 'Ah, but yer lovely,' she sighed. 'No wonder yer mammy thinks the sun shines out of yer little arse.'

She leaned over and gave the baby a gossamer kiss. 'Sure, the way she carried on, you'd think I weren't capable of looking after a baby!'

Mimicking Sonny, she reeled off a list of instructions. 'Don't forget to feed her ... change her bum ... bring up her wind this way and brush her little curls that way.' She threw out her hands in a helpless gesture. 'God love us, I've had children of me own,' she said, exasperated. 'But yer a special little angel, so ye are.'

Smiling down on the sleeping face, she thought how more like Sonny the child grew every day. The eyes were already changing from blue to green and the fine wispy hair had taken on a soft brown glow. 'The pair of yer will have to learn how to be away from each other now and again,' she said sternly. 'It isn't good for a mammy and child to be inseparable.'

She climbed back into her own bed, still tutting. 'The way yer lovely mammy clings to yer, anybody would think you were about to be stolen away, so they would!'

Tony Bridgeman coaxed the car along the street. Having left home in a hurry he hadn't realised how low the Jaguar was on petrol. So far all the garages on the way had been closed, but now he was sighing with relief because here was one with its lights still burning.

'Be open, you bastard!' he said, driving the car into the forecourt. It was coughing and spluttering, starting and stopping, and he was getting more and more irritated.

Two yards from the pumps the car came to a halt. Scrambling out, Tony gave it a vicious kick. 'Shouldn't do that, mate,' came a Lancastrian voice. The attendant was in his twenties, with a big round face and a flat cap perched over his fair hair. 'It won't do you no good.'

Tony was in no mood for chit-chat. 'Push it to the pump, will you?' He stood back, waiting for the young man to exert himself. 'And be quick about it.'

The man looked him up and down, taking an instant dislike to this arrogant southerner. 'I sell petrol,' he said. 'I'm not your bloody lackey!'

Tony stuck a fiver in his hand. 'Push it to the pumps,' he said again, 'and fill it up.' He stared at the man with hard, unfriendly eyes, 'Afterwards there might be another fiver if you give me some information.'

'Okay.' The attendant closed the driver's door and went to the rear of the car. Setting his legs apart and his back square he bent to the task.

It wasn't easy. At first the Jaguar wouldn't shift. There was a minute when the young man looked at Tony, silently wondering if he was going to give a helping hand. 'Some work, some watch,' he muttered, swearing under his breath when Tony sauntered over to the pumps, urging, 'Get a move on, man. I've got important business to attend to.'

Panting, the young man eventually rolled the car alongside the nearest pump. He filled the tank and held out his hand for the money. 'She's a thirsty bugger,' he commented, lingering a minute to admire the Jaguar's sleek lines. 'Cost a bob or two, I'll bet.'

'Which is no concern of yours.' Normally Tony would have bathed in the flattery. But not today. Not when he was so close to Sonny.

By the time the attendant got to the cash register in the tiny office, his breath recovered, he was whistling cheerfully. It would take more than a snotty bugger like this one to get him down, he thought.

Tony followed him into the office. 'Which way is Samlesbury?'

'Do you want the quickest way or the prettiest?' He corrected himself. 'Being as it's still not daylight, you'll not want the prettiest, will you?'

'Get on with it!'

'Right.' He gave Tony his change, then began whistling again. When Tony gave him the second fiver, the whistling stopped and the attendant's face was wreathed with pleasure. 'Straight down this road,' he advised. 'Turn left at the end and follow the lane for about six miles. That should fetch you straight into Samlesbury.'

Tony thrust a piece of paper under his nose. 'I'm looking for this address,' he said, pointing to his own handwriting. 'Do you know it?'

'Sefton House?' The young man irritated Tony by chewing his top lip while he thought.

'Come on, man!' Tony took out a pound note and held it in front of the man's face.

It did the trick. 'After you've gone through the village, keep going straight on for about two miles. Turn down by the Red Lion pub, and you'll find Sefton House about three miles along the lane, on your right-hand side. It's a big house, set back behind tall iron gates.'

He stared through the office window as Tony roared away. 'More money than manners,' he muttered, making a rude gesture. Then he fell into the comfortable armchair, lit a fag, and put his feet up. 'First time we've been open all night long,' he reflected, 'and I'm already eleven quid ahead.'

Tom Sefton was by nature a heavy sleeper, but since losing his wife he had rarely slept right through the night. He missed her warm body next to his; he missed her gentle snoring; and he hated the mornings, when he would wake and she was not there.

Tonight, for some reason, he couldn't sleep at all. He had watched the night thicken and fade, and now he stood by the window, watching the morning make its mark on the day.

'See that, my lovely?' he asked, pointing to the bright, golden rim in the heavens. 'Looks like it'll be one of those lovely crisp days you so enjoyed.' He made a soft sound, like a sob. 'It's such a beautiful sky,' he whispered. 'If only you were here to share it with me.'

His eyes filled with tears and now, as his thoughts turned to his daughter, there was an almighty ache in his heart. 'We raised a bad 'un, my lovely,' he muttered, as if continuing a conversation with someone close and very dear. 'Sometimes, God forgive me, I believe it were her that took you from me, and then other times I think it's so awful it couldn't be true.' Unbearable pain darkened his eyes. 'If I thought . . .' He gulped back the tears. 'But, no! I won't believe she could be that bad.'

He often cried in the darkness, when he was alone and no one but his lovely could see.

Now, in these early hours of a new day, he did his crying and was about to dress and start his day when his eyes were drawn to a car's headlights in the lane. Intrigued, he poked his head out of the window. 'Somebody's coming to the house,' he muttered in astonishment. 'Who can it be at this time of morning?'

When the car drew to a halt, he quickly retreated in case he should be seen. 'One of her fancy blokes, I shouldn't wonder!' Ashamed and disgusted, he had long given up on his despicable daughter.

Startled by the insistent knocking on the front door, Cathy Sefton jumped out of bed. The fear of being found out was always with her. It made her late to sleep; it filled her sleep with nightmares; and such was her guilt that every unusual sound, every strange knock on the door, filled her with terror.

She ran to the window. In the light from the lamp outside the front door she saw him. She did not recognise him, but when her eyes caught sight of the long white car she knew it was not the authorities.

Bolder now, she threw open the window, 'What do you want?' she called out.

Tony Bridgeman looked up. 'I'm here to see Sonny Fareham.' He worried about revealing his business to a stranger, but felt he had little choice.

Intrigued, Cathy told him to wait, she'd be right down. 'Well now!' She could hardly hide her delight as she rushed about making herself presentable. 'So who might this be, come to see our little friend?' Her devious mind was working fast. 'He could be the baby's father – the husband maybe?' She was praying that, whoever this man was, he had come to take her rival from these parts. 'This should give David food for thought. And with a bit of luck it might get her out of our lives for good.'

When she opened the door, the visitor seemed taken aback by her appearance. Cathy Sefton was at her most devastatingly attractive. She had on a white silk negligee and her long auburn hair was loose about her shoulders. 'You've come to the wrong place,' she said. 'Sonny Fareham doesn't live here.'

He stepped towards her threateningly. 'Just now I saw someone at an upstairs window. Was that her? Has she told you to send me away?'

'My, you are a suspicious devil! The person you saw at the window was probably my father . . . he has a habit of not sleeping.' She could hardly keep the loathing from her voice. 'As for sending you away, that's the last thing I want.' She opened the door wider. 'Come in. We can talk better inside.'

'I haven't driven hundreds of miles to stand and talk with you.' He glared at her. 'I've had a hard drive. I haven't eaten, and I'm totally shattered. Now, just tell me where she is and I'll be on my way.'

'She's away until this evening, so you won't get to see her yet.' Cathy looked him up and down, liking what she saw. 'I make a strong cup of coffee, and I always keep a full larder,' she teased. 'And you look like you could take the weight off your feet.'

'She's away, you say?'

Her smile was insinuating. 'She's away overnight . . . with her boyfriend.' Giving him an intimate wink, she let him think the worst.

Her implication sent him crazy. Thrusting his way past her, he growled, 'You're a liar! She's here. I know she is!' He ran across the hall, throwing doors open one by one and peering into the rooms. 'I'm not leaving without her.'

Still smiling, Cathy closed the front door. 'I've already told you, you won't find her here.' Amused, and beside herself with glee at his obvious obsession with Sonny, she stood calmly aside while he went through all of the downstairs rooms.

When he flung open the kitchen door, he was faced by an angry elderly man. 'This is my kitchen.' Tom

Sefton squared up to the intruder. 'What d'you want?'

With one vicious swipe, Tony sent him flying across the room. It meant nothing to him that Tom hit his head on the coal-scuttle as he went down.

Cathy Sefton had heard her father make the challenge. She heard the thud and knew he had been hurt. She came to the door and looked inside. Tom was struggling to get up, his head bleeding badly, and his legs giving way beneath him. 'Serves you right!' She spat out the words. 'You'll never learn, will you?' She made no effort to help him.

Behind her, Tony had raced upstairs and was running from room to room, calling out Sonny's name, telling her how much he loved her, and how he wanted to take care of her and the baby. 'What you heard that night at the house ... it was nothing. *She's* nothing! I want rid of her. It's you I want ... you and the baby. Why didn't you tell me you were pregnant? You had no right to keep it from me! It's *my* child. *Why didn't you tell me?*'

When at last he realised that Sonny was not in the house he came down the stairs, a weary, vengeful man with only one thought in his dark heart, and that was to find her.

'I told you she wasn't here.' Cathy Sefton met him at the foot of the stairs, her brown eyes boring into his. 'Now will you believe me?'

He spoke in a harsh whisper, his eyes unflinching as he wound a hank of her hair round his fist and drew her to him. 'This boyfriend she's with. Who is he? Where are they?'

Pain excited her. And he excited her. But that was

one thing, and Sonny Fareham was another. 'Ask the old man,' she told him, jerking a thumb in the direction of the kitchen.

Tony pushed her away with such force that she almost lost her footing. When he went at a run towards the kitchen, she went too.

Tom Sefton had heard and was waiting. 'I don't know anything,' he said as they approached. 'And if I did I wouldn't tell you.'

Tony hit him harder, but still he insisted that he knew nothing.

'Leave him to me.' Cathy pressed her face so close to her father's that the blood from his gashes coloured her skin. 'I know he asked you to mind the horses until he got back this evening. What I don't know is where he and that – ' her face convulsed with hatred – 'woman have gone.'

'I don't know where they've gone. He didn't tell me.'

'I didn't believe you when you told me that before,' she told him. 'And I don't believe you now.'

Tony took Tom by the scruff of the neck. 'I don't know what goes on between you and her – ' he flicked a glance over his shoulder at Cathy – 'and I don't care. All I want is for you to tell me where Sonny and the man are, and I'll be gone from here.'

Tom spat in his face.

Incensed, Tony put his hands around Tom's weathered throat and began to choke the life out of him. 'No!' Cathy Sefton surged forward. 'Don't. You'll kill him.'

He laughed. 'I wouldn't have thought that would bother you.'

'It doesn't,' she answered. 'It's just that he can't tell you anything if he's dead – and I don't want the authorities here.' The same old fear crept back but she managed to compose herself. 'Besides, it doesn't matter. She'll be back this evening. I'll take you to her then. Meanwhile, there's food and drink here, and you can rest.'

He considered that for a minute. He was ravenous. A shot of whisky wouldn't go amiss either. And he was so weary he could hardly think straight. 'You could be right,' he answered, letting the old man fall senseless to the floor. 'I don't want Sonny to see me like this . . . tired and unshaven.' He touched the bloodstain on his jacket. 'Can you get this out?'

'Don't worry about that,' she told him, 'I'll get it out.' She slipped the jacket from his shoulders and laid it on the back of a chair. 'Sit down, before you fall down. I'll get you some hot food.' She threw open a cupboard. There were two half-empty bottles, one of gin, one of whisky. 'Don't touch the stuff myself,' she said. Her gaze dropped to Tom Sefton lying face up on the quarry tiles. 'But he likes a drop now and then.'

'Whisky.' Tony slumped into a big pine chair. 'And don't stint.'

While Cathy poured she chatted. 'So! You're the father of her baby? I wondered . . . thought she might have run away from a bad marriage.' She eyed him up and down. '*Are* you married, you and her?' She gave him the drink and watched him throw it down his throat. She poured him another, but he refused it. 'Hot food, you said.' He needed to keep a clear head for when he came face to face with Sonny.

Cathy laughed. 'The strong silent type, eh?'

Tony closed his eyes and ignored her while she bustled about cooking him a huge bacon omelette. She made a mountain of toast and when the meal was ready, placed it in front of him. He wolfed it down, aware that she had her eyes on him the entire time.

When he was finished he wiped his mouth on the back of his hand and leaned back in the chair, addressing her in angry, clipped tones. 'The jacket. Do it now.'

She did as she was told. This man was here to help her. The least she could do was help him.

While she stood at the sink, rubbing at the stain on his jacket, he asked, 'What do you know about this man she's with?'

Satisfied that the jacket was free from stain, she hung it carefully in front of the range. 'The heat will dry it gently,' she promised.

'I asked you a question.'

Cathy looked down at her father. His colour was beginning to return. 'You nearly finished him off,' she said with a scornful little laugh, 'That's for me to do, in my own way.' Her way was more subtle; she would wear him down, make him weary of life – so weary that he would end it.

Sensing her visitor's growing impatience she came and sat opposite him. 'His name is David Langden.'

Tony sat forward in his chair. 'I want to know all about him,' he said. 'And her. I want to know what's been going on.'

Chapter Ten

Sonny looked radiant. She had had a good night's sleep and a refreshing shower and she had chosen to wear her favourite outfit. Blue was her best colour; it brought out the sea green of her eyes and the golden glow in her brown hair. She didn't have too many clothes – most of her earnings went on beautifying the flat and meeting the needs of baby Louise. The straight-skirted two-piece was a new addition to her wardrobe. When David had asked her to accompany him to the art exhibition in Scarborough where his sculptures would be on display, she'd gone straight out and bought the suit. It was smart enough for David's big occasion and feminine enough to turn heads as she walked into the breakfast room.

'You look wonderful,' he said as she sat down. 'But,' he added regretfully, 'I don't think you should come to the exhibition after all.'

Sonny was deeply disappointed. 'But I thought that was why you invited me,' she protested. 'I've been looking forward to seeing your work exhibited. It means a lot to you, I know, but it means a lot to me as well. Now suddenly you don't want me there. Why?'

His blue eyes twinkled. 'Because everyone will be looking at you, when they should be looking at my carvings!'

Her smile was one of relief. 'That was wicked of you.' But she liked him that way. He had a wonderful smile and beneath that hard, aloof exterior beat a sensitive and loving heart. She had seen it when he talked to Ellie and the children and, just occasionally, she had sensed it when he looked at her.

The waitress remained by the door, giving Sonny time to decide what she wanted. 'She's a good-looker, I'll give her that,' she remarked to her companion, a skinny girl with drooping eyes and a magnificent mop of hair.

'Generous too,' said the skinny one. 'When the porter took her bag to her room last night she gave him five bob.' Usually it was a shilling or, on a good day, half a crown. 'But she weren't showing off or nothing like that. She even stopped to have a friendly chat with him ... told him how she and the young man had come to sell his carvings at that art exhibition at the Centre.' She pursed her lips and regarded Sonny through admiring eyes. 'Do you think this is the first time she's been in a posh hotel like this?'

The other waitress also regarded Sonny, but for a different reason. 'Dunno,' she answered. 'But I'll tell you this ... I reckon she's been through hard times.'

'Never!' Now the skinny one was scrutinising Sonny more closely, observing the cut of her fine two-piece and the manner in which she wore it, like someone who knew how to. 'Been through hard times?' she echoed. 'I can't see how you've come to that conclusion,

Doreen. I mean, just look at her. That two-piece must have cost a pretty penny. Look how she's smiling ... like she hasn't a care in the world.'

Doreen was more philosophical. 'Clothes don't make the man,' she said. 'Nor the woman. You have to look in the eyes. Beneath that smile her eyes are sad ... kind of haunted, if you know what I mean.'

The skinny one dug her in the ribs. 'It's your turn,' she said. 'Go and get their order, or you'll have the fellow after you.'

Doreen giggled like a schoolgirl. 'Wouldn't mind that neither.' She winked. 'He's the best-looking bloke we've had in here for years. A wood-carver, you say? Well, I'm telling you, if I thought he'd lay a hand on me for not taking his order, the pair of 'em could sit and wait till Kingdom come!'

However, she did take their order, because she had a job to keep and bills to pay, and a bloke like him wouldn't look twice at somebody like her, not when he had a picture of loveliness sitting right across from him. Funny though, she thought, scribbling their order into her little white pad, they weren't lovers, because if one guest crept into another guest's room in the middle of the night the maids were the first to know and the waitresses the second. These two had spent the night in their own beds. Shame. A crying shame, that's what it was.

'Two teas,' she confirmed, looking from one to the other. 'A full breakfast for the gentleman.' She gave him one of her nicest smiles, going weak at the knees when he smiled back. 'Scrambled eggs for the lady. And toast between you.' She pointed to the buffet counter. 'Help yourself to juice and cereals,' she said, hurrying away to get the order.

Over breakfast David outlined his plans for the future. 'I expect there'll come a time when all my energies are devoted to raising horses,' he revealed. 'I've got two more filly foals, and another on the way. The horses and the land have always been my main interest, the main source of my income. Carving started as a hobby, something to take my mind off...' He lowered his gaze, reluctant to go on. 'I'm sorry,' he said, embarrassed. 'I'm sure you don't want to hear all this.'

Sonny got the feeling that he wanted to talk but didn't know how to start. 'You're a very talented man,' she said. 'Your furniture is much in demand and the carvings are beautiful. It would be a crying shame to give it all up. You know, David, I envy you.'

'Oh?' Folding his arms, he gazed at her across the table. 'And why's that?'

'Having the best of both worlds, when some of us struggle just to make our way. You have magic in your fingertips. You can take a dead twig and bring it to life, creating a scene straight out of Nature... a rabbit peeping with big eyes... birds and butterflies.' She had never in her life seen anything as beautiful as his carvings. 'Then you have the land, where you can wander at will, with the earth beneath your feet and the skies above your head. A mare gives birth to a foal, you raise it, care for it and love it, until it becomes a magnificent animal, and then you won't let it go until you've vetted the people who want to buy to make sure they love it too.'

She thought of the man she had fled from. She thought of his selfishness and how he had talked of killing her. He was a man of evil. David was a man of honesty and goodness and, though she believed it would never come to anything, she loved him with all her heart.

Saddened by the thought that he might not use the gifts he'd been blessed with, she tried to convince him. 'I can understand how you might feel there will come a time when you have to choose between your art and the land, but – can't you see? – it's all one and the same. The land, the horses and the carvings are all part of the same, perfect picture.'

For a long moment he continued to gaze at her, shocked to his soul by the conviction and passion in her voice. She had touched a chord in him, and now at last he knew he could never let her go.

In the softest whisper, he said, 'Thank you for that. And yes, you're right. I should be grateful.'

'You won't make any hasty decisions then?'

His smile enveloped her. 'I wouldn't dare.'

An hour later they had finished breakfast and had driven the short distance to the Exhibition Centre. Now they were making their way to the room where David's carvings were on show. 'I don't know how you managed to arrange this,' David said as they came into the long, grand room, 'but I suppose I shouldn't be too surprised. I've learned to respect your business instincts.'

Sonny laughed. 'You mean you've forgiven me for

raising the figures on the price tags?' When he brought a carving to the shop David would put a price on it. The minute his back was turned she would change it to a higher one. The pieces sold, and he was always astonished that anyone was prepared to pay such vast sums for his works.

'I'll think about it,' he said. But there was nothing to forgive. There were others he could never forgive, because they had destroyed his faith in human nature. Sonny was different. If only she had come into his life years ago he might have known happiness of a kind he had only ever dreamed about.

The attendant said there had been a 'lot of interest' in the exhibition and that, according to the number of tickets that had been sold, a good attendance was to be expected. 'Mr Wilson, the organiser, should be here soon,' he said. 'But, as you can see, we're all ready.' The walls were clothed in pastel drapes. Round platforms erected at different levels and columnar pedestals strategically placed around the floor made splendid displays. As well as David's wood-carvings there were oil paintings by two local artists and, though the subject matter and media were very different, the work was all of an extremely high standard.

'We're still early,' Sonny remarked, looking around for a telephone. 'I ought to give Ellie a ring.'

'She won't thank you,' David warned. 'You rang twice on the way here, while I was filling up with petrol, and again last night. She'll think you don't trust her to mind the baby.'

He was right of course. But: 'Just once more, then I'll

leave her in peace until we get home,' Sonny promised.

As she went to the phone, she thought of her life now, of the laughter that was beginning to creep back into it, of her new interests and, most of all, of her tiny, delightful daughter. It was strange, she thought, how the shadows seemed to be lifting from her heart. Strange, too, how she was beginning to put the past behind her. Tony Bridgeman still haunted her dreams, but less and less as time went on. Softer dreams. Forbidden dreams.

Four times she tried Ellie's number and each time it was engaged. 'Telling the butcher off, I expect,' she chuckled. 'There'll be too much fat on the pork chops, or the sausages have split open in the frying pan, or some such catastrophe.' There was an ongoing feud between Ellie and the butcher . . . and the milkman . . . and the paper boy, who always tore the pages when he dropped the paper through the letterbox. 'I'll try again later, when she's finished putting the world to rights.'

She wasn't to know that Ellie was in fact talking to Martha, and that it was a conversation with disturbing implications.

Frustrated, she returned to the exhibition hall. David was deep in conversation with Mr Wilson.

Leaving them to it, Sonny wandered around the room. It was a light and spacious place, with high windows and a pale green ceiling – just the right ambience for an exhibition of this kind. She had chosen eight of David's bigger carvings for the exhibition – four of them from the shop and four from his studio. They were of living creatures of the earth and sky. They were some of the finest things he had ever done. Sonny knew in her heart she had chosen well.

David's voice interrupted her thoughts. 'This is the young lady who arranged it all,' he was telling Mr Wilson. 'When she makes up her mind about something she's very determined.'

'Nice to meet you at last.' Mr Wilson was a little man, with a little head and a little smile. He had a little voice and a little hand, which he held out for her to shake. 'We've spoken several times on the telephone,' he recalled, 'but it's always nice to put a face to a voice.'

When the public came through the doors at nine-thirty, the little man greeted everyone with the same jolly words: 'Bit warmer today, don't you think?' Soon the place was heaving with bodies and his words became very apt – the room grew warmer and warmer, until he had to open one of the ceiling vents. 'They like your carvings,' he whispered to David and his smile broadened as he said, 'you do realise, of course, that I take ten per cent on all sales?'

'Can't we get out of here?' David said to Sonny, feeling out of place. 'Wilson keeps bringing people over to meet me,' he moaned. 'It's embarrassing.'

'You're a celebrity,' Sonny told him with a mischievous grin. 'I told you they'd love your carvings.'

They loved them so much they bought them all. One old dear paid fifty pounds for a litter of fat puppies playing around a fallen log. A thrush feeding its fledglings went for seventy pounds. One man paid the astonishing figure of a hundred pounds for a woman seated on a bench with a kitten draped over her shoulder and in her palm a tiny robin. The woman was round-faced and plump. 'She reminds me of my mother,' the man said.

At the end of the day, Mr Wilson was delighted. The paintings had sold well also – only two remained. 'It's been a good day,' he declared, sticking out his little chest. 'A very good day indeed.'

While David chatted to the two painters, Sonny made arrangements with Mr Wilson. 'Mr Langden will be looking forward to receiving a cheque,' she reminded the little man.

'And I shall be looking forward to the next exhibition.'

By four o'clock David and Sonny were leaving Scarborough behind and making for the moors. 'Wilson mentioned a quaint old pub up here,' David told her. 'I think we should celebrate, don't you?'

'If there's a phone there, I'll try Ellie again.'

David appeared not to have heard. He was looking at the changing landscape, his mind brimming from the events of the day, and thinking of Sonny. He wanted her so much. Yet he felt he could not tell her.

Sonny was deeply moved by the beauty of the moors. 'Oh, look!' she cried. 'Please stop!'

When he stopped the car she got out and stood on a low bank by the road. They were so high up it was like being in another world. 'See there,' she called out as he came to join her. 'There's the North Sea.'

The view was magnificent. From where they stood, the hill dropped down into the valley below. Far away there was a fringe of forest. In between was a wide bay, with silver sand and lapping water. Beyond that was a sky of palest blue. 'It's so beautiful!' Sonny was enchanted. There wasn't another soul to be seen. The breeze was surprisingly gentle, and you could even hear the whispering of the trees in the woods below. 'It's as if we're the only two people in the whole world,' she murmured.

While Sonny was enraptured by the beauty all around them, David was captivated by her – by the way the breeze lifted her rich brown hair; by the sparkle in her lovely green eyes and by the way she stood, with her slim arms outstretched and on her face the look of a child at Christmas. It was months since she had given birth, and somehow she seemed even more alive because of it. 'Oh, David!' she sighed. 'Have you ever seen anything so beautiful?'

When he didn't answer she turned and was instantly caught in his arms, locked in an embrace so fierce that it took her breath away. Murmuring endearments in her ear, he told her he loved her, that he had loved her from the first moment he saw her. He brushed the back of his hand down her face, tenderly, lovingly. She could smell the wool of his coat. It brought back memories of a dark and rainy night when she had been lost and alone and he came to help her.

After a while he released her and looked down into her astonished face. 'I've tried so hard not to let this happen,' he groaned. 'Tried not to love you, not to let you into my heart. God knows, I've no right, but I do love you, Sonny . . . love you so much that I can't think straight any more.'

Before she could say anything, he covered her mouth

with a kiss. It was all-enveloping, shaking her heart with emotion. She felt herself being drawn down, until she was lying in the grassy hollow and he was lying beside her. His dark blue eyes smiled into hers and there was no turning back.

Right there, in a sheltered dip where the breeze couldn't reach them, with the sun shining down on them, and the moors all around, they made love. It was love of a kind Sonny had never known, a warm and tender merging of body and heart, a giving, a taking, a bond that fused them together for all time. It was a wonderful, glorious love.

But, all too soon, it was over.

On the way home David was quiet. He spoke only once, to apologise. 'It won't happen again,' he murmured. 'Don't hate me.'

'I don't hate you,' Sonny answered softly. She wanted to say more, but she couldn't find the right words. How could he think she could hate him? Now, God help her, she loved him all the more.

At first she'd believed she could never love another man, but now she realised how wrong she'd been. She wanted to tell him this, to confide in him the truth about why she had come to Blackburn. She wanted to tell him about Tony Bridgeman, about how blind and foolish she'd been, and how she'd fled in fear for her life and that of her baby.

She needed to talk with him, to have him confide in her, to tell her the reason why he felt he could not let himself love her. All of these things she wanted, *needed* to say. But she did not know how.

They didn't stop at the quaint old pub Mr Wilson had mentioned, and only once did they stop for petrol. Sonny asked if there was a telephone, but there was not. The remainder of the journey was marked by traffic queues and faulty traffic lights. They got stuck behind a lorry for eight miles along a country lane, and by the time they got to the outskirts of Blackburn it was already nine o'clock and the night was thick and dark.

'I'll have you home soon,' David told her, making no reference to that wonderful interlude on the moors.

'I'm glad you sold all your carvings,' Sonny told him, trying desperately to sound casual. 'It only goes to prove what I said . . . they're very special.'

And so are you, he thought. So are you.

He was tempted to tell her she was everything he'd ever wanted in a woman. He wanted to say how much he loved her, how desperately he wanted to make her his wife. But he too was still unsure, and still afraid of what the future might hold.

Ellie was fast losing her temper. 'I've already told you, she's not back yet.' This was the third time Cathy Sefton had knocked on her door, and it was the third time Ellie had made it clear she was not welcome at her house.

'I'm sorry, but it is important.' Cathy Sefton was also losing her patience, but because she knew how much Ellie disliked her she forced herself to reply amiably. 'You said she would be back by teatime.' In the light from the hall, she glanced at her watch. 'It's nearly half-past nine.'

'Sonny's a grown woman,' Ellie retorted. 'Sure it ain't my business to tell her what time she should be back. It ain't your business neither.' Behind her the baby started crying. 'Now see what you've done!' she snapped. 'Bugger off! I swear, if yer knock on this door again I'll tip a pan of Irish stew over yer head, so I will!'

Climbing the stairs, she called out, 'It's all right, me beauty, Ellie's on her way.' Under her breath, she mumbled, 'I hope I won't have to throw a pan of stew over her head, 'cause it will be a terrible waste of good food, so it will.'

Outside, Cathy Sefton climbed back into the car. 'She won't be much longer,' she said hopefully. 'We'll just have to be patient.'

'I've been patient long enough,' Tony snarled. 'Why don't I just go in and wait for Sonny inside?' He was dangerously on edge, and itching to hurt someone.

'Ellie Kenny's a funny old sod. She won't even let *me* through the door, let alone you.'

'Is that right?'

Tony was sniggering, and that worried Cathy. 'Force isn't the answer either,' she said. 'Just stick to the plan. When they get out of the car you let him drive away, then you can go after Sonny.'

'I still haven't decided whether I want him to drive away.'

'Don't play games with me. I've already told you, there's nothing between them. Just get her and the brat away from here. Leave David to me.'

377

'Fancy him rotten, don't you?'

'None of your business.'

'You'd better not be lying to me about there being nothing between him and Sonny.'

'What reason would I have to lie?' If it meant keeping David out of this she would lie through her teeth. Not because she didn't feel he deserved to be punished, but because she felt it would suit her purpose better if Sonny was just to go, and she could then pick up the pieces.

Besides, if David knew that Tony had come to take Sonny and her daughter away, he would try to protect her. Better, then, if he didn't know, until after she'd gone. The last thing Cathy wanted was for David to dissuade Sonny from leaving these parts for good. 'When you get out of the car to go after her, I'll make myself scarce,' Cathy promised. 'Don't mention me to anyone.'

'Why don't you go now?'

'Because I want to make sure it all goes right.' He was a nasty, scheming bastard, she thought. Sonny Fareham was welcome to him.

'I won't be sorry to see the back of you,' he grumbled.

'The feeling's mutual,' Cathy replied, her surly manner matching his own. 'And I hope I never clap eyes on you or her ever again.'

And so they waited in silence. Each burning with passion for someone they could never have.

David drove in from the bottom end of the street. Tony was parked in the shadows at the top end. Neither Sonny nor David saw the Jaguar.

Ellie didn't see them arrive either, because she was upstairs. The crying of the baby had disturbed the other two children, who had gone to Ellie's room. Here they sat and talked, with Kathleen rocking the baby in her arms and Mick asking his mammy whether David would give up his land and horses. 'I hope not,' he said thoughtfully. 'Because I was thinking of asking him if he would teach me how to school the horses when I leave school.'

'You're very fond of David, aren't you?' Ellie remarked softly.

Mick nodded. 'If I had a brother, I'd want him to be like David.'

'I know,' she murmured, tousling his hair. 'I know something else too.' When he looked at her with quizzical eyes she lowered her voice. 'I know you miss having a father, and I can never make it up to you for that.'

'It's all right,' he answered, trying not to show his true feelings. 'I've got you, haven't I?' Though it would be so wonderful to have a father. Someone he could talk to about manly things. Someone he could look up to. Someone like David.

'You're a good lad,' Ellie murmured, her eyes shining with love for him, 'but just having a mammy isn't enough. Especially,' she said with a wry little smile, 'especially when you're a young man in the making.'

In the half-light she quietly observed her son, a fierce pride rising inside her. He was becoming a fine fellow, with his strong limbs and strong features, and those blue eyes that reminded her of his daddy – reminded her and made her angry. That bugger was a wanderer, she thought with a flicker of amusement, and it would take a better woman than her to tie him down.

'What did Martha Moon say?'

Ellie was surprised. 'Have you been eavesdropping on my telephone calls, young fella-me-lad?'

'No, but I heard you talking to her,' Mick explained. 'You've been worried ever since.' He hadn't said anything before because he was worried too.

'I wasn't so much worried,' Ellie answered honestly. 'Martha wanted to talk to Sonny. When I said she and David had gone to Scarborough, and that I wasn't exactly sure where, Martha said I was to ask Sonny to call the minute she got back. She said it was very important.' Ellie scratched her chin thoughtfully. 'There's something going on, but I'm not sure what. I hope everything's all right.'

'I expect she's missing Sonny.'

'I expect so.'

'Mam?' While rocking Louise to sleep Kathleen had been listening intently to the conversation between mother and son. Now she was looking at Ellie with curious eyes.

'What's the matter?' Ellie was growing tired. She'd been on her feet all day and if the children would let her she'd roll over on the bed and fall right off to sleep, sure she would!

'Lots of children don't have daddies, do they?'

'No, they don't, which is a great pity.'

'They don't have mammies either, do they?'

'No, bless yer heart.' Ellie hadn't realised how closely the girl had been following her conversation with Mick.

'But youse two *have* got a mammy. For as long as there's breath in me body.'

'Baby Louise has a mammy.'

'Aye. She's got a mammy who loves her like I love the two of youse.'

'She hasn't got a daddy though.'

Ellie was momentarily taken aback. Out of the mouths of babes, she thought, truth and innocence. 'Oh, she's got a daddy right enough,' she replied, going to the cot and stroking the baby's head. 'Just like you've got a daddy. Only sometimes a daddy might go wandering off, and it might take years for him to come home again.'

She realised it was not a suitable explanation, but on the spur of the moment it was the only one she could think of. She was too ashamed to reveal how she had let herself get pregnant, first by the elusive Arnie, who was Mick's father, and then by the merchant seaman who was Kathleen's. And she didn't know enough about Sonny's circumstances to make a statement of any kind.

It would have been a shock to Ellie if she'd known that Louise's father was sitting outside in his sleek white Jaguar, and that he had sworn not to leave Blackburn unless Sonny and Louise went with him.

Cathy Sefton was concerned that he might make a false move and spoil her plans. 'Wait!' she hissed. 'Let him drive away first.' She clutched at the cuff of Tony's jacket. 'It'll go easier if he's out of the way.'

He didn't answer. His eyes were on Sonny as she got out of the car. The mother of his child, he thought rapturously. 'Just look at her,' he whispered, as though to himself. God! He had forgotten how lovely she was. Now he wanted her all the more. In his arrogance he didn't believe for one instant that she would refuse him.

Reluctant to see David go, Sonny kept the car door open for a moment longer than necessary. 'Goodnight, David,' she said softly.

'Sonny?'

'Yes?'

He turned in his seat. 'It's all right. It can wait.' But for how long? He was aching to take her in his arms. He loved her. Adored her. Wanted to spend the rest of his life with her. But instead he was torturing himself. Did she want him in the same way? Yes! Yes! Or why would she have let him make love to her? All the way home he had been burning with so many things he had to say. So many things he could not say. He cursed himself for behaving like a fool. Why couldn't he bring himself to tell her the truth?

Sensing his dilemma, Sonny lingered. In the light from the streetlamp, he seemed so sad. 'If you're worried about . . .' She blushed fiercely, hesitating. 'I mean, about . . . what happened, please, don't be,' she pleaded. 'We were both responsible.'

Reaching out, he squeezed her hand. 'Goodnight, Sonny,' he said. 'You'd best go in. Tell Ellie I'll see her later in the week.'

As he drove off she remained on the pavement, watching him go, trying to compose herself for when Ellie questioned her about the trip. 'It'll be hard keeping the truth from her,' she said with a little grin. 'She seems to know what I'm thinking even before I do.'

Something – a sound, an instinct – made her turn. When she saw the face of Tony Bridgeman grinning at her she froze with horror.

'You've led me quite a chase,' he said in a sinister voice. 'You ran off and never even told me I was about to be a father.' He tutted. 'Shame on you, Sonny. Still, now you've had your fun and are ready to come back with me I expect I can forgive you.'

When he took a step forward she backed away, her eyes stark with horror. 'I'm not going anywhere with you,' she said. 'Go away! Leave me alone!'

His face darkened with anger. 'Don't fool yourself. If you refuse me, I'll move heaven and earth to take the child from you.'

This was what she had been afraid of. This was why she had run away. He had the power to do that. And, by the look in his eyes, he would still consider murdering her to get her baby.

In her desperation to lead him from Ellie's door she turned and fled. Her high heels and the rough cobbles made her stumble. Kicking off her shoes, she made a frantic effort to escape him, but it was only moments before he was on her. She fought like a wild thing, but she was no match for him.

'Now you're making me angry.' Tony shook her so hard she banged her head against the wall. 'Don't make me hurt you.' He tried to kiss her, but she bit his mouth, making him curse. 'Make no mistake,' he warned, pressing his hand over her mouth and stifling her screams, 'now that I've found you, I mean to keep you and the child.'

From the car Cathy Sefton watched. She saw how desperately Sonny struggled, how Tony had his hand over her mouth to prevent her from screaming, and she was delighted. Another minute and I'd better make myself scarce, she decided. It's best if I'm not seen.

Suddenly, everything seemed to happen at once.

Still disturbed by Martha's phone call, Ellie had looked out of the window to see if there was any signs of Sonny. When she saw the two figures struggling on the pavement she couldn't be certain . . . but there was something familiar about the woman. Quickly, she made her way downstairs.

Unhappy about the way he and Sonny had parted, David came back – to tell her he couldn't leave matters as they were, that there were things she had a right to know.

He saw the two struggling figures at about the same time as Ellie was opening the front door.

When he realised that one of them was Sonny he stopped the car and jumped out. In a minute he had Tony by the scruff of the neck. He didn't stop to ask questions. He knocked Tony to the ground with a hefty blow to the chin and went to Sonny's aid. She was bleeding from the head and dazed. 'Hold on to me,' he told her. 'I'll get you inside.'

He didn't ask questions. This was no time for questions. But they were burning in his brain. Who was the man? Why was he attacking Sonny?

His questions were answered when Cathy ran at him, trying to separate him from Sonny. Incensed and driven to desperate measures, she screamed, 'She's a slut! Tony

Bridgeman is married. They were having an affair, and she had his child.'

Suddenly Ellie's voice was calling out a warning. 'The car! *David! Look out!*'

Knocked dizzy by the powerful blow from David's fist, Tony was on his knees, struggling to regain his senses. When Ellie called out he looked up to see a car bearing down on him. He felt the thud against his body, but couldn't understand what had happened. He could hear Ellie screaming . . . a car revving up. Confused and in pain he peered through the dim light. The car was bearing down on him again. Her car! *Celia's car!* He screamed out her name. 'Celia! *No!* NO!'

She didn't hear. She knew too much. In the instant when she had seen him forcing his kisses on Sonny her love had turned to loathing. Now only revenge would satisfy her. She wanted him dead.

She wanted them all dead!

Again and again she ran over Tony's writhing body. There was nothing anyone could do. Cathy Sefton ran down the street, crying with fear. David did his best to stop Celia, clinging to the side of the car and desperately trying to wrench open the driver's door. Several times he was thrown aside. Each time he scrambled back, yelling at her, banging his fist on the window.

But she was beyond all reason. She had to be certain that Tony would never lie to her again and that no woman could ever again come between them.

When it was all over, she turned the car on Sonny.

Leaning against the wall, head bent and face running with blood, Sonny was still dazed and confused. She hadn't fully realised what was happening. Unable to protect herself, she looked up and was blinded by the car's headlights.

Knowing he couldn't stop the car, David ran to her. Grabbing her by the waist, he yelled above the noise of the engine, 'I've got to get you inside! Hold on to me!'

He got her to the door, where Ellie was waiting with open arms. 'Get her inside,' he ordered. 'Call the police.'

'They're on their way,' she told him. Then she took Sonny inside and closed the door. 'Don't open that door for nobody!' she told the horrified children. 'Not even if St Peter himself was to call!'

Convinced that she was to be the next victim, Cathy Sefton ran for her life. Behind her, David urged, 'Make for the alley. You'll be safe there!'

Other residents were out in the street by this time. 'Keep back!' David told them. Curious and excited, they gathered in little groups. Some of the men had only just returned from the pub, where they had imbued false courage, and now it was all David could do to stop them from being heroes.

As Cathy emerged from the alley she was astonished to see her father waiting there, quietly smoking his pipe in the cab of his old truck. 'Get in,' he told her, throwing open the door. 'I'll take you home.'

As she clambered in, a great bang rocked the truck. 'God Almighty! What was that?' Fear trembled in her voice. A mushroom of smoke and flames rose high in the air above Ellie's street. 'Get me away from here!' Cathy demanded, slamming the cab door shut.

'Lucky I was here!' Tom Sefton chuckled. 'Lucky I hung on to this old truck!'

'Why didn't you sell it to the scrapyard, like I told you to?'

'Because she's not ready for the scrapyard.'

Cathy peered at him suspiciously. 'What were you doing here?'

He didn't care to answer.

'How long have you been here?' she demanded angrily. 'Did you see what happened?'

'Most of it.' He put the truck into gear and drove off, still smoking his old pipe.

'I might have been killed!'

'But you weren't.'

'No thanks to you.' She snatched the pipe from his mouth, tearing the skin of his lip and making it bleed. 'You know I can't stand the smell of pipe tobacco, you old bastard!'

Negotiating the corner, he gave her a scathing glance. 'Did you think that *she* might have been killed?'

'Who?'

'Sonny Fareham.'

'Pity she wasn't.'

'And David? Did you wonder whether he might get hurt, even killed?'

'He wasn't supposed to be there. Just them – Tony Bridgeman and Sonny Fareham.' She gave a sigh of relief. 'He wasn't hurt. Just his pride. But he should be grateful. He found out what she was, just in time.'

'And he has you to thank for that, does he?' He gave her a sideways look. It was a little unnerving. 'I heard you and that fellow talking. You arranged it all, didn't you?'

'What if I did? She was never good enough for David.' Cathy gave a self-satisfied smile. 'He'll see that now.'

Shifting uncomfortably, she threw an old rag from the seat to the floor. 'You keep this cab like a pigsty,' she grumbled sourly.

'It's my cab.'

'Not for much longer,' she taunted. 'I've had enough of you living in my house. I want you out . . . you and your filthy belongings.'

'Oh? Any special reason?' He opened the window and spat out of it, as if there was a nasty taste in his mouth.

'I'm thinking of getting married.'

'To David?'

'Yes. To David.'

'What makes you think he'll have you?'

'With her gone, he's got no one else.'

'Is that what you thought when he lost his wife and family?'

'He's over that now. He was almost ready before, until Sonny Fareham came along and spoiled it all.' Her face was a study in cunning. 'But he won't want her now. Not now he knows what a tart she is. He'll soon come round to my way of thinking. He'll soon realise I'm the right woman for him. He'll realise what a good wife I'll make him, you'll see.'

'You would do anything for him, wouldn't you, Cathy?' There was a strange compassion in her father's voice.

'*Anything!*' She laughed softly. 'After what I've done, he belongs to me.'

'What *have* you done, Cathy?'

'Bad things.' Tucking her legs beneath her, she curled up like a kitten.

He slowed the truck. 'When he married your sister you were jealous, weren't you?'

'*I hated her!*'

'Did you hate the baby too?'

'Yes.'

'And your mother?'

'She was always talking about them.' She mimicked her mother's thin voice. ' "David's such a fine young man" . . . "When are you going to get married, Cathy? Dad and I would love to see you settled, like your sister." ' In a burst of temper, she kicked at the dashboard. 'Couldn't she see it was David I wanted?' Her eyes were black with loathing as she stared at him. 'I hated her for loving them too much, and I hated you for not loving me enough.'

For a long moment he let her simmer, then, fearfully, he asked, 'Did you hate enough to kill?'

She laughed aloud. 'What do you think?'

He pressed his foot gently down on the accelerator. 'I think you were driving the car that day. I think you deliberately turned it over.' He half turned to look at her. 'You know these roads like the back of your hand. You would have been in control. You could have chosen the right spot . . . planned it so you had the best chance of surviving.' He smiled, his voice taking on a tone of admiration, 'You always were the clever one.'

She enjoyed the praise. 'It was so easy.' She was talking to herself, reliving the event and bursting with pride. 'And you're right about me being clever.' She was scathing again. 'But you're stupid. Old and stupid. Because you're wrong about one thing.'

'You did kill them then? Your own mother and sister? And that innocent baby?' He choked on the words, wanting to end her life there and then.

Something in his voice made her sit up. 'You're making me say things I don't mean,' she protested.

He pressed his foot harder on the accelerator, swinging the truck round a bend and making her lose her balance. 'Shut up!' The pretence was over.

'Why aren't we on the road home?' she asked, staring out of the window. 'Where are we going?'

'I said shut up!'

She started screaming. Just for a second, until he slapped her across the mouth. 'I should kill you,' he murmured, 'like you killed my entire family. Three generations . . . and you gloat about it.' He smiled, screeching to a halt. 'Now it's my turn.'

She tried to scramble out of the truck, but he was too quick for her. Grabbing her by a hank of hair he pulled her across the seat. To her horror, she realised he was holding a shotgun. 'I want you to tell them what you've just told me,' he said, pointing to the building alongside them.

It was a police station. 'If there's any justice in this world, you should hang,' he said, and there was such sadness in his face that he looked unbelievably old.

Cathy started screaming. But as he marched her

through the doors she stopped screaming and began to yell abuse. 'You've gone mad!' she told him. 'You'll live to regret this day.'

Her threats meant nothing to him. She had hurt him too much over the years. 'She has something to tell you,' he informed the constable at the desk.

Seeing the shotgun the startled constable signalled through the communicating window to two of his colleagues who were talking in an inner room. The two of them came quietly into the outer office. 'Don't be foolish,' one of them, a sergeant, urged Tom. 'Put the gun down.'

Tom kept his back to the wall. By this time he had Cathy's arm twisted awkwardly behind her back. 'Tell them!' he urged, prodding her in the side with the shotgun.

'I don't know what he's talking about,' she cried. 'He's gone mad.'

'You murdered them all!' he shouted, bending her arm back until she groaned in agony. 'My wife, my daughter, and my grand-daughter.' She could feel the end of the barrel in her side. 'Tell them how you did it, or I swear I'll blow you in half!'

She was sobbing now, her voice breaking as she rounded on him. 'It's all your fault!' she cried. 'Yours and hers. Neither of you ever wanted me. It was always Alice this and Alice that. You never had the same time for me, did you? If it hadn't been for her I could have had David. But she took him from me, just like she took everything else. She was never the angel you thought she was. I told you that, but you didn't believe me.' Her voice was shrill with emotion. 'Yes, I murdered them, and I'm glad I did. I only wish to God you'd been with them on that day!'

There was a gasp of disbelief from the policemen, but they daren't move while he had the shotgun so close. 'You've got what you wanted,' the sergeant said. 'Now let her go. We'll take it from here.'

But Tom Sefton wasn't finished. He held Cathy tighter than ever. 'You said I was wrong about one thing.'

She smiled into his face. 'You thought I was driving the car.' She tried to shake her head but he held her too tight and she was made to cry out. 'Alice insisted on driving. I had it all planned. I would take the car close to the edge of Brewer's Hill, then, when I knew they wouldn't stand a chance, I could just jump out and let it go over the top, with all of them inside.' Her face filled with disgust. 'But she got into the driving seat instead. I had to rethink all my plans. When we got to the top of Brewer's Hill I grabbed the wheel and forced her to the edge. She was screaming ... they were all screaming.' Her eyes closed again in anguish. When they opened again it was in rage. 'I was afraid someone might hear. I had to fight her ... snatch the wheel out of her hands. When it went over, I only just managed to get out.' Horror filled her face. 'I could have been killed myself!' She had even climbed down the hill, to make sure it looked authentic.

The sergeant's persuasive voice intervened. 'It's over now,' he told Tom. 'Give me the gun.' He held out his hand and took a step forward.

'Stay back!' Tears careered down Tom's face. 'It isn't

over, can't you see? She murdered them. I always knew it, but I didn't want to believe it.'

'She'll pay for what she's done,' the sergeant promised. 'Do as I ask. Give me the gun now.'

Tom wasn't listening. He was talking to his daughter. 'You shouldn't have done that terrible thing,' he told her. 'You were so wrong. We did love you, your mother and me. We worried for you, because you were born bad. When you were small you tore the legs off frogs and burned your sister's hair. You were always selfish . . . greedy . . . wanting what everyone else had. We should have hated you, but we couldn't. You were our flesh and blood, you see. We had to love you. We loved you both. And now there's only you and me left.'

Her eyes turned up to his, his tears wetting her face. 'I'm so sorry,' he whispered, kissing her tenderly on the forehead. 'So sorry.'

In that moment she knew he really did love her. But it was too late.

The sound of the gun exploding was muffled by the softness of her flesh. A second shot, and for them the furore was over.

While all around there was pandemonium.

PART FOUR

1957

Love

Chapter Eleven

The whole country was shocked by the series of events which had taken four lives. Tony Bridgeman had never been well liked but he was respected by his business rivals. In the world of construction and property development he had had a reputation for being an aggressive and successful man with an eye for the main chance and an insatiable thirst for power. Some said he deserved his violent end. Others said nothing, because they knew what it was to be married and to have 'a bit on the side' and they hoped their own sordid little secret would remain undiscovered.

Most people saved their sympathies for Celia. 'It was her money that got him started,' they muttered. 'She worshipped the ground he walked on,' some said. And, 'She deserved better.' Driven mad by jealousy, she had killed her beloved husband. And then, eaten up with guilt and grief, she had deliberately driven her car into the side of a house. By God's good grace there was no one in the house at the time, but the car burst into flames on impact and Celia Bridgeman was killed instantly.

The sad tale of Tom Sefton touched everyone's hearts.

That he should have lost his family in such a brutal way was shocking in itself, but that his daughter had subjected him to such indignity ever since was unforgiveable. 'No wonder he killed her,' they said. 'There isn't a man alive who wouldn't have done the same thing.' And it was right, too, that he should have taken his own life, they agreed: 'If he had lived he would never have found another moment's peace.'

The Bridgemans were taken home to be buried. Ironically, it was Tony Bridgeman's new secretary, Sonny's replacement in that office, who made all the arrangements. The joint funeral was well attended, although few were there to mourn.

For the funeral of Cathy Sefton and her father the church was packed to bursting. People cried genuine tears and prayers were said that the Almighty might afford both these 'murderers' peace and forgiveness. But when the congregation bent their heads to pray it was Tom Sefton who filled their minds, to whom their hearts went out.

There was talk of burying Tom in land outside the church boundary. But, after much consultation and argument, his bones were laid with those of his wife, his elder daughter and his grandchild.

The one who had put them there, the one who had been ruled by passions beyond her control was interred separately. But not so far apart that an onlooker could not take in both graves in a single sweep of the eye.

Sonny stood in the shop. Her green eyes were sad as she looked around. The shelves were almost empty.

There was a carving of rabbits in long grass, another of two otters playing in some reeds. There were smaller studies – of a fox, of a pair of robins and of two fieldmice. Against the far wall stood a small chest of drawers and a beautiful chair. That was all. Nothing more. Nothing had been added since the tragedies that had unfolded around them.

'Are you closed, dear?' An elderly woman poked her head round the door, startling Sonny out of her reverie.

Sonny gave her a warm smile. 'Please, come in.' This was what she wanted. Someone to talk to. A stranger. Someone who knew little of what she was really feeling.

Thankful to come in out of the cold, the woman entered and closed the door. She was shivering, although she was wrapped in a warm red coat and wearing a little hat. 'Brr! The wind's blowing fierce round yer arse today,' she declared, astonishing Sonny, who had thought the old lady looked quite refined.

Sonny didn't know what to say, so she just smiled, before glancing at the child in its pram. Baby Louise was sleeping. The bell above the door hadn't woken her, thank goodness.

The woman's eyes followed Sonny's gaze. 'Oh, isn't she a little darling!'

Sonny had to laugh. 'You wouldn't have thought so if you'd been here at two o clock this morning,' she said. 'I walked the floor for over an hour and couldn't get her to sleep whatever I did.'

The woman looked coy all of a sudden. 'Aye, well,' she said, with the wide-eyed look of an old owl, 'children have a way of sensing things. I mean, what with everything that's happened, and you right in the middle of it, well, it isn't surprising she's so restless.'

Sonny's smile fell away. 'All that's behind us now,' she answered calmly. 'It doesn't do to dwell on things.'

The woman tutted and shook her head. 'Terrible thing,' she murmured. 'It's true what they say. There's no greater force than human emotion. Sometimes it can rob a soul of all dignity.'

'Was there something you wanted?' Eager now to be rid of her, Sonny gestured to the half-empty shelves. 'There isn't all that much left, as you can see.'

The woman was still dwelling on the reason for it all. 'Aye . . . when passion comes in the door, common sense and reason fly out the window.'

For the briefest moment Sonny saw the truth in what she was saying and she recalled the people who had played their parts in the events of that night: Tony Bridgeman, obsessed with her and the child; his wife, Celia, obsessed with him; and Cathy Sefton, her mind and heart set so fast on David Langden that she believed that by murdering his wife she could earn his love.

In everything that had happened that night there seemed no sense, no reason and no dignity.

This woman, with her bright red coat, little hat and old-fashioned philosophy, had said all there was to say.

Tapping the woman's hand, Sonny asked, 'What exactly are you looking for? Only we've had a sale and there isn't very much left.'

'Oh, yes!' She looked up with sharp eyes. 'I heard you were closing down, and of course it's understandable that Mr Langden wants to move away. There are rumours that he's selling the big house and all the land and buildings to a hotel consortium. I expect they've made him a handsome offer. Though, to be honest, he's worked that land and lived in that lovely coach house for so long now, I should think he'd miss it terribly. But there you are. No doubt there are too many bad memories there.'

She didn't wait for an answer. Instead she gabbled on, making Sonny think, making her regretful. 'Besides, I dare say he misses the old fellow. He and Tom Sefton were good friends for a long time, weren't they? This dreadful business has upset everybody.'

She gave a cough and while she took a deep breath Sonny seized the opportunity to tell her, 'If there's something you want to buy, you'd best be quick, because I was just about to lock the door and go out.'

Realising she had overstayed her welcome the woman shifted her gaze to the shelves. Her mouth fell open. 'Oh! Look at this!' Hurrying to the shelf, she picked up the small carving of the fox. 'By! He's a little rascal and no mistake.' She swung round and nearly knocked over the robins. 'How much?'

'Mr Langden's given instructions that I have to use my own judgement on what to charge.' Sonny thought for a moment. 'The fox is a particularly good piece,' she commented. 'Normally I would be asking twenty pounds.'

'Oh, I can't afford that!' The woman looked disappointed. With great reverence she replaced the piece on the shelf. 'I really like him too,' she said, stroking the fox's smooth head.

It was one of Sonny's favourites. She wanted it to go to a good home, not just to someone who had enough money. This woman, though she had a lot to say about recent events, did seem a genuine old soul and, more importantly, she was really taken with David's carvings. 'All right,' Sonny said kindly. 'How much can you afford?'

'I can't afford twenty pounds, or even half that.'

'What can you afford then?'

'Maybe five pounds, at a push.'

Sonny knew the woman loved the piece. Against all her business instincts she followed the dictates of her soul. 'I know you'll look after it,' she decided. 'Take it home, with my and Mr Langden's blessing.'

The woman looked at her in astonished disbelief. 'What! You mean . . . I can have it for nothing?'

Sonny wondered what David would have to say about it. After all, it wasn't hers to give away. 'Take it quickly,' she advised, 'before I change my mind.'

She was rewarded when the woman gave her a kiss on the cheek. 'I'll cherish it,' she said and, with the sparkle of a tear in her eyes, she went out of the shop with the fox in her bag and her faith in human nature restored.

Sonny stood for a moment surveying the shop's depleted contents. 'What now?' she wondered aloud. 'Where do we go from here?'

Louise was still sleeping in her pram. 'You may well sleep,' Sonny told her with a wagging finger. 'Your poor mother feels like a light gone out, thanks to you.' She rolled her eyes to the ceiling and gave a little smile.

'Come on then,' she said, lifting the child out of its pram. 'We're off to see your Auntie Ellie.'

It took only a few minutes to dress the baby in a warm romper suit and coat, with the hood pulled down to keep out the cold.

Sonny put on her black ankle boots and long coat, and wound a blue silk scarf over her shining brown hair. 'Right!' she announced to herself in the mirror, her green eyes twinkling with the merest hint of a smile. 'Let's see if the old dear was right. Let's see if the wind really is "Blowing fierce round yer arse today".'

It was. And the rain was just starting. 'She wasn't telling lies, was she?' Sonny asked the baby as she laid her in her carrycot on the back seat of the car. The baby looked up and gurgled. 'It's all right for you,' Sonny told her. 'You haven't got a worry in the world.'

She had, though. Because in two weeks' time she wouldn't have a home and she wouldn't have a job. She was still an unmarried mother with all the problems that entailed and for reasons she couldn't understand, or didn't want to, she didn't really want to leave her home.

When, twenty minutes later, she was walking down the passage into Ellie's front room, she told all of this to her friend. 'Apart from Patricia and Aunt Martha, there's nothing to go back for,' she confessed. 'The truth is, I want to stay around these parts. I feel I really belong here.'

'And so you do,' Ellie declared. 'You're part of this family now. My children would throw a fit if you went off and left them.' She led the way through to the kitchen. 'We can talk in peace,' she said. 'The kids won't be home from school for another hour.'

It wasn't too long before the kettle had boiled and the two of them were sitting comfortably, each with a mug of hot tea and a slice of Ellie's bread-and-butter pudding. 'David was in not five minutes since,' Ellie said. 'He left here to go and see you, but he'll be disappointed, won't he?' She was disappointed too. In spite of what had happened, or maybe because of it, Ellie still had high hopes of Sonny and David getting together.

Sonny was dismayed. 'We must have passed each other on the way. Do you know what he wanted to see me about?'

Ellie winked. 'Happen he's about to propose.'

Sonny blushed to the roots of her hair. 'You're a wicked woman, Ellie,' she chided.

'What else could it be about then?' Ellie asked mischievously.

'The shop maybe?' Sonny shrugged her shoulders. 'Or perhaps he's concerned about how quickly I can get out of the flat upstairs. Are you sure he didn't say what it's about? Is it important, do you think?' She glanced at the phone on the sideboard. 'Should I ring the shop? See if he's there?'

'Good idea. Why didn't I think of that?'

Sonny tried three times over the next few minutes. She let the phone ring and ring, and still there was no reply.

'Happen he's already gone.' Ellie's face was a picture of dejection. 'He'll be disappointed not to have seen you.'

'What do you mean, "Happen he's already gone"?'

Sonny had awful visions of never seeing him again.

Just then the phone rang. Ellie raced to pick it up. 'Who's that?' She always answered with a question. 'Oh! It's you! We've just been trying to reach you. Yes, she's here. Been here fifteen minutes and more. She reckons yer must have passed each other on the way.' She grinned from ear to ear. 'What? O' course yer can. All right. Take care of yerself, and I'll see yer when yer get back.'

She beckoned Sonny over. 'He wants to talk to you,' she whispered. 'It doesn't matter what he has to say. Just tell him how yer feel, that's what's important.' She had her hand over the mouthpiece so David couldn't hear what she said.

Sonny knew what Ellie meant, but she couldn't admit it. 'I don't know what you're talking about,' she said. 'Are you going to let me talk to him, or what?'

Ellie gave her the receiver. 'Tell him, that's all I'm saying, me beauty. Just tell him how yer feel.'

While Sonny was listening to what David had to say, Ellie waited with Louise, who was contentedly sucking her fist in her carrycot. 'Yer mammy starving yer, is she? Well, give her a minute and I'm sure she'll find a juicy little tit for yer to suck on.'

Sonny sounded puzzled, and more than a bit disappointed. 'How long will you be away?' She daren't show her feelings. She couldn't let him guess how much she wanted to share the rest of her life with him. If he wanted the same, he wouldn't be going away.

'A day. A week. I don't know for sure,' he answered. 'Does it matter?' He hoped it did.

'No, no,' she lied. 'What you do is your business.' She

was on the verge of saying, 'I love you. Please don't go.' But since that day when they made love on the moors he had never mentioned it, and neither had she. It was almost as though that particular day had never happened. Yet, for as long as she lived, she would not forget.

'What will you do while I'm gone?' he asked, desperately afraid she might not be there when he got back.

'I'm not sure,' she replied, her heart sinking. 'I have to find a job, and a place to live.'

There was a silence so long she thought he had gone. 'David?' She spoke his name, but the silence continued for a moment longer.

Then he said, softly, turning her heart over. 'Will you be all right?'

She laughed. 'Why shouldn't I be?'

'Well, I have more or less put you out on the street.'

'You have a right to sell your own property, David, and under the circumstances I do understand. You mustn't worry about me. Anyway, I didn't intend living over a shop forever.' She would live in a tent as long as he was there with her.

'Can you put Ellie back on the phone?'

'Goodbye, David.'

Through the silence she could hear him breathing. For one precious minute she thought he was about to say something intimate. But he only asked for Ellie again.

Sonny called to Ellie. 'He wants to talk to you.'

Ellie put the receiver to her ear and listened. 'Don't worry,' she told him, 'I'll take care of it.' After a minute or two she put the receiver down and came to where Sonny was feeding the baby.

She was astonished to see her feeding the child with a bottle. Wrapped in towelling, and tucked in the bottom of the baby's carrycot, it was now just the right temperature. 'What's wrong with a good old-fashioned titty?' she demanded.

'Nothing,' Sonny replied with a patient smile. 'Only my milk wasn't satisfying her, so the nurse suggested I feed her with a bottle, and anyway, you managed with a bottle when I was away for a night.'

Ellie tutted. 'Don't mean I hold with all these new-fangled ideas!' She tutted again. 'While you're feeding the babby I'll make us both a hot drink . . . keep the chill out, eh?'

From the kitchen doorway she watched Sonny feed and wind the baby. She watched her change her nappy and thought there could never be a happier picture than that of mother and child together. 'Have you been to the Registrar's yet?'

'Not yet,' confessed Sonny. 'What with one thing and another, I just haven't been able to find the time.' Or the heart, she thought worriedly.

'Yer can't fool me, Sonny Fareham,' Ellie remarked sadly. 'I know why you've been avoiding it. But the child has to be registered.' She sighed, biting her lip for a while, trying to keep the words from spilling out. But they would not be kept back, 'You know as well as I do, me beauty, they won't leave yer be, until she's legally registered. They'll be on yer back like a pack o' bloody wolves.'

'I know, and I will do it, I promise. When I can find the time, I'll go into town and see to it.' She was dreading it. But, as Ellie rightly pointed out, there was no escape; not even for a little innocent like Louise.

'What I can't understand is how yer managed to get out of hospital without the Registrar catching yer.' In spite of the seriousness of the situation, Ellie had to chuckle. 'What! The bugger was there half an hour after Kathleen popped into the world.'

Sonny gave a whimsical little smile. 'Whenever I saw her coming, I hid in the lavatory until she'd gone.'

Looking up with serious eyes, Sonny confessed softly, 'I can't bring myself to do it, Ellie.' Her voice trembled as she gazed down on the child's face. 'What do I write in the line where it says "Father's Name"?' When she looked up her eyes were moist with tears.

'It's a cruel world, my beauty.' Ellie's heart went out to Sonny in her dilemma.

'And I'm faced with a cruel choice ... either I write "Father Unknown", or I write *his* name.' Sonny shook her head. 'I can't tell her what an evil man her father was.' She was appealing to Ellie, and yet she knew there was no satisfactory answer.

'I can understand what yer saying,' Ellie declared, 'and I don't blame yer for being in a quandary.'

'If you were me, what would you do?'

Ellie wished there was a good piece of advice she could give, but there wasn't. 'This is summat you must decide for yerself, me beauty,' she confessed. 'And I don't envy you the task.'

Sonny was desperate. 'I hope you don't mind my

asking, Ellie, but what did you put on your children's certificates?'

'It weren't so hard for me, lass, because thank the good Lord my two had decent enough fathers though one buggered off on the high seas, and nobody ever knew where the other bugger was from one day's end to the next.' She was thinking of Arnie, and feeling awfully lonely suddenly. 'I wrote their names on the certificates. If there comes a day when the children want to seek out their daddies, that'll be up to them.' She rolled her eyes to heaven. 'Let's hope it's long after I'm gone, eh?'

Sonny felt ashamed. 'I had no right to ask you that. I'm sorry.'

'Don't be,' Ellie pleaded, 'I've grown a tough skin over the years. You've a difficult decision to make and I don't envy you it. I only wish I could advise yer, but I can't.' No one was more sorry than Ellie.

'Here,' she said. 'Give me that dirty nappy and I'll drop it in a bucket of warm water and rinse it through.'

By the time she returned to the living room the baby was back in her carrycot and happily playing with a row of miniature teddy bears strung across it. 'You didn't tell him, did yer?' Ellie complained. Seating herself opposite, she put Sonny's mug of tea on the fender and took a great gulp from her own.

'Tell who?' Sonny asked, her mind still on the baby.

'David. Yer didn't tell him.'

'What did you want me to tell him?'

'That yer love him and yer don't want him to go away.'

'I can't tell him that.'

'Oh, and why not? Yer do love him, don't yer?'

'Yes, I love him very much.'

'Well then, damn and bugger it!' Ellie was exasperated. 'Why can't yer tell him?'

'Because I don't want to put him on the spot. I don't want to embarrass him or make him feel guilty or feel that he's obliged to feel the same way towards me.' She bent her head, recalling his tenderness when they had made love on the moors.

'Yer talking in riddles, so ye are,' Ellie declared with a firm shake of the head. 'Why should he feel guilty?'

'Because we made love, and because I'm sure he's regretted it ever since.'

'What!' Ellie was beside herself. 'Well, bless me. And yer never said, yer crafty little bugger. When did this happen?'

'It was on the way home from the art exhibition. We stopped on the moors. They were so beautiful . . . as if mankind had never set foot on the earth.'

'Bugger that!' Ellie wanted to know. 'What happened?'

Sonny wasn't sure herself how it had happened. 'We got out to take a look at the beautiful scenery, and the next minute I was in his arms and we were on the grass.' She blushed so fiercely she could feel the heat creeping up her neck. 'He told me he loved me, and it just happened. That's the beginning and end of it.' But it wasn't. She had loved David before that day, and now she loved him more than ever.

'So what's gone wrong?' Ellie was a simple, uncomplicated soul. 'What's happened that yer can't tell him how yer feel?'

'Nothing's happened,' Sonny replied. 'But that's the point. Since that day David's never mentioned it, and he seems further away than ever ... sort of quiet and preoccupied as if he wished it had never happened. I think he's embarrassed and guilty, and that's what I mean when I say I don't want him to feel obliged ... that I read more into it than he really felt.'

'But you said he told yer he loved yer?'

'In the heat of the moment, maybe. It had been an exciting, successful day.' She sounded bitter. 'Maybe he wanted it to end the same way.'

'I'll not deny there are some men who say one thing and mean another,' Ellie admitted. 'Look at that useless bugger, Arnie Laing. One minute he's telling me he'll never leave me again and the next, when my back's turned, he can't get away up the street fast enough.' Her voice trembled a little as she realised that, where Arnie Laing was concerned, all her hopes had come to nothing. Since Christmas, she had seen him only once, and even then she was afraid to make her feelings known. Anxious and rejected he was presently keeping a distance. 'But that doesn't sound like my David,' she affirmed. 'If my David said he loved yer, he must have meant it.' She had another reason for believing that too. 'Else why would he ask me to take you and the babby in, and look after yer both?'

Sonny was surprised. 'So that's what he was talking to you about?' She didn't know whether to be pleased or annoyed. 'That should tell you something, Ellie.'

'Oh?'

'I was right. He *is* feeling guilty. He's afraid I might think he owes me something ... that I might make a claim on him. Well, he couldn't be more mistaken! What happened on the moors meant no more to me than it did to him.' Anger flared into rage. 'And he needn't offload his guilt on to you, Ellie, because by the time he gets back I'll be long gone. I'll leave his premises clean and tidy. I'll arrange for the bits and pieces in the shop to be safely stored, and then I'll be on my way.' She was on her feet now, pacing the floor, making plans, her blood boiling. 'What right has he to decide things for me?'

Ellie was about to argue, but a knock on the door made her jump up. 'Who the hell's that?'

It was Arnie.

And he gave Ellie the shock of her life. 'I've come to say I'm sorry for letting you down again,' he told her. 'And I've come to ask if you'll marry me?'

Speechless, Ellie stared at him. Standing there with the wind blowing his carrot-red hair, and a lost forlorn look on his homely face, he looked like a naughty boy. 'Have yer gone mad?' Ellie gasped. 'Are yer really asking me to wed yer?'

'I know I don't deserve you,' he said defensively. 'And I can't promise I'll not clear off again, but I'm a bit older and a bit wiser and I think a lot of you, Ellie. I always have. And, yes, I want to wed you ... if you'll have me.'

Ellie's face crumpled, and her eyes half closed as the tears ran down her face. 'Yer a bugger so ye are, Arnie

Laing,' she cried. And he didn't know whether to take to his heels or throw his arms around her.

Sonny had heard it all, and now she came up behind Ellie and laid her hands on those big, trembling shoulders. 'Say yes,' she urged in a whisper. 'You know he belongs here, with you and the children.'

Ellie gave her a strange look. She wondered how much Sonny had guessed. 'Yer right,' she murmured, then, turning to Arnie, she told him softly, 'get in here, yer daft old sod, before yer catch yer death o' cold.'

Then, while Sonny made her way out of the house with her baby tucked up in the carrycot, Arnie went inside. It was not surprising that Ellie was too preoccupied to notice that Sonny had discreetly crept away.

That night she had a long talk on the phone with her Aunt Martha. 'It's time you came home, dear,' the old woman said.

And, against all her deeper instincts, Sonny agreed.

Early the next morning she left a note for David:

Dear David,

Thank you for all your kindness, but I think it's time for me to leave.

I have arranged for Mr Bartram, the butcher, to keep an eye on the place until you get back, if you ever do.

I'll leave the keys with him.

I hope everything goes well for you, and that the sale goes through as you want.

Thank you again. I don't suppose our paths will ever cross again.

Love,

Sonny (and Louise)

She then wrote a letter to Ellie, telling her how glad she was that Arnie had come home. 'Don't lose each other again,' she wrote. 'I would have phoned you, but I was afraid you might make me change my mind and stay.' She explained that she was going back to Aunt Martha and promised to keep in touch. Then she put the letter into an envelope, wrote the address on the front, and tucked it into her handbag for posting on the way.

Now that her mind was made up it didn't take her long to pack her bags – just her clothes and the baby's belongings. 'There's nothing else here I want,' she murmured, looking around. 'Best to make a clean sweep.'

At ten o'clock she turned the key in the lock for the last time. With her suitcase and the baby aboard she drove down to the butcher's shop, where she delivered the key and left the letter for David.

Ten minutes later she was on the road again, heading

towards the A5 and the south. As she drove the tears blinded her eyes. 'Oh, David! All you had to do was ask me,' she murmured as she left Blackburn. 'And I would have followed you to the ends of the earth.'

Chapter Twelve

Patricia's scars had healed, and she was fighting fit. 'I'm glad Tony Bridgeman got what he deserved,' she told Martha and Sonny. 'But I'm sorry for his wife. She didn't deserve to die like that.'

'She didn't deserve a husband like Tony either,' Sonny remarked.

Martha had her own views on the subject. 'Celia Bridgeman was obsessed with her husband. I'm sure she would rather be dead than living without him.' She had thought about it a lot, and was convinced Fate had taken a hand. 'It wasn't your fault that she flew back from Jersey when she couldn't get him on the phone.'

'Maybe not. But when she turned up at the hospital I needn't have told her that he'd gone to find Sonny, and where he'd gone.' Patricia looked at Sonny with remorseful eyes. 'My God, gal, I could have got you killed!'

'Well you didn't so stop worrying.'

'Fancy Celia Bridgeman having a daughter, though,' Martha exclaimed. 'I was amazed when I read it in the papers.'

'Hmm!' Patricia was a little envious. 'It seems she'll inherit everything. Lucky little devil. That's why the business is being sold, and that's why me and Lonnie are out of work as from next week.' She turned to Sonny. 'Really, you know, some of that inheritance belongs to Louise. If it was me I'd fight tooth and nail for it.'

Martha intervened. 'Sonny and I have already discussed that, and she wants no part of it.'

Patricia was mortified. 'Me and my big mouth,' she said, addressing Sonny. 'I don't blame you either. Best if nobody knows Louise is Bridgeman's daughter, eh?'

Sonny's voice was fired with determination. 'Nobody ever will. At least not from me or Aunt Martha.'

Patricia gaped at her. 'No, and not from me neither!' she declared. 'I promised I'd not say a word, I haven't, and I never will,' she went on. 'Not even to Lonnie.'

Sonny was relieved. 'Thank you for that.'

This was the second morning Sonny had been back at the cottage, and though she loved her Aunt Martha dearly her thoughts were constantly with Ellie and David . . . wherever he was.

Thinking of him, and of what might have been, she asked Patricia, 'Have you and Lonnie set the day yet?'

The three women were sitting in Martha's little cottage, setting the world to rights and mulling over past events. Patricia had called by to tell them that she and Lonnie were to be married. Sonny was thrilled for her friend. 'You don't want to leave it too late,' she said cheekily. 'He might change his mind.'

'He'd better not!' Patricia got up to leave. 'We haven't set a date yet, but somehow I fancy being a June bride.'

She laughed out loud. 'By that time he should be able to walk me out of the church.' A shadow crossed her face. 'Mind you, if we're both still out of work there won't be two pennies to rub together, let alone pay for a wedding.'

Sonny was also thinking of looking for work. Martha had offered to mind baby Louise, but it was not an ideal situation. Still, there was time enough yet. 'What about that job you went for at the Co-op?' she asked Patricia.

Patricia shook her head. 'No go. They wanted someone on the till, and you know how useless I am with money.'

Optimistic as ever, Martha told her, 'You'll find something, I'm sure.'

After ten letters and umpteen interviews Patricia was not so certain. 'I'd better get going,' she said. 'Lonnie's out of his wheelchair today, and I want to be there to cheer him on.'

With Patricia out of the way Martha felt free to broach another subject. 'Have you heard from David?'

'No.' Sonny busied herself with Louise. 'There's no reason why I should.'

'So that wasn't him on the phone when I was upstairs earlier?'

'It was Ellie.'

'Has she heard from him?'

'She didn't say, and I didn't ask.' But she had wanted to. Oh, how she had wanted to.

Martha was not convinced by Sonny's display of casual disinterest. 'I know how you feel about that young man.'

Sonny turned to look at her. 'I expect you do,' she said with a half-smile. 'There isn't much you miss, is there?'

'I'm so sorry, my dear.'

She would have said more, but Sonny stopped her. 'Please, Aunt Martha. I'd rather not talk about it. David doesn't want me, so there's no point in talking about how I feel,' she said. 'Now, if I'm going to the Registrar's, I'd better make a move.'

Martha came to her. 'Have you decided what you'll put on the certificate?' She knew how torn Sonny felt about this delicate issue.

Sonny didn't need to say anything. She just slowly shook her head. Right into the early hours she had thought and thought, and still she hadn't made up her mind. But she had to register the baby, and she would.

'Nobody can help you on this,' said Martha. 'It's for you to decide.'

Sonny smiled, 'That's just what Ellie said.'

Taking the hint to change the subject, Martha asked, 'Did Ellie say how she and Arnie are getting on? Will he stay, do you think?'

Sonny had to smile. 'If he doesn't he won't get his foot over the doorstep again. But they seem to be getting on all right, and the children think he's wonderful.'

'I'm glad.' Martha liked Ellie, in spite of her rough edges. 'Though I have to admit I wouldn't want a man cluttering up my life.'

'We're all different,' Sonny remarked. There was only one man she would ever want, and that was David.

Sonny tucked Louise into her carrycot, dropped it

into its wheeled frame and pushed it to the door. Here she took her coat from the back of the door and put it on. 'I have to call in at the agency and see if there are any places to rent.'

'I've told you, you're welcome to stay here for as long as you want.'

'Thank you, you're a darling.' Sonny returned to give her aunt a grateful kiss. 'But it will suit us both if I find a place for me and Louise.' She wouldn't hear of any excuses. 'I'm used to her keeping me awake until all hours, but it's not fair on you.'

'It's up to you,' Martha told her. 'But this is your home, yours and the baby's, for as long as you want.' Though since Sonny had been gone she had learned to value the peace and quiet of her own company.

Unclipping the carrycot from the frame, Sonny lifted both into the car, the frame into the boot and the cot into the back seat. 'See you later.'

'Be careful now,' Martha warned. 'And mind how you drive past Hawthorn Rectory. That new vicar is an absolute maniac when he gets behind the wheel of a car.'

Ten minutes after Sonny had turned out of the lane, another car turned in.

This was going to be a red-letter day for her, and she didn't even know it.

Bedford town centre was teeming with people. It took five minutes to get from the car park to the accommodation agency on Midland Road, and half an hour to get to the head of the queue that was waiting there.

It seemed everybody and his uncle were looking for places to rent. 'We'll let you know,' the man said. Sonny thanked him.

She was even more downhearted twenty minutes later, when she got to the Register office. 'Fill out this form,' grunted a clerk, peering at her over his little rimless spectacles, 'I'll be back in a minute.'

He was good as his word, only Sonny wasn't finished. In fact, she wasn't even started. 'Is there a problem?' he asked impatiently.

'No, it's all right, thank you.'

'Right. Well.' He glanced at his watch. 'I'll give you another minute, but we close for lunch soon,' he snapped.

When he returned five minutes later, Sonny handed him the form, with seven shillings and sixpence.

Shoving his glasses along his nose, he perused the document. 'This won't do,' he said, exasperated. 'You've forgotten to enter the father's name.'

'Do I have to?' Sonny asked simply.

He stared at her. 'Of course you do! It's a legal requirement.' Thrusting the document at her, he moaned, 'It's a simple enough thing. Write the father's name then we can all go to lunch.' He looked at her strained face and then he looked at the child in its cot. 'Is there a problem?'

Sonny reached out to take the document.

She almost collided with the man standing behind her. 'Careful!' a familiar voice murmured. Her heart almost stopped. She looked up and there he was, her own love echoed in his dark eyes. 'Fill out the form, sweetheart,' he said with a slow easy smile, 'the man wants his lunch.'

His name fell from her lips. 'David.' He looked down on her with such tenderness that her heart melted. She tried to fill out the form but her hand was trembling too much.

David took the form and in the space where it said 'Father's Name' he wrote in a sweeping hand: 'David John Langden'.

He gave the clerk the form, and the man gave Sonny a sour look. 'I should report you for registering this child late,' he threatened. 'But I don't suppose it would do anybody any good.'

Seeing them out of the office, he grumbled and moaned, and almost fell over the doormat in his haste to be rid of them. 'A simple thing. Father's name, that's all.' When they were gone he slammed the door and left them, laughing together on the doorstep.

Later they sat on a bench in the small park off Midland Road, holding hands, lost in each other's company. 'On the day my wife was killed she was making arrangements to leave me,' David confessed. 'I'd suspected for a long time that she was seeing someone else. When I confronted her, she admitted it. She said her daughter was not mine at all. That was the hardest blow. I had fallen out of love with Alice long ago, but I felt we should make the marriage work for the sake of the child. She didn't agree. Eventually we decided there was no future for us together.'

Sonny's heart went out to him. 'I'm sorry.'

He took her hands in his and drew her to him. 'Sometimes, Fate can be cruel. But here we are, you and I, so much in love and ready to embark on a new life together.' He gazed at her long and hard. 'I've just got back from London. I was on the verge of selling Sefton House, and everything with it. But I couldn't do it. Oh, I know it had unhappy memories but once it was a beautiful, happy place where two people, very much like you and me, started out with dreams and plans and there was laughter and joy. Tom Sefton used to sit in the barn while I was working and reminisce about how it used to be.' He grew excited. 'I want it to be like that again, Sonny. I want you and me to bring the house back to its former glory, to throw open the windows and let the sunshine in. And children . . . Louise will be the first of six, maybe even seven. Children's laughter, echoing once more from the walls of that lovely old place. What do you say? Will you marry me, Sonny? Will you?'

He was on his knees, and she was laughing and crying at the same time. 'Get up,' she chided, 'people are looking.' And they were. And she didn't care. She only saw David's face, adoring and handsome. And, yes, she would marry her David, and have his children, and, God willing, never look back.

On 4 June, 1957, the church in Blackburn town centre was packed to bursting, 'Three weddings!' one fat lady sighed as she waddled into a pew. 'Isn't it romantic?'

First came Sonny, dressed in a lovely ivory gown and carrying a simple posy of red roses. Before God, she joined her oath with David's and everyone said they had never seen a happier and more handsome couple.

Next came Ellie and Arnie, the pair of them looking

ten years younger in their best bibs and tuckers.

Patricia and Lonnie were last, and yes, he was able to walk her out of the church and into the sunshine, where everyone laughed and chatted, and the two attendants, Kathleen in her blue dress and Mick in his best dark suit, posed with the three brides and grooms and had their photographs taken for posterity. Then each couple had their photograph taken and afterwards, at the newly renovated Sefton House, the reception went on until the early hours.

The day after the wedding Ellie had a secret to tell, and it was this: Arnie was not only Mick's real father but David's father too. Mick was thrilled. 'I've got a real dad,' he cried, 'and a brother.'

There were a few anxious moments while Ellie explained how she had to give David away, in order for him to have a better life. But love shone through, and all was well in the end.

Over the years Sonny and David became the proud parents of eight children – six strapping boys and two pretty lively daughters. Louise grew up believing that David was her father and between them a very special bond was formed.

David and Sonny farmed the land and reared horses and their love grew stronger with every day. David took time out for his wood-carving, but his great joy was Sonny and the children.

Patricia and Lonnie came to live in the gatehouse. Lonnie was given the job of tending the horses. They had two children, a boy and a girl, and over the years remained firm friends of Sonny and David.

Mick displayed a talent for show-jumping, and won many trophies across the world.

When she was eighteen Kathleen fell in love with her mammy's homeland and went to settle in Kilkenny. Two years later she married an Irish fiddle player and they had three mischievous red-headed sons.

Ellie had her Arnie, and he never again wandered.

Martha paid many visits to Sefton House and each time her visits grew longer. 'She'll live to be a hundred,' Sonny laughed when her aunt talked about learning to ride a horse; though she gave up the idea of learning to ride when Ellie informed her, 'By the time it's taken you round the field twice you'll be bow-legged as an old coot!'

David and Sonny had been twelve years married when one day they climbed to the top of the hill and surveyed the scene below. The sun was shining and the old house stood proudly amidst lovingly tended gardens. Wafting up on the breeze, the sound of their children playing below made Sonny smile. 'Do you love me enough?' she asked David, who was gazing at her with quiet eyes.

'Enough for what?' he asked.

'Enough to let me win if I race you down the hill?'

'Oh, I don't know about that,' he teased. 'The children are watching. A man has his pride after all.'

Before he finished speaking she was away, running down the hill to the loud cheers of the children. 'You can do it!' shouted young Arnie, and all of them were dancing up and down with glee as their parents came tumbling down the hill.

When David caught her in his arms, and the two of them came roly-polying down, the laughter and the screeching were deafening. 'I love you!' David yelled, holding her tight.

'No you don't,' she called out. 'You didn't let me win!'

As they crashed to the bottom of the hill the children piled on top of them and it was a free for all until Louise called out from the kitchen door that the jam tarts were ready and if they wanted one they'd better get a move on.

Everyone raced to the house except Sonny and David, who stood by the horse trough, kissing each other with the same love and devotion that had carried them through the years past and would carry them through many, many more to come.

At long last the old house was filled with joy and laughter. 'Are you happy?' David asked, holding Sonny close.

'Happier than I ever dreamed possible,' she said.

In the golden sunlight her green eyes shone with joy and her heart was filled to overflowing. 'Take me home,' she whispered.

And he did.

Headline hopes you have enjoyed reading THE DEVIL YOU KNOW and invites you to sample the beginning of Josephine Cox's compelling new saga, A TIME FOR US, now out in Headline hardback . . .

Chapter One

'Give us a kiss!' One brown eye gave a cheeky wink.

'Shame on you, Mike Nolan.' In spite of the laughter bubbling inside her, Sally managed to keep a straight face. 'And me a married woman, too!'

'The man doesn't deserve you.'

'I'm glad you think so.'

'Don't you sometimes fancy a change?'

'Wouldn't tell you if I did.'

'Go on, Sally, be a devil,' he pleaded. 'One kiss, that's all.' He winked again, making her smile. 'What he doesn't know won't hurt him.'

She feigned indignation. 'Do I look like the kind of woman who would cheat on her husband?'

The mischievous brown eyes looked her up and down. 'Hmm.' He rubbed his chin and smiled at her. 'Perhaps not. But all I need is a quick cuddle behind the vegetables.' He glanced towards the shop doorway. There was no one about. He grew bolder. 'And if you're feeling extra generous, I wouldn't say no to a bit *more* than a cuddle.' Grinning like a naughty boy, he raised one eyebrow quizzically. 'If you know what I mean?'

Flattening her hands against his chest, she pushed him away. 'You randy old bugger!' Pleasure lightened her pretty blue eyes fleetingly. 'I know what you mean all right. And the answer is still no!'

Groaning like a man in pain, he grabbed her by the waist. 'You're driving me mad!' he cried. 'I'VE GOT TO HAVE YOU!'

'Have you any idea what you look like?' She could hardly contain her laughter. 'Cabbage stains on your overall, and the smell of carrots in your hair. What woman could fancy you?'

'Jesus, Mary and Joseph ... you're a wicked woman.' With great difficulty he tried to drag her round the back of the counter. 'Five minutes on the floor should do it,' he promised, going red in the face as he tried to lift her off her feet.

'Put me down, you daft devil!' she laughed. 'The time's long gone when you could sweep me off my feet.'

Keeping his arms round her, he demanded in a hurt little voice: 'Mrs Nolan, are you insinuating that I'm past it?'

Now it was her turn to eye him up and down. 'Well, you must admit you aren't as slim as you used to be,' she answered kindly.

'Neither are you.' He squeezed his arms tight round her waist. 'But I'm not complaining.'

'And you'd better not!' She touched her finger against the end of his nose, her voice falling tenderly as she told him, 'We might as well face it, my love, we'll never be eighteen again. We're both a bit thicker round the waist ... a bit dafter as the years go by.' She ran her finger over his mouth. 'But I still love you, Mike Nolan. More than ever.'

It was a moment before he could speak. In that moment he looked into her wistful blue eyes and his heart was full. 'You're as lovely as the day you walked down the aisle,' he murmured.

'And you're still the most handsome man I've ever met,' she told him. 'Just as cheeky . . . just as much fun.' Giggling like a schoolgirl, she reminded him, 'Just now, though, when you were pretending to be my lover, anyone might have walked in and heard the conversation. *Strangers* even!' She blushed a fierce shade of red, 'God knows what they would have thought.'

'Strangers?' He looked astonished. 'This is a family greengrocer's, known to all and sundry, from one end of Blackburn to the other. The only "strange" person who might have caught us acting the fool is old Polly Entwhistle.' Making a face that was uncannily like that of the old troublemaker, he even sounded like her. 'I'll have a pound o' them there apples . . . nice and soft so me teeth won't come out. Oh, an' mek sure there are no worm-holes in 'em. Oh, yes, and I've brought back the bananas you sold me last week. They've gone all yellow, so I want me money back, an' no argument!'

Sally couldn't help but laugh. 'Serve you right if she did walk in and give you a piece of her mind,' she warned glancing furtively towards the door.

'Do you love me?'

'I must do, or I wouldn't put up with you.'

Contented now that he had made her say that, he let his mind roam back over the past twenty-five years: the

433

courting; the doubts when they'd found she was pregnant; the rushed marriage, and the wonderful, happy years that had followed.

Sally had been eighteen when they met. He was twenty. Two years later they were hastily married, and everyone warned the marriage wouldn't last.

Their love for each other had proved everyone wrong, thank God. Seven months after they walked down the aisle, they were blessed with a precious daughter whom they named Lucy. The years following had been more wonderful than he could ever have imagined. He and Sally were in their forties now, and as much in love as ever. Not a day passed when he didn't pray there might be many more wonderful times to come.

In the twenty-two years since she had been born, Mike's daughter Lucy had become his pride and joy.

His wife was his very life.

Now, with such love inside him that it hurt, he held her small, pretty face between his hands. Gazing with unashamed adoration into her bright blue eyes, he whispered, 'What in God's name would I ever do without you, eh?'

Lucy Nolan and her friend Debbie turned into Penny Street.

The two of them were laughing and chattering, enjoying each other's company and sharing little snippets of gossip in the way of young women.

Lucy and Debbie had gone through school together. They'd endured puberty, courted boys, shared secrets, loved and lost, laughed and cried, and always found consolation in each other. On leaving school six years ago, they had found work in the same garden nurseries. Here they had grown from girls to women, and their friendship had flourished and strengthened. These two shared a special bond, a fierce protective instinct towards each other. A unique and wonderful friendship that others could only envy.

'Do you think there'll ever come a time when you leave here?' Debbie asked.

Lucy didn't answer right away. But when she did, there was such conviction in her voice that Debbie was subdued. 'One day,' she said quietly, nodding her head, 'one day, when I'm ready to make my way in the world, I expect I'll have to pay the price.'

With a little shock, Lucy realised that leaving Penny Street would be the hardest thing she had ever done. Yet in some instinctive, inexplicable way she had always known she was not meant to spend the rest of her life here.

In a minute they were outside the shop. Both of them saw the intimate little scene through the window, but it was Debbie who commented, 'Cor! Look at them two!' and giggled. 'Kissing and cuddling like a pair o' lovers.'

It was true. Blissfully oblivious to any onlookers, Mike and Sally were locked in each other's arms. 'They love each other,' Lucy declared proudly, 'what's wrong with that?' She continued to gaze at her parents, her young heart filled with devotion.

'Nothing!' Debbie whispered. 'Only sometimes you wonder about older people, don't you?'

Lucy turned, grey eyes puzzled. 'What do you mean?'

For the briefest of moments, Debbie looked embarrassed. 'Well ... you know ...' She shrugged her shoulders and wished the earth would swallow her up. 'Making love and all that. Older people. I've often wondered how old you have to be before you stop?'

Lucy smiled. 'No wonder you forget to water the plants,' she said. 'If that's the sort of thing that fills your head when you're supposed to be working.'

'Got to think about *something*, or I'd go stark raving mad.'

'That's funny.'

'What is?'

'Well, I thought you were already!'

'Bitch!'

'I know.'

They giggled, and Debbie persisted, 'When *do* older people stop having sex?'

'When they stop loving each other, I expect.'

'Not them two, though, eh?' She drew Lucy's attention back to her parents. 'They look as though they're still madly in love.'

Lucy smiled, a quiet, knowing little smile. 'They are,' she murmured. 'When Jack and I have been married for as long as they have, I hope we're as happy as Mum and Dad.'

'So you are gonna marry him then?'

'If he asks me.'

'You lucky bugger! I wish I could get a man like Jack Hanson. Matter o' fact, if you decide you don't want him, I'll always take him off your hands.'

'No chance.'

Debbie sighed. 'I didn't think there would be.'

Suddenly the shop door was flung open. It was Lucy's dad. 'What are you two hanging about for?' he demanded light-heartedly. 'Waiting for a bus, are you?'

'Hello, Mr Nolan.' Debbie smiled. 'No, we're not waiting for a bus. We're waiting for you to stop kissing and canoodling.' Nudging Lucy, she remarked in a serious voice, 'These older folk. Isn't it terrible the example they set?'

'Terrible,' she agreed. 'There ought to be a law against it.'

Lucy's mam called out from inside the shop, 'You two! Stop embarrassing my husband.' Before the last word was spoken, she appeared at the doorway. ' "Kissing and canoodling" wasn't invented just for the young,' she said. 'Me and this handsome fella's been married long enough to do what we like, whenever the fancy takes us.' Giving Mike a peck on the cheek, she asked, 'Isn't that right, love?'

MORE THAN RICHES

Josephine Cox

'*You'll never let it go, will you?*'

Taken aback by the hatred in her eyes, he wanted to tear out her heart. 'I'll let it go when you stop wanting him!' he hissed. Then he covered his head with his hands and cried like a child.

When Rosie's parents were involved in a train accident, her mother was killed and her father was left crippled, unable to earn a living and relying on Rosie to keep the wolf from the door.

With her mother gone and her sweetheart Adam away in the army, Rosie is lonely. She eagerly awaits the letters from him, but they never come. As she grows more disillusioned, Adam's best friend Doug goes out of his way to be charming and attentive. Alone and confused, Rosie blossoms under his evil influence. Soon she is carrying Doug's baby and her father has thrown her out of the house. Realising she has no choice, she agrees to marry Doug.

As if she isn't in enough trouble, Rosie's whole world falls apart when a warm and wonderful letter arrives from Adam . . . telling her he's on his way home.

'Driven and passionate, she stirs a pot spiced with incest, wife-beating . . . and murder'
The Sunday Times

FICTION / SAGA 0 7472 4657 2

A LITTLE BADNESS

FROM THE BESTSELLING AUTHOR OF
MORE THAN RICHES

Josephine Cox

*Rita Blackthorn's heart was barren and hard. In
all of her life she had never truly loved. But she
had hated. She hated now, so deeply she could
almost taste it. Beneath the loving gaze of her
daughter's soft green eyes, her heart swelled with
dark and dangerous emotions.*

Young Cathy Blackthorn has never experienced
any loving response from her mother; it is her
beloved aunt Margaret, with a heart as big and
warm as the summer sky, who has been more of
a mother than her own could ever be. And when
Cathy's father Frank Blackthorn brings home a
London street urchin and announces this will be
the son he and Rita have never had, Cathy
despairs of ever winning her parents' love. But
Cathy is a generous soul, and tries to give the
young lad a chance to prove himself – one way
or the other – but, unlike her best friend, David
Leyton, something about him makes her more
than uneasy . . .

'Driven and passionate, she stirs a pot spiced
with incest, wife-beating . . . and murder'
The Sunday Times

FICTION / SAGA 0 7472 4831 1

Now you can buy any of these other bestselling books by **Josephine Cox** from your bookshop or *direct from her publisher*.

FREE P&P AND UK DELIVERY
(Overseas and Ireland £3.50 per book)

Looking Back	£5.99
Rainbow Days	£5.99
Somewhere, Somebody	£5.99
The Gilded Cage	£5.99
Tomorrow the World	£5.99
Love Me or Leave Me	£5.99
Miss You Forever	£6.99
Cradle of Thorns	£6.99
A Time for Us	£6.99
The Devil You Know	£6.99
Living a Lie	£6.99
A Little Badness	£6.99
More Than Riches	£6.99
Born to Serve	£6.99
Nobody's Darling	£6.99
Jessica's Girl	£6.99

TO ORDER SIMPLY CALL THIS NUMBER

01235 400 414

or e-mail <u>orders@bookpoint.co.uk</u>

Prices and availability subject to change without notice.